A NEW BEGINNINGS
ANTHOLOGY

NICOLA JANE   TRACIE PODGER   ELLE M THOMAS
SIENNA GRANT   KATE BONHAM

FOREWORD

This is a collection of stories are part of The New Beginnings Anthology, raising awareness and money for the charity Living Without Abuse because everyone has the right to live without domestic abuse. The authors taking part in this anthology have agreed that all proceeds will be donated directly to the charity.

Living Without Abuse (LWA) believes that all people have the right to live safely and without fear of violence and abuse. On this site we offer information and advice to anyone experiencing domestic abuse and/or sexual violence. We can also provide support services to anyone living in Leicester, Leicestershire or Rutland. We are committed to raising awareness of domestic abuse and sexual violence, working towards its prevention and eradication, and assisting those affected by this crime to determine their own lives. https://lwa.org.uk/

Anyone experiencing any abuse please know that you are not alone and seek support.

Living in the UK? Find help here:
https://www.nhs.uk/live-well/getting-help-for-domestic-violence/

Living in the USA? Find help here:
https://www.thehotline.org/get-help/

Living in the AUS? Find help here:
1800RESPECT - 1800 737 732 (Available 24 hours, 7 days a week)
https://www.whiteribbon.org.au/helplines/

PLEASE be aware that these stories maybe a trigger for anyone experiencing or having experienced domestic violence so please proceed with caution.

VOLUME 1

BREAKING FREE

A NEW BEGINNINGS STORY

NICOLA JANE

BREAKING FREE

A NEW BEGINNINGS STORY

NICOLA JANE

Meet The Team:

Cover Designer: Francessca Wingfield @ Wingfield Designs

Editor: Rebecca Vazquez, Dark Syde Books

Proofreader: Jackie Ziegler, Dark Syde Books

Formatting: TBR Editing & Design

ACKNOWLEDGMENTS

Thank you to my readers who love whatever I write. I appreciate every comment, share, review, and TikTok.
X

This story holds a special place in my heart. To anyone that's survived domestic abuse, you're amazing. To anyone going through it, reach out, there is help available, I promise. There is life after abuse and it's not always an easy path with a hero waiting to rescue you, each story looks very different. But if you reach out for help, your story could have a happy ending.

SPELLING NOTE

Please note, this author resides in the United Kingdom and is using British English. Therefore, some words may be viewed as incorrect or spelled incorrectly, however, they are not.

A NOTE FROM THE AUTHOR

Some people may find this story triggering. However, it's been written as part of an anthology to raise awareness for Domestic Violence and how easy it is for victims to be drawn in and held there through fear or mental abuse.

If you, or someone you know, might need help. Here are some useful websites:

https://www.womensaid.org.uk/about-domestic-abuse/

https://www.nationaldahelpline.org.uk/

The freephone, 24-hour National Domestic Abuse Helpline 0808 2000 247

PLAYLIST

When She Cries – Britt Nicole
i can't breathe – Bea Miller
Bad Thing – Jesy Nelson
Sociopath – Olivia O'Brien
Titanium – Madilyn Bailey
What He Didn't Do – Carly Pearce
lovely – Billie Eilish ft. Khalid
Narcissist – Lauren Spencer-Smith
One Day – Tate McRae
All I Want – Lauren Spencer-Smith
Fighter – Christina Aguilera
Both Sides Now – Luke Sital-Singh
Praying – Kesha
Beautiful – Christina Aguilera
Warrior – Demi Lovato
Bird Set Free – Sia

CHAPTER ONE

8 YEARS EARLIER...

TESSA

I CHECK my outfit one last time in my full-length mirror. Callie rolls her eyes impatiently. "Can we just go, please?" She's eager because her new boyfriend is waiting for us in the car outside.

"Are you sure he won't mind me coming?" I ask.

"I told you already, he's fine about it. We're going to a house party, and there's gonna be loads of people there."

We rush down the stairs, and my care-worker pokes her head around the kitchen door. "Going somewhere nice?"

"Cinema. Mike cleared it," I lie.

"Ten o'clock curfew," she shouts after me as we head out. The care home where I'm currently living is nicer than most places I've stayed, but it's strict on curfews and rules. I've spent my life in care, passed around several different foster homes, and now, at the age of sixteen, I'm here. They no longer call them children's homes, but that's what it is—a home for the kids no one wants. They say if you haven't been adopted by eight years old, you've missed your chance, and for me, that's the case.

I climb into the back of the black BMW. I can't lie, I'm a little impressed. Callie gets in the front and leans over to kiss the guy in the driver's seat. He then turns to me, smiling, and I catch a glimpse of a gold tooth. "I'm Jase," he introduces, and I try not to look shocked. He's a lot older than me and Callie. She never mentioned that part.

"Tessa," I say warily. He winks, then turns back around and starts the engine.

We drive around for a half-hour before he pulls up outside a house. It's huge, much better than the houses on the estate where we live, and there's music pumping from inside. As we get out the car, I see people hanging around in the garden. They all look older than me and Callie, and I hook my arm in hers and lean close so Jase doesn't hear me. "You never said you were dating Hugh Hefner," I hiss.

She laughs. "He's not that old."

"Yet he's not that young either."

She rolls her eyes. "Come on, Tess, lighten up. He's twenty-five, hardly a grandad, and he thinks I'm eighteen, so don't say a word."

"Where did you meet him?"

"A bar. Live a little and let your hair down. These parties are amazing."

I look around doubtfully as we head inside, trailing behind Jase. He stops occasionally, shaking hands and chatting with the other partygoers, but eventually leads us over to a couch. He waves down a passing girl carrying a tray of drinks and takes two glasses of wine, handing them to us. I hate wine, but Callie gives me a warning glare to keep quiet and smile gratefully. When he turns to chat with someone else, another woman places a tray on the table with lines of white powder neatly sectioned and some black straws.

"Is that what I think it is?" I hiss, and Callie nods. "You're not gonna do that, are you?"

Jase crouches at the table and takes a straw, sniffing as he guides it along the line of powder. He grins at us before offering the straw to Callie. She takes it, and I watch in horror as she does the same. She turns to me, but I'm already shaking my head. "Come on, Tess, don't be a bore."

"I'm not a fucking bore, Callie. If I go home out my face, they'll kick me out." I'm proud of the fact that I haven't gone down the route so many kids in my situation do. I've never done drugs or smoked, and I only have the occasional drink.

"They'll kick you out soon, anyway," she mutters, handing the straw back to Jase. She's right, I can only stay at the home until I turn seventeen, and then they'll point me in the direction of a hostel or a bedsit. The thought terrifies me because I've never lived alone. I've always been surrounded by other kids.

"You're an idiot," I mutter. She's only doing this crap to impress her new boyfriend. He's not even that nice-looking.

"If you're going to nag, go away," she snaps. Standing, she wraps her arms around Jase and kisses him. I shudder, watching as he leads her away towards the stairs. *Great, now what?*

The atmosphere in the room suddenly changes. People begin to shift uncomfortably and then they part, almost like they're waiting for a storm to pass through. A group of men appear, all dressed in smart suits with gold watches on show and shades covering their eyes. I feel like I'm watching a movie scene, and I want to laugh at the ridiculousness. They stop in front of me, and one of the men lifts his shades, revealing his piercing blue eyes that stare hard into mine. "Move," he says clearly.

I look behind me to make sure he's speaking to me. When I see he is, I frown. "No."

He stares a little longer, unsure of what to say. I don't suppose many people tell him no. Another guy pushes to the front. "Who's she?" he asks, also lifting his shades to eye me suspiciously.

"Who are you here with?"

"Jase," I reply.

They both exchange a smirk. "Where is he?"

"With my friend."

"What the fuck are you all doing?" Another man appears behind the two, and they both spin to face him.

"Sorry, boss, we got distracted."

The man watches me with an intrigued look on his face. "Remove this shit," he tells them, pointing to the tray of powder. "And get me a drink." He loosens his tie slightly and takes a seat beside me. "Dante," he says, holding out his hand.

"Tessa," I reply, shaking it. My breath catches in my throat. He's gorgeous, maybe the most handsome man I've ever set eyes on.

"Where's your boyfriend?"

I feel myself blush. "I don't have one."

He smirks, leaning back and placing an arm over the back of the couch. I feel the heat from it like a red-hot fire, searing my back. "Lucky me."

Present day . . .

I HEAR the lock click and dread fills my stomach. I try to steady my breathing as I lay as still as possible on the floor. It's my usual trick, thinking maybe if he sees I'm sleeping, he'll leave me alone, though it very rarely works.

His footsteps move closer and it's almost impossible to stop myself from tensing. I feel him crouch behind me before running a finger down my spine. The sudden touch after three days of being in here startles me and I flinch. "Good morning, Tessa. How are you feeling?"

I don't know if this is a trick question. I don't understand what answer he wants, so I slowly turn onto my back, wincing from the pain that causes, and force a smile. "I've missed you, Dante," I whisper. My voice is hoarse from the lack of water.

He grins. "Good. We have guests arriving in one hour. I've promised them a traditional roast beef dinner." I push to sit and immediately feel dizzy, so I squeeze my eyes closed. "What are you waiting for?" he asks.

I look down at my naked body. "Can I wear clothes?" I whisper, almost ashamed to ask.

He laughs. "Hurry, Tessa, I don't want my guests waiting for food." And then he leaves.

It takes me five minutes to stand and be steady enough on my feet to get out the room. It's on the top floor, and as I slowly take the three flights of stairs down to the kitchen, I have to cling onto the wall and handrail for support.

The ingredients for dinner are laid out on the kitchen island. There's no way I can make a roast in one hour, and if I'm a minute late, I'll pay for it. So, I unwrap the beef, place it in the air fryer, and select roast cook. I've spent years learning ways in which to outsmart Dante. He sets me up to fail all the time, so if I can cheat my way out of it, I'll do it. I prep the rest of the food and set it all to cook.

Half an hour later, Dante enters the kitchen, looking around with that smug glint in his eye. "Everything going to plan?" he asks.

I smile. "Yes, of course. Can I get you a drink?"

He holds up his glass of bourbon to indicate he's already sorted it himself, and I curse myself for not making sure that was the first thing I did. "Sorry, I was distracted with dinner."

"Do you have anything to say to me, Tessa?" he asks, tipping his head to one side and eyeing me.

I move closer, my nerves on edge in case it's the wrong thing to do and I set him off. "Dante, I'm so sorry for upsetting you," I begin. He remains still, and I carefully reach up to his face and place my hand against his cheek. "I wasn't thinking, and I hate that I upset you. I deserved longer in the room, but I'm glad you let me out to cook for you. It's the least I can do."

He inhales sharply, a sign he wasn't expecting me to be so sincere. "I've left your clothes on our bed," he says firmly.

"Thank you." I'm relieved to gain this small victory.

"Shower and change."

I nod, placing a gentle kiss against his mouth before rushing back upstairs to do as he's asked. Once locked in our en-suite bathroom, I clench my fists and silently scream. *I hate him, I hate him, I hate him.* I repeat the chant while I shower.

NERO

I PACE THE ROOM, my stress levels off the chain today. When my handler finally walks in, I stop and give her a steely glare. "No contact. That's the fucking rule, right?"

"They're getting restless, Nero. Tell me you have something."

"What I have is a fucking target on my head whenever you call me away like this. You know how this works, damn it. Don't contact me again. I'll tell you when I have something."

I head for the exit, and as I pass her, she grabs my arm. "In case they're watching," she whispers.

I clench my jaw, unable to shake the anger. "I mean it, Callie, don't call me like that again." I place my hand behind her head and tug her to me, kissing her hard.

CHAPTER TWO

TESSA

"SO, what happened? Where did you go?" I ask Callie. She looks tired and pale. She disappeared at the party, and I didn't see her again for the rest of the night. "In case you were worried about leaving me all alone, I was fine. I met some guy called Dante and he drove me home. Thanks for that, by the way, leaving me in a place with a bunch of strangers."

"Stop acting like a kid," she snaps. "It's not always about you, Tess."

I raise my brows in surprise. "What's up with you?"

She scrubs her hands over her face. "Nothing," she mutters. "Don't worry about it."

"Everything okay with Jase?"

At the mention of his name, she scowls. "Who's Dante, anyway?" she asks, changing the subject, and I come to the conclusion she's been dumped.

I shrug. "He came and sat with me after you left me. We

only talked a bit. We were interrupted a million times by either his phone ringing or people stopping to talk to him."

"Nothing happened between you?"

I scoff. "No, he was way too old for me." I give a dreamy smile. "But he was so fit." She smirks. "And he was surprisingly nice," I add.

THE BARROW PUB is the only place we can drink without being asked for I.D. It's an old-fashioned place with dark carpets and a landlord who squints like he can't see a thing. Our friend, Emerson, got us some fake I.D.s a year ago when we turned fifteen. The women in the photographs look nothing like any of us, so we're wary of trying them out anywhere more upmarket, but it doesn't seem to matter in this place. "I think we should go down the road to the Duck and Partridge," says Callie.

Emerson almost spits her vodka and Coke out. "No way, that place is full of dodgy people."

"And drugs," I say pointedly, because I didn't raise the issue of her snorting coke at that party, but I need her to know I haven't forgotten and I won't let it go.

"But this place is dead, like the people in it."

I look around at the old men supping their Guinness. "We'll never get served in there," I point out. "This bar is safe. They never question us."

"We can try," mutters Callie, grabbing her jacket. "I'm sick of this place."

THE DOORMAN at the Duck and Partridge eyes us suspiciously and stares down at our I.D.s. "This isn't you," he says, glancing back and forth between the photograph and me. "What's your date of birth again?"

An arm snakes around my shoulder. "Leave it out, Jonny, they're with me." I glance up at Jase, and he grins back at me.

The doorman sighs heavily, handing us our I.D.s back. "I ain't taking the blame if Dante kicks off," he mutters, opening the door for us to enter.

"Stick with me, ladies," says Jase, waltzing inside like he owns the place. I catch Callie's expression. She looks worried, but when she catches me watching her, she forces a smile.

Inside, the place is heaving. Emerson hooks her arm in mine. "If my dad finds out I've been in here, he'll go mad."

There's space towards the back of the bar, but as we make our way there, I spot Dante and the men he was with at the party. I have no idea if he'll recognise me, so I stick with Jase and the girls. Jase passes us each a drink from the bar and then throws his arm around Callie. "You've been avoiding me, gorgeous," he says, kissing the side of her head.

"Jase." We look to the source of the voice. It's one of the men from Dante's group.

"Enzo," Jase mutters, removing his arm from Callie. "I didn't know you'd be in here."

"I bet you didn't," Enzo says, smirking. "The boss wants a word." Jase swallows hard, nods, and follows Enzo over to where Dante is.

"What was that all about?" I whisper, glancing back at the group.

"Fuck knows. He's weird," says Callie, shuddering.

"I thought you liked him?"

Emerson gasps. "He's way too old for you."

"You don't have to worry, I'm not with him anymore. I just haven't told him yet."

A commotion from behind me gets our attention and I turn in time to see one of the men laying into Jase. "Oh shit," I mutter, stepping back with Callie and Emerson behind me. "We should go."

A loud bang rings out and I drop my glass. The pub falls silent and one of the men stands on a stool. "Lock the doors," he shouts, and the doors are suddenly bolted shut with everyone inside.

"Oh my god," Callie whispers, grabbing onto my arm in a panic. "Jase is dead."

We all stare at Jase's unseeing wide eyes, a pool of blood surrounding his chest. "Holy shit," whispers Emerson, squeezing my other arm tighter. "We need to go."

I take a steadying breath. My heart is racing so hard, I don't know how they can't hear it. "Let's stay calm," I whisper back. "Just keep quiet. We don't want to draw attention to ourselves."

"He's fucking dead," hisses Callie. "Dead."

"I know," I say through gritted teeth. "But no one in here is bothered. Look around. This must be normal to them."

Emerson suddenly lurches forward and vomits. I stare wide-eyed, hardly daring to look up because I know we now have the attention of the men standing around the dead body. "Way to stay fucking calm," I hiss, then she begins to cry.

I look up in time to see Dante moving towards us. There's concern in his eyes. "Get the lady some water," he barks to no one in particular. "Are you okay?" he asks Emerson, gently rubbing her arm.

She nods, wiping her eyes on her sleeve. "Sorry, I must have drunk too much."

He smiles, taking a glass of water from the barmaid and handing it to her to sip. "Come sit down in my corner." He takes her hand and leads her away from Jase to a corner the opposite side of the room. We follow, and I don't think he recognises me at all.

He points for us to all sit down in the booth, and we do. "Sorry about that," he says, also sitting. "Things get heated sometimes."

"Is that how you sort all your problems?" mutters Callie, and I kick her under the table. She yells out and scowls at me.

Dante doesn't seem to mind her question. He grins. "Sometimes." He catches my eye and recognition hits him. "Jailbait," he says, winking. "I thought I recognised you." He then turns to Callie. "And your name is?"

"Callie Woods."

"Woods," he repeats. "Any relation to Bob Woods?"

Her eyes widen slightly. "My dad."

He gives a knowing nod. "And you?" he asks Emerson.

"Emerson Grey."

This time, Dante looks surprised. "Frank Grey's daughter?" She nods. We're not surprised—everyone knows Frank. "Does he know you're in here?" She shakes her head, and he laughs. "Nah, I bet he doesn't."

He whistles to get the men's attention, and one of them rushes over. "Boss?"

"Take these lovely ladies to my place. Stay with them until I get there."

"No, thank you," says Emerson. "We should get home."

Dante looks at his watch. "You have less than two minutes to get out of here before your dad turns up, and I don't think you want me to tell Frank you were here. So, go with my friend and do what I say."

"You can't tell us what to do," snaps Callie, and I glare at her in disbelief. We just watched this guy end someone and she's sassing him.

Dante suddenly leans over to her, pushing his face in hers. I squeeze my eyes closed in panic as I feel Callie tighten her grip on my hand. "You don't know who I am, little girl, but you're about to. I don't get told no. Ever. People who tell me no, end up like your friend, Jase. So, I suggest you get a move on."

I grab Callie by the hand and edge out of the booth with Emerson following. Something tells me it's safer to do as he tells us.

Present day . . .
TESSA

I SLICE the beef as he likes it, sauté the vegetables just right, and cream the potatoes to perfection. I lay the hot dishes in the centre of the table just as Dante's guests begin to arrive.

I join them in the living room and stand beside him with my head slightly lowered so that later, he can't accuse me of eye-fucking his guests. The usual men are here. Kai is Dante's right-hand man. He's known him his whole life, and they're more like blood brothers than friends. Enzo is Dante's advisor and very good friend. And there's another man I've never met, so I make sure not to be anywhere near him and glue myself to Dante's side.

Eventually, he takes my hand and uses his other hand to tip my head up to look at him. "I want you to meet Nero. He's going to be around a lot more." I don't move my eyes from Dante, not until he tells me I can. He smiles, placing a gentle kiss on my nose. "Good girl," he whispers. "Nero, this is my wife, Tessa. Tessa, Nero is your new bodyguard."

NERO

BODYGUARD. *Bodyguard. Fucking bodyguard.* His wife looks just as surprised as me, but she shuts it down, giving me a neutral expression. "Boss?" I say like I'm asking the question, cos fuck knows he didn't speak to me about this.

"Problem?" asks Dante, tipping his head to one side like he's daring me to challenge him.

"No, Boss. Just wondering what my duties will entail."

"My wife has prepared a meal. Shall we go eat?" he asks, turning back to his wife and running his hand through her hair. She winces slightly, giving the impression he's tugging it. "Will you serve us, Tessa?"

She smiles politely. "Of course."

The tension in the room is almost unbearable. I've sat with gangland killers, Mafia bosses, and nutters who would kill their own mother. Yet sitting here in silence while Tessa serves us food is worse than any of it. She's nervous. Her entire body is stiff as she walks round to each of us to place beef on our plates. Dante has his eyes fixed on her the entire time, not moving them for a second.

Once our plates are full, she begins a retreat to the kitchen. "Aren't you joining us?" I ask. All eyes turn to me, including Dante's. "It's just, she cooked us this food, isn't she going to have some?"

"Why are you concerned with whether my wife eats?" asks Dante.

"Just a question," I mutter.

***

I get back to my shitty little temporary apartment and throw my car keys on the side. Fuck, that was heavy. Minutes later, the door opens and Callie comes in. "So, how did it go?"

I shrug out of my jacket. "What the hell is going on with him and his wife?"

She sits on the couch. "Domestic violence. I told you."

"Nah, it was weirder than that. I mean, she's scared to death, it's obvious, but you feel the tension in every room. It's like the violence is clinging to every wall and silently screaming. He didn't take his eyes off her the whole time she was around us. It's like he was watching for the smallest mistake."

"He probably was. Men like him enjoy complete control. Anyway, we're not there to deal with the wife. Are you in?"

I nod, unable to suppress my smile. She claps her hands together. "Yessss!"

"But . . ." She flops back into the couch, groaning. "It's not exactly what we hoped for."

"We can't keep dragging this out, Nero."

"Hear me out," I say, taking a seat beside her. "I'm the wife's bodyguard."

She sits up straight. "What?"

"Yeah, surprised me too. No word of warning. He introduced me, then told her I was her new guard. I've got to go back tomorrow for a full briefing."

"A year," she snaps. "An entire year and all you get is babysitting duties?"

"Actually, this could work to our advantage. She could be our in. She hates him, you can see it in her face. I can try and get information out of her."

"She's not going to know anything, Nero. Come on, you know he plays his cards close to his chest. She's a battered housewife and no fucking use to us."

I pinch the bridge of my nose. "Then what do you suggest I do, Cal? Tell him to fuck off, refuse to do as he's ordered me? Then I'll be out and it'll all have been for nothing." I sigh. "Look, I'll be in the house, able to watch the comings and goings. I can listen in on conversations. Frankly, I don't have another option."

CHAPTER THREE

8 YEARS EARLIER...

TESSA

"WHAT DO WE DO?" asks Callie, staring out over London from the apartment that apparently belongs to Dante.

"This is your fault," I snap. "If you hadn't arranged to meet Jase in the first place, we wouldn't even know any of those men."

"Are you fucking serious?" she yells. "I just watched him get shot, and you're standing here blaming me?"

"Don't play the victim. You didn't seem too keen back there when he was pawing all over you."

The door opens and we fall silent. Dante shrugs out of his jacket and throws it on the side, then he loosens his tie. "You," he says, pointing to Callie, "come." He crooks his finger, but Callie stays rooted to the spot. I can see the annoyance on his face and I don't want to see him mad, so I give her a nudge and she goes to him. He gently runs his fingers through her hair, then suddenly grabs a handful and yanks her head back aggressively. "You breathe a fucking word to anyone about tonight, about Jase, about me, I'll kill your entire family. I know your dad, I know where your mum works, and I even know your little sister goes to Clairemont Primary School. Do I make myself clear?"

She doesn't speak, and he pulls out his mobile phone and opens it. He then shows her a picture, and she begins to cry. "That's your sister's bedroom, right?" She nods. "The man outside, the one who took this picture, will set that house alight if you don't agree. So, Callie, are we on the same page?" She nods again, desperately fighting back her tears. "Good." He shoves her away and turns his attention to Emerson. "Your dad will go to prison if you breathe a word. I have so much shit on him, he doesn't stand a chance."

Emerson nods. "I won't tell a soul." Her dad isn't exactly squeaky clean, so she's used to keeping secrets.

I'm trembling so hard and fighting the urge to vomit when he turns his attention to me. "Now, jailbait," he grins, "there's no one in your life I can threaten you with." I shake my head, wondering what that means for me. "Follow me." I hesitate as he marches towards a door down the passageway. "Enzo, take the other two home."

Present day . . .

I LAY in bed and count to ten. Breathe in, breathe out. It's no good—my heart is racing, and it's hard to ignore the way my stomach growls in hunger. "I know you're awake," Dante announces as he steps from the shower. "The beef was cooked to perfection," he adds, wrapping a towel around himself. "How did you do it in that short space of time?"

I force a light smile. "I didn't want your guests to wait," I say. "I was thinking of them."

He sits on the edge of the bed and tucks my hair behind my ear. I tense. "Did you use the air fryer?" I nod. "I asked for roast beef."

I smile again. "I still roasted it. You said yourself, it was cooked to perfection." His eyes darken in that way they always do when he's working himself up. "You gave me an hour," I add, trying to make him see reason, "and I didn't want to let you down and cause embarrassment."

He grabs my face, digging his fingers into my cheeks. "You were trying to be clever," he hisses, and spittle lands on my face. "Always trying to be fucking clever, jailbait."

I try to shake my head. "I wasn't, I promise. I was doing as you asked."

"Take yourself to the shed," he orders.

I stare in disbelief. It's cold out, frosty even, and as usual, I'm naked. I'm always naked when he's home, unless he gives me permission to wear clothes, and even then, he chooses them. "No." I don't fight Dante, not anymore, as I always end up worse off, but I refuse to go outside in these temperatures.

"Say it again," he whispers, his voice menacing.

I try to smooth my hand over his cheek. "Please, Dante, be reasonable."

"Unreasonable would be sending you to sit in the garden. I'm giving you shelter."

"For cooking the beef to perfection?" I cry. "For doing as you asked?"

Dante stands, taking me by the arm and hauling me from the bed. I try to prise his hand from me, but it's no good. He drags me from the room, pulling me angrily along the passageway and down the stairs.

I lose my footing as he pulls me through the kitchen, but it doesn't slow him. He continues dragging me behind like a rag doll. Opening the back door, he pushes me out into the garden, slamming the door in my face. I bang my hands against it, yelling his name over and over. We don't have neighbours, so no one will come to my rescue. I slide down the door and hug my knees to my chest.

NERO

DANTE ANDERSON SITS BACK in his office chair and stares at me. He does this a lot, mainly to show his authority and to intimidate, and on a normal man, I imagine it works. "I want you to have sex with my wife," he says clearly.

I sit straighter, my mouth opening and closing like a goddamn fish. No one ever catches me off guard, but this has. "Sorry?"

"You heard correctly." He clasps his hands in front of him and stares me dead in the eye. "I want a child, but it's something I can't give her."

I frown, rubbing my forehead. "You want me to have sex with your wife and get her pregnant?" He nods. "And what does your wife think about this?"

"She doesn't know."

I almost laugh. "You haven't asked her?"

"She can't know."

"Dante, with the greatest respect, I can't fuck your wife, get her pregnant, and not tell her. Besides, she's married . . . to you. I don't think she'll willingly sleep with me."

"That's why I hired you as her bodyguard. Get to know her. She'll fall for anyone who's nice to her." He sounds bitter, and I wonder for a second if she's ever cheated on him. *Of course, she hasn't . . . she'd be dead.* "I realise I'm asking a lot and it's an odd request."

"You're not fucking kidding," I mutter.

"The bottom line is, I want a child and I can't have one. Tessa doesn't know I can't have children. No one knows."

"Why me?" I ask.

"Kai tells me you're loyal, hardworking, that you want to be someone." I nod. "You've worked your arse off to get here, by my side." I nod again. "This is your chance."

"Hardly," I mutter. "What happens if I agree to this? Once she's pregnant, you won't want me around."

"I'll make you head of another division." I try to remain impassive, but this is huge. To get there, he'll need to let me in more and show me how he runs things. "I'll take you under my wing, show you the way and set you up in an area of your choosing."

"How will I know you'll stick to your word?"

"If I don't, you can tell Tessa everything."

"You could kill me so I don't get the chance."

He smiles. "I guess you'll have to trust me. Look," he rubs his forehead, the only sign he's letting his guard down, "Nero, I never go back on my word, ask anyone close to me. I'm giving you my word. I can't use any of my other men—they're too close, and I can't send them away after. You, I don't know, but I have my men backing you, telling me you're keen and loyal. I can send you away."

"ARE YOU FUCKING SHITTING ME?" Callie screeches.

"I'm just as spun out about this as you."

"Surely, you're not considering it?"

"If I don't do this, I have to walk away. He'll never let me hang around knowing what I know."

"I'll never get this approved. You've lost your mind."

"So, don't approve it."

She glares at me. "Don't act crazy. This is our career. I'm pulling this case."

"No. Don't you fucking dare. This can work. We've come so far, it has to work."

"Listen to yourself, Nero. This is madness. You're losing your mind. You've been in there too long."

"Come on, we've been deeper than this, in more shit than this, and we never pulled out."

"This is different. This is Dante fucking Anderson, and he's asking you to get his wife pregnant. It's too far. You're bringing an innocent life into it."

"What if I don't get her pregnant?" I pause. "What if he thinks that's what I'm doing, but I don't. It's not like he can ask her."

Callie runs her hands over her face. "I don't know. It's too risky. This could end very badly."

"We both know Dante gets what he wants. If it isn't me, it'll be someone else. I can string this out for as long as I need for him to take me under his wing. It's an offer we'd be stupid to ignore."

CHAPTER FOUR

TESSA

MY MIND IS RACING and I'm struggling to breathe, like my lungs aren't fully taking in the air. The room feels hot, too hot, and I pull at my shirt to generate a slight breeze. I perch nervously on the edge of the huge bed inside Dante's bedroom. He stares at me for an uncomfortably long time, adding to the stress I already feel.

"You have no one," he repeats.

"I won't say anything," I mutter, and my voice sounds weak and so unlike me.

"I know." He takes my hand and pulls me to stand. He gently brushes some hair from my face and then he lowers his mouth to mine. My heart slams harder when I realise I can't pull away because his hand is gripping the back of my neck. His lips are rough against my own, and his stubble scratches against me. When he pulls back, his eyes are full of lust. "You're going to stay here, with me."

"Huh?"

"You're staying here, jailbait."

I laugh nervously, waiting for him to tell me he's joking. When he doesn't, my smile fades and I swallow the lump in my throat. "You're crazy."

"Have you had sex before?"

Panic replaces the nervousness, and I frown. "What's that got to do with anything?" I pull free and head for the door.

He snatches my hand in his, yanking me back to him. "Are you a virgin?" I shake my head, suddenly scared to be here, trapped in this room with a man twice my age. A man I've seen do the unspeakable. "Shame." He slips my top from my shoulder, and I shrug him off. He narrows his eyes. "I always get what I want, Tessa, and I want you. We can do this the easy way or the hard way." I shove him, but he hardly moves. Instead, he grins. "The hard way is fine by me."

———

THE NEXT DAY, Dante slows the car outside the care home. "Hurry."

"They'll ask questions," I mutter, gently running my fingers over the bruise above my knee.

Dante catches my chin in his grasp and pulls my face to look at him. I wince. "Hurry, or I'll come in there and find you."

Josey rushes towards me the second I close the door. "Jesus, what happened?" She checks my black eye.

"I got into a fight," I mumble, turning my head away. "I'm fine."

"You didn't come home last night. You have a curfew."

"Curfews are for kids, and I'm almost seventeen. Another month and you'll be kicking me out anyway." I rush upstairs and slam the door. I fall onto my bed and cry hard, pushing my face into my pillow to muffle the sound. I want to tell Josey the truth and beg her to help me, but Dante said if I tell anyone, he'll kill Callie and Emerson. They're the only people I truly care about, and after what he did to me last night, I fully believe he'll kill anyone who stands in his way.

Taking a deep breath, I push to sit up and look around the room I've lived in for the last two years. I don't know what Dante has in store for me, but it's not anything good. Judging by last night, I'm heading to live in hell.

Present day . . .

I EXAMINE the packet of biscuits before placing them in my shopping trolley, then I glance at Nero, who follows a few steps behind. I've never been allowed out alone. I spend days either locked up in the house or following Dante around while he does business. This is the first time I've been allowed out of Dante's sight and away from the house, and I can't deny I feel sick with nerves. When he announced Nero would be my bodyguard, I didn't realise it meant I'd get more freedom, and now, other questions are plaguing my mind, like why Dante would suddenly ease up on me. It makes no sense. All I can come up with is that it's a trick and, later, when I return home, he'll punish me.

Dante gave me a bank card this morning at breakfast and ordered me to do some food shopping. Usually, he takes care of that by ordering everything online. It's been a long time since I did anything like this. I'm already on the third aisle in the supermarket and I'm finding the whole thing overwhelming. Eventually, Nero steps closer. "Is everything okay, Mrs. Anderson?"

I nod, then shake my head and decide to come clean. "Actually, no."

He frowns. "You're not sure what to get for dinner?"

I look around. "I'm not sure how to do any of this," I admit. "At all."

"You usually have someone who does this for you?"

I nod. "The shopping always gets delivered to the house, and it's always the same things."

He almost smiles but then sees I'm serious and goes back to frowning. "When was the last time you did a supermarket shop?"

"Never," I mutter. "I mean, I've been into shops, but not for a long time, especially not on my own."

"Well, things haven't changed much in the last year or so," he says, smiling again.

I bite my lower lip and glance around. "Since I was maybe sixteen," I admit, and his mouth falls open in surprise. "And at that age, I mainly bought magazines and chocolate."

His frown deepens. "Right, okay. Well, firstly, you're not alone. I'm here, and I know how to navigate around a supermarket. Secondly, tell me what you like to cook and I'll show you where the things are."

"On Mondays, we have chicken."

"Every Monday?" I nod. "Why don't you change things up a bit and go for steak?"

I bite my lower lip. I don't want to give Dante an excuse to punish me. "I think Dante prefers chicken on a Monday."

He shrugs. "Right. Follow me."

Nero shows me where to find the chicken and then the vegetables. I want to try the different varieties, but I don't think Dante would approve, so I stick to the usual potatoes and green beans. "Maybe I could get some things for baking," I suggest quietly.

"If you want to, it's your choice."

Those words make me nervous. I've been so used to having my choices limited, it seems alien to me now. "I used to love baking."

He stares for a moment. "So, why did you stop?"

I shrug. "I just did." I can't tell him I stopped doing all the things I loved when my life became Dante's.

———————

AFTER SHOPPING, we load up the car and Nero turns to me. "We should get coffee." I shake my head and climb into the passenger side of the car, then he gets into the driver's seat. "You don't like coffee?"

"Dante didn't say I could . . ." I trail off, wincing at my slip-up. "I mean, I didn't tell him, and he'll worry."

"I'll clear it with him, don't stress."

Panic rises in my chest. He might think it was my idea and he'll accuse me of flirting. "No. I want to go home."

Nero eyes me for a second before nodding. "Fine, your call."

Dante isn't home when we return. Nero carries the shopping into the kitchen, and I begin to put things away. He turns on the coffee machine. "Want one?" he asks. I guess now we're home, it's okay, so I nod.

I continue to put things away as Nero takes a seat at the kitchen island, watching me.

"What do you have to do once I'm home and safe?" I ask.

"Just hang out here."

"All day?"

He nods. "Boss said to do whatever you want. I can take you wherever you want to go, and if you want to stay home, I should keep you company."

I frown. Dante's never bothered about me having company before, especially male company. "Are you gay?" I blurt out, and he laughs.

"No, I'm definitely not gay."

"Married?" He shakes his head again. "I don't understand why Dante would ask you to stick around. It's not like him."

"What is he like?"

I bite my lower lip. Dante would hate me talking about him. "I just don't understand," I repeat.

"Maybe stop trying to," he suggests. "Just relax, and we can get to know one another."

"Why?"

He smirks. "Because that's what people do? Besides, if we're going to be spending time together, it's only right we know each other."

I must work out what Dante is playing at to stay ahead of the game. Something is off with this whole situation.

NERO

TESSA IS SUSPICIOUS. She's also jumpy, like all the time. At the slightest noise, she looks around nervously, as if she's expecting something bad to happen. Dante has a reputation for violence, but I can't see any signs of bruises. I'm not stupid, I know not all domestic violence is physical, and even when it is, perpetrators can be very careful about the marks they leave and where they leave them.

"Do you have siblings?" I ask, trying to get her to relax. She shakes her head. "What about your parents, are they still together?" She shrugs, looking more uncomfortable by the second. Maybe I should get Callie to look into Tessa's background. We didn't bother because it's Dante we want, and it's obvious Tessa has no control in the relationship. I doubt she knows any of his business dealings, and my only hope is she's one of those women who linger in the background, listening to everything that's said. She looks the type to hold secrets. "You're gonna have to help me out here, Tessa. I'm trying to get to know you."

She places her hands on the worktop and stares at me with suspicious eyes. "I don't know how much you know about my marriage, Nero, but it's complicated. If Dante finds us chatting like besties, he'll shut it down and I'll pay the price." She turns her back to me and begins washing dishes.

"What does that mean?" I ask, glancing at the dishwasher and wondering why she isn't using it.

"I think it's best we don't talk."

"What, ever?" I ask, smirking. "How will I know where you want to go? And can I ask why you're handwashing the dishes when you have a dishwasher right there?"

"Dante likes the dishes handwashed."

"So, why have the dishwasher?"

"Because . . . I don't know. Why do you ask so many questions?"

I try a different tactic, figuring she'll never tell anyone anyway. "I have a sister. She lives in Ireland, so I don't see her as much as I'd like. She's a headteacher in a primary school. My parents are both dead." I see her watching me from the corner of her eye. She's intrigued. "I'm not married and I don't have kids. Not that I know of." I laugh to show I'm joking.

"Sorry about your parents."

"Don't be, you didn't kill them."

She gasps. "They were killed?"

I nod. "Drunk driver. He hit their car when they were travelling to the airport to see Luna. That's my sister."

"That's awful. Did they find the driver?"

I nod. "Yeah, he's in prison."

"It must be hard. I don't know my parents . . . not anymore, anyway. I was taken into care when I was younger. I grew up in foster care and, eventually, I went into a care home."

I breathe a sigh of relief that she's finally talking. "Wow. And look at you now, living in this huge house."

A sadness passes over her face. "Yes, I'm very lucky."

"Did you stay in contact with any of your foster carers or people you grew up with?" She shakes her head. "How did you meet Dante?"

She dries her hands. "My friend. She was dating someone he knew."

I grin. "Love at first sight, was it?"

She frowns. "So, how come you're single?"

"I've been away for a long time, so I never really got the chance."

"Away?" she repeats.

"You know the life, Tessa," I say, finishing my coffee.

"What did you go away for?"

I grin, standing. "I'll tell you when we know each other better."

***

"How did the first day of babysitting go?" Callie asks, handing me a beer.

"She's hard work. Can we run some checks on her?"

"Already did. There's nothing. She grew up in care. Never been in trouble with the police, not even a speeding ticket. She's never held a job, and there are no family on record."

"Yeah, she said as much. Weird, though, that she's not even worked. How long she been with Dante?"

Callie shrugs. "I have no idea. The marriage was registered eight years ago."

"So, she was what, sixteen?"

Callie nods. "Young."

"She's a nervous wreck. She jumps at the slightest noise."

"Just focus on the job, Nero. We're not there to rescue little miss gangster wife. We've bigger fish to fry."

CHAPTER FIVE

TESSA

I STILL REMEMBER the first time Dante hit me outside the bedroom. He accused me of flirting with a barman. I wasn't, I'd just smiled and thanked him for my drink, but it was all the excuse Dante needed to lose his mind. He punched me so hard, my ears rang for hours. Everyone around us in the bar turned the other way. They didn't want to call Dante Anderson out and get themselves into a bother. After that day, I was a little more cautious of how I spoke and the smiles I gave.

So, now, as I cover a black eye with makeup, I fight tears from falling. I hate myself a little more every time this happens. And it isn't every day—some days, he's the sweetest man. But then there're days like today, where whatever I do or say is going to get me hurt because he's just in that sort of mood. I know the signs now. The look in his eyes, which darken in anger and narrow slightly. And the way he questions me, asking for every single detail, warns me that things are going to go badly for me. And no matter how much I try to defuse the situation, I somehow only make it worse.

The bedroom door opens and Dante lingers there, watching me. "Wear the black dress." I nod. "And lose the makeup." I stare at his reflection in the mirror. No makeup means people will see my eye. "What?" he asks, daring me to speak what's on my mind. I shake my head and force a smile before taking a makeup wipe to remove what little I'd already applied.

———

HOOKING my arm into Dante's, he leads me into the bar. We spend most Saturday nights in here. Most of his business associates are here too, and they play poker and drink whiskey.

Some of the other men's wives sit together, but I've never been invited to join them, and Dante wouldn't let me even if I was. He always takes my hand and keeps me close.

Dante is speaking with Kai, and I have an urgent need to use the bathroom. He releases me, but as I move towards the bathroom, I feel myself being tugged back by the hair. I fully expect it to be Dante having changed his mind, but as I turn, it's Emerson glaring at me. "I thought that was you," she snaps. I haven't seen her or Callie since that day in Dante's apartment. He'd taken my mobile phone from me, and I hadn't been allowed to leave his side, so it's been impossible to contact either of them.

"Emerson," I gasp. "I . . . I . . ." My eyes fill with tears because there's so much I want to say but can't. I have no doubt Dante will come searching for me if I don't hurry.

"You look a mess," she spits, and I frown. I'm confused by her anger. "Don't you have anything to say to me?"

"I'm so sorry," I begin. This angers her more, and this time, she reels back and slaps me hard across the face. I cry out, gripping my cheek.

"I thought we were friends, but the second he comes along, you dump us for him. You know he's a monster, don't you, Tessa? But then you always did love the danger."

I'm crying into my hands as I feel Dante touch my back. "Emerson, it's been a while."

"A whole year. I can't say I've missed you . . . either of you."

"Emerson, what the fuck are you doing?" Her dad rushes towards us. "Mr. Anderson," he adds, holding out his hand for Dante to shake, but he stares at it coldly until it's retracted.

"Your daughter just hit my wife," Dante says through gritted teeth.

"Jesus, I am so sorry," Emerson's dad rushes out. "Shit, Emerson, apologise."

"It's fine," I mutter feebly, wanting to get away from it all.

"It's not fine. Hit her back," Dante orders.

I glance up at him. "Huh?"

"You heard me. Hit her back."

I shake my head. "No."

"Hit her, or I will."

I swallow, glancing at Emerson, who looks outraged. "I don't want to."

Dante grabs a handful of my hair. "You're fucking weak," he hisses.

"Please, Mr. Anderson, I can't apologise enough. I'll have strong words with Emerson," her dad pleads.

Dante releases me, shoving me to Kai, who takes my

arms and begins to pull me away. "Please, Dante," I yell. "Please don't hurt her."

I'm almost out the door when I see Dante backhand Emerson across the face.

Present day . . .

DANTE STANDS in the kitchen doorway, watching as I finish off scrubbing the kitchen floor. My hands are sore and my knees ache. Drying my hands on my top, I push to stand. "I lost track of time," I say, standing on my tiptoes and kissing him on the cheek. "Did you have a good day?"

"Leave dinner tonight. I'm taking you out."

"I've cooked chicken," I say, glancing back at the oven. "It'll be just a minute."

"I'm taking you out. Go and get dressed." He hands me a bag containing a dress before he saunters off to his office, and I sigh. I'm shattered from the housework, and the last thing I want to do is spend the evening watching my every word in case I upset him. I turn off the oven and rush upstairs to do as asked. He doesn't like to be kept waiting.

By the time I'm ready, he's at the door, and he watches as I descend the stairs. "Beautiful," he mutters. Dante rarely compliments me these days, so I smile politely.

He drives us to his favourite Greek restaurant. We're seated in his usual spot by the window, and he orders our meals without checking the menu—soutzoukakia for him and a Greek salad for me.

"How was your day?" he asks, pouring some water into my glass. Dante never asks about my day, so it only adds to my suspicion.

"It was fine," I reply carefully. "I got dinner like you asked."

"Good. Did you go anywhere else?" I shake my head. "Why?"

"You didn't say I could."

He smiles, satisfied. "Good girl." I relax slightly, knowing I did the right thing in coming straight home. "And what do you think of Nero?"

I nervously tap my fingers on my knee under the table. I don't know how to answer him without setting him off. "He's very professional."

"Do you feel safe with him?" I nod. "I've asked him to take you more places. I'm sure you'd like to go somewhere other than the supermarket."

Sickness bubbles in my stomach. "There's nowhere I need to go."

"Tessa, you've been by my side or locked up in that house for years. Don't you want more freedom?"

I think over my answer carefully. "I want whatever you want."

"And I want you to have some freedom."

"Why?" The word is out my mouth before I can stop it, and I try to calm the panic I feel at such a stupid mistake.

But Dante just smiles, relaxing back in his chair and watching me with amusement. "Maybe I'm getting bored of you," he muses. I stare at him, not daring to speak. "Maybe I've met someone else." I don't react. "Or maybe, my darling wife, I just want to see you smile for once. It's not fun staring at your miserable face." And there it is, the cruel look in his eye.

"Have you met someone?" I ask. I'm not sure how I feel about this potential new information. I've never really thought about what would happen if Dante met someone else. Would it mean I'd get freedom? Probably not, as he's not the type to let me walk away. That thought sits in my mind while I wait patiently for him to answer.

"You used to smile," he continues like I haven't spoken. "Even in the early days when you hated me." I don't point out that I've always hated him. "There were times when you'd almost look happy." I grit my teeth together until they ache. He's fucking delusional. I've been in survival mode since the day he forced me to pack my things and live with him, and any smile I may have sent his way was purely to keep him from hurting me. "When I showed you the new house, that was a happy moment." He's talking like he's lost in thought and I'm not really sitting here wanting to scream. "I want to see you smile again." *He just needs to stop torturing me with his sick games.* "I think we should have a child."

"No!" I yell, almost jumping out my seat. Dante arches a brow, and I bite my lower lip, glancing round nervously at the few people who look over at my outburst. I take a breath and lower back down. "I mean, I don't think it's the right time."

"You talk like I need your permission."

The food arrives and he takes my plate, scraping half the salad from it before placing it back in front of me. Controlling my food is one of his favourite things to do. He doesn't care if we're in a restaurant, entertaining friends, or alone, he always removes something from my plate. I stare down at the green leaves I'm left with, most of the olives and feta now on a napkin. My stomach growls in protest and I fight back my tears.

"If you want a child, I'd need to eat properly," I mutter, unable to stop myself.

"You also need to be a healthy weight," he snipes, and I

bite my lip. Answering him a second time will result in a painful night. The truth is, if I lose any more weight, I'll be bones.

"I'd also have to see medical professionals," I add. He'd hate that. Not only because they might see the bruises he leaves on my skin, but also because they might reach out a hand to help, and fuck knows I'd take it. I haven't seen a doctor or nurse since before I met him eight years ago.

"I'd never deny you medical treatment, Tessa. What are you trying to say?" He's daring me to call him out. When I don't reply, he smirks. "You're clumsy, and you bruise far too easily, right?" I nod begrudgingly. He's drilled it into me so many times that it would always be my word against his, and who would believe me? A messed-up kid who grew up in a care home. The police could never fully protect me, and he'd kill me, I have no doubt about that, but then he'd find Callie and end her too. My mind wanders back to Emerson and that same feeling of sickness and pain swills around in my stomach.

I push the plate of leaves away. "I'm tired. Can we go home?"

He smiles. "When I've finished eating."

NERO

"YOU'RE VERY QUIET TODAY," I say, watching Tessa as she scrubs the spotlessly clean kitchen cupboards. "Have you eaten breakfast?" She shakes her head but continues scrubbing. "Didn't you clean those just the other day?"

"I don't need to go out today. Feel free to go and keep busy," she mutters.

"Dante insisted I take you out today."

She stops, and her hands fall to her knees. I hear her silently sobbing and rush over. "Tessa, what's wrong?" I gently touch her arm, and when she jumps in fright, I hold my hands up. "Sorry, I was just checking you were okay." She jumps down off the kitchen worktop and sways, grabbing hold of the side to steady herself. I catch her, and she has no choice but to lean on me as I guide her over to a stool. "You haven't eaten properly in days, have you?" I ask, and she shakes her head. "Let me get you something."

"I'm fine."

I ignore her and open the kitchen cupboard. It's empty. I frown and go to the next, then the next, but they're all bare. She watches with terror in her eyes. I go to the fridge, but again, it's empty apart from a small amount of milk and butter. "Where's the food?"

"I . . . I, erm . . ." She puts her head in her hands, and I go back to her, crouching down and tugging her hands away.

"Tessa, what's going on?" Her tears fall silently with a look of hopelessness on her face. "Why isn't there any food in the house?"

"I need to go shopping."

"Why didn't you say? I can take you shopping."

"Dante didn't . . . he didn't . . . I don't have any money."

"What about the card he left you yesterday?" She shakes her head but offers no explanation. "Okay, I have an idea." I stand, pulling her with me. "Let's go and feed you."

"I don't think I should—"

"Eat?" I finish, and she nods. "I don't care what's going on with you and Dante, Tessa, but you're eating today. As your bodyguard, I'm forcing you."

"He'll be mad," she whispers.

I gently swipe her tears away with the pads of my thumbs. "He doesn't have to know."

———

I HAND the menu to Tessa, and she stares at it in a panic. "Choose anything, my treat," I reassure her.

"What's good?"

I frown. "Most of it. I like the Angus steak burger personally."

"I'll take that," she says, closing the menu.

I re-open it. "Tessa, look at the menu. Choose what you want."

She stares at it and a tear escapes down her cheek again. She slams the menu down and wipes her cheek angrily. "I bet you think I'm pathetic," she mutters, but I shake my head. "I wasn't always like this. I used to make decisions and choose food."

I like that she's opening up. "What changed?"

She thinks for a moment. "Dante."

"Well, he isn't here now," I remind her, nodding at the menu. She smiles sadly and goes back to looking. When the waitress arrives, I patiently wait for her to say what she wants, smiling when she orders salmon and potatoes.

Once the waitress leaves with our order, I put my full attention back on her. "Tell me about your life before Dante." When she hesitates, I place my hand over hers. "You can trust me, Tessa. I won't tell him anything you say."

"He pays your wage."

I nod. "He does, but I still have my own opinions and, honestly, I don't like what I see between the two of you."

"There's not much to tell," she says. "I grew up in care, then I met Dante and he saved me."

"Saved you?" I repeat.

"I was about to be sent out into the big bad world. I was almost seventeen, and they encourage you to leave the care home and be more independent. I'd have gotten a bedsit, but I would have been alone."

"You didn't have friends? You mentioned before that you did."

"I had friends, but everyone moves on as you grow up."

I shrug. "I don't know about that, I'm still in touch with friends I grew up with."

"Lucky you."

"Did you choose to lose contact, Tessa, or did Dante prefer it that way?"

The food arrives and she takes the chance to change the subject.

CALLIE ISN'T IMPRESSED when I give her the rundown of my day. The phone line on her end goes silent for some time before she inhales sharply. "Have you forgotten the reason you're there?"

"Of course not, but I can't ignore this."

"You can, Nero. You have to because it's distracting you. While you were playing babysitter and feeding her, where was Dante?"

"I don't know."

"Exactly, and you should know because he's our target. You need to push your way in there."

"Tessa is the way in," I remind her.

"No, Nero. No, she isn't. She doesn't know anything. She's his bitch. There's no secret there—you already know he beats the shit out of her. We can't get him on domestic violence or starving his wife because it's not big enough."

"Maybe we can get her out of there, put her in a safe house."

She sighs heavily. "Listen to yourself. So, we get her out, then what? What do you tell Dante, that you lost his wife? What do you think he'll do then? He's paying you to watch her, fuck her, get her up the duff. If you lose her, he's going to kill you, and then whole operation fails. No, you have to keep her in there and begin worming your way into Dante's good books. If I were you, I'd tell him she's confiding in you. He'll soon shut her up, then you can concentrate on the important stuff."

"Christ, were you always this harsh?" I ask.

"Yes. It's why I'm at the top. Now, sort your head out and get me something on Dante Anderson before the whole thing collapses."

I disconnect. She's right, until I get something on him, Tessa is stuck there.

CHAPTER SIX

TESSA

I'M in bed when I hear the front door slam. Holding my breath, I wait for his angry footsteps to hunt me down. There's a commotion downstairs, but I don't move. It's best not to see whatever is going on. I learned that very quickly.

Almost twenty minutes later, I hear his footsteps. I can't control the panic taking over my body. The bedroom door opens, flooding the room in light. I squeeze my eyes closed and try to slow my breathing. "There's a guest downstairs." I don't respond, hoping he'll think I'm sleeping and leave me alone, but he rips the sheets away. "Get up, Tessa," he says through gritted teeth. I get out of bed, and he grabs my wrist, dragging me like a toy doll behind him. "You embarrassed me tonight," he snaps.

"I didn't mean to. Emerson is my friend. I couldn't hit her."

"Do you let all your friends hit you?"

He shoves me into the living room, and I freeze. Naked on the couch is Emerson. Sitting on the end of the couch, topless and with his jeans unfastened, is Enzo. "She's good, Tessa, but she isn't you," Dante hisses in my ear, and a sob escapes me. "Now, hit her." I shake my head. She's passed out cold, but I can see bruises beginning to form on her body.

"You've hurt her enough," I whisper.

He grabs my hair and pushes me closer. "She disrespected you, which means she disrespected me. Hit her or you'll face the same punishment."

"I don't care," I whisper, letting tears flow freely down my cheeks. "I won't hit her. I'm not you."

He laughs, turning me to face him and slapping me hard. I fall to the floor, right beside Emerson. Scrambling to my knees, I move the hair from her face. "Em, wake up. Em," I whisper urgently. She stirs, groaning when she tries to move.

Dante slaps her arse, and she cries out, her eyes springing open. And then, as if the memories rush back to her, she sits up wide-eyed and begins to scream. Dante places his hand over her mouth, pulling her against him. "Now, now, gorgeous, let's not cause a scene again."

"Please, Dante. Do whatever you want to me, just don't hurt her anymore," I plead with him.

Emerson's eyes find me, and we share a pained look. "Are you sure you won't hit her?" he asks, and I shake my head. "Okay, then everything that happens next is because of you." He places his hand on Emerson's forehead and the other wraps around her chest, and then he pulls, yanking her head to one side fast and hard. There's a sharp cracking sound and her eyes widen before she drops to the floor, her gaze still fully on me but now lifeless.

I stare open-mouthed. "All you had to do was hit her back," he continues as if nothing happened.

"What did you do?" I whisper, crawling over to Emerson. I hold a shaky hand over her, hesitating before I touch her. When I do, she's still and completely lifeless. I begin sobbing and shaking her. "Wake up," I beg. "Wake up, Emerson."

Dante drags me up off the floor. "She's fucking dead, Tessa. That's your fault."

I shake my head frantically. "No, no, no."

He gives a satisfied smile. "I want you to sit here," he orders, pushing me to my knees beside Emerson, "all night. Don't fucking move and don't go to sleep. You should think about what you've done tonight, the heartbreak you have caused to her family."

"But . . . I don't . . . I can't . . . please, Dante."

He slaps me hard, so hard it feels like my brain is bouncing around in my skull. "Don't move or I will find Callie and she'll join her."

I watch as Dante and Enzo leave, closing the door behind them.

I gently move Emerson's hair from her face before closing her eyes. Then I curl up behind her and wrap my arm around her waist, just like we used to when we were younger. I remind her of the times when we were carefree and how we'd laugh at stupid things. I tell her how sorry I am, and how I only lost contact with her to save her. But in the end, I couldn't.

And then I beg God to hear me and free me from this hell.

Present day . . .

I STARE at myself in the full-length mirror. The bruises littering my body are colourful, if nothing else. Dante has been true to his word over the last month. He's trying hard to get me pregnant, and whenever he's home, we have sex. Cold, hard, forceful sex, and each time, I wonder why the hell he would want to bring a child into this mess. He can't even try to conceive it with love and kindness. These bruises aren't from his fists, for once, yet somehow, it feels worse because I'd rather his fists beat me than him force himself on me to get me pregnant.

I'm thankful for one thing—Nero. He's kept me sane these last few weeks. He's kept his word and hasn't told Dante anything. He feeds me secretly every day. He's kind and funny, and he finds places to take me so I'm not stuck in the house. I'm even noticing a slight tan on my skin from our days spent sightseeing.

Today is my birthday. I'm excited because Nero has plans for our day, and he's been teasing me all week, giving me clues. I can't dress in anything that doesn't cover me up, so I choose jeans and a shirt, and when I glance back in the mirror, I decide to unfasten the top two buttons. It's hardly revealing anything, but I smile as I bounce downstairs. Today, I feel beautiful, and I haven't felt like that in such a long time.

Nero is waiting in the kitchen. He picks me up and spins me around until I laugh. "Happy birthday." He puts me back on my feet and produces a small box. I take it, biting my lip to hide my smile. "It's just something small."

"You shouldn't have," I whisper, carefully removing the wrapping paper. I haven't celebrated my birthday since I met Dante, so getting a gift feels alien. I open the box to reveal a delicate silver bracelet with a tiny diamond. "It's your birthstone . . . April," he explains.

I throw my arms around him. "Thank you so much. I love it."

He wraps me in his strong arms and something shifts between us. As I pull back, we stare into each other's eyes, and for a second, I contemplate kissing him. *Fuck, I really want to kiss him.* But then the front door slams and we pull apart. I shove my gift into the nearest drawer and turn just as Dante walks in. "Happy birthday, my gorgeous wife," he says, smiling bright. I frown as he pushes a bunch of flowers into my hands and kisses me on the head.

"Thank you," I mutter, feeling confused. Nero smiles awkwardly.

"And here's a special gift," Dante adds, placing a long, thin, wrapped box in my hand. "Nero, we won't be needing you today," he adds, and I feel my heart crush in my chest. I was so excited about today. "I have plans that involve my wife and our bed," he says, winking.

Nero nods once and steps towards the exit. "Okay, Boss." We lock eyes before he turns and leaves.

Dante pulls my face up to look at him. "Why do you look so sad? It's your birthday."

"I didn't think you knew," I mutter.

He laughs again. "Of course, I know your birthday. I know everything about you. Now, open your gift."

I rip the paper and my heart stops. "It's a pregnancy test," I mutter.

"What better gift? If this is positive, we can celebrate." *And if it's not . . .*

He leads me to the bathroom, taking the test from me and unboxing it. "Pee in this," he says, handing me a small plastic pot.

"I don't know if I can pee on demand," I admit.

"Don't talk crap, Tessa, just piss in the damn pot."

I do as asked, and he takes the pot, placing it on the side. I watch as he dips the stick and lays it flat beside it. Then he turns to me and wraps his arms around me. "This could change our lives," he says, kissing me. "I can't wait to be a dad," he adds, tugging my hair and kissing me harder. "I've always wanted a son I can teach. He can take over from me when I get too old." He laughs as I cross my fingers behind my back and pray to God it's negative. Damn the consequences.

NERO

"CAN you come back to the house?" Dante asks when I answer his call.

"Of course. Everything okay?"

"Just get here," he mutters, disconnecting.

"Dante?" asks Callie, and I nod. "You think he's got some work for you?"

I shrug. "I only left them a couple of hours ago, but maybe."

DANTE IS in his home office when I arrive. There's no sign of Tessa. "Everything good, Boss?" I ask, closing the door and stepping closer to his desk. He throws a white plastic stick on the top and glares at me. I take the stick, turning it to see the word 'negative' in the window. "Is this a pregnancy test?"

"It's been six weeks," he snaps. "Why the fuck is it negative?"

I place it back. "These things take time, Boss. She took a while to open up to me."

"Every day, you're with her and you tell me you're fucking her. You tell me things are going well, and yet here we are with no fucking pregnancy."

"I was supposed to be spending the day with her today, remember," I ask, "but you surprised us by coming back." I sigh. "I'll keep trying, Boss. Relax."

"Relax?" he yells, slamming his hands on the table. "I'll relax when she's pregnant. Work harder. I'm going out of town today for two nights. I suggest you spend them in the bedroom."

IT'S BEEN two hours since Dante left for his trip and Tessa still hasn't appeared. I go upstairs and gently tap on her bedroom door. "Tessa, it's Nero," I tell her. "Are you okay?"

The door opens and Tessa stands before me in her underwear. I gasp, not because she's practically naked but because her body is covered in bruises. She's been crying, her cheeks are red, and her eyes swollen. "Jesus," I whisper. She falls into my arms and breaks out into fresh sobs. I walk her backwards into the bedroom, kicking the door closed. "Tessa, what the fuck happened?"

"We're trying for a baby," she sniffles. "Every morning, every night . . . I hate it. I hate him," she cries. It's the first time she's told me how she feels about Dante. Usually, she makes excuses, and she's never told me about the abuse, not really. "And today, my birthday gift was a pregnancy test. He wasn't happy it was negative."

"Fuck," I mutter, stroking a hand down her back.

"Tessa, I'm so sorry, I didn't realise." And I mean that in a different way to how she's taking it. Because what I really mean is I didn't think about him taking this shit out on her.

"Ask me," she says, sitting up and looking me in the eye.

"Ask you what?"

"What everyone wants to ask. Why am I still here? Why haven't I left him?"

"I'm sure you have your reasons."

"If I left right now . . . if I packed my bags and just walked away, what would happen?"

I think about her question. "I guess he'd kill me."

"Exactly. There's always someone he can hurt, someone he can hold over me. I can never leave because he'll kill people I love, then he'll come for me. He'll track me down and end my life in the worst possible way imaginable."

I choose not to go into the details of that last statement. "I thought there were no friends or family, so who could he hurt apart from me?"

"I had two friends before. We went to school together and were inseparable. We witnessed something, Dante threatened them and their families, and then he told me I had to move in with him or he'd kill my friends."

"So, what happened to them?"

"I'm not sure." She looks away, and I sense that she's lying. "But I have a feeling Dante would still find them or their families and he'd make sure I knew what he'd done."

"You ever witness him hurting people before, Tessa?"

She scoffs. "You'd be surprised at the things I pick up while hiding in the background."

"Like?"

"I wanted to kiss you before," she blurts out. "After you gave me my gift."

"But Dante walked in," I say. I know the exact moment because I wanted to kiss her too.

"Would you have let me?" she asks.

I turn to her, brushing the hair from her face. "Tessa, you're in enough danger. Kissing me would make everything so complicated."

She blushes. "You're right. Sorry, I'm a mess." She stands. "Oh god, I'm so embarrassed."

I rise to my feet, pulling her to look at me. "Don't be. I'm not saying I don't want to. I do. It's just—"

"You do?" she asks, her eyes hopeful. I nod. We stare at each other for a moment, and then I move closer, unable to stop myself. She moves too, until our lips are a breath apart.

"I do," I confirm. I gently brush her lips with my own, and she inhales sharply. Cupping her face in my hands, I do it again, this time letting my lips linger. She opens, giving me access, and I close my mouth over hers in a gentle, slow kiss.

TESSA

WE'RE KISSING. We're actually kissing, and it feels so good, like I'm alive again. My entire body tingles, and when he swipes his tongue against mine, I curl my toes. I've never felt like this, and I don't want the moment to end, so I push my hands under his T-shirt, feeling his warm, smooth skin. I run them over his hard chest, desperate to feel his body against my own. As if he's read my mind, he reaches for the hem of his shirt and tugs it over his head, briefly breaking our kiss. He skims my shoulders with his hands and my bra straps fall. He stops kissing me and rests his forehead against mine, looking down at my breasts. I pull the bra down completely, then I take his hands and guide them there. He cups them, rubbing his thumbs over my nipples, and I want to cry out in pleasure. His hands feel so good, so gentle.

I walk backwards until my legs hit the edge of the bed. I tug the button on his jeans, popping it open, and then I slide back onto the bed. He stands before me, and I rest on my elbows, watching as he removes his jeans, then his boxers. His body is perfect, from his muscled chest to his tight abs. My eyes trail down to his erection as he swoops down and grabs his wallet from his jeans. He pulls out a condom and rips open the packet. He rolls it down over his shaft before crawling between my legs and settling there.

"You sure about this?" he asks, kissing me, and I nod. I've never been surer of anything. I'm going to make the most of my two nights of freedom, and then I'm going to free myself forever. I'm going to join Emerson.

CHAPTER SEVEN

NERO

I WAKE AND STRETCH OUT. Tessa is naked beside me, lying on her stomach. We spent the entire night worshipping each other, and now, reality is setting in. Because despite all my training and experience, I don't know how to handle falling for someone while I'm on the job. They don't tell you what to do. They just tell you how to avoid it and then say that if you can't, go with it, because once the job is complete, you'll pack your shit and move on to the next. But as I count the bruises on her perfect skin—*eighteen just on her back*—I find myself trying to work out a way I get to keep her.

I go downstairs and call Callie. She's my handler, so she'll know what to do. "You didn't call in last night," she says. "I was getting worried."

"Sorry. Dante flipped out. He made Tessa do a pregnancy test and, of course, she was negative. It didn't go down well."

"Shit. What'd he say?"

"He left town for a couple nights so I could work harder." I give a humourless laugh. "Prick."

"Where did he go? Is he doing business?"

"I don't know. He beat the shit out of Tess and left."

"So, what did you do?"

"That's why I'm calling . . ."

"Oh, dear God, tell me you didn't do what he asked."

"Not completely. Well, as in, I used protection."

"FUCK!" Callie yells. "Are you joking? You had sex with his wife?"

"I had permission," I remind her.

"Not funny, Nero. So, now what?"

"I need to get her out of here."

"No, no, you don't. You leave like you were never there, and we find another way to get Dante."

"I can't, Callie. I can't just walk away and leave her here knowing what he's doing."

"If she hates it so much, why doesn't she leave? Ask yourself that."

"I asked her, but he's threatened her and her friends. She had no choice."

"There's always a choice. Get out of there and we'll pass it on to the local beat for DV. They can pick it up."

"He's got the police in his back pocket. She'll never talk to them."

"I don't care. Nero, she's not our problem. Get out of there. I'm pulling you."

I disconnect as Tessa wanders into the kitchen. "Good morning," she says, smiling shyly. I pull her to me, grabbing her arse in my hands and kissing her.

"Don't act all coy with me. I've seen you naked," I tease. She giggles, and it warms my heart. "Get dressed. I'm taking you to breakfast, and then we're celebrating your birthday just like we planned yesterday."

WE HAVE breakfast in a small deli in central London. It's good to see Tessa eating so well. She's slowly gaining weight and she looks amazing for it. I pay the bill while she goes to the bathroom, then I step outside to wait for her. "You ignored me," snaps Callie, marching over.

I glare at her. "What the hell are you doing?" I hiss, glancing inside the deli to make sure Tessa isn't coming out. "You're breaking every fucking rule by being here."

"I've pulled the plug on this, you have to step away."

"I told you, I can't just walk away."

"You don't have a choice, Nero. I've spoken to the chief, and he's in agreement with me. You've gotten in too deep. This is a direct order."

"Bullshit. I've done this a thousand times and walked away. I'm the inside, I know when the right time is, and it's not now."

The door opens, and I groan. Callie turns her back, but it's too late, Tessa's spotted us. Then she does something unexpected—she throws her arms around Callie and begins to sob. "Oh my god, Callie, it's really you." Callie avoids eye contact with me. "I didn't know if you were dead or alive or—"

"You know each other?" I ask.

"She was one of my friends that I told you about," Tessa says through her tears. "How do you know each other?"

I arch a brow for Callie to explain, and she turns to face Tessa, unhooking her arms from around her. "Tessa, long time," she mutters, smiling tightly.

Tessa wipes her eyes, nodding. "I've thought about you so much."

"I'm in a rush to get to work. Great to bump into you, Nero. Nice to see you again, Tessa." And then she rushes away.

Tessa stares after her, frowning. "How do you know each other?"

"I used to work with her. Come on, on to the next surprise," I say, grabbing her hand and pulling her in the opposite direction.

TESSA

I'VE NEVER BEEN clothes shopping. Dante always bought my clothes, usually a size too big. I stare at myself in my bedroom mirror and take in the outfit that Nero insisted on buying for me. The jumpsuit fits well, hugging in at the waist to give me a figure I didn't know existed. I smile as I lightly run my fingers over the delicate necklace he gave me while we sat in the park and enjoyed a picnic. I wish I'd met Nero all those years ago, because now, it's too late. Dante will be home tomorrow, and I have a plan that I need to carry out before he returns. I take a deep breath and release it slowly. I have tonight, and that's all I'm going to think about right now.

As I descend the stairs, Nero is standing by the door, staring down at his mobile phone. He looks up and smiles wide. "Wow, you look hot."

I blush at his compliment as his appraising eyes take me in. "Thank you. You don't look too bad yourself."

He does a slow spin to show off his shirt and jeans. "Thank you." He hooks out his arm for me to take. "Let's get you wasted on tequila and beer."

THE ONLY BARS I've ever been in are the ones run by Dante or his friends. They're the kind where dangerous men hang out and everyone knows everyone else.

So, when we enter a bar in central London with twinkling fairy lights and bright décor, I gasp out loud. It's beautiful, and there's not one dangerous-looking gangster in sight. I relax instantly, and Nero leads me to the bar. "I want to open up a tab," he tells the bartender, handing over a bank card. "We've booked a booth, number ten," he adds. The bartender nods, handing him an electronic device, and then he leads me over to a booth.

"What's that?" I ask as he places the device on the table.

"You tap it when you want service."

"Wow." I glance at the menu, looking at the different types of drinks. "I've never heard of any of this."

"Didn't you go to these sorts of bars when you were younger?"

I shake my head. "We were too young, and the doormen would never have believed our fake I.D.s. We stuck to local bars. Emerson, my friend, her dad was well known, so we could drink in our area and it didn't bother anyone."

"Oh yeah, what's his name? I might know him."

I shrug, not wanting to tell him in case he knows what happened to Emerson. Her dad is still in the area, and I see him when I go out with Dante, but he doesn't speak or even look in our direction. There's been so many times I've wanted to go over and tell him how sorry I am and that I laid with her all night until Dante ripped me away kicking and screaming. "Do you know Callie well?" His jaw tightens, and it's clear he doesn't want to talk about her. "Were you two a thing?" I ask, smirking.

He nods. "Yes, and I really don't want to ruin our night talking about exes. I haven't seen her in a long time before today. I don't know her anymore."

"You're right, it's not important. Let's have fun tonight and worry about everything else tomorrow. But I would like to speak to her again. Maybe you could get me her number?"

I DRINK shots like I'm sixteen again and it feels good. I like the buzz alcohol gives me, and I like how brave I feel. Maybe that's why Dante hardly lets me drink—he knows I'll speak my mind. I lean closer to Nero. "Before Dante, I was happy," I say, my words slurring. "Everyone assumes kids in care are sad and angry. I wasn't. I loved being surrounded by people. I was always supposed to be surrounded."

"What was the bad thing?" asks Nero. "You said before, he threatened you and your friends because you witnessed a bad thing."

I smile, tapping his lips with my finger. "I can't tell you his secrets, Nero. He'll kill me."

"I won't tell him."

"You might." Emerson's face flashes through my mind. "Yah know, it's kind of all Callie's fault," I add. "She met a guy and dragged us all down with her."

"Oh yeah?"

I frown, thinking back to his earlier words. "How did you work with her when you've been in prison? Is that how you met her, through work? How did you end up together?"

"I thought we weren't talking about Callie?" He kisses me and thoughts of Callie leave my mind.

NERO

TESSA IS WASTED. I feel terrible, she's slurring her words and lounging all over me, but I'm desperate for any information that'll get Callie off my back, and the more she drinks, the more she talks. I top up her glass and encourage her to drink it in one.

"Why were you in prison?" she asks.

"I'll tell you my secrets if you tell me yours," I say.

She sighs heavily. "I can't have children," she confesses.

I lean closer. "What?"

"I've known since I was fourteen. I had something wrong with my ovaries and had to have an operation. It left scarring, so the chances of me conceiving are extremely low."

"Fuck, Tessa, but Dante doesn't know?"

She shakes her head. "He doesn't deserve to know. That's why I can't stick around."

"You're leaving?" She nods. "Do you want money or a place to stay?" I'm reeling from so much information. She's not set up to just leave. She has no access to anything and doesn't have anyone she could go to. Fuck, she doesn't even know how to shop without me telling her.

She smiles. "No, I've got it covered."

"Well, if you're leaving, you can tell me what you and your friends witnessed that caused all this in the first place," I push.

She thinks for a moment. "He killed someone."

I arch my brows, trying to act indifferent. "Fuck. I heard he was brutal. Someone you knew?"

She shrugs. "Not really. Callie had just met him."

I frown. "So, Callie knows all this?"

"Yes. Me, her, and Emerson, we all saw it."

"Let me get this straight. All three of you were there when Dante killed someone, you all saw it?" She nods. "Where was this? When?"

She thinks again. "It was in the Duck and Partridge, on Porchester Road. I was sixteen. I didn't know his full name, but we called him Jase." I let that information sink in. What the fuck is Callie playing at?

"Christ, Tessa, no wonder you feel so trapped and alone. And you never saw your friends after?"

A sad look passes over her face. "I saw Emerson," she almost whispers. "Just once."

"I bet they were scared. What did they think of you moving in with Dante?"

She bites her lower lip and tears balance on her lower lash line. "I didn't get a chance to explain the deal."

"Deal?"

"Dante said if I moved in with him and stayed, they'd never come to any harm. I thought if I did that, then eventually, I'd escape. Then I could tell the police and they'd keep us safe."

"So, what happened?"

"I was sixteen and stupid. I soon realised that the police were in his pocket, and even if I did make it out somehow, Dante would find me again. Then he'd kill Emerson and Callie and probably make me watch. But in the end, it didn't matter, not for Emerson."

"Did something bad happen to Emerson?" I push.

A tear rolls down her cheek and she nods. "When I saw her, she was mad. She slapped me, and Dante saw. He sent me home, and I thought he'd probably teach her lesson, maybe hit her, but he did so much worse."

"He killed her?"

She nods. "Him and Enzo, they," she sniffles, "they raped her. She was a mess when they brought her to the house. And Dante demanded I hit her, but I wouldn't, so he . . . he . . ." She breaks down, and I pull her to me. "I need the bathroom," she whispers, pulling away.

I watch her go and take out my mobile phone, angry that I've been kept in the dark. I make my way out to the smokers' terrace and call Callie. She answers right away. "I've been trying to call you," she snaps.

"When were you going to tell me?"

"Tell you what?"

"About Jase?" The line goes quiet. "In case you're interested, I got her to open up. Once she started, she couldn't fucking stop. She's witnessed shit. But then apparently, so have you."

"We should meet to talk," she mutters.

"You're a fucking copper, Callie, and you held out on something huge. And now I know too, what the fuck am I supposed to do?"

"Let me explain."

"Explain that you could've brought Dante down all alone? But instead, you kept your mouth shut and let me go undercover for fucking months?" I turn and find Tessa right behind me. She's staring open-mouthed. "Fuck. I gotta go." Tessa turns and runs, pushing her way through the crowd. "She heard me," I tell Callie. "Tessa knows."

CHAPTER EIGHT

TESSA

I DON'T REMEMBER the last time I felt so drunk. I stumble through the crowd and break out onto London's busy streets. It's easy to get lost in the crowds. I hear Nero calling my name, but I don't stop until I feel him right behind me and realise I can't outrun him. He wraps his arms around my waist, lifting me off the ground and holding me against him. I kick and scream, but we're in London and no one bothers to stop and check if I'm okay. "Let me explain, please," he whispers.

"Explain that you lied," I cry. "That you're not who you fucking said." My heart feels like it's shattered into a million pieces and my throat feels tight.

"I am. What I've told you is true . . . everything but my job."

I suddenly feel exhausted. "Take me home."

NERO FORCES me to drink lots of water before guiding me upstairs to bed. I can't bear to look at him let alone speak to him, so when he turns the light out and leaves, I'm relieved. I cry into my pillow. I've been such an idiot . . . again.

I drift off into a restless sleep, tossing and turning, and dreaming of Callie and Emerson. I wake with a start when the light floods the room. Dante leers over me, and the fear I'd left behind for a couple days soon returns. "Dante," I whisper.

"Get up." I sit and the room spins. I hold my head. Fuck, I forgot what a hangover feels like, and it's not good. "Are you sick?"

"No."

"Where's Nero?"

I frown. "I don't know." Last night comes flooding back, and I suddenly feel worse. I should tell Dante. If he finds out that I knew and didn't say anything, he'll be so angry.

"I have breakfast downstairs. Let's go." I follow him down, smelling the bacon as I get closer. The last thing I want to do is eat. "I had someone come in and cook for us," Dante says as we enter the dining room. I stare at the table full of food.

Minutes later, Nero appears with Kai. He gives me a strange look, and I think he's silently pleading with me to stay quiet. "Everything okay, Boss?" he asks.

Dante points to the seat on his right, and Nero sits while I sit to the left. "I thought we could have breakfast and a catch-up." He begins to pile food on my plate. There's no way I can eat, but if I tell him that, he'll punish me, so I pick at the bacon.

"Do you wanna talk in private?" Nero asks.

"No. Let's get it all out in the open." Nero glares at me.

He thinks I've told Dante. "Shall we start by talking about this?" he asks, holding up a condom wrapper. It's the condom wrapper Nero used.

I begin to panic, my body shaking as I try to think of an answer quickly. I open my mouth to speak, but nothing comes out. "It's mine," says Nero.

"Clearly," snaps Dante. "What I want to know, Nero, is why the fuck there is a used condom in the bathroom?"

"I'm so sorry," I cry. "I'm sorry."

"Shut the fuck up," Dante growls as he turns back to Nero. "I gave you a simple instruction. Fuck my wife, get her pregnant. You fucked my wife using a condom. Do you not understand basic sex education, or should I show you?" The words hit my brain and confusion follows. Dante gives a cruel laugh. "Oh, wifey, you didn't think he actually wanted to fuck you?"

"Tess, ignore him. Listen to me," shouts Nero, standing. Kai rushes forward, grabbing Nero's arms and pulling them behind his back. "It was real. It was all real," he continues to yell.

I stare, open-mouthed. His words sound distant as Dante laughs harder. "I hired him to get you pregnant, Tessa. He doesn't give a shit about you. All he wants is to work his way up in my firm." My heart breaks, shattering into a thousand pieces. "All the dinners, the little dates, the picnic in the park," Dante hisses, "I cleared it all."

"That's not true," yells Nero. "He's lying."

"So, now you have a choice—fuck my wife, or I'll find someone who will." Dante grabs my hair and pulls me to my feet. He shoves me over the table, pinning me face down. "What do you say, Nero? You or Kai? Who wants to go first?"

I rest my face against the hard wood and stare at Nero.

He looks devastated, and somehow, that hurts me too. He deserves to hurt. I should blurt out some of my own truths, but I don't want him to feel pain. I don't want him to feel the same as I do because it's too much. No one deserves to feel like this. Dante pulls my shirt up over my arse, and I hear him laughing over the whooshing sound in my ears. This must be how Emerson felt. *Poor Emerson.* My heart twists painfully.

My hand slides slowly across the table to the fruit knife. Nero is struggling to free himself as Kai shouts for Enzo to come and help. In all the commotion, they don't notice me take the knife, and I smile because, for once, Dante's dropped the ball. For once, I'm going to win.

I don't feel the blade go in. I thought I would. In fact, this feels nothing like I'd imagined. Maybe Emerson is helping from the other side. She knows I'm ready, so she's making the pain feel less. I pull my hand up to my face to check and, sure enough, it's coated in sticky, red blood. I smile wider, relief flooding me. I'm going to be free. *Finally.*

"Tessa?" Dante yells, pulling me up and turning me onto my back. He assesses me with his eyes, freezing on my now bloody inner thigh. "What the fuck have you done?"

"Jesus, if she's hit the femoral artery, she'll die in minutes," shouts Nero. Those words bring me comfort and I close my eyes, waiting patiently for death to come.

NERO

KAI RELEASES ME, and I take off my shirt, ripping it down the middle and wrapping it around Tessa's wound. "Call an ambulance," I demand.

Dante shakes his head. "It's what she wants," he mutters.

"You fucking piece of shit." He's got no intention of saving her.

There's a loud bang at the front door. No one has time to react before the house is full of police officers yelling to us all to get on our knees and place our hands behind our heads. Callie smiles at Dante. "Dante Anderson, I'm arresting you on suspicion of the murders of Jason Collins and Emerson Grey."

Another officer grabs my hands and cuffs them. "She's bleeding out," I shout. Paramedics rush in and begin to tend to Tessa as I'm dragged out the house along with the others.

CHAPTER NINE

TESSA

I OPEN my eyes and blink a few times. A nurse comes into view, smiling. "You're awake," she whispers. Glancing around the room, I take in the bright lights and realise I'm in hospital. There's a crushing feeling in my chest and I realise it's disappointment. "Let me get the doctor," she adds. I want to scream. This isn't part of my plan. I shouldn't be here. I ball my fists angrily at my sides and glare at the ceiling.

The doctor checks all my vitals, occasionally making notes. "You're very lucky, Tessa. A little deeper and it would have severed the femoral artery. I hear the man who did this to you is in police custody." I frown. "There's an officer waiting to see you. Shall I send him in?" I don't bother to reply. Sadness claws at me so hard, I have no energy to find words.

Nero appears minutes later, and I almost gasp. The memories flood me with everything that's happened, and the pain is suddenly overwhelming.

I turn my head away, squeezing my eyes closed tightly. "You scared the shit out of me," he mutters, taking my hand, but I pull it free. "I thought I'd lost you."

"Are you here on official business?" I ask coldly.

"Tessa, look at me, please." I don't. "I know you're upset, and you have every right to be, but I couldn't tell you who I was. I couldn't risk it."

"Get out," I whisper.

He grabs my hand a second time, desperately holding on to it. "My name is Tristan Neroli. I've been an undercover police officer for ten years." I begin to cry, keeping my face away from him. "Everything else was true. What we have, that's real."

"Just leave, Nero," I whisper through my tears. It hurts too much.

"Tessa, please. Don't be like this. The dates we went on and getting to know each other, it was all real."

I finally turn to look at him. "It wasn't real, and if you think it was, you're a bigger dick than I thought. Now, get out."

THEY KEEP me in the hospital for a week. Various professionals come to see me, including the officer now in charge of my case. Nero told the police that Dante stabbed me in the leg, so on top of his existing charges that are stacking up, attempted murder has been added.

I've also given a statement about everything—the murders, the abuse, and everything in between. It felt freeing but scary. I had a support worker with me every step of the way, which made it a little easier, but I know the scariest moments are yet to come.

My support worker, Cath, arrives just as I'm finished dressing and packing my hospital bag. She's holding a set of keys which she hands to me. "Are you ready to go and see your new place?" Through the help of the local women's centre, they've found me a flat in a different part of the city. One not controlled by Dante or his men. Eventually, I'll move out of the area completely, but while there's a court case pending, I've agreed to stick around.

The drive takes us an hour, and when we stop outside a tall building, I feel a sense of calm. "I know it's not much," Cath begins.

I stop her because anywhere is better than being with Dante. "It's fine."

We head to the first floor, and I unlock the door to my new place, smiling as I step inside. "Other women in similar situations to you stay here." I run my hand over the green couch. It's ugly, but I love it already. "There's a microwave and a kettle. The laundry room is across the way in block two," she continues. "Here's some money to get you started," she adds, handing me twenty pounds. "You'll get your benefits within the next couple weeks. It's all going through." I nod, grateful that she's helped me this far because I wouldn't have had a clue. The paperwork for the benefits agency was long and painful. I couldn't answer half the questions, and without Cath, I'd have given up. "I'll let you settle in. I'll call in a few days to check in on you, and you have my number if you need me. The public phone is at the end of the street."

Once she's gone, I explore the one-bedroom flat. It's small and basic, but I'm grateful for anything right now. There's a set of new sheets on the bed that I unwrap and make up.

A knock on the door distracts me from the half jar of

coffee I found in the kitchen. I answer it to find Callie, smiling awkwardly. She's the last person I expected, but a part of me needs to hear what she has to say. "Can I come in?" I open the door wider, and she steps inside. I follow her, wondering why she's here. I've had a lot of time to think things over while in hospital, and every time, I come back to the same conclusion. She was a police officer and knew what shit I was in, and she let it happen.

"How are you?" she asks.

"Sore. Tired," I mutter.

I point to the couch, and she takes a seat. "Green," she mutters, running a hand over it. "Who the hell made this and thought it looked good?" She attempts a laugh, but I don't join her. "Yah know, we thought you'd left us behind and you were living a great life with that murdering scumbag," she begins. "We were so angry you'd choose him over us." She scoffs. "And then Nero told me the truth, that you did it to keep me and Em safe." I lower onto the couch. "I don't know what to say," she whispers, and I see the vulnerable teenager I used to know. "I read the case file. Your statement. I read about all the things he did. All the things you had to put up with." Her eyes water. "You did that for us."

My heart melts a little at the sight of her tears. "I wanted to tell you. That was my plan, to do as he said and then run away and find you both, but once I agreed, I wasn't allowed out of his sight. Not for a minute. He took my phone, and the only people I saw were him and his men. They were too loyal to him to help me."

"We didn't bother to find you. We talked about it, but we were mad so . . . anyway, my dad moved us to Australia for a few years, and I lost contact with Em over time. We grew apart."

"You moved away?" The news surprises me.

She nods. "Dante sent men to warn my dad. They smashed the house up and put the windows in. The next day, we drove to the ferry and went to France. From there, we moved around until we eventually went to stay with family in Australia. My parents were worried one of us would end up dead."

"It was a mess," I mutter.

"And I keep thinking, if I'd never met Jase, if I'd have not tried to be the cool kid and snort that shit he kept giving me, none of this would've happened."

Part of me wants to agree, but we were teenagers. "We were kids. We didn't know what we were doing. And he was older, old enough to know better. It wasn't your fault. It wasn't any of our faults." The words leave my mouth and I feel like a huge weight is lifted.

"Dante killed him because he owed him money for the drugs. I didn't know. If I had, I would've ran a mile in the other direction. And then Emerson . . . poor Em," she whispers, her eyes filling with tears again.

"I still see her when I close my eyes," I admit. "She was broken."

"So were you," says Callie, taking my hand. "Yah know, I joined the police to help stop men like Dante Anderson. I didn't want other kids to go through what we did."

"Do you think he'll get out of this?"

She shakes her head. "Not if Nero and I have anything to do with it." At the mention of Nero, I look away. "He's not the bad guy, Tessa."

"Isn't he? He lied, just the same as Dante lied. I thought maybe I'd found someone who understood me, and all along he was playing me."

"His feelings weren't a lie. I tried to pull him when I realised he was falling for you, but he wouldn't leave."

I shake my head in disgust. "He could've saved me way before. He's a police officer and he knew what hell I was in. How long would it have gone on if I hadn't found out the truth? If you hadn't burst in when you did, would he have raped me to keep up his lie with Dante?"

"No," she says firmly. "He'd never have done that." She takes a shaky breath. "This job is hard, and Nero is good at it. You have to think on your feet, be alert all the time, and when Dante asked him to get you pregnant, he was never going to do it. He told Dante he was sleeping with you even though he wasn't. He was buying time."

"Who for?" I snap. "Did you see the photographs, Callie? The ones of my bruises? And they're just the marks he left on my skin. Everything else is under the surface. I was already trying to survive while drowning, and Nero gave me hope. Turns out it was bullshit, and now, I feel like a fool."

"You're not a fool, and if he made you smile, even for a few weeks, then surely, he's not so bad. And look, you're free. You're out of there, and Dante is locked away."

"For how long?" I mutter.

NERO

I TAP the steering wheel impatiently. Callie walks towards me, getting in the car. "She's not going to see you, sorry."

"Did you ask?"

"Sort of. She's not in a good way."

"What's it like inside?" I ask, looking at the tall building.

"Not great. Basic. Social gave her a bit of money until her benefits come in."

"It's shit. How the fuck can she live off the pittance they hand out? And why should she when her husband is fucking loaded?"

"There's a hold on all his money," Callie says. It's police procedure to hold everything we suspect is the profit of criminal activity.

"Do me one last favour," I ask, and she groans. "You lied to me, Cal, it's the least you owe me. I'm gonna do some food shopping for her. Take it to the flat?"

———

JUST AS I pay for the shopping, Callie gets a call from the Chief to get back to the station. She pats me on the shoulder before rushing off. I can't wait for Callie to come back, she could be hours, and the supermarket is a short walk from Tessa's new flat.

I place the bags on the doorstep and knock loud. Then I turn to walk away quickly, but the door opens before I round the corner. "Nero?" I turn back and give her a guilty smile. "What's this?"

I head back to her. "Just a few things for the cupboard."

"No. I don't need anything. Take them back."

I smile. "I know Social only gives you twenty quid to last you until your benefit payments start. That could be a couple weeks yet. And I know how bad you are at shopping." I add a grin, which she doesn't return.

"You shouldn't be buying me things. Actually, that reminds me." She reaches up, unclasping the necklace from her neck, followed by the bracelet I brought for her birthday. She holds them out to me, but I make no move to take them. "Please," she whispers.

I shake my head. "They were presents."

"To keep me from finding the truth," she says. "I don't want them."

"They were presents because I wanted to make you smile. I wanted to do something nice because you deserved it—"

"So, it was guilt?"

I sigh. "No, Tessa. I lied because I had to. I didn't know you when I made that agreement. If I did, maybe I wouldn't have. Either way, I can't take it back now. I'm sorry . . . so fucking sorry." She looks torn, so I move closer, picking up the bags. "At least let me carry these in for you." I don't wait for her reply. Instead, I go inside.

I take in the chipped paint on the walls and the worn-looking couch. "It's through there," Tessa says, pointing to her kitchen. I place the bags on the side. The kitchen is outdated like the rest of this shit pit.

"Jesus, this place isn't liveable," I mutter.

"It's just fine."

I begin to take the shopping from the bag before stopping and turning to her. "I don't want to leave you here. Come home with me. Or I can get you a hotel if you're not ready to forgive me."

"I've spent my adult life with a man controlling my every move. I'm happy here with my freedom."

"Tessa, I'm not like him. I'd never control you."

"Can I be honest with you, Nero . . . or Tristan . . . whatever your name is?"

"People call me Nero," I tell her.

"Meeting you was like a breath of fresh air. I'd spent so long being invisible, and you made me feel seen. The reason I slept with you was because I'd made my mind up —I was planning on taking my own life." I brace myself on the worktop at her confession. "And I wanted to have one last good memory because I don't have many of those. But then I found out the truth and I don't know if you'll ever understand what that did to me. With Dante, I knew he was bad, so I expected each nasty remark or punch. I didn't see that coming with you and it hurt so much more. You lied to me. Even after you supposedly liked me, you didn't come clean. Not only that, but you used me to get to him. Every punch and every kick after you walked into my life was one you could have prevented." I lower my head, unable to look her in the eye. "So, I can't forgive you, and I can't let you back in, because I've made a promise to myself not to ever let a man treat me badly again, especially a man I can't trust. And I can't trust you, Tristan."

There's a lump in my throat that I swallow down before looking her in the eye. "It was real, Tessa. Every kiss, every touch. That was real."

"The night you took me out to celebrate my birthday, did you drink alcohol?" she asks. I look away, and she smiles sadly. "You plied me with drinks so I'd talk. Do you see why I can't trust you?"

I nod. "I was desperate. They were gonna pull the plug on the operation, and that meant I had to walk away from you, ghost you."

"Is that what happens with these things?" she asks. "How many women have you done this to then ghosted?"

"Tessa, I lo—"

"Don't," she cuts in. "Don't you dare say it."

"Just because you won't let me say it, doesn't mean it isn't true. I've never felt like this before."

She folds her arms over her chest. "You should go now. Please, don't come back."

"You don't mean that."

She nods. "I do. We're over. I don't want to ever see you again." She follows me to the door. "Do you know the worst thing, Nero?"

I stand on the doorstep. "What?"

"I would've told you everything if you'd have asked. Do you know how long I'd waited to find someone who could help me get out of there? I'd have told you whatever you needed to get him put away."

CHAPTER TEN

TESSA

LIFE FEELS BETTER. I can't say it's great just yet, but I'm heading in the right direction. I have therapy once a week, group therapy twice a week, and the support of some wonderful warriors I've met in group, some of whom live here in the building I've been housed in. This will be my permanent home now, and although I was glad to have the small flat before, this is much better.

Jess passes me a cuppa, and I smile gratefully, placing my paintbrush in the pot and standing back to admire our handiwork. If someone asked me ten months ago how I thought my future would pan out, I'd have laughed and told them I didn't have one. Because back then, I could only see one day at a time. It was the only way to survive. But now, as I look around my flat at my new friends, Jess, Jo, and Amanda, I realise I'm not holding that ball of anxiety in the pit of my stomach anymore. I'm healing.

The doorbell rings, and I rush to answer it, excited at my first unexpected visitor. A man stands there holding a bunch of flowers bigger than half his body. "Tessa?" he asks, holding them out to me. I take them and thank him.

"Lucky lady," says Jo, downing tools to watch me open the card.

What we had was real. Congratulations on your new place. Love always, Nero.

Jess looks over my shoulder and reads the card aloud. "Wow, the copper?" I nod. "After all this time, he's still thinking about you."

I stuff the card in the flowers and place them on the table. "You're not going to say anything?" asks Amanda, smirking.

"There's nothing to say," I reply, shrugging. "He's in the past."

"I think we should raise this in group therapy tomorrow," Jo teases, and I throw a cushion at her. "Cath will want to talk about this," she continues.

"Maybe it's something to raise in your session," says Jess seriously.

"Come on, ladies. We talk all the time about moving forward, not looking back. Nero was during a bad time for me, and I don't need the trigger. He's in my past and he has to stay there. I've got the court case coming up, I don't need distracting."

But distracted is what I am when, for the next five days, I receive flowers every day. Each card reads the same thing:

It was real.

NERO

I GIVE my evidence in court. I stick to facts and brush over half-truths, like Tessa stabbing herself. I didn't see her stick the knife in, and all I have is her confession that she'd planned to kill herself. But I know for a fact she wouldn't have done that if Dante hadn't abused her for all those years, so I don't feel bad for telling the court he stabbed her when he realised she wasn't pregnant. Tessa gave her evidence this morning, and as I step out into the corridor, I see her with her army of support, wiping her eyes with a tissue. I head over, and the women step aside, eyeing me suspiciously.

"I hear you did well in there," I say, and she looks up through glassy eyes.

"Who are you?" asks one of her friends.

"Commander Neroli of London's Metropolitan Police."

"Give us a minute," Tessa mutters, and the army of women disperse.

I sit down beside her. "I've dealt with some criminals in my time, but that lot, they scare the shit out of me," I say, and she smiles a watery smile. "Why the tears, Tessa?"

"It's the end," she whispers, "and it feels good but scary."

"Understandable. But he's going down for this. You get that, right?"

She nods, wiping her eyes again. "You climbed the ranks?"

"They needed my experience to organise other officers," I say, smirking. And then I add with more seriousness, "It was time for a change."

"Congratulations."

"I understand if you want to say no, but would you go for a coffee with me?" I stare straight ahead, bracing myself for another brush-off.

"Will you stop sending flowers if I agree?" she asks, and I glance back at her. She smiles. "My flat looks like a damn florist."

TESSA

I WATCH as Nero orders the coffees. He's still as handsome as the day I first laid eyes on him, maybe more so in a suit. He places the coffees on the table and sits opposite me. "Callie said you did well in court this morning."

I shrug. "I told the truth."

"It took balls to stand up and tell a bunch of strangers everything."

"Well, I was behind a screen. At least I didn't have to look at him. But do yah know what pisses me off the most? He's not facing charges for what he did to me, the years of abuse or forcing me to live with him when I was still a kid really."

Nero smiles sadly. "It's a pile of shit. He should get life for that alone, but at least he's going to prison."

I nod, even though I don't agree. I want Dante to face up to what he did to me and be punished for ruining my life. I was close to taking my own life, yet he'll never spend a second inside for that.

"How's life going?" he asks. "You look great."

I smile. I have a hard time taking compliments, something we're working on in therapy at the moment. "Thanks," I force myself to say. "I'm doing good. As you know, I have my new place and we're decorating it to make it my own."

"We?" he queries. "You've met someone?"

I laugh. "No. And it's a good job seeing as you keep

sending me flowers."

He gives a coy smile. "I was hoping to wear you down. How's therapy going?"

"By we, I mean me and my friends. I met them in therapy, which is going amazing. I love my sessions and look forward to them. I feel like they're helping me rebuild my life."

"That's amazing. So, you're in a better place?"

I nod, confident that, for once, I'm not faking. "I don't think I would've got through it all without the girls. They've been a massive support."

He grins. "Was that the motley crew back there?"

"Yeah, Jess, Jo, and Amanda. They've all been where I am at some point. They're warriors like me."

"I'm glad things are going good for you, Tessa. You deserve it."

I fiddle with a napkin. "And you?" I ask. "How's life treating you?"

"Good. I just bought my first place after spending years renting. It's hard to put down roots in my line of work, I was always moving around. Now I'm settled, it feels good."

"You said before that you have a sister, was that true?"

Guilt passes over his expression at the mention of our past. "Yes, it's true. Luna lives in Ireland. I have a little nephew on the way, actually. She told me last week."

"Don't you miss her?"

He nods. "All the time, but we call regularly and we video chat. I didn't want her here, so when she decided to move to Ireland, I encouraged it. My line of work was dangerous, and I didn't want her getting dragged into anything. She's safer there than here."

"Even now you've changed your job?"

"She's settled now. Maybe one day she'll decide to come

home, but right now, she's happy, which means I'm happy."
He checks his watch. "We should get back to the court.
Lunch is over, and they might recall witnesses."

AS IT HAPPENED, they didn't call up any more
witnesses. After three weeks, I was glad the jury retired.
They're expected to be out for a couple days, which means I
can breathe a little. The legal team seems pretty confident
that Dante will go down for many years. My therapist and
support worker have broached the subject of what I'll do if
he gets off, but I can't even think about that. Callie said I
have the option to go into witness protection, that they'll
relocate me and do everything they can to protect me from
him, but deep down, I know he'll come for me. Besides, I'm
making a life for myself here, and the thought of leaving that
behind again because of Dante makes me more determined
to be strong.

Jo groans when the doorbell rings, disturbing our cosy
slumber party. It's something we do every Friday. All us
girls get together and we watch films, chat, and chill. I think
we've all lost friends in the past due to our abusers, so
having this time is important to us all. Amanda gets up to
answer, returning a second later with Nero.

I sit up quickly, brushing a hand over my crazy hair that
I decided to let dry naturally after my shower. I'm regretting
that decision now. "Hey," I say, "do you have news?"

"No, shit, sorry. I didn't know you had company. I can
come back," he says, turning.

"Don't you dare," says Jo, also pushing to sit up. "If you
run every time we're here, it'll make us suspicious."

He smiles. "You're right, sorry. I'm Nero."

"Um, the flower guy," says Amanda, flopping down on the couch.

"The liar," adds Jess. I kick her under the blanket, giving her a warning glare.

Nero winces. "She told you about that, huh?"

"She tells us everything. You should take a seat, let's talk," says Jo, pointing to the chair.

Nero stares at me warily, but I'm enjoying this way too much to help him out, so I sit back, folding my arms over my chest. He sighs, lowering into the chair. "Why are you here?" asks Amanda.

"I wanted to check Tessa was okay after everything lately."

"Didn't you do that over coffee today?" asks Jo, arching a suspicious brow.

"We did," says Nero uncomfortably, "but I . . . shit, I don't have a reason other than I needed to see her because I had this uncontrollable urge to just be near her."

I see Amanda almost swoon and I nudge her. She needs to be stronger than falling at the first hurdle. "Quite the charmer," Amanda says, recovering quickly.

"What's with the lorry load of flowers this week?" asks Jo.

"I wanted her to know I was thinking of her because I knew it would be hard to stand in court and talk about everything."

"What are your intentions?" asks Jess, and we all turn to look at her. "What? I saw it in a film."

"Usually asked by a father figure," Jo points out, laughing.

"Don't pretend we're not curious. We want to know why he's hanging around," says Jess.

"Honestly—" Nero begins.

"You don't have to answer that," I cut in, feeling uncomfortable.

"I messed up before. I let a wonderful woman go and I hate myself for it."

I stare down at my hands, unable to look at him and take the compliment. "So, you want another chance?" Jo questions.

"Why should she ever give you another chance?" asks Jess.

"She shouldn't," says Nero simply. "I don't deserve it after what I did. But I'd like the chance to start over, as me. No lies, no secrets."

"Can you give us a minute?" I ask. The girls go into the kitchen to replenish snacks and drinks.

Nero looks nervous as I turn back to him. "I know you're probably about to give me the reasons you can't give me a chance, and I get it, I know why you'd be wary. But let me just say this." He takes a breath. "I spent the last six months working on myself. To be better. I changed my job, got a house, put down roots. That's huge for me. But most of all, I did it because I wanted to be a better man for you. That's what you deserve. I did courses on domestic violence, so I could understand it better. I don't ever want to be that police officer who doesn't get it. I've thought about you every day, driving myself mad because I've forced myself to stay away until I'm good enough for you. And now I think I'm there, I can't bear to think you'll send me away without at least giving me one chance." My heart aches at his words. "But it is your choice. Completely. So, if you tell me that I have no chance and you want me to leave and never come back, this time I'll go. Because I understand it must be your choice, just like I get this all needs to be at your pace."

I stand, and he does the same, hurt filling his expression. He hangs his head and takes a few deep breaths, bracing himself for my rejection.

I hold out my hand, and he glances up in confusion. "Hi, I'm Tessa Cole."

Relief floods his face as he takes my hand. "I'm Tristan Neroli, but people call me Nero."

"I like Tristan," I tell him.

He grins. "Tristan it is."

The girls rush in and throw themselves around us so we're all in one big hug. "Something tells me you were listening in," I accuse.

"We were ready to bust in here and make you forgive him after that speech," says Jo.

"Tristan, these are my friends, Jo, Jess, and Amanda. They're part of my package," I explain, because I'll never choose a man over my friends again.

He laughs. "I kind of figured that out." We break apart, and he takes my hand. "So, what are you girls watching?"

We all sit together on the couch, me and Tristan crushed in the middle. Jo throws the blankets over us all. "Disney's *Cinderella*," she tells him, pressing play on the remote control.

He looks at me quizzically. "It's tradition," I tell him. "We only ever watch films with happy endings."

He smiles, placing a gentle kiss on the end of my nose. "I love a happy ending."

His words warm my heart. I've dreamt so long for a happy ending, and I find myself hoping I've finally found it in Tristan.

The End

AFTERWORD

Breaking Free is a story of hope. I know many stories out there, real life stories, aren't as simple. I encountered an abusive relationship when I was just thirteen. Not myself, but a couple who I babysat for. I witnessed very small snippets of a terrified woman, scared to say the wrong thing in case she set off her partner, and he'd fly into a rage. We'd often leave in the middle of the night, grabbing the baby and whisking her to her grandparents. It was a sad situation, one she eventually found the courage to leave.

When I was sixteen, I found myself in a similar situation. A man much older than me pressured me into a relationship by using threats against my family. I thought I was old enough to deal with it, and it's only now, when I look back, that I realise I was just a kid, and the grown ups around me that should have helped, didn't. Instead, I was blamed, not the man who was twenty years older than me. But hey, that's another story.

So although I'm no expert, I, like so many others, have either witnessed domestic abuse in some shape or form. I have been exposed to it. And I understand that it's not easy to just walk away. And it comes in many forms.

I decided to take part in the anthology to help support a small charity that helps victims of domestic abuse. These small charities are often overlooked, but they do many great things.

To see more about Living without Abuse, head here: https://lwa.org.uk/

ABOUT THE AUTHOR

I'm a UK author, based in Nottinghamshire. I live with my husband of many years, our two teenage boys and our four little dogs. I write MC and Mafia romance with plenty of drama and chaos. I also love to read similar books. Before I became a full-time author, I was a teaching assistant working in a primary school.

If you'd like to follow my writing journey head here: https://linktr.ee/NicolaJaneUK

ALSO BY NICOLA JANE

VOLUME 2

AMBER'S FALL

A NEW BEGINNINGS STORY
TRACIE PODGER

Publisher: S&P Publishing

Cover Designer: Francessca Wingfield @ Wingfield Designs

Formatting: TBR Editing & Design

CHAPTER ONE

PRESENT DAY

I RESTED BACK on my heels. My blurred vision was clearing and the white noise that screamed in my head fell silent. The smell was awful–blood and... was that shit? Could I smell shit on the carpet? I wanted to heave. I looked down at my hands, they were stained red and for a moment I was confused why.

A large carving knife sat on the floor beside me, its blade no longer silver but the same red as my hands. I knew there would be splatters over my face and I wondered about the pattern. The cream painted wall had an arc of colour and I smiled as I stared up at it. It looked good. I made a mental note when I redecorated I'd see if I could replicate that. I would need to redecorate, wouldn't I?

I needed to move because I could feel the numbness creep over my feet. I winced as I climbed to them, aching bones, tired muscles, exertion, and exhaustion were all taking its toll. Perhaps I'd have a nap. I wondered if I had time for that. Or time to clean myself up, even. The least I could do was to clean my hands.

I walked to the bathroom and ran the tap; impressed

with the fact I thought to use my elbow to flick the water on. I used anti-bacterial wash to remove the red. When only a pink tinge remained, I used the nailbrush to scrub my skin. With clean hands, I then returned to the living room.

Nap or phone? Nap or phone? I ran the words through my head until I decided I needed to make that phone call. I was sure the stench would overwhelm me at some point.

I walked back into the living room and picked up the telephone. I dialled and waited for the call to be connected to the police.

"Police, what is your emergency?" I heard once the call handler had answered.

I took a deep breath in. "I have killed someone," I said.

At first, there was a pause. "Oh, I'm sorry, I need to give my details." I then rattled off my name and address and waited for that to be repeated back to me.

"Who have you killed?" the handler asked.

I looked over to the other side of the room, to the prone form that was bloodied and very much dead. I caught sight of the arcs that crisscrossed the wall. They distracted me for a moment.

"Hello? Who have you killed?" There was urgency in her voice.

"I'm sorry. My husband... I've killed my husband. I'll wait here," I said, and then I disconnected the call to wait.

I found my shoes and put them on my feet. One was discarded in the hall, the other, I found under the sofa. I thought, with the way I'd toppled over the heel might have broken, so I was pleased to see it still intact.

I could hear the sirens getting louder as the police approached. I could see blue and red flashing lights through the window and was pleased to not have neighbours to disturb, I would have hated that. A banging on the front door startled me and I was unsure what was protocol. Do I wait for them to break in, or should I open the front door?

I decided on the latter. As I unlatched it, it was pushed open, and I stumbled back against the wall. I held up my hands, and that's when the shouting started. Too many people shouting too many things. I couldn't concentrate on any of them. I spotted a woman, and I focussed my gaze on her.

"Mrs Stowley?" she enquired. I nodded. "Did you make the call?" I nodded again.

From then on it was a blur again. A hand gently pressed on my head to stop me from bumping it as I was encouraged into the back of a police car, and I wanted to laugh. I didn't deserve their care or attention. I was driven to the station, and I gave basic details such as my name and address. I was taken to another room and my clothes were removed, my nails were scraped, my mouth and ears were checked, although I wasn't sure why. I was given a white cotton overall to wear. Questions were fired at me, and I didn't answer one of them.

I wasn't being obtuse. I wasn't acting tough, as was suggested. I wasn't the cold-hearted killer they called me. I was paralysed by fear.

"I was meant to feel free," I whispered.

CHAPTER TWO

THE PAST

"PHEW, THANK FUCK THAT'S OVER," I heard. My best friend, Patty, walked beside me as we strode through campus. She slid her arm through mine. "Party like we've never partied before!"

We had just finished our final exams. Three years of hard slog at uni was finally over. I'd nearly quit multiple times but kept going, mostly because Patty nudged me along. I wasn't academic, and I still didn't know what I wanted to do with my degree. I most certainly didn't want to be the teacher Patty was pushing for. She wanted me to join her on a teaching course, so we could work at the same school and stay friends for life.

I chuckled as we walked.

"What are you laughing at?" she asked.

"Just thinking of you and me working in a school."

"Are you going to sign up for the course?"

"Nope. I can't imagine anything worse that working with kids."

I had five younger siblings, bickering, shitting, puking babies I'd had to care for. My useless non-care giver, as I called my mother, kept pumping them out hoping each father would hang around long enough to actually pay for the kid.

I loved them, but they were the only reason I ran away to university. Although I wished I'd run away to a foreign country. A permanent gap year was my thing. Working my way around the world, experiencing different cultures, different lovers, even.

Patty had thought that hilarious. I was still yet to lose my virginity. It wasn't because I didn't have fellas after me, more so because I just couldn't *give it up* to someone without knowing there might be a next time. I didn't want to be my mother.

We parted ways, she to her shared house, and me to my small bedsit. We had started uni life living together, but I didn't like her friends. I didn't like the drugs or copious amounts of alcohol consumed every night. I didn't like not eating because we spent money on weed. Having the electric cut off and then thinking it was wonderful to sit in the dark wasn't my kind of thing at all.

I promised to turn up for the first of many end of uni parties she was hosting before she was finally kicked out of the shared house. Whether or not I would keep that promise, I wasn't sure.

As it turned out, I fell in love instead.

I WENT to the party after all. I dressed up, did my makeup, and found my one pair of high-heeled shoes. As I walked from my bedsit to the house, I passed a bar with a group of men also celebrating. However, these guys didn't look like uni students. Suited and booted, their ties were askew, hair messy. One swung a bottle of champagne, sipping from it periodically. They were brash and rowdy but looked like they were having fun.

Before I realised what had happened, one guy had lurched onto the pavement from the doorway, he collided with me, knocking me to the ground. As I stumbled, a heel broke, and I landed awkwardly on my side. It hurt, and I cried out.

Hands reached down for me, and lifted me to my feet. "Oh my God, I'm so sorry. Are you hurt?"

It wasn't the chap that had knocked me to my feet, but one that seemed a little more sober than his friends.

I could only nod as tears welled in my eyes. My hip was painful, as were my palms and knees. I guessed I'd placed my hands on the pavement to break my fall. I looked down at my broken shoe and torn stockings.

"Shit," I said, kicking off my shoes. I leaned on the guy that had held me up and removed my stockings.

"I don't think anyone has ever removed their underwear after being thrown to the ground for me," he said, smirking.

I raised my eyebrows and glared.

"I'm not about to walk down the street with one shoe on and torn stockings."

"Feisty, too," he said. Then he held out his hand. "Andrew Stowley. And I'll apologise for my drunken colleague. We've just bagged a huge account, earned some amazing bonuses, so we thought we'd blow off some steam."

"Well, that's very nice for you. Now, if you don't mind, I'll have to hobble home."

"Would you do me the honour of allowing me to accompany you?"

I stared at him and then laughed. I hadn't heard something as old-fashioned in a long time.

He held out the crook of his elbow, and I placed my hand around it. "Miss...?"

"Anderson. Amber Anderson."

"Well, Miss Anderson, which way?"

I chuckled as we set off. All the way he asked me questions, wanting to know about my degree and what I planned to do after. I confessed to not have a clue but wanted to travel. He told me of his times in Asia and the more he talked, the more fun I thought he was.

It disappointed me to actually arrive home. More so when he walked me to my door, then bowed and stepped back.

"Once again, Miss Anderson, I apologise for the ruined shoes and stockings, and if you'd allow me, I'd like to replace them."

"No need. I doubt I'd get much use for them, anyway."

"Amber, a beautiful woman like yourself must be having all the men bashing on you door wanting to court you."

"You'd think, but... no. Anyway, thank you. I think I'll take a hot bath to bring out those bruises quicker."

He held out his hand, and I took it; he placed his other over the clasped palms and squeezed. "I would like to replace the items. Perhaps I could call on your again?"

Again, that old-fashioned speech, and I believed he was sincere. I coloured a little. "Perhaps," I replied.

He bowed again and grinned. I opened my door and paused. "Thank you, again," I said, then stepped inside and closed the door.

I leaned against it, my heart pounding in my chest. Then I laughed. What an evening! And what a super guy!

CHAPTER THREE

THE FOLLOWING MORNING, I opened my door to collect the milk and found a white shoe box. Initially, I frowned, a little confused, and then I laughed. I picked up the box and opened it. Sure enough, sitting on white tissue paper were a pair of black high-heeled shoes. They looked way more expensive than my broken pair. I grabbed the milk bottle and heading back inside.

After placing the box on the kitchen unit, I tried on the shoes. They were a perfect fit and wearing my bobbly old dressing gown and pink PJ's, I paraded around the flat in them. They were a dream to wear. Under the tissue paper, I found two pairs of silk stockings. I opened one packet and let the material slip through my fingers.

"Expensive," I whispered to myself.

The one thing that concerned me was the lack of a name or address. I had no way to thank Andrew Stowley. No idea where he lived or worked, only the pub he had been in. Then, I guessed, if he'd wanted me to contact him, he would have left some details.

I decided on a bath and to then get ready for the day. I

was sure that Patty would knock on my door at some point. I doubted her telephone would work, she never paid the bills, so I couldn't call her and explain my absence.

Sure enough, an hour later there was a knock on the door and a dishevelled and very hung over Patty stumbled in. She stunk of stale booze and weed. It was then I noticed the tears in her clothes.

"What on earth happened to you?" I said, suddenly noticing the tears streaking down her cheeks.

"I don't know," she stuttered. "But I hurt, down below."

I ushered her into the bathroom and ordered her to strip, finding her covered in bruises.

"We need to call the police," I said.

Patty shook her head. I sighed. It was the early 1980s, the police hadn't woken up to the fact that a woman could get drunk or high and for that not be a reason for an assault. Patty had clearly been assaulted.

"Let's go to the hospital." I said.

Whether we'd get any more sympathy there was another issue, but if she hurt, she needed a doctor. I encouraged her to slip into some loose trousers and placed a thin T-shirt over her head. I hadn't noticed she was barefoot until that moment and found some large slippers that would fit. Together, we headed off to the local hospital.

Four hours of waiting and she was finally seen. I wasn't allowed to accompany her, but paced up and down a corridor until a doctor came and found me.

"I'm afraid your friend has suffered some trauma. We'd like to keep her in for a day or two." Of course, he didn't elaborate on the trauma, but he never seemed to meet my eyes, either.

"Can I see her?" I asked.

He nodded and gave me instructions on where I'd find her.

Patty lay with her eyes closed in a hospital bed in a mixed ward of about ten people. My heart sank when I gently sat beside her, and she cried. A mixed ward really wasn't the place for her.

"They said I've been raped. I don't remember a thing," she said.

"Perhaps that's not a bad thing?" I replied, not really knowing how to respond other than with honesty.

She nodded, and a tear tracked down her cheek. "One minute I was dancing, the next, I woke up outside behind the house in the alley. I think someone drugged me."

"Have they taken bloods for testing?" I asked.

She raised her hand to show some bruising. I guessed that meant they had.

"What now?" I asked, gently.

"I don't know. They want to just monitor me for a day or two, but they didn't say what for. There's that disease, that Aids thing. Do you think they're worried about that?"

Aids was the newest disease to hit the streets. Mostly among gay men, but everyone was worried. No one really knew where it came from and how it spread.

"I don't know, Patty." I really wanted to offer some form of comfort but couldn't. I also released her hand, wanting to rub my palms on my jeans to clean them.

Thankfully, she hadn't noticed.

"Is there anything that you need?" I asked.

"Would you tell my mum? I'm sure she'd want to know."

I nodded. I knew her mum, of course, I'd met her many times when I'd stayed with the family over breaks. I grabbed a pen from my bag and tore the end of an envelope off so I could write the number. There was a pay phone in the hospital. I could call her from there.

"I'll do that now. I think they want me to leave," I said, eyeing a nurse who was staring at me.

Patty nodded her head, turned it away, and then closed her eyes again.

"Try not to worry, Patty. And think about telling the police, please?"

She didn't respond.

The first thing I did was to wash my hands in the bathroom. I scrubbed them until they were red. I highly doubted she would have contracted anything that could be passed to me, but this disease was new and scary. The government were sending leaflets to every home and there were endless adverts on the television about it.

I then headed to the pay phone to call Marilyn. She informed me she would head straight to the hospital, whether or not it was visiting time, and she'd let me know any further updates. She thanked me for helping her daughter. I wondered if she would have still thanked me had she known how I wanted to scrub my skin in case I caught Aids from her. For the second time, I felt awful.

I had been home for a couple of hours when Marilyn called. Patty needed some surgery to repair some internal damage, and the police informed. I was glad that had happened. Whoever had raped my friend needed to be punished. Although, I was more than aware of the hell Patty would go through at the hands of the police and the courts should it get that far. It saddened me greatly that the country was in such a mess where dealing with women was concerned.

Once Patty could leave the hospital, Marilyn was taking

her back home. I told her to keep me up to date and I'd visit as soon as she'd settled.

―――――――

LATER THAT DAY, as I settled on the sofa with a cup of tea, I heard a knock on my door. I smiled as I looked through the spy hole and smoothed down my hair. I pinched my cheeks to give them some colour, then opened the door.

"I wanted to see if you'd received the new shoes?" Andrew said.

"I did, and since you didn't leave any contact details, I had no way of thanking you. Perhaps you'd like a cup of coffee?"

He nodded, and I opened the door so he could enter.

"I like what you've done here," he said, looking around.

"It's small, but it's mine."

I walked to the kitchenette and pointed him to the sofa. The bedsit was small, just the one main room and a separate bathroom, but I'd tried to section of areas. I'd placed a tall shelving unit at the bottom of the bed to give the illusion of a wall, then a sofa facing the kitchenette. I had a television that I rarely watched and shelves of books. And plants. I had plants everywhere, and I loved them.

I made two coffees and perched on the footstool opposite the sofa.

"Thank you for the shoes and stockings. But you really didn't need to," I said, raising my cup to him.

"I wanted to. I'll have my chum reimburse me, of course," he said, his posh clipped tone hid any humour in his words. Then he laughed.

"Well, thank your *chum*," I replied.

We chatted about his job in the city and my plans for

the future. I told him I wanted to travel before deciding on what career to settle into. He was engaging and fun, we had a second, and then a third cup of coffee.

I then told him about Patty. He was sympathetic, moving to sit beside me and place his arm around my shoulder.

He wanted to know all the details, sighing and shaking his head as I spoke. He seemed so concerned for her, and me. He told me he wanted me to keep a rape alarm in my handbag, and to have his telephone number should I ever need it. I wrote it down on a piece of paper and placed it in my purse. His concern for me was warming. I hadn't had that before.

"I best be going. I'm sure you've got tons of things to do," he said, slapping his thighs and standing.

I didn't, but I also didn't want him to think I was a loser with no friends and nowhere to be.

"Once again, thank you for the shoes. I'm sure I'll have to find an occasion to wear them soon."

"How about dinner? Tomorrow night. You could wear them then," he asked.

I paused for all of about thirty seconds before replying. "Sure, why not. It would be nice to get dressed up for a change."

"Perfect, I'll collect you at, say, seven?" His smile was wide displaying perfectly straight and white teeth.

I nodded in reply, then showed him to the door. He hesitated, then leaned down and kissed my cheek.

"I look forward to seeing you in the shoes tomorrow," he whispered. There was something a little erotic in his words, but I put that down to my virgin brain having a melt down at his closeness.

He walked away whistling to himself.

I was on cloud nine. I floated around the flat, picking up his mug and holding it to my lips. The following evening couldn't come quick enough, I thought.

I picked up the telephone, ready to dial Patty before I remembered she wasn't at home. I felt guilty about having those few hours just about me. Patty was a force of nature and everything we did was usually her idea with her friends, and all about her. I loved her and she was my best friend, but it felt good to have someone else who wanted to spend time with me.

Marilyn called that evening. Patty had spoken to the police, but it didn't look hopeful there would be an investigation. She'd been drunk and high, she'd admitted, unable to be sure what had happened to her. She received a lecture about not putting herself in a vulnerable position in the future, and that was it. Marilyn and I both felt that time out of the city would be beneficial for Patty. Although Marilyn lived just outside London, apparently, there was a family member in Norfolk they could visit for a while. I told her I'd make a point of seeing Patty as soon as she arrived home and before they left for the coast.

CHAPTER FOUR

I TRIED on several outfits before settling on one that I thought matched the stockings and shoes. One that was sophisticated enough for a date with my posh boy. I was excited and nervous. I wished I could call Patty to chat through what I should do or say. I hadn't dated much, always being known as the geeky friend, not the party girl. But I made an effort with my hair and makeup and was ready at ten minutes to seven.

"Wow, you look stunning," Andrew said when I answered the door.

I blushed and giggled. "Thank you, and you look rather dapper yourself." He was wearing a smart blue suit, crisp white shirt that was open at the neck.

"I opted to go without a tie. That's okay with you, isn't it?" he asked, and I was taken aback.

"Erm, of course." I thought he was so thoughtful in asking.

He held out the crook of his arm and I threading mine through it. We set off along the high street. We chatted about our days. He told me all about his work and the deals he was working on. He was pleased when I'd compliment him, placing his arm around my shoulders and squeezing me to him.

We eventually stopped at an Indian restaurant. I'd never eaten Indian food before and was hesitant, but Andrew clearly knew what he was doing, so I allowed him to order for me.

The smells were a little overwhelming, but I moved past that by listening to him tell me all about his life. He was an only child; his mother had been a stay-at-home mum and his dad was a banker. Both were still alive and lived in the Cotswolds. It seemed he'd had a wonderful childhood romping over fields with Labradors and ponies. I loved to listen to him, his life had been, and was, so different to mine.

He asked about Patty, and I told him she'd be heading off to Norfolk to recover. He thought that was a good idea but seemed a little hesitant when I told him I wanted to see her before she did.

"You know, she might be better off not seeing anyone from here for a little while in case it reminds her of what happened," he said, as our starters were placed in front of us.

"I hadn't thought of it like that," I replied. He then told me what dishes were which and encouraged me to taste from them all.

"Well done," he said, when I'd finished eating. "I want to teach you all about different foods."

I smiled, bemused, but also pleased that he wanted to take the time to do that.

When our mains arrived, he did the same. He encouraged me to taste and comment on each dish. He held a fork to my lips, his hand under my chin, and there was something erotic about it. Especially when he'd use his thumb to wipe sauce from my lips, then suck on it himself.

"I love that you want to learn new things," he said.

"I guess it will help when I travel," I replied, chuckling.

"Well, I hope you're not rushing off just yet."

We continued our meal talking about nothing and everything. When it was time to pay the bill, I offered up half which he declined.

"What kind of man would I be if I let my date pay?" he asked. Again, I warmed inside. No one had taken care of me before.

He held out my coat, even buttoned it up and then gently kissed my cheek. He opened doors for me, made me walk on the building side of the pavement, and held my arm all the way home. Just before we got to my door, there was a homeless man sitting on the curb. He called out as we passed, asking for money. His voice slurred, he was clearly drunk.

Andrew kicked his legs away so I could pass. "You need to get a job, mate," he said, spitting the words at him. "And don't ask my lady for money again."

At first, I was shocked. He was just a harmless man sitting on the floor. We didn't know his circumstances, why he found himself homeless. I would have had more compassion and probably given him a pound or two. But Andrew explained that a lot of them were con artists. He'd see them in London pull up in their smart cars and then pretend to be homeless. It was a lucrative business, he said and I began to doubt my generosity.

"And if he's using that money for alcohol, you're not really helping him," he said gently.

"Gosh, I hadn't thought about it that way before," I replied.

We continued to walk the path to my front door. I had half the ground floor of a two-storey house. I'd wanted the basement because that had a separate bedroom but couldn't afford it. Andrew stopped at the door and smiled at me.

"I've so enjoyed this evening. Can we do it again? Soon?" He looked so shy, kicked his toes on the concrete path and looking down.

"Yes, and soon is good for me," I replied.

His smile was broad, and he took a step closer. "I just... I have a feeling about us," he said. He then leaned down to gently kiss my lips.

He brushed some hair from my forehead. "I love your hair like this," he said, tucking it behind my ears.

I'd always hated my ears, but if he loved them, I'd wear my hair like that every day, I thought.

"Let me have your telephone number so I can call you."

I hastily fished in my handbag for a pen and piece of paper, wrote it down and gave it to him. "Call me whenever you can," I said.

He nodded and then left. I watched as he walked back the way we'd come and again kicked the feet of the homeless man as he passed.

MARILYN CALLED to say that she was collecting Patty and would I like to join her. I agreed and we arranged a time to meet at the hospital. Marylin and Patty take a taxi back home and then straight off to Norfolk. Since the hospital was a short walk away, I'd make my own way there and home.

I met Marilyn at the door. "How is she?" I asked.

"Not too good. Physically, she's better, but mentally...

Well, she's remembering things, I think, and it's traumatic. Seems there was more than one bastard!" Marilyn had to stop speaking and take in a deep breath. "If I got my hands on them..."

I placed my hand on her arm. "Time away from here is going to be a good healer and maybe, if she writes everything down, you could go back to the police to reopen the case." I didn't know if that was possible, of course.

Marilyn nodded, took another deep breath in, and straightened her headscarf. "Right, let's go get her."

Patty though, was a shocking sight to see. Although it had only been a week, she had changed. She'd lost a lot of weight and her hair was lank and greasy. Her skin was sallow, sickly looking. My heart skipped a couple of beats.

"How are you?" I asked, sitting on the edge of the bed while she packed her things into a carrier bag.

"I've been better," she replied, and smiled weakly at me. "Glad to see you, of course."

I felt a tinge of guilt that I hadn't visited her.

"You're going to love Norfolk, getting some sea air will do you wonders," I said.

She huffed. "Won't stop the nightmares, will it?"

I wasn't sure what to say to her. I wanted to reach out and touch her, hug her like we'd done a thousand times before, but she looked so frail and ill, and...

"Did you get all the results back from your blood tests?" I asked.

"No, still waiting on the important ones. If those bastards have given me aids, I'm going to hunt them down." The venom in her voice startled me. I'd never heard her use that tone before.

"We'll hunt them down together," Marilyn said. She

helped Patty pack her things and after a final okay from the nurse, we walked from the ward.

Patty didn't speak much until we were outside. "Does anyone have a cigarette?" she asked, knowing I didn't smoke.

Marilyn shook one from a packet and I couldn't help but notice how much Patty's hand shook when she held the thing to her lips, accepting a light. Marilyn's hands shook just as much.

Patty took a long drag and exhaled slowly. She turned to me. "Will you come and visit us?"

"Of course I will. We'll take a nice stroll along the beach, maybe grab a pint in the pub, or something," I replied. I meant every word.

Patty just nodded and then Marilyn informed us the taxi was waiting. There were no hugged goodbyes, just a nod. I felt tears brim in my eyes as I watched my friend leave and wondered if that would be the last time I'd see her. Would I really travel to Norfolk to have that stroll, that pint? I wasn't sure.

I took a slow walk home.

CHAPTER FIVE

I HEARD from Patty just once the following week. She called me and it was a stilted and difficult conversation. I don't know what had changed, but there wasn't the natural flow we usually had. I tried to tell her about Andrew and our dates, but she wasn't interested, and I understood that. It had to be hard to hear of someone else's happiness when so consumed by sadness. I just didn't know what to say to her.

"I felt awkward," I told Andrew that evening. He was sitting at the small table in my flat and I was cooking him dinner.

"Did you tell her about us?" he asked.

"I did. She wasn't very interested. I get it, though."

"Well, you've always been in her shadow, Amber, so she probably doesn't like it now you're branching out on your own," he replied.

I nodded absently while stirring the gravy. I'd made us a roasted chicken, about the one thing I did well. Of course, Andrew was used to more upmarket cooking, he told me, but he was looking forward to my roast. He'd brought a bottle of wine, one he loved and proceeded to tell me about. I was impressed with his knowledge of wines, and he made a comment that perhaps we'd travel to France to taste some wines one day.

The thought of travelling through the French country-side with wine tasting was certainly appealing.

I dished up our meal and sat opposite him. Andrew smiled at me. "I do think that you've bloomed, Amber, and maybe Patty doesn't like that."

I shrugged my shoulders. He might have a point. She hadn't wanted to know anything about him. "Like I said before, and I know this is hard, my darling, but talking to you might remind her of what happened here."

I nodded. "I wondered that, as well. Maybe I'll have a word with Marilyn and see what she says."

"I'd leave it for a little while before you do that. It might have been a one off where Patty was concerned, and you don't want to alarm her mum. Perhaps leave it for a while and see what happens."

Andrew was full of wise advice, I thought. He patted my hand and tucked into his meal.

"Mmm, this is delicious. I don't think I've had roast chicken as lovely as this," he said, and my heart swelled.

I knew I wasn't as sophisticated as him, I wasn't as worldly, so when he complimented me or something I'd done, I was thrilled.

When we'd eaten, we snuggled up on the sofa with just a couple of standard lamps giving a warm glow over the room.

"I'd like to take our relationship a little further," he said, nuzzling into my neck.

"So would I. I've never done anything before, though."

He pulled back and looked at me. "I'm glad to hear that,

Amber. There is something unsavoury about women who have had multiple partners."

It was the 'old fashioned' Andrew that I loved the most. He was obsessed with my safety, wanting to know where I was going and insisting that I called him when I was home each evening. I felt cherished and wanted.

At no time did I think there was anything wrong in his behaviour.

I lost my virginity to him that evening. I can't say it was the special moment I was hoping for. I wasn't left feeling elated and fulfilled in any way, but, as Andrew had said, the first time isn't always the best. It was about *breaking me in*. Maybe next time might be better.

Andrew didn't stay over as I was hoping. He had an early start, he said.

"Thank you for this evening, Amber. I can't tell you how much it pleases me to be your first," he said, holding me to him.

I inhaled his scent and wrapped my arms around him. "I'm glad it was you," I replied.

He gave me a brief kiss and then left, promising to call me in the morning before he left for work.

Calling me three times per day had become our norm. He'd ring before he left for work to wish me a good morning, then at lunchtime to check I was okay and that I'd eaten. He'd then call in the evening if we weren't seeing each other. Although it had only been a couple of weeks, the relationship was already intense.

"I have a business dinner tomorrow night. Will you come with me?" he asked during one of our telephone conversations.

"I'd love to. I'll have to find something nice to wear, though."

"How about I take you shopping? We can go as soon as I've finished work," he said.

"Oh, I'm not sure you need to do that. I mean, I'm sure I can find something here."

"Amber, if I'm going to show you off to my work colleagues, I want you to look the best woman there. I want my chums to be jealous," he said, laughing at the same time.

I laughed along with him. "Then, yes, let's buy a new dress."

He told me to be ready for five thirty, he'd leave the office a little earlier than usual. It was a Thursday; late night shopping had recently started in London on a Thursday. I was excited to be dipping in and out of shops, looking for that perfect dress. I already had it in mind, something demure, lacy perhaps. Or raunchy and sexy in red. I played with my hair, wondering if I could get a last-minute appointment to have it cut. It hadn't been cut in a long time. I bunched it on top of my head, looking this way and that. Yes, piled up in a messy bun with tendrils escaping around my face would look perfect.

I fished around in my bedroom for some costume jewellery, I was sure I had some faux drop diamond earrings somewhere. And, of course, I had the perfect shoes and stockings.

Yet again, a pang of sadness washed over me. I had no one to tell about my *business dinner* with Andrew. I shook it off when I remembered what he'd said one time.

You don't need a bunch of friends who are just going to be jealous of you. You just need us.

He was right, I just needed him. I'd even stopped taking calls from my siblings for fear that they wanted something from Andrew. He'd mentioned once before about my sister calling and wanting money that I didn't have to give. He'd said that I needed to be careful. If they discovered I was moving up in the world, they'd want to tag along and they'd never fit in. He was right, of course, I thought.

ANDREW HAD DECIDED on the shop that he wanted to take me to. I thought we'd take a leisurely Stoll along Oxford Street, browsing the windows before deciding. He said we didn't have time for that, and I wondered if he had something exciting for us to do. He held my hand as we entered the shop, and he walked straight to a rail of evening dresses.

He swept through them, discarding ones I thought were lovely, until he found what he liked. He held it up to me.

"Oh my God, Amber, this is you. So you! Everyone is going to be envious of you in this dress. Go try it on."

He ushered me to a changing room, and I got caught up in his excitement.

I hung the dress up without really looking at it, and then undressed. I slipped it over my head. It clung to my curves, and the neckline was a little revealing for my liking. I could see the top of my bra.

"I'm not sure this will do. It's a little too low cut," I called out.

"Let me see," he replied.

I held the dress up and walked out of the changing room.

Andrew wolf whistled.

"I need to get you home quick," he whispered while holding his crotch.

I laughed, both embarrassed and elated I had that effect on him.

"Take the bra off," he instructed. "Turn around."

I did as I was told, and he unhooked the old greying bra I wore. I slid it from my shoulders, then turned back to him.

"Now, that's better. You have an amazing body; you need to show it off."

I turned to look in the full-length mirror. The dress was red sexy but not close to the one in my mind. I hadn't realised how revealing it was. It was miles away from anything I would have chosen or had worn in the past.

"I guess, with a wrap, it will be okay," I murmured, twisting and turning to see the back.

"No wrap needed. If you're going to be on my arm, my darling Amber, I want the world to see what a cracking woman I have."

I patted his cheek and he looked so lovingly at me, that my stomach fluttered.

"Then this is the dress," I said, returning to the changing room.

Andrew insisted on paying for the dress, and I was glad considering I had a small budget for clothes and that would have taken it all.

"Now home, I want to ravish that body of yours," he said.

I chuckled and the warmth of knowing I was wanted, desired, flowed through me.

However, our lovemaking wasn't much better than the previous time. I had nothing to compare it to, of course, but I just had a feeling of dissatisfaction, of something missing.

Andrew was *teaching me* how to pleasure him and I enjoyed that, but I wanted pleasuring as well. My stomach felt empty as he slid to the side, beaming with delight, and having come himself.

I kept telling myself it will get better the more experienced I became.

As before, he left, stating he had an early start. As I closed the door behind him, for the first time, I had a pang of disappointment. I pushed it to one side, however. I'd never had sex; I'd never had a *proper* relationship. Nothing to compare how I felt with Andrew, or how he made me feel. I shook my head. I was probably just nervous about the dinner. I made myself a cup of tea and snuggled back in bed. I'd worry about it another time.

CHAPTER SIX

THE FIRST TIME Andrew hit me was during the business dinner. Thankfully, not in front of anyone.

He'd collected me and once again, marvelled at how amazing I looked. I felt a million dollars. I'd pinned up my hair, applied my makeup carefully and was sure to wear the flimsiest, laciest pair of knickers I could find.

I held his arm as we entered a country club, the venue for his dinner, and walked into a room full of people. He, of course, wanted to arrive last, to make an entrance, he'd said. I guessed it wasn't the entrance he'd hoped, though. He didn't seem overly happy not to have everyone turn to greet him.

We walked to a small group of people, and he slapped some backs, shook hands, and kissed cheeks of the women in the group. Then he introduced me as his partner.

"Doesn't she look amazing?" he said, pushing me forward. "I bought this dress, and the shoes and stockings," he added with a laugh.

I wasn't sure why they needed to know what he'd bought, but I smiled at him and introduced myself by name.

One woman, the wife of one of his colleagues, complimented my outfit but remarked more on the earrings. She wanted to know where I'd gotten them.

"Probably some flea market," Andrew said, placing his arm around my waist. "No need to shop there anymore."

"A friend made them, actually," I said, correcting him. "She's an amazing costume designer, hoping to work in theatres."

He pinched my side, hard. I turned to him with a puzzled look, but before I could speak, he silenced me with a brief kiss on my lips. "Let's find our table, shall we?"

I was confused, I mean, it was just a pinch, once that would bruise, but I had no idea what it was for.

He took my hand and led us into the dining room. "Excellent, we're near the boss. Will you do me a favour?" he asked. I turned to him and smiled. "I need to impress the big boss. Be nice to him and if he talks to you, tell him how wonderful I am?"

He placed his palms together and fluttered his eyelids like a child would do. "Pretty please? We can go to France with the pay rise I'd get if he promotes me."

I laughed. "I'll tell him how super you are and that he'd be mad not to promote you, how's that?"

He kissed the tip of my nose. "You are amazing, do you know that?"

The meal was actually very pleasant, and the *big boss* spent time talking to everyone on the table. I made a point of talking only about Andrew and how much he loved his job and the company, knowing Andrew was listening in.

He patted my knee as if thanking me.

Once the meal was over, we returned to the bar area. One or two of his colleagues were already drunk, and I spotted the one that had knocked me over. He weaved his way to us.

"You banged her then?" he said to Andrew. I stepped back a little. "With those tits, I'd do her as well. Fancy a threesome, love?"

I recoiled in shock, but made the mistake of laughing. I really wasn't sure how to respond and the laugh was more from embarrassment and certainly not because I found him funny.

Andrew gripped my wrist and led me out towards the toilets.

"Slow down, I can't walk that fast in these heels," I said, chuckling.

Before we got to wherever he was leading me, he halted abruptly. He slammed me against the wall, holding me with his hand on my chest.

"Did you have to laugh?" he asked.

"I'm sorry, I don't know what you mean?"

I felt panic rise in my throat. "Bet you'd fucking love his cock inside you, wouldn't you?"

The vulgarity of his words shook me to my core. He'd been nothing but well-spoken until then. I opened my mouth to speak but couldn't form the words.

He slapped my face.

I gasped.

I tried to push him away, and he only stepped back when a couple of women walked down the corridor heading to the ladies.

I turned to look at them and before they could speak to me, he leaned in and kissed me hard. He forced his tongue down my throat, they chuckled and carried on walking. I guessed they assumed we were happily making out.

When he stepped back, he looked so full of remorse. His eyes were brimming with tears.

"Oh God, Amber, I'm so sorry. Please, please forgive me. I got so jealous for a moment. I can promise you that will never happen again. My ex, she cheated on me, and when I saw you laugh, I thought of what she did. I can't bear that I've hurt you. Please let me make it up to you?"

He rambled on, holding my face in his hands, trying to soothe the soreness on my cheek.

"I can't believe I did that. If you want to leave me, I'll accept it. What I've done is unforgiveable. But when you laughed, I thought it meant that you wanted that to him."

"I don't want him at all," I replied, my voice a little croaky from emotion.

"He's going to think that."

"You can tell him I don't, can't you?"

"Yes, of course, my darling. I wouldn't let him touch you! Do you forgive me?"

We were back to the child and, stupidly, I believed him.

I sighed. "Yes, I forgive you, but please don't do that again."

"Pinky promise," he said, holding up his little finger and smiling at me.

I rolled my eyes and laughed.

"Let's go home, shall we?" he said. I was hoping he meant to his house, one I hadn't visited.

Instead, once outside, he flagged down a taxi and gave my address.

Once inside, he asked if I'd undress in front of him. He kept his hand down the front of his trousers, pleasuring himself as I did. I wanted to please him, to make him happy, more so after the evening we'd had. I was sure I'd made him mad by laughing inappropriately at his friend's comment, and I wanted to make that up to him.

We made love, and it was getting better. He spent some time touching me, kissing my body, but it was still so short lived. Ten minutes later, he rolled to his back and sighed in contentment.

"How about we have a round two?" I asked, turning on my side and running my fingers over his chest.

"Was that not good enough for you?" he asked, and the tone of his voice startled me.

"Of course, so good I just wondered..."

"I have work in the morning. It's been a trying evening, Amber. It's okay for you, you can lounge around here all day. I mean, maybe it might be time to look for a job?"

"Erm, yes, I... I'm sorry. Of course, you're right, you've got a busy day ahead. I'll make you a nice cup of tea while you dress."

I slid from the bed, not because I was desperate to make him a cup of tea, but so he wouldn't see my tears. He confused me.

He wanted me, then he didn't.

He complimented me, then he didn't.

I was standing in a robe stirring the tea when he came up behind me. "You make me so mad because I want you all the time. I love you, Amber, and it's like a fire inside me."

He nuzzled into my neck. It was the first time he'd said he loved me.

I didn't answer him. "Don't you love me?" he asked.

I turned in his arms.

"Of course I do. You're so passionate. I just want more of that."

"And you'll get more. Now, I have to go. I'll call you in the morning."

I didn't get a peck to my nose that evening, he just left with me holding the cup of tea that I'd made him.

I sat for a couple of hours thinking about the evening. Eventually, I'd convinced myself that Andrew was right. I shouldn't have laughed at the comment, and I vowed to do better. Andrew was obviously insecure over his previous relationship, and I had to make sure that I didn't give him any cause for concern. I would never cheat on him, or anyone, and I would make him believe that. I headed to bed.

It was with a better frame of mind that I took his morning call.

"Hi, I was thinking. Perhaps I could cook for you this evening?" Andrew said when I answered his call.

"That would be lovely. At your house?"

"Or yours, whichever is easier."

I hadn't been to his house, although he had talked about it. It was a small mews house that he rented with a friend. I guessed a romantic candlelit dinner might not be that romantic if his friend was around.

"Come to mine, at least we'll have the place to ourselves," I offered. "Would you like me to do a shop?"

"No, I'll bring what I want with me. I'll see you later."

I busied myself for the rest of the afternoon cleaning the flat. I knew I should be job hunting, but I also wanted to talk to Andrew about travelling. I couldn't see myself heading off alone and wondered if he'd take a holiday with me at least.

The urge to fulfil my dream of travel was still strong, but it was battling with my need to have Andrew in my life.

CHAPTER SEVEN

LIFE BOWLED ALONG and we settled into a routine. There were still the three calls per day, and I'd postponed my travels in favour of getting a job. I hadn't known what I wanted to do with my degree, so settled in a local small building company as a secretary. It was only a temporary thing until I chose a career. Andrew insisted on accompanying me to the interview, he wanted to vet those who I was going to be employed by.

As he said, *you never know what creeps are out in the work place nowadays.*

I enjoyed the job; I didn't enjoy the attention I was getting from some of the men. There were the usual sexist comments, the 'make me a cup of tea, love' crap that I'd expect from the workplace dominated by men, and I quickly learned not to tell Andrew any of it. Just one small comment about having a conversation with a colleague sent him in a temper, to the point he threw his plate of dinner across the room.

Of course, he apologised profusely afterwards, cleaned the place up, kept kissing me, then insisted on making love. I didn't view it as making love. Our intimacy was more about him getting all the pleasure and me being left unfulfilled.

"You don't look too happy, love. What's up?" I heard one morning.

I looked up from my desk, my boss was standing in front of it.

"Oh, I'm sorry, I'm fine. Just concentrating," I said, adding a laugh.

"Nah, you don't look happy. But it's okay if you want to keep it to yourself. My door's always open, though."

He was a nice guy, married with a couple of kids, one of which worked as a builder. I'd met his wife a couple of times and really liked her as well. She'd come to visit and always bought me a cake. She'd warn me about some of the men, encouraging me to answer back to their silly, suggestive remarks. I remembered her saying, *they aint brave if you go back at 'em, love.*

I sat for a moment wondering how miserable I looked, and if I was miserable? I wasn't sure. I had a successful boyfriend; one many girls would love to date. Okay, so the sex wasn't great, but was that the be all in a relationship?

I sighed. I'd make more of an effort in the bedroom department, maybe take the lead a little more and see what happened. Perhaps I'd buy a book. There must be one I could read to gain a little insight in how to please both Andrew and myself.

With a resolution in mind, I was happier.

"I'VE BEEN INVITED for drinks after work by the boss tomorrow. He wants to thank us all for this quarter's results," I said.

Andrew and I were flicking through estate agent's brochures having decided to move in together. My flat was too small, and he shared his, so we'd decided to start afresh.

"Did you tell him that you couldn't go?" he said, not looking up. "Here's one that might suit and in a good location for my work."

He pushed a leaflet towards me.

"No, I said I would go. I didn't think you'd mind. And what about my work?"

My flat was close to where I worked, and his close to his company. Neither were that far away from each other, but the property he was showing me was miles away.

"I think it's more important that we worry about mine, don't you? I'll be the bread winner after all."

We hadn't got to the discussion about who was paying what. I assumed we'd just go halves on everything.

"I'm not sure I could afford my half of that property," I said, sliding it back.

His jaw tensed and his eyes narrowed as he slowly looked up at me. "I don't think I like your tone," he said, standing.

"I don't have any kind of tone; I'm just saying that might be a little too expensive for me. I don't want you to think that you have to pay for me."

He slammed his palms on the table, scattering the brochure and loose leaflets.

"Am I not good enough for you now? Been asked out by the boss so you don't want to live with me, is that it?"

I had no idea how he'd reached that conclusion. I stood and moved around the table to his side. I placed my hand on his cheek.

"You are way more of a man than my boss. You're more respectable, you earn more, you're my partner." I'd learned that making Andrew feel better than anyone else often calmed him down. "I don't want to go out for drinks with them and if you feel this is the right property, then let's book an appointment."

He took in a deep breath.

"Why do you have to always spoil things, Amber? This was meant to be exciting, now I don't know if I can be bothered."

He sat back down and picked up the television remote. I tidied up the papers and then sat next to him.

"Let me make you feel better," I said, rubbing my hand over his crotch.

He leaned back, not taking his eyes off the programme while unzipping his trousers. He freed his cock and then grabbed the hair at the back of my head.

"Want to make me feel better? Suck that," he said, forcing my head down.

I gagged at first, but then complied. I understood it aroused him to be forceful where sex was concerned, and I'd do whatever was necessary to stop the temper flaring further.

When he came, he pushed me to one side and headed for the bathroom to clean up. I rinsed my mouth in the kitchen sink, pouring bleach down the plug hole after it. I wanted to cry, but I wouldn't, not in front of him.

I felt his arms creep around my waist. "Thank you," he whispered into my hair.

I simply nodded. He returned to the table as if nothing had happened.

"So, this apartment? Shall I book a viewing? We can go tomorrow evening if you like."

It was the same evening work had invited me for drinks,

but going to the apartment with Andrew was more important, I guessed.

"It's going to be so exciting, Amber. Just think about it, we'll have a lovely apartment. I don't think any of my colleagues have one as nice as this. It has a swimming pool in the basement, and a gym. You could join and get fit, lose those pounds around your hips," he said, smiling away at me.

"It does sound lovely," I confessed.

And it did. It was in Canary Wharf, a blooming part of London that had great access routes into the City. I wasn't sure how I would get to work, but I'd have to figure that out should we move. Both of us had a small amount of savings, and Andrew had said we'd need to place a deposit down.

"You know, if we decide on children, you won't work anyway, so this could be perfect for you. Shops nearby, there are some lovely restaurants as well."

I hadn't planned on children, and we'd certainly never had a conversation about them or made any formal arrangements for our relationship. We'd only been dating a few months.

I walked behind him, placing my arms around his shoulders, and kissed the top of his head. "It sounds perfect, give them a call," I said.

He slid the telephone towards him, and I left him to it.

It was times like that that I longed for a conventional apartment. Not because I wanted to live with Andrew, but to be able to move to a different room to gather my thoughts and process what had happened. I knew I was bending to his will too much, but I didn't seem to be able to stop it.

I had no one to talk to. I hadn't contacted or been contacted by Patty at all, and it seemed, the longer that went on the more unlikely rekindling our friendship would be. I felt embarrassed that I'd let it slip, but also knew that Andrew wouldn't have approved. He mentioned his dislike for *loose women,* as he called them, often. He'd even gone as far as saying that Patty had got herself into a vulnerable position, so what did she expect?

He discouraged any kind of relationship with my work colleagues, but we regularly dined with his. I kept quiet, answered questions when required to, and avoided the gaze of any of the men. Some of the women tried hard to befriend me, but Andrew's painful squeeze of my thigh would stop me taking that up.

He didn't want to share me, he'd say. Whereas once I'd felt elated at that, there was a small part of me that knew I was losing my identity.

CHAPTER EIGHT

WE VIEWED THE APARTMENT, and it was amazing. It had a small balcony and views of the River Thames. It was way above our budget, but Andrew decided, there and then, that we wanted it. We completed the paperwork and waited.

I finally got to see Andrew's house when I visited to help decide on what furniture to take with us. Well, deciding was up to him, of course. My wishes weren't as important. However, had the more modern furniture, and as he said, it would be more befitting of the apartment than my second-hand mix and match pieces.

There was no sign of his house-mate other than some strange toiletries and hairbrushes in the bathroom. Andrew assured me those belonged to the house-mate's girlfriend before they broke up. He grabbed the items and shoved them in the rubbish bin.

We made a list of what items he wanted to take and then headed to the local pub to celebrate. I was caught up in his excitement and plans for dinner parties and entertainment. We talked about decorating and art, where we'd place some items and by the end of the evening, I was more than ready to move.

The following day, I began sorting out my flat. I took lots of items to the charity shop. We decided to keep my bed as it was larger than his, and my dining table. It was an extendable one and would be suitable for those dinner parties he wanted to throw.

My boss wasn't as pleased when I told him I was moving, however.

"Are you sure that's the right thing to do?" he asked.

We were sitting in the pub, not that I told Andrew, of course. A group of us regularly nipped next door for a pint during our lunch break. The boss always paid the bar bill.

"Of course. Why do you ask that?" His comment took me aback.

"You don't seem very happy. It's either the job or your love life causing it," he replied, chuckling.

"I love my job!" I did. I loved the lads, the builders, and even the apprentices that were tasked with asking me for an invisible ruler, or some other item that didn't exist.

"So, it's the love life then?"

I clamped my mouth shut. "It's a big move, that's all."

He nodded. "Remember, my door is always open. We're having a bar-b-que at mine at the weekend. Bring him along."

I nodded, knowing full well he wouldn't attend. I'd already come up with all sorts of reasons why we were busy, and I knew my boss wasn't fooled.

I mentioned it to Andrew, anyway.

"Sure, let's go. I haven't met your colleagues yet," Andrew said. I blinked rapidly.

"Are you sure?" I asked.

He stared at me. "Are you ashamed of me, Amber? Do you not want me to meet your colleagues?"

"No, and yes. It's just you've never wanted to before. You'll love them, real down-to-earth people." I smiled at him.

"I'm sure they are. Now, let's get down to more important things."

He went on to making notes in his diary about up-and-coming events at his company, scheduling in a dinner party in our new apartment when we moved in. I thought it premature but didn't say anything.

———

THE SECOND TIME he hit me was at my boss's bar-b-que. Like before, thankfully, not in front of anyone.

I was nervous as the taxi pulled up outside the property. It was a large house with electric gates. Perfect lawns laid either side of the drive. Already there were cars parked and a couple of the builders were lounging against one holding bottles of beer in their hands.

"That's Tom and George," I said, as we exited the car.

Tom called out. "Here she is. We had bets on whether or not you'd show."

"Can't help having a life, Tom," I replied. I received a slight nudge to my ribs. "Let me introduce my boyfriend."

Andrew strode forward, holding out his hand. He wore a dark blue suit, white shirt, and a rugby club tie. Not that he'd ever played rugby.

"Andrew Stowley, Amber's soon to be husband," he said.

I came to an abrupt halt. There had been no mention of

marriage and he hadn't proposed. I swallowed hard and attempted a neutral expression.

"I didn't know you were engaged," Tom said. "Congratulations."

"Thank you," I replied. Andrew then introduced himself to George.

"Shall we?" Andrew said, indicating to the front door.

We walked into the house and stood in the hallway. "Tacky isn't it?" Andrew whispered. "New money, I bet."

I thought it was tastefully done, but I nodded anyway.

"You came," my boss said, striding over. He leant to kiss my cheek, and I froze. He hadn't done that before, and I knew it was just a gesture of greeting, but Andrew wouldn't like it. I didn't dare look at him.

"And you're her boyfriend?" he asked, holding out his hand.

"Yes, Andrew Stowly. It's a pleasure to meet you, finally," Andrew was the perfect gentleman, but I noticed a tic that had started at the side of his jaw.

"Bill Sanders," my boss replied. "We're thrilled to have Amber working with us. She's sorted the office out a real treat, keeps all the lads in line," he said, laughing.

"Does she now?" Andrew said, his voice lowering.

"Come outside, meet the rest of the team."

I let Andrew walk ahead with Bill and it was only then I caught Tania, Bill's wife watching us. She smiled and came to my side.

"You know, if there's anything you'd like to talk about, Bill and me are here for you."

It seemed a strange thing to say, but I smiled in response.

"You look terrified, and I've seen that look before, Amber. I was you once, before I met Bill. I'm here for you."

"Oh, I... I'm not sure what you mean."

I knew damn well what she meant, but I couldn't acknowledge it. Bill shouldn't have kissed me; Andrew would have every right to be cross. I'd be the same had some woman kissed his cheek, I thought.

We followed the men into the garden.

There was a pool filled with inflatables and children splashing around, a chef behind a cooking station. It wasn't a bar-b-que, more a fully fitted outdoor kitchen. A couple of people came over to introduce themselves, and Andrew was polite. I was on edge. He hadn't said a word to me. I placed my hand on his arm, and he finally turned to me.

"Shall I get you a drink?" I asked.

"I'll have a glass of wine, thank you." He clipped his reply. I hoped that he would stick at just the one glass, he could be vile when drunk.

I grabbed him a glass from a passing waitress and a Coke for myself. The tension rolling off him was palpable. I wanted to keep my wits about me.

I'd seen him angry a few times, but his stiff body and tense jaw were new.

He gulped down his glass. "If we have to mix with the riff-raff, might as well do that drunk," he said, a little too loudly.

Tears sprang to my eyes. I liked my boss, his family, and the guys at work. They treated me well and I started to pray he wouldn't embarrass me in front of them.

The more he drank, the less I did. He was chatty and seemed to get on well with my colleagues. We ate and he started on the beers. Whenever I moved slightly away from him, he'd grip my arm. I had wanted to join the ladies, but he wasn't having any of it. Instead, I had to listen to him bore people with talk of his job. He was a trader in the city, a serious job, he'd tell them. He failed to add that he was still a junior trader and not quite up with the big boys he bragged about. I was sure he was trying to make them feel small and inadequate around him. Thankfully, they seemed to take it on the chin. I was guessing they'd come across lots of Andrews in their time. The posh twit who thought everyone was beneath him. I started to get cross.

When he started talking about how he'd found me in the gutter and that he was training me up to middle *classdom*, I walked away. I snatched my arm from his grip and headed for the toilets. Andrew was laughing, swaying around, and I couldn't care less whether he fell into the pool at that point.

After a few tears, I came out of the toilets, Tania was there. "You okay?" she asked.

"He's drunk and being an arse. He isn't like this normally," I said, rubbing under my eyes to get rid of any smeared mascara.

She nodded, but I could tell she didn't believe me. "I think you should take him home. He might end up getting a bop on the nose here," she said, smiling kindly at me.

"A bop on the nose?" we heard, and I closed my eyes briefly before turning to face him.

"I think it's time we left," I said.

"I'll leave when I'm good and ready," he replied, slurring his words.

"You'll leave when I ask you to, which is now. You're insulting people," Tania said.

He stared at her, and, unlike me, she held his gaze. "You can't bully me, mate," she added. "I'll call you a taxi."

He grabbed my arm and dragged me to the front door. I stumbled down the steps. "Stop pulling me, I'm going to fall!"

He stopped and turned to me. "I'm so sorry, Amber. Let me go back and apologise to everyone."

He was a Jekyll and Hyde, for sure. One minute spitting insults, the next, all apologetic and remorseful.

"Let's just get home."

He turned and walked to the road. I followed, rubbing my arm, knowing I'd have a bruise there.

The taxi didn't take long, and he didn't speak to me at all. I kept my head turned, looking out the side window and paid when we arrived at my flat. I hadn't wanted him to come in but didn't want to stir the hornets' nest by telling him that.

We walked in and I kicked off my shoes. Before I could remove my jacket, he punched me square in the face. I was so stunned that for a few seconds I didn't move. I was frozen. Then I fell backwards, hitting the small coffee table.

"Do you normally let him kiss you?" he said, looming over me. His fists were clenched tight.

"No, and you bloody well know that," I said, trying to scoot back and out of his way.

"You embarrassed me in front of your colleagues," he shouted.

"You embarrassed yourself," I said, shouting back at him. That earned me a kick to my hip. I cried out in pain.

Tears began to slip from my eyes. "Just go, Andrew. We'll talk about this tomorrow," I said, desperately wanting him out of my flat.

"There's nothing to talk about, Amber," he dragged out the sound of my name. "You're having an affair with him, aren't you? Bet his wife doesn't know. Mind you, he can have you. I'd rather his wife anyway. We can do a swap. How about that? Bet she's fucking great in bed. She can suck my cock any day."

I closed my eyes, not wanting to see the spittle that left his mouth, and he bent down close to me. He grabbed the front of my shirt and tried to lift me from the floor. I clawed at his hands until the material tore, and I fell back down.

"Nothing but whores, the lot of you," he said. He started to mumble something before collapsing onto the bed.

I lay still for what seemed like an age. When I heard him snoring, I slid out from under his legs and stood. I hurt. My nose was bleeding and my eye stung. Andrew was flat on his back with his feet still on the floor. I didn't want to touch him, move him, for fear of him waking up. I walked to the bathroom and locked the door.

At first, even though I stood in front of the mirror, I didn't want to look. I kept my eyes closed, but I could hear a drip and taste the blood that ran from my nose and pooled on my lips.

When I finally did open my eyes, I cried out.

My nose was red and bloodied, swollen, and I had a black eye. I peeled down the top of my trousers to see a large black bruise on my hip. I silently cried some more.

I ran a bath, hoping that might help the bruising come out quicker. I could still hear him snoring and knew I wouldn't leave the bathroom until I felt safe. I sank into the bath and wetted a face cloth. I placed that over my nose and eyes, hoping the warmth and steam would help. I wanted to sob, but I was too afraid to make a noise.

I think I drifted off; until a knock at the door startled me awake.

"Amber, can we talk?"

I didn't answer him.

"I know you're in there," he added.

"You need to leave," I said.

"I can't do that until we've spoken."

"I have nothing to say right now. Leave, Andrew."

I felt braver behind the locked door, but still apprehensive. It has such a flimsy lock he could kick the door open in a few seconds. He didn't, though. I heard him shuffle and then the front door open and closed.

I sighed. I wasn't rushing out of the bath, however. I wasn't stupid enough to think he might have actually left. And I was right. Ten minutes later, he knocked on the door again.

"I will call the police if you don't leave," I said, shaking with fear and the cooled water.

"No you won't, Amber. You love me. I love you. This is just a blip, nothing we can't get over," he said.

I frowned. "Do you really believe that?"

"Yes, we're made for each other. I know, I was an arsehole, and I'll apologise to all involved, I promise. I get jealous, you know that. I—"

"You're not blaming me for this one, Andrew," I said, interrupting him. "You've gone too far this time."

He didn't respond, and a few minutes later I heard the door open and close again. I gave it another ten minutes before I climbed from the bath, stiffly, and wrapped myself in a towel. I sat on the edge of the bath, listening. There was nothing, no noise at all. I felt safe enough, then to open the bathroom door.

Andrew had left. I rushed to the front door and slid over the safety chain. He didn't have a key, but I wasn't taking any chances.

I then made a cup of tea. My hands shook, but I needed the warmth. As soon as I sat on the sofa, the telephone rang. I looked at it, not answering. After ten rings, it stopped, only to start again. That went on for about an hour. By the end, I was curled up in a ball on the bed and sobbing. I should have left it off the hook. I should have called the police, but I was so confused, I just didn't think straight.

I didn't go to work the following day; I called in sick. Bill asked me what was wrong, and I put it down to *women's problems*. Usually that stopped any further chat, but he asked me if I wanted Tania to call by. I declined his kind offer, disconnected the call, and pulled my duvet up over my head.

I didn't see Andrew the following day, or the one after. In fact, I didn't see him for the entire week. It was the following Friday that I felt okay to go back to work. No one said anything and everyone was pleasant, but I knew they knew. I'd done what I could to conceal the bruising, but nothing would hide the swelling. I had cups of tea made for me, cake bought, and sandwiches placed on my desk at lunch time. I wanted to cry at their kindness, and I appreciated their silence. I wasn't up to answering questions.

CHAPTER NINE

IT WAS on the Sunday that I decided to take a walk around the local park. I'd worked all day Friday and Saturday to catch up and needed some fresh air. When I got back, my heart sank in my chest. Sitting on the doorstep with an enormous bunch of flowers was Andrew. He looked dishevelled, like he hadn't slept. His eyes were red rimmed. He stood as I approached.

"I'm sorry. So so sorry. I won't take up much of your time, because I know I don't deserve it, but I wanted to give you these."

He thrust the flowers into my chest.

"I don't want flowers," I said, quietly. I didn't want to rile him.

"Then I'll give them away. But please just hear me out. I'm going to counselling. I've booked my first appointment. I can't believe I hit you like that; I don't know why I get so jealous. I know you love me, and you won't cheat on me, but..." He took in a deep breath. "No buts. I'm going to counselling and I just wanted to know if you'd wait for me."

He looked like a lost boy. His tone of voice was eager and he wrung his hands together.

"I'm not sure," I said. He nodded.

"Can I at least speak on the telephone to you?"

It was my turn to nod. And I only did that to appease him in the hope he would leave.

"Thank you, you won't regret it," he said.

He stepped to one side so I could open my door. "Erm, I'll hear from you another time then, I guess," I said, stepping into the flat.

I closed the door and then slid down it. As I sat on the floor, I heard him. "I'll leave the flowers out here."

I didn't open the door until later that evening when a neighbour called through the letterbox.

"Amber, it's Joanie. You know you got flowers out here?"

I opened the door and took them in. "Sorry, I didn't realise they'd been delivered."

"Been a naughty boy, has he?" she said, laughing.

"Something like that."

She waved as she headed to her flat up the stairs and I placed the flowers on my table. They were expensive lilies, ones that made me sneeze, but beautiful all the same. He'd even had the florist removed the stamen.

I didn't want to keep them, but I found a vase and filled it with water. It wasn't the flower's fault, I thought.

And that's how the next couple of weeks went.

Andrew would call three times per day, and at first I was irritated by that. However, he was charming and polite, he didn't pressure me to meet with him, and he told me about his counselling sessions.

He understood how his father's infidelity had affected him, and how his mother just accepting it had skewed his thoughts on women. It sounded so plausible.

When the gifts started, I wavered. At first it was just a box of chocolates, or a bunch of flowers, always left by the front door or delivered by courier. One gift was a pair of earrings, a pretty silver flower shape with a small diamond in the middle.

Another gift was a book, the newest release from my favourite author.

I thanked him and we chatted about books. It was a different Andrew I was speaking to, one not so bullish and, for the first time, interested in me and what I liked.

"How's the new flat?" I asked him. He'd told me he'd moved in, and I assumed he'd informed the landlord that he'd done that alone.

I was thankful that I hadn't handed in my tenancy and still had somewhere to live.

"You'd love it here. The views are amazing. I love to sit in the evenings just looking out. Do you remember the floor to ceiling windows? I put a couple of chairs facing them with a small table between. You said about doing that, didn't you? Anyway, in the evenings it's fantastic."

I could picture the scene and smiled.

"I bet it is."

"Perhaps you'd like to come and see. Nothing more, just a visit," he said.

I hesitated. "Perhaps," I replied.

"No rush. Now I have to go, got an early start. Did I tell you I got that promotion?"

"You didn't, congratulations. You worked hard for that, but don't let it take up all your life," I said. I was genuinely pleased for him; he'd wanted that promotion for a long time.

He laughed. "I have a new life to look forward to. One, I hope that you'll be part of."

"Maybe," I replied.

We said our goodbyes, and I slowly placed the handset back down. I did enjoy talking to him. I missed him. I was still very wary of him, though.

He wore me down eventually. Only a month later, I stood in his lounge looking at the view he'd told me about and agreeing how wonderful it was. I walked around as he talked about all the new appliances the flat had. How the shower was so powerful, and the bath so deep.

"Do you want a glass of wine?" he asked.

I stared at him. "I'm not drinking, but I'd like to offer you one," he added.

I nodded. "Okay, and please don't think you can't have a glass with me. I'm sure you've learned what your tolerances are now."

He smiled as he uncorked a bottle of red. He sniffed the cork. "That trip to France, the vineyard I told you about. That's where this wine came from. I'd still love to do that trip one day. You said you wanted to travel."

"I still do, I just never seem to have enough money anymore."

The rent on my flat had increased, shopping bills were going up, the country was heading for a recession, so we were told.

"I'd still love if you moved in here," he said, quietly.

I didn't answer. He stepped towards me until we were toe to toe. I tried hard not to flinch. "Can I kiss you?" he whispered.

I nodded. He lowered his head and gently kissed my lips. He pulled back just a fraction, his eyes searching mine. He kept his arms down by his side. I placed mine around his neck and he kissed me hard. He took my breath away with his passion. It was the kiss I'd dreamed of; one he'd never given me before.

I moaned gently, and that, I guess, was his cue.

He lifted me up and carried me to the bedroom. I didn't protest at all when he undressed me and then fell to his knees. He kissed my body, all of it, before returning to my lips.

His love making was the kind that I'd been desperate for from the beginning. He spent time to make sure he's satisfied me, that I orgasmed for the very first time. When he slid himself above me, he stilled.

"I love you, Amber, so much."

It was the love making I'd read about. The passionate combining of two bodies. Everything that came before it was forgotten. It was just us in the moment. I wanted to shed tears. This was what I deserved.

A week later, I handed back the keys to my flat and moved in with Andrew. It was a bittersweet day. I'd loved my little flat. It had served me well for the years I'd spent at uni. My landlady was sad to see me go, Joanie shed a couple of tears. I promised her that I'd visit, knowing full well I doubted I would.

Bill, however, wasn't as gracious.

"I think you're making a huge mistake, Amber," he said when I gave him my new address. "A leopard never changes its spots."

"Thank you for caring about me. I really do appreciate it, but he has changed. He's having therapy, he'd different, I promise you."

I wanted to convince everyone that I was doing the right thing, that he had changed. He was becoming the Andrew that I first met, the charming old-fashioned gentleman in a young man's body.

I brushed off all concerns.

Maybe Andrew had been right when he'd said that

there were a lot of people jealous of our relationship. We had it all, a beautiful apartment overlooking the Thames. We both worked, even though Andrew had said that I didn't need to if I wanted to take time out. He earned more than enough for both of us. The only downside to that was the hours he worked.

He was tired during the week; it was late nights and early starts. But he kept telling me it was all for our future. We'd be able to buy our own house soon. He wanted a nice car and holidays. I wanted all that as well. I worked, and I cared for him as well. I made sure the flat was neat and tidy, that his shirts were ironed, and his suits dry cleaned. He had a hot meal prepared every evening, and a bath ran when he wanted it.

We even got married. It was a surprise to me, of course. Andrew had booked the registry office and I only knew when I had to sign the paperwork with him. But I went along with it. He had changed. I was sure. It was all going to be fine. With two witnesses off the street, I became Amber Stowley.

For a while, nearly a year, it was bliss.

CHAPTER TEN

ANDREW WAS MOVING up the ladder fast. He was about to be promoted to Associate, the youngest in his firm to achieve the title. It would mean a lavish dinner in celebration.

"I need a new dress," I said, looking through my wardrobe.

Andrew sidled up behind me. "Now you've lost that bit of weight, you certainly do. You deserve a new dress for all you've done for me lately," he said.

Although he had changed, he hadn't lost the snide comments. He had a knack of building me up and knocking me down in the same sentence. I had learned to let it go over my head, but it had eroded my confidence.

I didn't like to shop on my own. I preferred that Andrew chose my clothes. I couldn't get it wrong that way. Many a time I'd have to return a dress because he'd convince me it wasn't right. I trusted his judgement. I was often complimented on how I looked, so he must have been right.

I didn't have to shop for that dress after all. Andrew

returned home one evening with a lavish paper bag tied with red ribbon.

"I bought you something," he said, presenting it to me.

"Wow, a gift?"

"Sort of. Open it."

I pulled the ribbon, and the bag came open. Inside was tissue paper, which I removed. Nestled further down was a dress. I pulled it out. It was a stunning peach coloured silk dress. It had thin spaghetti straps and a cowl neck. It was backless though and I worried how I'd pull it off.

"Try it on," he said, pushing me gently towards the bedroom.

I laughed. It was probably the most extravagant dress he'd bought me. I had no idea of the label; I didn't do designer, even though Andrew always wanted me to wear expensive things around his colleagues.

I slipped out of my work clothes and pulled the dress over my head. It slid down my body, one that was thin with exposed ribs and hips. Andrew like to see my bones, he'd say. I mostly starved myself to keep that androgenous shape.

The dress was stunning. Whether I could carry it off was something else though. I grabbed a pair of nude-coloured shoes and placed them on my feet.

"Are you ready?" I called out.

"Yep, bring that body of yours out here, Amber," he said.

I strutted into the living room as if I was walking a runway.

He whistled slowly. "I think I might be in trouble at that dinner. No one is going to keep their eyes off you."

I stilled; my breath caught in my throat. "It's a joke," he said, as if hoping to quell the fear that rolled in my stomach.

"You look divine. Do you like it? I think it's perfect for you."

"I love it. Where did you get it?" I asked, twirling in front of him.

"There's a woman in my office. She always dresses so stylishly; I asked her to show me where she bought her clothes."

It was the first time he'd mentioned any female colleagues before, and I wasn't sure I liked it. "So, another woman recommended this dress?"

"No, and don't get snarky. She recommended a shop, that's all. I chose the dress."

I swallowed down my response.

"Don't spoil the mood, Amber. It's a beautiful dress and fits you perfectly."

I nodded and raised up to kiss him. "I'm sorry. I love the dress and thank you."

"That's better. Now get it off and let me see you in just those shoes."

As our relationship had grown, so had his sexual kinks. Andrew had started to prefer anal sex, something I hated. He liked to *fuck me,* as he called it. Gone were the days when we'd make love, and he made an effort to give me an orgasm. His selfishness had returned to the bedroom. If I complained, he got angry. He'd call me selfish for not wanting to satisfy him, especially after all the hours he put in at work to give us a lavish lifestyle. He told me I should be more than willing to do whatever he wanted in gratitude.

"I've got my period," I lied.

"Urgh, then I guess I'll have to pleasure myself," he said. "Or you can suck my cock. Think of it as a thank you for the dress." He laughed as if he'd said the funniest thing.

Of course, I complied, it just wasn't worth the argument that would follow if I didn't.

I HAD my hair done and nails painted for the celebration dinner. Even though I said it myself, I thought I looked nice.

"I think you should change that handbag. You took that one last time," Andrew said.

"Oh, okay, I thought this went better with the dress."

"You took that last time," he said, sterner.

Andrew had a thing about showing off his wealth. I wasn't to wear the same dress twice, but to have to change handbags was bordering on the ridiculous. It was just a handbag. But it wasn't worth the argument.

"Is this one better?" I said, holding up a cream clutch.

"Much. You know how I don't want you to look like you've only got the one thing," he replied, doing up his cuff links.

He wore the same coloured suit every day of the week, the same brand but a different colour when we went out. He had five pairs of the exact same shoes, seven of the exact same tie, so I just didn't get this logic.

Andrew had ordered a chauffeur to drive us. Gone were the days we'd ring the local cab company. He was waiting on a new car he'd ordered, a top of the range Mercedes. Neither of us drove much, we didn't need to where we lived, and it would sit in the underground car park most of the time, but it was a status symbol for him.

"Oh, I also contacted an estate agent about leaving the apartment. I think it's time to move. This is getting too small for us now."

I nodded. The apartment was perfectly suitable for the

two of us, but I had a secret that I had yet to share and perhaps, a larger property might be better.

"Tod just moved to a gated community in Sevenoaks, it's an easy commute into London so I think we should look there."

He finally looked up and cocked his head to one side. "You look stunning," he said.

"Thank you."

We were driven, mostly in silence, to the country club where the reception was being held. Andrew was on a fast track to becoming a Partner and I knew how important that was to him. He was feted by his peers, existing Partners, and the juniors under his control. And he loved it.

For Andrew, he had to be needed, to be wanted. He had to be better than anyone else, have more. It was important that he wore his wealth, as did I. I was just as happy in a pair of charity shop jeans, but not him. I'd pretended the charity shop jeans were the new shabby chic look that everyone was talking about. He fell for that.

Although Andrew earned extremely well, he kept control of the finances. I still had my job in the builders but had gone part time. Andrew didn't think I had enough time to dedicate to the house and him if I worked full time.

The problem I had was that I never had enough money. Everything had to be accounted for. I kept a household budget that he'd go through on a monthly basis, putting enough money into the house account to cover all the bills. Sure, I had nice clothes. But I didn't want nice clothes. I wanted to be able to walk to a coffee shop, sit and people watch while sipping on a latte. I wanted to head to a bookstore and fill my shelves with romance books—something Andrew hated with a passion.

To outsiders, we had the absolute best of everything. It

was stifling. And it was suffocating. I longed for a little freedom, to breathe clean air, and wear what I wanted.

I put on the fake smile I'd become so great at, and took hold of his hand.

"You deserve this evening, Andrew. You've worked so hard, and I'll do your proud. Now, who do I need to chat up?" I said, laughing.

His laugh was stilted, and I realised my mistake. "I mean, who do I need to tell how wonderful you are?"

"I'll point him out when we get there."

He puffed his chest out and lifted his chin. Arrogance was his cloak of armour.

Hand in hand, we strode into the reception to be greeted with champagne and cheers. I wasn't allowed to leave his side, not even when one of the bosses' wives beckoned to me. I had to be paraded around.

"Oh you bought the dress, then?" I heard a woman's voice say.

I turned to see a woman standing alone. She was stunning. "I'm sorry?"

"The dress. Andrew said you wanted a nice dress, so I recommended that one."

"It's lovely, thank you." So, this was the colleague he had mentioned. "Do you shop there often?"

"My friend owns it, designs a lot of the clothes herself."

"She's very talented." I saw the quick glance she gave to Andrew and the sternness in his face. She then left.

My instincts were on high alert.

"I think I need the ladies," I said.

"Now? We've only just got here. Can't you hold it for five minutes at least?"

He turned then to talk to some guys. Why he wanted me to be at his side was beyond me. He never introduced me; I had nothing to add to their conversation. It was strange.

We moved around the room and only when we got to the Senior Partners did he introduce me. He would joke that I was still in training to be a Partner's wife and generally act condescending. I would laugh and take it. Although one of the senior partners didn't find him funny. He held out his hand to me.

"Hi, Daniel Morgan," he said.

Considering Andrew worked for Morgan & Morgan Wealth Management, I assumed him to be one brother that owned the company.

"I think your wife is more than *qualified*, Andy."

I'd never heard anyone shorten Andrew's name before. I felt the grip on my arm tighten.

"I'm still learning about your business, Mr. Morgan. Andrew teaches me a lot about wealth management. I find it fascinating. And, of course, he's so good at what he does, he makes it easy for me."

Mr. Morgan looked at me. "Well rehearsed," he said. "Andy." He nodded at us both and moved away.

Andrew's jaw was ticking.

"He seemed nice," I said, not because I believed it, I didn't even know the man, but to have some words fill the void that surrounded me.

Andrew didn't answer. Instead, we were called into dinner.

I wasn't sure to be elated or dismayed to find myself seated next to Mr. Morgan. I genuinely thought him nice, but something was bothering Andrew. I would have switched the name plates around had we got to the table before anyone else, but Mr. Morgan was already seated.

"Amber, you appear to be next to me," he said, patting the back of the chair.

I looked at Andrew, who had fixed a false smile on his face. That was until the female colleague came and took the chair on the other side of him.

"This is a wonderful venue, Mr. Morgan. And such a lovely thing for you to do for Andrew. He works so hard to progress within your company."

These were words I had, as he'd suggested, rehearsed, and used frequently.

"Now tell me what you really think," he replied, leaning close and whispering. "Personally, I think this *bigging up an ego* is a load of bollocks."

He leaned back in his chair before I could reply. I opened my mouth to speak, but quickly shut it again. However, I couldn't stop the giggle that escaped.

He gave me a wink.

I daren't look at Andrew. Starters were brought around and placed in front of us. "Would you like some wine?" Mr. Morgan asked. I nodded.

I knew Andrew was looking at me, but I kept my gaze on my plate. Eventually I heard her speak to him and she diverted his attention. I breathed out.

"Amber?"

I looked at Mr. Morgan who held aloft a bottle of wine.

"Oh, yes, please, that would be nice."

He poured into my glass, and then his own. He then placed the bottle back on the table without offering to fill Andrew's. Not that it was needed, the female was busy filling up his wine and water glasses.

"So, tell me a little about yourself? I heard you work with an old friend of mine," Mr. Morgan said.

He had my attention, then. "Bill?"

He nodded and smiled. He had a kind face, sparkling blue eyes. "Bill and I were at school together. Our grand-dads were all in the workhouse at the same time, so legend has it."

"The workhouse?"

"Yes, those shitty places kids went to if they had no parents or were poor. Back in the thirties, I believe."

"The thirties?"

"Nineteen-Thirty-Nine. You've heard of the work-houses, I take it?"

"Of course. I have a geography degree, social economics through British history was one of my specialities."

"An educated woman, I bet Andy doesn't like that," he said, chuckling into his glass as he raised it to his lips.

I didn't know how to respond and was only glad that Andrew seemed engaged in a whispered conversation with the female.

"Dare I ask, you don't like Andrew?"

He laughed. "Does anyone? Do you, even?"

I blinked rapidly. I really didn't like the way the conversation was heading.

"I'm sorry. That was rather crass of me, and it was meant to be a joke. He's an ambitious young man, who knows what he wants and how to get it."

That was a rather polite way of saying he'd gotten the measure of the real Andrew, not the one lording it up at the dinner table with, I suspected, his mistress by his side. Call it female intuition, but the minute I caught the glances between Andrew and the female, I knew there was something more to their 'relationship.'

"Yes, he is, and does."

"He want's my job, I believe."

"That can't have been fun to hear, Mr. Morgan," I replied.

He laughed. "He doesn't have a chance and call me Daniel."

He raised his glass to me, and I picked up mine. I shifted my eyes to Andrew to make sure he wasn't looking before I clinked.

We then ate our starters, I chatted to some others on the table, ate our mains, and refused more wine.

During coffee, someone made a speech. Of course, it was all about Andrew, and he loved it. His smile was broad as he listened to all his amazing attributes, and at the end, the female stood to applaud him. Slowly, others got to their feet.

Andrew held his hand over his heart in a fake gesture of thanks. I expected a *shucks, you guy's* to leave his lips at any moment. Thankfully, it didn't.

With the plates removed, a band started to play.

"Would you do me the honour?" Daniel said. He'd stood and held out his hand.

I looked at Andrew. "Does she need your permission?" Daniel asked.

The tension was rising. "No, feel free to dance, Amber. Perhaps Petra and I will dance too."

So that was her name. Of course, it had to be something unusual. The four of us headed to the dancefloor. Whereas I kept a respectable distance between myself, and Daniel, Petra and Andrew were chest to chest, crotch to crotch. I ignored them.

"Does that bother you?" Daniel asked, nodding towards them.

"Andrew dancing with someone?" I asked, knowing full well what he meant. "No, of course not."

Thankfully, for the second dance, we switched partners. "He likes you," Andrew said, not looking at me.

"I doubt it, but he likes you. I think he's also worried about you. You're more than capable of doing his job and he knows it."

"Did he say that?"

"In so many words."

Andrew then smiled and I came down to Defcon level two.

For the first time ever, after we danced, Andrew walked off to chat to some people. I was left sitting at the table on my own. Of course, Petra was hanging off his arm.

"May I?"

I looked up and smiled. Bollocks to Andrew and Petra. "Absolutely, I was getting lonely sitting here."

Daniel sat and offered me another glass of wine. "I'm sticking with water for now, but thank you."

I never drank when Andrew did, I had to keep my wits about me.

And I certainly needed those from the minute we left.

CHAPTER ELEVEN

ANDREW DISAPPEARED, as did Petra. I scanned the room, all the while trying to hold a conversation with Daniel. When he finally reappeared, he had white power around his nose. He also had his zipper undone. Petra's hair wasn't as perfect as it had been.

"Andy, might want to adjust your zipper," Daniel said. "Oh, and wipe that shit from your nose."

Andrew immediately zipped up his trousers, and with the back of his hand, wiped across his nose. I'd suspected before he'd done cocaine at other parties. There was a certain look in his eyes, a maniacal attitude that he got. I closed mine in despair.

"Call me, Amber, if you need me," Daniel whispered, and slipped a business card in my hand. "Remember, Bill and I are childhood friends."

I assumed Daniel knew that Andrew had hit me on occasions.

I knew trouble was brewing from the minute we stepped out from the Country Club and into the waiting car. Andrew had held onto my arm so hard; his fingers had left bruises.

"Please don't hold me so hard," I said, rubbing my arm.

He glared at me, and then at the driver; his jaw clamped shut.

"It was a lovely evening, wasn't it? They all seem to enjoy your company," I added, trying to bring the conversation back to him and therefore diffuse any pending trouble.

It didn't work.

"Shut up, Amber."

We drove home in silence.

We hadn't got far from the car when he grabbed hold of my arm, swinging me around to face him.

"What the fuck do you think you're doing? Trying to make me look like an idiot, were you? Flirting with the one person I can't stand."

"I wasn't doing anything, and I wasn't flirting. I didn't know you didn't like Daniel."

"Daniel! Daniel is it? On first-name terms, are we? I bet you want to fuck him, don't you?" He pushed me hard, and I stumbled back against the wall.

"You're not doing this again, Andrew."

He stepped close, his face just an inch from mine. "Do what, Amber?"

"You're being unreasonable and you're not manhandling me," I replied.

He laughed manically. "Manhandling me," he said in a childlike voice. "Bet you wouldn't say no to him *manhandling* you."

I sighed. "You're being ridiculous. I was doing what you asked me to do. I was—"

The slap to my face rattled my teeth. The second slap gave me whiplash.

Andrew grabbed hold of my hair and dragged me along to the lift. I cried out, screamed, but stairwell absorbed the sound.

He jabbed at the lift so hard I thought he'd break it.

"Andrew! Let go of me," I shouted. He ignored me, of course.

When the lift doors opened, he threw me forwards. I stumbled onto my knees, my hair falling from its bun.

"Not again. Not a-fucking-gain," I said, standing up. "You will not lay one fucking finger on me," I shouted, pointing at him. I was so angry.

He looked amused. "You have a disgusting mouth," he said.

And then he punched me just like a man would punch another. Like a boxer trying to score top points.

I cried, holding my face as I stumbled back. "You dare swear at me? Remember, I dragged you up from the gutter and I can put you back there. You're nothing without me."

I covered my ears and let the blood drip from my nose to the carpet of the lift. I looked up, hoping to see a camera, and when the lift pinged, I prayed someone would be there.

We were alone.

"Move," he said, pushing me along the corridor.

"I'm not going into that flat. I'm done, we're done," I said.

He laughed again. "Sure."

He held the back of my neck while he opened the door, then threw me inside. I watched as if in slow motion as he released the buckle from his belt. He slid the leather through the loops and wrapped one end around his hand.

The whoosh as it flew before connecting with me was louder than the crack as it hit the skin on my back. I was stunned at first. There was no pain, initially.

He whipped me again.

"I bet you like that, don't you?" he said, breathing so hard he had snot leaking from his nose.

He was manic, his hair standing up on end, his eyes red rimmed.

"You've been on drugs, haven't you?" I said, cautiously.

"What's it to you? And I fucked Petra in the toilets."

His spiteful words had the desired effect. They hurt more than the belt.

He grabbed me, lifting me from the floor and tearing my dress to shreds. "Now I want to fuck you." He dragged me to the bedroom.

I didn't have a choice. I wasn't strong enough to push him away. He placed a pillow over my head so as *not to see your ugly face* and he did what he had to do. Thankfully, and as usual, he didn't last longer than five minutes. But it was five minutes of hell. I was sore, I was bruised, bloodied, and broken.

When he slid to one side and fell instantly asleep, I curled into a ball and sobbed. I didn't care if he heard or not, but judging by his snores, he was dead to the world.

Dead to the world. Oh, I so wished he was.

I crawled into the bathroom and stood under the shower. I had makeup streaming down my face, making me look like a hideous clown. I had a swollen cheek and a split lip. When I turned in the bathroom mirror, I had five whip marks across my back. I cried again.

I placed my hands over my stomach. "I'm pregnant," I whispered to no one in particular.

There was a child in my body. Part of me, part of him. I knew I could never bring a child into our relationship. I couldn't trust Andrew not to beat me again, hurt the baby. I had to get out. I didn't care if I ended up on the streets. I had to protect my child.

I had to be free.

LEAVING WASN'T GOING to be easy. I had no money of my own, just a meagre wage. I could speak to Bill and Tania, but pride, initially, stopped me. I could have called Daniel. I still had his card in my clutch bag.

I would have to plan.

I left the bathroom and, in a robe, walked into the kitchen. I needed a drink and some pain relief. Could I take pills? I wasn't sure.

Before I could decide, Andrew walked into the kitchen.

"You made me do it, Amber. You promised you wouldn't anger me so much," he said.

"I didn't... Yes, I'm so sorry. Will you forgive me?"

"Come here," he said, and I stepped into his embrace. My stomach roiled with disgust. "You make me so angry sometimes, I lose my mind."

"I know. It's done now. How about a cup of tea?" I asked, anything to get out of his arms.

He nodded and, as if nothing had happened, I made us both a cup of tea. He sat at the table, and I sat opposite him.

"Are you having a relationship with Petra?" I asked.

His eyes clouded over, thunderous.

"Wait, hear me out. I think Petra is good for you. Perhaps she can offer you more, sexually, than I can. So, it's okay," I said, swallowing bile without him seeing.

He frowned at me.

"I fuck her. That isn't a relationship," he said, as if that explanation was okay.

I nodded. "I'm saying, and not that you need my permission, it's okay. I'm not upset by that."

He frowned some more. I needed to be very careful with my words. "Of course, it hurts, but I love you enough to share you."

The fact he thought I was hurting was enough to bring a small sadistic smile to his lips.

"She is a good fuck, Amber. Maybe you could watch, learn a few tricks."

"Perhaps, if you think that's needed." I resorted to the subservient. It served two purposes. It silenced him, but it also gave me a little satisfaction in knowing he wasn't getting a rise from me.

"I'll invite her over. You can cook for us; we'll play a game. You can be the maid that spies on the master while he fucks the arse of a woman. We will see you and make you join us. How about that?"

I clenched my jaw tight, drawing in a deep breath without him seeing. "Again, if you think that's what I need," I said.

He laughed and waggled his finger at me. "I know what you're doing, Amber. If you think I'm going to fuck you and her at the same time, you're wrong. She's what I need in the bedroom."

"Then I wish you luck." I rose. "If you'll excuse me, I need to tidy up the bedroom."

There was a bloodied towel on the floor, the pillow splattered with red. The sheet was wet. I was sure my bladder had given out on me, and his cum stained the duvet.

I wanted to burn it all. I bundled it up ready for disposal. I dressed gingerly, in loose clothing. Tears sprang to my eyes as the material brushed against the welts on my back.

I wish he would fuck her here, then I could stab the pair of them, I thought.

I shook the thought from my mind. I needed to get a plan together.

CHAPTER TWELVE

I DIDN'T SEE Andrew for the next couple of days, and I was so glad. It gave me time to pack some items of clothing in a small duffel bag. I then took that to work and left it there. I told no one for fear of him finding out.

I knew it would take some time before I could escape, and I was prepared to wait.

Each week, when I shopped, I would return a few items and collect the cash. Andrew would see the receipt and it matched the amount that left the account. He would never see the cash that came back and started to mount up.

I wasn't sure exactly how much I needed, but knowing I was going to leave my job, it had to be substantial enough to disappear.

Andrew would find me if I stayed in London, in England even, I thought. He might not want me, he might hate me, but he'd never want to lose face and have people know his wife left him. Oh, no, Andrew would concoct something to show him as the victim. But too many people knew about his beatings.

I would call upon those that offered help because I knew I couldn't do it alone. But only when I was able to.

In the meantime, I kept my distance from him. When he was home, I cooked and cleaned, then he would go out and not come home until the early hours. He'd be up and out to work before I rose. I prayed him burning the candle at both ends would give him a heart attack before I left.

I spent many hours hoping he'd die. Either he'd have a car crash or get run over. I'd laugh at the thought of him having an aneurism while fucking Petra. That would be funny. I could imagine the call from paramedics, or the police, and them having to tell me where and how they found him. I wondered if Petra would even say he had a wife at home.

I made sure to hide Daniel's business card in my desk for when I needed it.

"Hi, you seem really preoccupied at the moment," Bill asked.

I was sitting at my desk, lost in thoughts of Andrew's demise and ignoring the ringing phone.

"Oh, God, I'm so sorry. I was miles away. Let me get this," I replied.

"May I speak with Amber Stowley, please?" I heard.

My heart lurched in my chest. Was it the police? Had my dreams come true?

"Speaking."

There was a chuckle. "It's Daniel. I thought I'd put on my best telephone voice."

I laughed. "You fooled me, for sure. Are you after Bill?"

"No, you. You hadn't called and I think I gave you enough time, so I took action."

"I hadn't called?"

"I asked you to call me. Okay, I said, if you needed me,

and I'm guessing you don't right now, but I thought you might have."

"Well, I'm sorry to disappoint, Daniel." I glanced up at Bill, who smiled and walked away.

We chatted for about a half hour. Mostly about the freakish weather patterns we were having. It was rather surreal.

"I wondered if you'd like dinner sometime."

"Erm, oh. Erm, I'm married, Daniel," I said, not knowing how to respond.

"Yeah, right, on paper I guess. Come to dinner with me, just as friends." He snorted at first. "Please?"

I laughed. "Okay, when?"

"Tonight, after work. That way you won't have much time to think about it."

I totally surprised myself by agreeing. Andrew wouldn't be home that night. We had fallen into a pattern of him being away for the first half of the week, back for the second, then away again over the weekend.

I replaced the handset slowly. What on earth had I just done?

Bill smiled again when he walked past. "You could do a lot worse than Daniel... You do actually do worse, but you deserve someone nice."

"I'm married. Andrew would..."

"Beat the shit out of you?" He stopped and rested against my desk. "We see the bruises, Amber. I can't stand it. I hate that you're living that life. I want to smack the crap out of him. And I would if you let me."

"Whatever you give him, will come tenfold back on me. I'm working on it, Bill. I'm leaving as soon as I can. But there are things I have to get into place first. I'm pregnant, I haven't told him, I won't. I also know that I can't stay with him. If he doesn't kill me, he'd kill the baby. He doesn't want children; it would interfere with his career."

Bill shook his head. He came around my side of the desk. "Tania is your girl, Amber. You can't do this alone. We are here for you."

"I know that. I appreciate that. I will call Tania when I'm ready, when I've got everything in place."

"If it's money, I can give you some to get you on your feet."

Tears sprang to my eyes.

"That's so kind, but you know, I'll have to go, leave London. He won't let me just walk out. His ego wouldn't stand it."

Bill sighed. "I thought that. Tania had to leave Scotland and she loved it there. I mean what I say, though. You don't go anywhere until you've let us help you."

I patted his arm. He had turned into a good friend and one I knew would come through on his words.

"I can't believe I've agreed to dinner with Daniel!"

"You deserve something nice. Go home, get ready."

EXCITEMENT COURSED through my veins as I showered and washed my hair. I would tell Daniel that I was pregnant right from the get-go so he wouldn't get any ideas that I could enter a relationship with him.

It would be nice to have a friend, though.

I slathered on moisturiser and picked an outfit from the wardrobe. Just a simple shirt and trousers, with some medium sized heels. I dried my hair and applied some makeup. I'd lost even more weight, but I had a glow to my cheeks from the pregnancy. I knew I had to watch my diet and try to eat more for the baby. It was something I'd look into when I made the first doctor's appointment. I knew I was about three months gone at that point.

Just as I was filling my bag with keys and lipstick, Andrew walked through the door.

My heart stopped.

"Why are you home?" I blurted out.

He stared at me, not that he could focus. His face was puffy, his eyes bloodshot and drug fuelled.

"Last time I looked, I lived here. It's my name on the paperwork."

"I meant, I wasn't expecting you home. Do you want dinner? I could nip to the shops."

"You don't look dressed for a night in. Who are you whoring with?"

I sighed. "I was going out for a drink with Tania."

"Tania huh? That washed up old bitch."

I swallowed back my retort.

"I'll tell her I'm busy. Would you like dinner? Maybe have a shower while I grabbed something? How about a Chinese?"

He stepped closer to me. "You smell nice, Amber. A bit too nice just to be getting a drink with Tania. Unless... You and Tania aren't up to the naughty, are you?"

He laughed and licked his lips. His breath stank. When I looked at him, his shirt was crumpled and there was a dirty tidemark around the collar. His tie had a food stain on it.

Obviously, he didn't have a change of clothes at Petra's.

"No. Now, would—"

He grabbed my shirt and in my haste to pull back, I toppled over the arm of the sofa. I lost a shoe along the way.

"Don't fucking touch me," I screamed.

He was one side of the sofa and I was the other. "Touch

you? Are you out of your mind? Why would I want to touch you? You have a foul mouth, Amber. Gutter crawler, that's all you are."

His words didn't hurt, I'd heard them lots. It was his fists I worried about. The ones he had balled at the side of his hips.

He was between me and the door. Between me and my bag that contained a couple of hundred pounds. Not all that I'd saved. That was squirrelled away at work. I wanted to be able to pay my way when I met with Daniel.

He saw me look at my bag and reached for it. He shook out the contents. "What's all this then?"

"Nothing."

"Looks a lot like money to me, Amber. Where were you going?"

"I told you, out for a drink."

"That's a lot of money just for a drink."

I shrugged my shoulders. "We might do a little shopping."

He bunched the notes in his hand. "Where did you get it from?"

"My salary, I have a job, remember?"

"You don't earn enough to have any spare. Where did you get it from? Been out whoring have you?" he screamed the words at me, and I hoped a neighbour might hear.

"Yeah, while you're fucking Petra, I'm earning well on the street corner."

He flew over the sofa so fast it took me by surprise. He shoved me hard back against the wall and I cracked my head on the plaster. A piercing headache instantly had me close my eyes. I didn't see his fist coming. I had no chance to duck or weave out of the way.

He punched over and over, when he kneed me in the stomach, I panicked.

"I'm pregnant," I shouted, covering my stomach as I fell to the floor.

"And who's the unlucky father of your bastard child?" he asked.

"You. You're the father," I said, sobbing.

He kicked me then. I protected my child as best I could, but my hands weren't a match for his size eleven shoes.

He kicked and kicked. He stomped on my arm in the hopes I'd move it from my stomach. I heard the crack of a bone.

"I'll kick that bastard thing right out of you," he said, puffing with exertion.

I heard someone bang on the wall. It stilled him. They threatened to call the police but he only laughed.

That gave me a second to move. I rolled and sprung to my feet. Where I got the energy from, I had no idea. I ran to the kitchen area and grabbed a knife. When I turned, he was laughing at me.

"You don't have the guts, Amber."

"Don't come near me," I shouted. "Help!" I screamed as loud as I could.

He walked slowly towards me. I skirted along the wall until I was back into the living area.

"Do it, stab me. I bet you dream of that, don't you?"

"Yeah. I dream of killing you. I pray that you'll die. Want to know the funniest one? I hoped that you'd have a heart attack while fucking Petra. I laughed out loud at that."

"You're mad, you know that?"

"I am. I've finally lost it. So don't try me. I'm leaving and you're going to stand there and let me."

I reached to grab the money and shoved it in my pocket.

I never took my gaze from his. Before I could get to the door, however, he stepped closer.

"Do you think you'll get out of here? The door is locked, Amber."

He reached into his pocket and fished out his key. He swung it from side to side in front of me. My door key was in the bag on the floor.

He took another step closer. He was just a foot away. I was shaking, and my grip tightened on the handle of the kitchen knife.

"Do it. Put us both out of our misery."

I closed my eyes and thrust my arm forward. I heard a gasp and felt his fists connect with my skin. When I opened them, I had stabbed him in the chest. He hadn't died. He was fighting back. I pulled out the knife and stabbed him again. His eyes were wide with shock, clearly not imaging I would actually do it. As his fists rained down on me, I stabbed him again and again.

I lost track of time, so even when he was on the floor and not moving, I continued to stab. The last one being in the side of his neck. That was when an arc of blood, just the one, splattered over the wall. When the blood stopped spurting, I knew his heart had stopped.

I waited.

I waited for the feeling of freedom to come.

I felt calm. I felt serene, and extremely tired.

I needed a nap.

CHAPTER THIRTEEN

PRESENT DAY

TWO, or it could have been three, days later I woke in a hospital bed with a policewoman sitting beside me. I had dreams, or perhaps they were flashbacks of the time between killing Andrew and passing out. I wasn't sure what was real, though.

Tania sat on the other side. She jumped up as I opened my eyes.

"My baby," I croaked out the words.

"All fine, your baby is okay," she said, with tears streaming down her face.

I closed my eyes but couldn't stop the sob. "I killed him. If I hadn't, he was going to kill my baby, or me."

"Shush, don't say anymore," she said, looking over to the policewoman.

"I didn't hear a thing, love," the woman said, smiling kindly at me.

"What's going to happen now?"

"They can't charge you for murder. It was self-defence. Daniel has got you an amazing lawyer, he was here yesterday. And there is a neighbour, he heard you fighting and screaming for help. He called the police as well."

"Daniel? How long have I been here?" I wasn't concerned about the neighbour, not understanding the importance.

"A week. You've been out of it for most of the time. You've got some injuries that needed fixing."

I raised an arm covered in plaster. "It needed pinning. They had to do an operation, Amber."

I nodded and closed my eyes.

"I was meant to feel free," I whispered.

"You are, Amber. You're free now but it will take some time, my lovely. You've fallen and we're going to build you back up. When you're standing tall, you'll feel all the freedom, I promise you."

———

DANIEL CAME TO VISIT, and he held my hand. "You still owe me a dinner date, you know that, right? I sat there like a right pillock on my own."

I laughed. As much as my bruised and beaten face would allow me to.

"You'll have a few people visiting soon. The police, obviously. Your lawyer, and a woman from a domestic violence charity too. She'll help you through this, put you in touch with counsellors and what not," he said.

"You don't have to hang around, Daniel."

"Trying to get rid of me?"

"Look at me. I'm fit for nobody. I'm having a baby, his baby, and I have to... manage that."

I knew I would love my baby no matter what. It was a part of me, but it also carried his genes, and I would try my hardest to make sure there wasn't a trace of him anywhere.

"When you're ready, Amber."

"I still have a way to fall, Daniel. I've got to hit bottom before I can rise again."

"And I'll be here when you do."

I knew the mental damage would last way longer than the broken bones. Andrew had tried to kill my baby; I had no doubt about that.

I needed to sleep.

It was during the night that I woke again. I was in my own room, and the door was open. Light from the corridor filtered in. I could hear whispered conversations between nurses, the odd cry from a patient. The police woman walked in carrying a coffee.

"You're awake?" she said, stating the obvious.

"I am. Unless I'm medicated, I can't sleep. I keep seeing him. Do you know if he's really dead?"

It was something that came to me while I'd dozed. What if he was still alive? What if he was still out there waiting for his time to finish me?

"He's dead, love. And sounds like he deserves to be. He did a right number on you, didn't he? And not for the first time, either, so I hear."

I frowned at her.

"You had a ton of people come forward and give statements about how horrible he was to you. I'm no lawyer, but I can't see this even going to court. *Not in the public's interest,*" she said.

She was right. A week later all charges were dropped. There was some press activity, and, of course, there were some of Andrew's *chums* who tried to say what a lovely bloke he was until they were informed of my injuries.

Morgan & Morgan distanced themselves from him, sending me a huge bouquet of flowers.

But it was the cheque I received that finished me off. A large cheque from the life insurance policy the company had taken on Andrew. Daniel had brought it in, and I wanted to tear it to bits.

"You can tear that paper up, Amber, but the money is still yours. Think of the baby. This could set you both up for life."

It was a substantial amount; I could buy the apartment with it if I wanted to. Or the cottage in the country that I dreamed of.

I was staying with Tania and Bill and had yet to return to the apartment. They had given me clothes and toiletries to tide me over, but I knew I had to face that last hurdle.

Daniel had assured me the apartment had been professionally cleaned, and we made a date that I would go there with him to pack up my things. A charity would take everything else.

I wasn't in a position to have a relationship with Daniel. He was just a friend, and one that I loved dearly. He wanted more, but I made a point of telling him that I had no idea if I'd ever be ready for another man in my life. I wanted to be honest and not string him along. He, Tania, and Bill became my saviours. They supported me during the very brief police interviews to close the case, and then when I insisted on attending Andrew's cremation. No one else was there, but I wanted to be sure the bastard burned.

Only then did I feel free. Only then did I know I'd fallen as far as I could and there was nowhere but up.

I held Daniel's hand as we walked back to his car. I hugged Tania and Bill, and we made our way back to their house. I had a cottage to look at the following day, funnily enough, not that far from Daniel.

The future was, finally, looking brighter. I placed my hands on my tummy and felt my baby shift. I had no doubts that my child was going to be strong and tough, he, or she, had already sustained an attack and survived.

I smiled, looking forward to meeting my child. Looking forward to the future and a freedom I hadn't had in a long time. Another thing I looked forward to was reconnecting with Patty. It had taken some time, but I recognised that Andrew had done his best to isolate me from family and Patty. I had Marilyn's number, and it was the first call I'd make. I had my suspicions there was a reason Andrew had kept me from her and it wasn't simply because he didn't want me to have friends.

The End

ABOUT THE AUTHOR

Tracie Podger currently lives in Kent, UK with her husband and a rather obnoxious cat called George. She's a Padi Scuba Diving Instructor with a passion for writing. Tracie has been fortunate to have dived some of the wonderful oceans of the world where she can indulge in another hobby, underwater photography. She likes getting up close and personal with sharks.

Tracie likes to write in different genres. Her Fallen Angel series and its accompanying books are mafia romance and full of suspense. A Virtual Affair, Letters to Lincoln and Jackson are angsty, contemporary romance, and Gabriel, A Deadly Sin and Harlot are thriller/suspense. The Facilitator books are erotic romance. Just for a change, Tracie also decided to write a couple of romcoms and a paranormal suspense! All can be found at: author.to/TraciePodger

STALKER LINKS

https://www.facebook.com/TraciePodgerAuthor/

http://www.TraciePodger.com

https://www.instagram.com/traciepodger/

BOOKS BY TRACIE PODGER

Volume 3

WHAT DOESN'T KILL YOU

A NEW BEGINNINGS STORY

ELLE M THOMAS

Meet The Team:

Cover Designer: Francessca Wingfield @ Wingfield Designs

Editing: Bookfully Yours

Formatting: TBR Editing & Design

For all of the survivors

CHAPTER ONE

NOW

"AND HOW DID that make you feel, Danielle?"

God, I hated that question when anyone asked it in response to something where there was an obvious emotional response. The question felt like a set up some-how. I just hoped it wasn't going to become his go to. His expression didn't betray any acknowledgement that his use of Danielle had made me flinch sightly.

"Shit! It made me feel like complete and utter shit if you really want to know." I could feel the anger bubbling beneath the surface, threatening to boil over. But then, that could be the very point of the question, to push my buttons. This guy was a professional and it had taken me a long time to get to this point, and if I stood any chance of becoming me again, I needed to work with him, not against him, however, he also needed to respect my boundaries.

"Why?"

Okay, perhaps that question was his go to. "Doc, I realise you have a job to do, that I volunteered for this ther-apy, one that I am paying for, and I know I need to work through all of the shit to come out the other side a better person, but I can't do this, not today."

Sitting back in his chair, the counsellor nodded and offered me an empathetic smile. Empathy didn't rile me in the way that sympathy did. Sympathy pissed me off because I didn't need anyone to feel sorry for me, but if they tried to understand what I had been through and could somehow try to imagine and accept how I was feeling, then I was all good with that.

Silence surrounded us for a matter of seconds before I found my voice. "Could you call me Danni, please?"

"Of course, Danni." His expression looked almost proud. "We do this at your pace, although that's not to say that I won't push you beyond your comfort zone, I will, but you're truly in the driving seat here."

"Thank you." I didn't cry often. Very rarely now. The threat of tears caught me off guard. People giving me control over anything was my Achilles heel now and I was still growing accustomed to it.

"We're not even ten minutes into our first session, so why don't you tell me how you come to be here?"

I risked a frown in this man's direction and felt somehow relieved when a warm but genuine laugh left his lips.

"I know the official reason but tell me in your words."

I nodded but before I spoke, he did.

"Oh, and you don't need to work through anything to become a better person, there's nothing wrong with the person you are, always were, however, hopefully by the end of this you'll feel more like a whole person again."

"Whole?"

"Yes, whole, that over the course of weeks or months, you will rediscover who you are, who Danni is and then you can set out your stall for the world to see and know that you are complete, flawed, as we all are, but complete. That despite what has happened, you have survived. Become stronger. More resilient and that moving forward you are a fighter, a survivor, and you can be whoever and whatever you want to be."

Well, fuck me, that is not what I was expecting him to say. I don't know what I was expecting, but not that.

"Okay. In my own words?"

"They're the only ones that know how you truly came to be here."

THEN

STANDING behind the bar for a busy Saturday night shift was nothing new. I had been working here for almost four years and I could see light at the end of the tunnel now. My next year at uni would be the final one and then working for minimum wage and dealing with drunken idiots intent on causing trouble on a Saturday night would be behind me, although perhaps not if I ended up working in A&E.

I'd moved away at eighteen after acing my A-levels and with a choice of uni offers, I had opted to make the break from my family, not because we didn't get along, it was more to do with the fact that I wanted to be independent and to stand on my own two feet. At home, I was the princess, and the baby of the family to boot, so this was my chance to not only fulfil my dreams of becoming a doctor, but to also become my own person. I couldn't quite believe that in just a year and a half I would be preparing to start my foundation training and actually be working with senior professionals and helping real life patients. The smile I could feel breaking out across my face confirmed that this was what I wanted, all I ever wanted, and I was making it all come true.

"Hey."

I looked up and found an attractive looking man smiling at me.

"Hey," he repeated.

"Hey, sorry, I was miles away. What can I get you?"

He arched a brow and laughed, deliberately misunderstanding my obvious offer to take his drink order.

"To drink," I clarified but couldn't help laughing with him.

"To drink is a good start. Beer, please, and whatever you want yourself."

I got his drink and took a small tip and carried on with my work but couldn't help but keep the occasional glance on the man who appeared to have been joined by a group of friends.

The busy night continued and time flew by until it was closing time. When all of the customers had finally left, I helped to tidy up and grabbed my coat and bag. One of the other staff members and I usually shared a taxi on a Saturday but tonight she wasn't working so I decided to walk. It wasn't far and the route was busy enough that I felt pretty safe.

I was about halfway home when I heard a group of men calling and shouting from a bar on the opposite side of the road. Unsure if their words were for me or not, I continued to walk on, ignoring them. Yet one voice seemed much louder, closer. As I deliberated crossing the road towards a club with bouncers on the door, the voice spoke again and relief washed over me.

"Hey."

Spinning, my attractive customer from the bar came into the light of the streetlamp overhead.

"Shit! Sorry, did I scare you?"

Clearly my earlier nervousness was still evident on my face.

"A little," I conceded.

He held out a hand. "Mike."

I accepted his hand and shook it with a coy smile in response to his megawatt one. "Danni."

"You shouldn't be walking alone this late, there are all kinds of weirdos out and about."

"Are you one of them?"

He laughed and stepped closer. "Maybe, but not one of the dangerous ones. Look, I know you don't know me, but can I walk you home or get you a taxi, it really isn't that safe."

I nodded. I hated that I couldn't walk home alone and not have to consider my safety, but he was right. The neighbourhood wasn't a bad one in the grand scheme of things, but it also had its fair share of muggings.

"I only need to go round the corner, so I should be fine and your friends will be waiting."

"They won't, I told them I was going to do my good deed for the day."

"And I'm your good deed?"

He stepped even closer, forcing me to move back until we were concealed in a dark alley, a wall somewhere behind me as he almost caged me in. "Depends, am I going to do you?"

I was flustered, partly because as much as I'd known what I was doing with my suggestive question, I hadn't expected him to respond in quite this way, but also because I liked that he was close enough to touch, smell, feel, kiss.

"Mike." I had no clue what my simple use of his name was, a plea, a question or a rebuttal.

"Danni, do you want me to walk you home or get a taxi?"

"I don't know." What was the matter with me? He was a stranger, I mean attractive, friendly, amusing, and judging by how much he was focused on me getting home safely, he was also a genuinely nice guy, but I was ready to allow him to walk me home and I knew if he did that then I would definitely be his good deed for the day. He would indeed be doing me. I was no prude and after losing my virginity to a tutor in uni who was a little older, I had experienced a couple of one night stands that had been okay at the time but the following day they always felt a little lacklustre and unfulfilling.

"Or perhaps you'd rather I kissed you, right here, right now."

"Yes."

The sensation of my back colliding with the wall, being pressed between the rough bricks and the hard edges of his body, startled me briefly, but the feel of Mike's lips, moulding my own before accepting the invitation of my open mouth when our lips began to dual, combined with the sensation of his hands skimming over my clothed body, made everything other than him and me disappear.

Working in the bar I tended to wear trousers or jeans rather than skirts and dresses and tonight was no different, except as Mike grabbed at my arse and his fingers began to explore, for the first time, I regretted my inaccessible clothing.

All too quickly, our kiss was broken and we both stood, staring breathlessly at each other.

"Come on, let me walk you home." Mike's hand

stretched out as a broad smile spread across his face.

Willingly, I accepted his offer and his hand, hoping that once I got home, he'd kiss me again.

NOW

"MIKE SOUNDS QUITE THE CHARMER."

A sardonic laugh echoed around the room. Mine. "He was, or appeared to be, but what is it they say about not judging a book by its cover, well, I did exactly that and landed myself in a whole heap of shit."

"How?"

"That night we slept together and it was good, great even, and he was relentless in his pursuit of me for weeks, months; flowers, dates, endless flattery and attention, and then he wasn't."

"I see. What happened, or should that be what changed?"

"I don't know. Nothing, or perhaps, everything. It wasn't that clear cut, things changed, slowly, gradually, until I barely recognised myself, Mike, or the situation. Even now I'm not entirely sure how it happened, but it did, and I have the scars to prove it."

I found myself staring at the print of a boat, a small rowboat sitting slightly adrift on a pond, perhaps a lake, although I was fairly certain that should not be the biggest issue in my mind as I reflected on the lowest points of the last five years, and the demise of my relationship with Mike.

"You said that night, when you met and kissed, that you spent the night together."

I nodded.

"What happened, the next morning?"

CHAPTER TWO

THEN

WAKING, it felt comfortable, although slightly shocking to be in Mike's embrace. The sex had been good and he had been considerate of my needs as well as his own.

Unsure whether he was awake or not, I slid from his arms and the bed to use the bathroom before dashing to the kitchen to make some tea for us both. Whilst waiting for the kettle to boil I was joined by my friend, Jess, who was also one of my housemates. We had met on our first day at uni when we had been on the same floor of uni accommodation and just hit it off. We had quickly become good friends and when our first year ended we had decided to enter a house share together, the same house we still lived in with four other students.

"I thought you'd have slept through til Monday after all the excitement and activity of last night." She laughed while I turned a lovely shade of crimson at the realisation that she had heard me having sex.

"I assume as you have two cups, and I don't drink tea, that *Mike* is still all tuckered out from your shenanigans." Her emphasis on his name that she shouldn't know confirmed that she'd heard me use it whilst we were having sex. The truth was that she would have heard me moaning it.

Despite my embarrassment, I laughed. "Whatever."

"Wow! You are going to be a doctor, actually having people's lives in your hands, the top student of your cohort and *wow* is the best you can come up with which can only mean one thing . . . you've been dickmatized!"

I howled at her ridiculous vocabulary, but when I noticed her gaze move to the open door behind me, I turned and found Mike standing there, topless, looking wonderfully dishevelled. However, by the time my glance reached his face, he looked less than impressed, and then, in the blink of an eye, the dazzling smile was there and he was introducing himself to Jess.

Watching on, I felt relieved that Mike was making an effort with my friend, although, he didn't really know that she was my best friend, so maybe he was just a nice and sociable guy. They chatted, well, Mike chatted mainly for another ten minutes or so after I handed him his tea, and then with work to get to, Jess left us alone.

Suddenly I felt awkward. No. That wasn't it. I felt nervous, and I had no idea why. "I hope the tea was okay." Yes, my nerves were directing conversation if I was discussing his tea.

He nodded. "It was fine, thank you."

I suspected it had been less than fine judging by the fact it was only half drunk.

There was a pause before Mike continued speaking. "What is this? Us? I don't need promises or labels, but I need to know."

I opened my mouth to answer his question, not that I really had any answers for him. I hadn't been looking for anything beyond last night, and maybe today too, but the previous night, I hadn't thought beyond the present. Did I want to declare my intentions? Did I even have any? It didn't matter because before I could speak, he continued.

"You see, I like you, and last night was great, but this morning . . . you were talking about us to your friend, about sex, about my dick, and I don't like that. Whatever happens between us should remain between us. It's private and I don't appreciate it being something for you and her or you and anyone to cackle about."

He looked pissed off, the glimpse of the expression I had seen earlier was back and it was out in force. I mean, I appreciated what he was saying and although he had clearly misunderstood what he had walked in on, I respected the sentiment and truth be told, I didn't particularly like the idea of him discussing the details of what we had done with other people either.

"Sorry. I wasn't talking about us, telling Jess things—"

He cut me off. "So, it wasn't you she was referring to as being dickmatized by, ooh, let's think, my dick!"

Well, he had me there.

"Sorry," I repeated, unsure how to defend myself without making this more than it needed to be. "She heard us. Having sex. She heard me." Okay, perhaps I was going to attempt a defence after all.

"Then maybe you need to practice being quiet."

Mike was up on his feet and grabbing my hand to pull me back towards my bedroom and although I wasn't entirely sure what had just happened, and I was certain things were okay between us, I felt a little uncomfortable.

NOW

"WAS that typical of you at that time, to just let things slide in order to maintain peace, would you say?"

I laughed. "Not really. I wasn't confrontational in any way, however, I was, I am again, kind of stubborn, opinionated, and not afraid to challenge where necessary. I don't think I was ever hostile or arsy with it, but I wasn't the sort to just shut up and put up until . . ."

"Until?" The counsellor was on a roll.

"Until Mike."

"Why was that, Danni, or why do you think that might have been?"

"I don't know, not with certainty. I did like him, he was charming and sweet, kind of old fashioned but not in a dated way . . . he reminded me of my dad, the good things about my dad."

"Do you think that's why you trusted him enough to take you home and to stay with you?"

"Yes." I didn't pause never mind hesitate. "Not consciously, but believe me, over the last five years I have done a lot of questioning and soul searching and I really did trust him."

With a nod, a chew on his pencil and a pointed glance, he paused.

"What?"

"I am not suggesting that you didn't trust him, however, from your own account, there were points during his meeting with your friend when you admit to feeling uncomfortable, and you weren't looking for a boyfriend or a relationship, were you?"

This guy was good, he came with a good reputation and a hefty price tag and I could see why because he latched on to every minor detail I didn't even recall sharing.

"Perhaps it is now that I am recognising those things

and at the time, while it may have given me a sense of unease or something similar, maybe that was due to the fact that I didn't really know Mike."

Yet another nod. "That makes sense and seems perfectly reasonable to me. So, what happened with the two of you? Presumably you overcame those morning after wobbles and continued to see each other?"

"I honestly do not know how we ended up in a relationship because after that morning it was never discussed again and before you could say he's wrong 'un, we were very much in a relationship with labels and lots and lots of empty and broken promises."

THEN

SITTING in the first lecture of the morning, I smiled down at my phone that carried a message from my mother. It was simple and to the point.

> Mum: Mike seems lovely and you are
> perfect together. Don't be such a stranger
> once the school year is finished, either
> of you

I had taken Mike home to visit my family. We'd been seeing each other for almost a year and after Mike had cancelled several visits to meet my parents, I'd finally got him to come with me, and they'd liked him. My brothers and father had been slightly less enthusiastic than my mother, but I was still their princess. I wasn't sure when I'd be able to get back to see them, alone, or with Mike. I had a few more months before uni would end, and final exams, before starting my foundation. I had already been offered a place at a nearby hospital with a good track record on junior doctors and assuming my exams were passed, which they would be, the next two years would be busy.

A new message hit my screen, Mike.

> Mike: Come to mine, I need to fuck you

The bluntness of it startled me briefly. I was okay with the use of language and used to it because Mike usually spoke that way in the context of sex and I liked dirty talk and a dialogue, always had, but his bluntness could come across as cold and hard. This might be the first time he had sent me a message like this though, there wasn't even a kiss. Discreetly, I replied and hoped he wasn't going to get pissy, which he did occasionally when my plans didn't fit in with his. I pushed aside the thought that his pissy moments had become more frequent over the last few weeks, maybe the last couple of months, but then life was busy and we all had stresses. Perhaps as I was approaching the end of the school year and my exams, I was neglecting him and our relationship. This was one of the reasons why I had been determined to remain single until after graduation at least, but somehow, a handsome stranger on the other side of the bar had changed that. I smiled as I thought of him, that guy. I was reading too much into his text and his pissy moments of late and he was a good guy and I loved him, and he loved me.

> Me: Hey, I can't. I have lectures until after 4 and then I have work at half 5

Mike: Then you're cutting a lecture or going
to work late. I went to your parents and
spent the whole weekend in a guest room –
I haven't forgotten you refusing to let me
touch you so I will see you between uni
and work

Shit! Pissy or something similar was in the house.
Specifically, I suspected, horny was in the house. We spent
a lot of time together. Had done since that first night, and
we also had sex often, and it was great, for us both, and
when we didn't have sex, we both missed it, so when my
parents made it clear that we wouldn't be sharing a room
during our visit, I'd expected Mike to want to see me, but
assumed it would be after work. That's what I would do –
finish uni, head over to work and then head straight to
Mike's later. It was Monday, so I'd be finished by half nine
and be at Mike's by ten. If I had time, I could swing by
home before work, grab some sexy underwear to make up
for the fact that I'd refused to let him touch me during a
walk we'd taken my parents dogs on. Although we'd been
out of sight of my parent's home, it still felt wrong to me.
Mike hadn't been happy but he'd accepted it at the time, if
not now.

BY THE TIME I'd taken my break at work, my phone was
literally bombarded with messages and missed calls, each
one becoming more irritated than the last. I sighed as I
glanced down at it and wondered if I should simply go
home after my shift if Mike was already in this mood. I had
an early lecture the following morning so the last thing I
needed was to get into an argument, or more likely coax

Mike out of silence before making it up to him as that was likely to take hours but I couldn't just not turn up so I sent him a message.

> Me: Hi, sorry I couldn't make it between uni and work. I get that you're not happy, so maybe we should forget tonight and we can meet tomorrow instead

His response bounced straight back.

> Mike: If you're done with this, us, then just tell me rather than playing me and making me look and feel an idiot. I told you from that first day that I liked you and needed to know if you were serious or not, and if you're not . . .

Not what I was expecting.

> Me: Sorry, of course I'm not. I love you. If you still want me to, I'll come to you from here. I'll try to get off early

His next response was a thumbs up, no more.

I did manage to leave work a little earlier, so quickly changed into my good underwear and a short wraparound dress that I'd managed to grab from home, one I knew Mike liked, not that his face showed that when he eventually opened the door for me and walked away without a word meaning I ended up following him like a bloody lovesick puppy.

Entering the kitchen, I quickly found myself lifted up and pushed against the nearest wall. I expected him to kiss me, but he didn't, he instead proceeded to push up my dress and move my underwear to the side, and still, not a word passed between his lips.

I felt nervous with the silence that was stretching out as he pushed his shorts down, preparing to fuck me, and although I typically had no objection to that term, this felt different. Strange. Uncomfortable. Alarming.

"Mike, please," I began but his glared stoney expression cut me off short.

"You don't get to speak." Five words uttered and none of them a threat as such, but they carried an air of danger I hadn't felt before.

Pain and discomfort filled me as he thrust inside me and his hand that held my behind squeezed the flesh there.

"Condom, Mike, condom!" I was unsure if I was begging, pleading or somehow trying to reason with him, but we had never not used a condom before and I didn't want to do that now. I wasn't on the pill and although we had talked about alternative forms of contraception, it hadn't gone past the talking stage.

He looked through me as he began to thrust in earnest.

I opened my mouth to speak again, to repeat my request for a condom, but his free hand came up and covered my mouth, stemming any requests or objections. His movements increased in speed which in turn intensified my pain and discomfort. I was dry and as far from turned on as I had ever been and was internally hoping for this to be over soon. He only lasted another ten, maybe twenty seconds, but rather than coming inside me, he pulled out so he came across my inner thighs, underwear, and the dress that still sat bunched around my hips.

Looking down at myself, I was uncertain what to do or even how to feel.

Mike had no such qualms. "That was fucking hot."

I stared at him. Was he fucking kidding me? Had he actually experienced what I had?

"What?"

"It was hot. I mean, I know we only spoke briefly about fantasies and you mentioned a dominant man taking you."

I didn't hear his other words as I tried to accept that he thought he had just fulfilled a fantasy of mine. I had shared the fantasy he had described but I hadn't meant what had actually happened and surely if you were going to share fantasies with a view to living them out, you'd discuss details.

"You didn't wear a condom." There was clear accusation in my voice and he shrugged.

"I pulled out."

My eyes drifted down to the image of us, me still against the wall and Mike standing between my spread thighs, his penis still fully erect.

"You should have asked me."

He moved closer and I shuddered at the thought that he was about to go for round two. "I thought you wanted dominant."

Unsure what to say and fighting the tears that threatened, I dropped my gaze from his penetrating stare.

"You didn't even try to make it enjoyable for me, to make me come." I had no idea why that realisation had only just dawned.

"After your stunts today, I don't think you deserved to come."

Had he really just said that to me?

He continued, "Between refusing to see me, disregarding my feelings, and ignoring my calls, you didn't deserve it."

"I didn't—"

He cut me off before he even heard which part of his

sentence I objected to most. "Danielle, do not spoil a hot night by picking a fight."

He had never called me Danielle before, had he? In that second, I hoped he never would again, especially not when it was wrapped up in the greatest travesty of a 'hot night' I had ever known.

Instead of picking the fight he had indirectly told me we'd be having if I continued, I changed tack. "I should clean up."

He nodded and then as if this night hadn't been shocking enough, he made it even more so. "I have a busy day tomorrow so probably best if you go back to yours. Be sure to close the door when you leave."

He could not be serious. His expression confirmed that he was.

"Mike, I need to clean up, I am covered in cum!" I all but screeched the last word.

"Yes, you do, and yes you are, but perhaps had you not gone to work dressed ready to fuck, you wouldn't be." He allowed me to drop to my feet before pulling his clothes back into place. "Do you need me to show you out?"

NOW

"MIKE REALLY 'EMBRACED' that dominant thing, didn't he?"

With a short nod, I prepared to offer an explanation not that the counsellor made me feel like he was expecting one. "He did, except, it was more, wasn't it?" My question was rhetorical and as such I didn't need to wait for a response. "My first lover, not that there were many, but my first was special to me," I laughed as I saw the counsellor's face and the naïve sounding words I'd spoken. "I know everyone says your first is special, but he was, special to me. He was older than me, quite a bit older, he came to do a series of lectures at uni, and he made me feel safe and worshipped and he was dominant, but not like Mike."

"Were you hoping to recapture what you'd had with your first lover?"

I nodded, there was no point denying it. "I wanted dominant, but consensually dominant, with parameters we both knew and respected, but I didn't get that with Mike."

"Was it your first lover or consensual dominance you were seeking?"

"I'm unsure that I was seeking either, certainly not actively, but in Mike, I was hoping to find some of the qualities that my first lover had possessed."

He offered a very short nod and an expression that said he understand what I was saying. "Did you discuss what happened that night with anyone after you'd been sent home?"

Looking at the counsellor's expression, I knew he meant someone professional.

"Jess. I told Jess when I got home. I was upset and confused and she was still up."

"And what did your friend say?"

"She told me to dump Mike and to never put up with shit like that again." I hesitated. "Jess didn't like Mike. From the first time they'd met there'd been some tension. He had tried to charm her over the next year or so and she was immune to it. She tried to talk me out of seeing him again and had never tried to disguise how much she disliked him, in turn, he disliked her and that left me stuck in the middle of them."

"And how did you balance that, being stuck in the middle?"

I laughed, not that being in that position had ever been fun or funny. "Badly. Mentioning Mike's name resulted in eye rolls, huffs and many swear words, plus, Jess would tell me to dump him and list all of his faults."

"His faults?"

"Yes. I accept some responsibility for that because I think when I confided things in her, like telling her about that night, it influenced her view of him."

"Hmm, I can see why you might think that, but the things you told her that influenced her view, were they accurate or did you lie or exaggerate events?"

"What? No! Of course not . . ." Yeah, this man knew exactly what he was doing.

"Exactly. It may have influenced her views and opinions but that doesn't make them inaccurate."

"Thank you." I don't know why that was my response but I was grateful and for years had regretted confiding in Jess some of the things I had because ultimately it had put a divide between her and Mike and ultimately drove a wedge between her and him.

"How did Mike respond to your friendship with Jess?"

"He wouldn't bad mouth Jess as such, but he would point out that she was trying to make decisions for me and that she was jealous of what we had but also that my world didn't revolve around her anymore."

"And was that an accurate summarisation by Mike?"

I hadn't thought about this for years and now that I was, my view was slightly different to how it had been. "It was, kind of, or at least I thought it was at the time. Jess and I were super close and no matter who else came and went it was me and her. She was confused about her sexuality, not that I realised it at the time, and as such she experimented, but didn't feel ready to commit to a label or lifestyle meaning she had no real committed relationships and I was focused on my career, we both were, so we were a match made in heaven, until we weren't anymore."

"Until Mike?"

"Yes, until Mike. Mike's evaluation of Jess was accurate to a point, but I was blinded to the other side of things, that she could see things in Mike that were dangerous for me, those pesky red flags I refused to acknowledge beyond fleeting seconds of recognition."

"What happened after that night, when you told Jess what had happened between you."

I let out a loud and long hiss. "She hated him. She wanted me to go to the police because she felt I had been assaulted."

"And what did you think?"

"I don't know, not really, but I didn't see it as an assault, I mean he was my boyfriend and I hadn't been opposed to having sex with him, God, I'd even dressed for it, plus it was that fantasy thing . . ." My voice trailed off.

"Danni, we are all but out of time, however, what I need you to do before our next session is to think about that question again – what did you think? There are no wrong or right answers, however, I want you to think about it beyond what you initially thought."

"Okay." My voice broke on that one word because I wasn't sure that I wanted to go back to that time, but not because I wouldn't be able to answer the doctor's question, but because I feared I might, and the answer today, was going to be very different to the one I gave Jess. Poor Jess. All she had ever done was to support me and ultimately I had let her down, badly.

WITH MY VISIT to the counsellor over, I walked away feeling a little relieved. I hadn't really wanted to see him, or anyone. I didn't need to talk over this, keep trawling over the shit show of the last five years, or at least I didn't think I did, until now. Counselling hadn't been my decision. I had actively resisted it when my family, once they became aware of the things that had happened between me and Mike, suggested it. It was a nice doctor at the hospital who had got through to me and made me see that I had unresolved issues that I needed to address and resolve in order to move forward.

Not ready to go home, and with no work to go to, I decided on a little retail therapy. The local shopping centre was about a fifteen minute walk and as it was a fine day, I felt more than happy to take a steady stroll.

There was nothing I wanted to buy, but I always enjoyed window shopping. After an hour or so and a pitstop at a coffee shop, where, with a latte and sticky bun I gave some thought to the counsellor's question and went back to how I actually felt that night. Jess had known how wrong it was and that at best I had been coerced into doing something I hadn't consented to and at worst had been raped. When she had used that word, *raped*, I had lost my shit with her. Told her she was jealous because she was alone and lonely and would never find what I had with Mike . . . I really hoped that was true because nobody, least of all Jess should have to endure that. I had refused to even allow rape to be an option in my mind. I paused now to ask why that had been and I wasn't entirely sure; I loved Mike, thought I did, but not in a *I will die without you* kind of way. Looking back, I could be neutral and see it for what it was. Mike had made me dependent on him, telling me that without him, I was nothing, that nobody else would love me like he did, that nobody else would even want me. He never said those things in so many words at the start, but he got the message across loud and clear and as time went on, his words had been more direct and blunt. He hadn't loved me. I wasn't sure he knew what love was or how to show it appropriately. He'd wanted to control me, and then break me with no intention of putting me back together, and he had, but I wasn't broken any longer, a little damaged maybe, but not broken because I had put myself back together.

So, back to the question. How had I felt that night? Hurt, sad, scared, but there was more. I'd felt like a victim, not that I knew what of, but now I did. I had been the victim of a sexual assault and because it had been at the hands of my boyfriend I hadn't been able to see it at the time. I still wasn't ready to go as far as rape, because, well, I didn't know why, but at least I was finally acknowledging what had happened regardless of any label it was given. It hadn't been my fault, it hadn't been okay, or a sexual fantasy that hadn't lived up to my expectations.

CHAPTER THREE

NOW

SEVERAL WEEKS PASSED and I was opening up more and more to the counsellor, and although the revelations of those sessions haunted me in the days between, the appointments were helpful and I finally felt as though I was getting somewhere in ordering and processing the events of my time with Mike.

Today, entering the office, I had no clue what we'd be discussing but knew it would be beneficial in my life moving forward.

After a few pleasantries we got down to it.

"How long is it now since you saw Mike?"

"Two years." The answer is tinged with surprise and it was twofold because it meant it took me over three years to escape him and another two to come anywhere close to truly functioning.

"And in the last couple of years, have you seen anyone?"

I heard the question and understood it, and yet, I was confused by it. I wanted to answer literally, that yes, I had seen lots of people in the last two years, every day I saw them, in fact, I was seeing him right now, but that is not what he meant. What he was really asking was had I been on a date, had a boyfriend, a relationship.

I shuddered. "No."

"Do you imagine dating again, marrying maybe, perhaps even having children one day?"

It was a reasonable question and I wasn't yet thirty so everything he asked about were realistic possibilities, and yet, the thought of it made me feel hot, sweaty and nauseous.

"Danni, are you okay?"

Clearly I looked as unwell as I felt.

"Mike asked me to marry him . . . I never said yes . . . although I never said no. He asked me one time after things had been, erm, difficult. He already had the ring and forced it on my finger. It was too small but rather than admit he'd got the wrong size he told me I'd gained weight and even my fingers were fat."

"But you know that whether you had gained weight or not, you did not deserve that treatment, any of it, don't you?"

I nodded, I did, and I was unsure why the first tear had slid down my cheek, or perhaps I did when the next words left my lips. "I should have had a baby."

THEN

"I'M YOUR MOTHER, if I can't pop in for a visit, who can?"

I laughed at the image of my mother on my doorstep, but suspected there was more to her casual visit than met the eye.

"Mum, you live a three hour drive from here, so forgive me if you dropping in has come as something of a surprise."

"Okay, perhaps not, but I'm worried about you. You didn't come home for Christmas and I saw Jess. She's worried about you."

And there it was, the real reason for her visit.

"Am I going to be invited in or have I wasted my time in coming here."

Stepping back, making the doorway accessible for her to walk through, I closed my eyes and took a deep breath as I wondered exactly what Jess had told my mother and how I might explain the events of my life to her.

———

WE SAT EATING lunch and even that caused worry and anxiety to rise in me. I'd always had a healthy appetite but had gained a few pounds of late so was watching what I was eating, something my mother had raised her eyebrows at when I'd ordered an undressed garden salad.

"How is Mike? We haven't seen him since that first Christmas you were together."

"He's good . . . busy."

"Of course, and you, how is work?"

A loaded question.

"Yeah, good, great." I wasn't convinced by my own enthusiasm so I was pretty certain she wouldn't be.

"Dr Danielle King, it has quite a ring, doesn't it?"

Fuck! She knew and had backed me into a corner because now I needed to lie to her face or come clean. Maybe I could defer the question, if only for a little while.

"Where did you see Jess?"

One of her beautifully natural eyebrows arched at my

obvious avoidance tactic. "Strangely enough, your father and I went to Dublin and Jess happened to be there with some friends."

The idea of Jess being anywhere with friends and me not being one of them stung, although I knew it was my fault that we were no longer friends, well, not my fault because she had backed me into a corner and forced me to choose, so I did. I pushed down the voice in my head that questioned if I had made the correct decision.

"Your father spotted her first and rushed over expecting you to be with her, after all the two of you are, *were* inseparable."

I shrugged off her pointed *were*.

"Mum—"

She didn't let me get any further. "Danni, what happened between the two of you?"

"We just grew apart, you know how it is."

Her scowl suggested that she wasn't buying that line for a second.

"We wanted different things and she was possessive over me and our friendship. It wasn't fair on Mike."

My mother stared at me and I wasn't quite sure what her expression was for a few seconds and then it clicked; sadness, concern. "I'm worried about you Danni, very worried. You look unwell, you've lost weight and colour. Your spark has been snuffed out and I can't help thinking that is down to Mike."

I wanted to cry and throw myself across the table until I was nestled in the safety of my mother's lap and her embrace but I didn't, instead I became defensive. "You have no idea what you're talking about. I don't suppose Jess told you how argumentative she became or how offensive and rude she was to Mike until he refused to come to the flat. I would put money on the fact that she didn't tell you that she told me I had to choose between our friendship and Mike."

My arms crossed tightly across my chest.

"She told us all of that and more, actually. Danni, your father and I love you and we want you to be happy, but we need you to be safe, and although when we met Mike we did like him, he was charm personified, we no longer believe he makes you happy or keeps you safe."

Rooted to the spot for long drawn out seconds gave my brain enough time to scramble and resettle before speaking and then, the words I spoke weren't the ones I planned on saying, not that I really knew what I was planning on saying. "Mike loves me, and you're wrong about him wanting to keep me safe because you have no idea the lengths he goes to in order to do that. Don't make me choose, Mum. Do not make the same mistake Jess did or you will not see me." Up on my feet, I was preparing to leave but not before more words I hadn't planned left my mouth. "Nor will you see your grandchild." I stroked a protective hand across the tiny swell of my belly only I knew was there before turning and leaving.

<u>NOW</u>

THE COUNSELLOR LOOKED at me over the top of his glasses that had slipped down his nose slightly. "Why weren't you going to tell your mother you were pregnant?"

I was fearful of speaking the words aloud, and instead chose to talk around the answer to his question. "Have you ever had a dream where you get everything you ever wanted only to wake up and find that none of it was real and that you're actually living your biggest nightmare?"

A cock of the head and a slightly arched brow were his only responses, leaving me to continue.

"My dream was to be a doctor. I wanted to see the world in all its glory, to have a nice home and eventually a family like the one I grew up in. Mike said he wanted those things too, and I believed him and truly thought I could have it all. I couldn't."

"What makes you say that?"

"Experience and life. My reality was that I was pregnant and didn't know if I was going to keep the baby. If I told Mike I was pregnant, there would be no going back, and if I didn't tell him and ended the pregnancy and he found out afterwards it would have ended my relationship."

"And you didn't want the relationship to end?"

"No. I should have, but I didn't. I became dependent on Mike and on being with him . . . or perhaps it was more that he made me believe that I couldn't be without him, not that I realised it at the time. When I was a little girl I was confident, over-confident." A smile and a roll of my eyes was my reaction to the memory of a younger me. "I was the baby of the family and the only girl. I was protected and in that I was allowed to fully express myself. At school I was popular enough and had friends but got along with everyone, and academically I was bright, like *really* bright, straight A bright, and I'm not being cocky."

"You don't have to apologise for being academically gifted."

A frown marred my brow at his words. "Did I apologise?"

"Not in as many words but your tone and demeanour were apologetic."

"Ah. I always wanted to be a doctor. I had a *Barbie* doll,

lots of them, but the doctor one was my favourite and that was what I always planned on becoming, until Mike."

"I thought you said he wanted the same things as you?"

"What I said was that he said he wanted the same things."

"He didn't?"

"No. The clues were there but I ignored them. I wanted him to be everything he said he was."

"What he said he was?"

I was being pushed now. Pushed into really acknowledging what Mike had and hadn't said as opposed to what I believed he could be. "What he inferred with his words and actions, the illusion I had created in my head rather than the man he was. Looking back I can see that there were enough red flags to use as coronation bunting, but at the time, I missed them all."

"Missed them?"

Yes, he was pushing me hard. "Ignored them."

"So, the baby and your future?"

"In the beginning Mike would encourage me to miss lectures, something I never did unless I was genuinely ill, like physically incapable of being there. I resisted and over weeks and months I gave in. He wore me down. We'd stay up late and drink too much so when I did go, I wasn't firing on all cylinders. I completed uni and as I said, I'm very bright so somehow managed to bag a really good degree. I had my foundation training secured and was looking forward to starting the real journey to becoming a doctor, and then I found out I was pregnant and the shit really hit the fan."

"You told Mike?"

"I told Jess."

CHAPTER FOUR

THEN

"YOU'RE PREGNANT?" Jess' words were definitely a question but carried an element of disbelief and horror.

I nodded, unsure what else to say and desperately trying to keep a hold of any semblance of calm I had, however, the truth was that inside I was freaking out badly.

Jess began to pace around the kitchen, circling the table I sat at, a constant hum sound radiating from her. This continued for several minutes before she eventually rejoined me.

"Have you told Mike?" Her expression was unreadable from where she sat on the opposite side of the table.

Shaking my head, I had a feeling what was coming next when guilt filled my mind, wondering why I hadn't told him and had instead told Jess.

"Okay . . . decide what you want to do before you tell anyone else, *anyone*, okay?" She didn't wait for a response. "I can't tell you what to do, this needs to be your decision, and I do mean yours, but a baby will change your life and your career plans won't be possible."

I shook my head and felt my anxiety and irritation

rising, but why? Was I angry with Jess or myself for being in this position? After all, she was right and she was saying everything I already knew to be true. "I could still do my foundation. It might just take a little longer . . ." The trailing off of my voice and the threatening tears suggested I wasn't even fooling myself.

Jess was already at my side hugging me. "I thought you were being careful." She interrupted herself. "Sorry, no contraception is foolproof."

"There have been a couple of times when we haven't."

That was enough to exhaust my friend's sympathy. "Why? Why would you risk ending up in this position?" While she remained at my side, she had put some distance between us and was studying me. "Ah. This is Mike's doing, right?"

I wanted to defend him. To protest and explain that we had been in agreement. We hadn't. He had wanted me to go on the pill. I had been on it as a teenager to regulate periods that were horrendous, and I had a really bad reaction to it with awful mood swings and bruising all over my legs. The doctor had taken me off it and said it wasn't something I should take again which I now knew was more to do with the clotting rather than the moods. So, I'd told Mike I couldn't take the pill and he had tried to argue that I could try and that not using a condom would be special between us. I had stood my ground and he seemed to accept it, however there had been at least three occasions I knew about when we had not been protected during sex, twice, I hadn't realised we hadn't used a condom until after the event, and now here I was pregnant.

Jess continued to fix me with a heavy stare until possible realisation dawned. "Mike. Shit! He has done this on purpose, Danni. This is a humungous fucking trap and he has well and truly sprung it. Even if you desperately wanted a baby, would it be with him because once he knows, you are never going to be rid of that man." She spoke with complete contempt for Mike. I'd known she didn't like him but thought she might come to in time, but she hated him and apart from anything else, I had no clue why.

"I don't want to be rid of him. I love him." I sounded pathetic but I did love Mike, didn't I? Plus, I wasn't sure that I could cope without him anymore. We spent huge amounts of time together and were planning a future. When there were practical things I couldn't do, he would laugh and ask how I managed before him and then he would tell me that I'd never survive without him. One thing I wasn't good at was cooking and he would tease me about it when we first got together but now he would say that it was a good job I was with him because no other man would put up with a woman who was so clueless in the kitchen. Pushing down the times he'd said similar things about the bedroom too, I focused on Jess and it was as though she could see exactly what was going on in my head.

Jess rolled her eyes several times before speaking. "He is a dickhead, and I don't like him, but I could put that all aside if he treated you as you should be treated. He puts you down at every opportunity, and with subtlety in company so not everyone will notice, he controls where you go and what you do, he has sexually assaulted you at least once, and now he has knocked you up without your consent. Now tell me, what is there to love about that?

Preparing to protest, Jess got to her feet, I thought as preparation to leave me. She didn't. Instead, she leaned down to give me a hug I didn't know I needed as much as I did.

"I love you, Danni, and whatever you choose to do is

your decision and I will try to support you any way that I can, but Mike is bad news, bad for you and his kid, the kid who will ensure that for the rest of your life, Mike will be in it, one way or another, so think really carefully about what you do next."

Now she did leave me alone with her words and my thoughts.

———

SEVERAL DAYS PASSED and I still wasn't sure what I was going to do about telling Mike. The words Jess had spoken about my plans not being possible rang loud and clear, and yet I knew there was a way I could still make my dreams come true, but I would need to work twice as hard and I would need Mike to be there and support me, especially with the childcare. My parents would normally be the ones to jump into the breach with that, but they lived too far away. Mike didn't have a good relationship with his parents, so that left just the two of us, and being a junior doctor would involve long and unsociable hours with studying on top. It would be hard. I corrected myself, it would be impossible without Mike's support, support I wasn't sure would be there. Jess was right. I'd known it all along but she had voiced it and I knew that is why I had chosen to confide in her. The question now was whether I told Mike or not because if I didn't and we remained together, I would need for him to never find out, and if I told him, I needed to accept that he would have an opinion that may be very different from my own.

———

JESS and I hadn't spoken about my pregnancy or her feelings towards Mike. Instead, she went about her life and I went about mine. In my head, I knew what I needed to do, and whilst I had no moral objection to termination, it wasn't something I ever imagined having to go through. I called a clinic and arranged an appointment. It was all set and then, as is the case with best laid plans, it all went to shit.

Mike had been staying with me over a bank holiday weekend and by the Monday, he was suspicious of my early morning fleeing to the bathroom and the telltale sounds of vomiting. Returning to bed on that morning he asked me if I was pregnant, and I couldn't deny it. I had expected him to be pleased, however, I couldn't have been more wrong.

"You had better be fucking joking!" Mike was up and pacing around the bed. The sight of him pacing whilst naked would be funny under other circumstances, but not these. Annoyance rolled off him. With a murderous expression fixed on me, he continued. "How could you be so fucking stupid?" He laughed but there was no amusement in it. "A straight A student my arse! You're not clever, you're a fucking imbecile, you idiotic bitch!"

"Mike—"

"No!" That one word was a roar. "You've trapped me, haven't you? I know you're insecure but fuck me, I didn't think you'd sink this low." He dropped into a sitting position at the bottom of my bed, and a little calmer, I approached him.

"I didn't. I think when you didn't use protection it must have happened."

I felt him stiffen. "We, Danielle, when *we* didn't use protection."

The use of my full name caused me to shrink and as much as I wanted to protest that it hadn't been my decision to not use contraception, I didn't, instead, I apologised. "Sorry, I really am."

"Your timing couldn't be any worse . . ." His voice trailed off and I sensed there was more to his outburst than my unplanned pregnancy, I even ignored the reference to my timing as I felt that under the circumstances, I was incidental to being pregnant. "I lost my job a couple of weeks ago and there's nothing out there."

"Oh, Mike, I am so sorry, what happened?" I didn't even raise why he had waited until now to tell me.

"That's so typically you!" He spat as he sprang to his feet. "Accusations about what I've done wrong. We can't all be the perfect teacher's pet." He laughed again and I felt as though there was a heavy stone lodged in my stomach and the sensation was nothing to do with pregnancy. "Do you fuck them? The teachers, lecturers, because I find it hard to believe that anyone as *clever* as you is getting top marks on intellectual ability." His eyes half squinted as if he was struggling to focus on me and then, having confided in him about my sexual encounter, he threw it right back at me. "I mean you have a track record for it, don't you? The lecturer who popped your cherry. How easy were you for him, Danielle?"

There was my full name again.

"Did you agree your A+ before he fucked you? What other tricks did you have to turn to secure the highest of marks? I mean it must have been more than you've given me, or was it the blood on his sheets that got you the extra marks? Perhaps I've misjudged you because as much as I accuse you of being stupid, you've fucked your way this far when you can't cook, trip over nothing and you're actually scared of the dark! Fuck me, you're not even attractive or have a banging body anymore."

I was crying, but the accusations and the verbal blows kept coming. I had no clue where all of these insults and revolting words or sentiments came from, but the worst part was knowing there was no escape from any of this. I could have simply walked through the door because Jess and my other housemates were all around and what would Mike do if I told him to shut the fuck up and get out? It wasn't as though he abused me, was it? He'd never hit, not beyond the odd spank to my arse. I know he could be a bit rough in his handling of me, but—I became aware of his words continuing to flow.

"Your personality and personal hygiene are questionable, and honestly, you'd better hope that this bastard child doesn't add stretch marks and flabby skin to your C.V."

He dropped to his haunches in front of me and I thought he was going to apologise, explain that he was freaking out and he hadn't meant any of the things he had said and that he loved me. He didn't.

"You're stuck with me now."

Jess' words came back to me. This is what she had warned me about.

"And so long as you at least try not to let yourself go completely." His hand gestured down my body and his contemptuous expression followed. "I might throw you a sympathy fuck from time to time, but you let go any further and I can't promise I won't look elsewhere."

Tears and snot flowed now and still he showed no compassion or concern.

"You, however, won't ever look elsewhere. You are mine until I tell you otherwise." He laughed again. "Nobody else would fuck you more than once anyway with your awkward fumbling and inability to fully pleasure a man."

Turning, he moved towards the chair where his jeans

were and I assumed he was leaving. Hoping he was. Instead, when he turned, his jeans thrown to the floor, he held up a condom and that is when I noticed that his previously flaccid penis was now fully erect, but why? Was he actually getting off on this horrid situation and the vile insults he had thrown my way.

"At least we won't be needing these. Now get on your hands and knees because the last thing I want to see is your deceitful, whiny, snot covered face."

In my head, I refused, I told him we were done, that I was not his and never would be, that the condoms were irrelevant because he would never touch me again and that my timing of being pregnant was irrelevant too because I had made plans to no longer be pregnant. I said none of those things, instead, what I did was to get on my hands and knees and like a well-trained animal, I waited for my trainer to make a move or give a command.

The bed dipped beneath me. "I don't know which is worse to look at, your face or your fat arse."

The tears flowed in the silence of the misery that had become my life.

NOW

THE SIGHT of the counsellor's outstretched arm, offering me a tissue from the box in his hand was the first indication for me that the mere recollection of that time had resulted in fresh tears, years later.

"Danni, we can end things for today, if you'd rather?"

Blowing my nose, I shook my head. "It's fine. I don't know that I'd planned on telling you all of that. Is it normal to tell you things this way, like out of sequence?"

A small smile curled the lips of a face I was beginning to

trust in ways I didn't think I ever would. Truthfully, I wasn't sure I had it in me to trust anymore, but it seemed I did, even if this was a professional trust. "There is no right and wrong way to talk, not with me. Some people will literally start from their first memory and then move forward chronologically, and others allow each memory shared to lead to another, so, no wrong or right."

"Okay, but I suppose for me it's just good to say these things out loud and to hear how messed up it was."

"You know all of those things, those awful things and the words that left Mike's mouth, they were about him not you, don't you?"

Did I know that? I wasn't sure I did, not entirely, but I was more convinced of it now than I ever had been before. I expected him to pick up a thread from all I had revealed. He didn't, instead he went with something completely different.

"What happened between you and Jess?"

"Mike. That's the short answer."

"And the long answer?"

I laughed, a single short sound. "Still Mike really. After he discovered I was pregnant, after that morning, he took great pleasure in telling Jess and it was clear she was horrified, although she already knew but Mike didn't know that. He really rubbed her nose in the fact that he was there to stay and as the father of my baby he would trump her role and what I think he saw as her authority."

"How did Jess take it?"

"Badly. It was another couple of days before we got some time alone and that is when she asked why I had told Mike when I hadn't been entirely sure that I was going to have the baby. She repeated her concerns for me and for my future. I felt overwhelmed and things got out of hand and somehow we ended up arguing. She told me that she couldn't stand by and watch me ruin my life. I felt strangely protective of the baby I'd had no intention of having and reacted defensively to what I perceived as her attacking it. She did say that she would support me if I had the baby, but not while Mike was on the scene."

"Why do you suppose she said that?"

I knew exactly why and he was pushing me to acknowledge it. "Because she knew that he hurt me, not physically, not really, but she saw me afterwards and picked up the pieces."

"Didn't he hurt you physically?"

That wasn't where I expected him to go.

"He didn't hit me." I heard the defensiveness enter my voice and somehow he had found my issue. I didn't consider myself to have been physically abused and this was what I clung to, that no matter what he had subjected me to, I had drawn the line at that.

"So, you're saying that because he didn't hit you, there was no physical abuse?"

I said nothing.

"What happened with Jess?"

Why had he raised the issue of physical abuse if he was just going to let it go? In my head I knew that he had broached the subject in order to force me to consider it, perhaps not now, but it was now in my head so would have to be addressed at some point.

"By the time Jess said that I should visit my parents alone, talk to them, tell them about the baby, my head was spinning. I hadn't even considered my parents in this and suspected that what she really meant was for me to tell them about Mike. My face must have showed my shock at the notion of telling my parents and that they would see how bad things were between us."

"I imagine as your friend, that was her aim, to have your parents in your corner and maybe she thought they could succeed where she must have felt she'd failed."

He wasn't wrong. "She told me I was stupid to think this was ever going to work out well. She said that I was an idiot if I kept the baby and thought I would ever be rid of Mike, that he would ruin my life and that the baby would facilitate that."

"That made you defensive?"

"Yeah. I hadn't planned on keeping the baby but hearing anyone speaking ill of my baby that way hurt, especially as it was Jess. We argued and she laughed when I maintained that I could have my baby and my career, and she was right to think I couldn't, but I wasn't prepared to admit it at that stage. She then repeated that if I wanted to keep the baby, she would support me if it was what I wanted, however, she wouldn't sit back and watch me be further destroyed by Mike."

"An ultimatum?"

"Yes and that's not something I respond well to, so with my end of year exams done and the lease on the house share coming to an end, I ended up moving into Mike's while Jess moved about an hour away to take up her foundation.

"What about your foundation training?"

CHAPTER FIVE

THEN

"MIKE, please, I have to get ready."

Mike rolled his eyes, still not understanding why I was so insistent on pursuing my dream career, especially now that I was pregnant.

"It makes no sense to do this now. Just ditch it and maybe once the kid starts school."

I didn't hear anything else he might have said because the world turned black as I realised that Mike expected me to take that long a break in my pursuit of a career.

"No!" Turning, I saw the scowl marring Mike's brow and knew this was going to become an issue.

"What do you mean, no? Have you already made your plans with no consideration for my thoughts or feelings?"

"That's not what I am saying, but five years is too long. I will continue until as late on in the pregnancy as possible and then, so long as everything goes to plan, I could probably return to work twelve weeks later. I can catch up, I am sure . . ." My words stopped at the look of pure fury I was met with.

"And who the fuck is looking after the baby then?"

I should have stopped, said no more, maybe even back-tracked but I didn't. "Obviously we could work things between us and you'd be here in the evenings and at week-ends if I wasn't, then we could look at a nursery of childminder."

"Me?" He laughed but he was a far from amused as anyone I had ever seen. "You trapped me, not the other way round, so if you think I am spending my evenings and week-ends babysitting your kid while you play doctor . . ." He paused. "Or is that it, that you plan to play with the doctors while I stay at home? Forget it, Danielle. You will be the one at home, in the day, at night and at weekends."

Looking across at the clock that told me I was going to be late, I felt sick, not least because if we were using my full name, this was about to take another turn for the worse. Suddenly, my belly let out a loud rumble.

"Sit down." Mike's voice was softer, confusing me at the quick change in mood and his next words confirmed a change in topic too. "Eat some breakfast."

Reaching for a slice of toast and a banana, I prepared my escape and at that very second, that is exactly what it felt like, an escape. I had realised, perhaps a little late as I was almost four months pregnant that I could not do this. I wasn't sure I could terminate my pregnancy, but I could call Jess, and my parents and explain everything and they would help me. It had been ten weeks since Jess and I had fallen out and probably a month since I had outed my pregnancy to my mother, but I knew they'd be there for me.

"Sit down," he repeated and kicked a chair out for me to sit.

Protests were on the tip of my tongue, but I swallowed them down.

"Eat."

The toast stuck in my throat, possibly more so because Mike was silent, not another word was said, instead he just stared at me. Part of me wished he'd let rip at me with insults and accusations.

"You need to take care of yourself, or at least the baby."

I assumed he was referring to my rumbling stomach. "I am trying to make sure I eat."

His laughter caused me to stop. "Your eating is not in question. Your spare tyre and multiple chins will attest to that."

I felt myself shrink at his barbed and hurtful words that were yet another dig at my weight. I didn't believe I had put a significant amount of weight on. Even the sonographer a couple of weeks before had commented that I was *all baby*.

"Come on, I'll walk you to the door."

He was mercurial at the best of times, but this morning was something else.

As we entered the hall, I faced him and wanted to see something kind and loving in his eyes like there had been at the very start. Kindness and love had been present then, right? If they hadn't, then how the hell did I come to be in this hideous predicament?

I wasn't quite sure how it happened, but as we moved into the hallway, the arm around me turned into a tight grip on my arm and body and the next thing I knew, I was being bundled into the cupboard under the stairs and then the sound of a lock echoed around the dark, empty space.

NOW

"HE LOCKED YOU IN THE CUPBOARD?"

My depth of the fear I felt in that moment came flooding back to me. My whole body shook, the tears flowed and the sobs were the only sound in the office. I had no idea how long I cried for but once my emotions slowed and eventually stemmed, the counsellor spoke again.

"Can you tell me what happened, in the cupboard?"

"It's not so much what happened. I think I said before that I was scared of the dark, and that Mike had made reference to it, critically so, but yeah, my fear was real, irrational, but real."

"Fears are rational to a point, however, it's when they take over your life or limit how you live your life that they become an issue."

"I don't even know where the fear came from, not really. I don't remember a time when it wasn't a fear I had. My parents would leave a light on at night and as I got older, I coped with going to bed without lights on, however, if I was somewhere new or it was pitch black, it caused panic in me."

"What did that panic look like?"

"I'd feel sick, sweat, cry and my mind would go into overdrive, thinking of a million different things, all the terrible things that could happen to me in the dark, things that rationally weren't plausible, but my fear allowed them to become real scenarios."

"I don't think I have heard fear so accurately described. Did Mike understand the depth of your fear? Not that I am suggesting using anyone's fear against them on any level is acceptable."

"We went to a theme park and one of the rides we went on was in complete darkness. I hadn't realised that the ride was pitch black and I had a panic attack in the middle of it. Mike had been great, held me, talked me through it and reassured me until we got off the ride. We talked about it afterwards and we didn't speak about it again until we had arguments when he would make a comment about my ridiculous fear, he'd ridicule me, tell me how pathetic I was. Then he locked me in the cupboard."

"What happened, that day in the cupboard?"

"I'm still not sure how long I was in there, but it was a long time, long enough that when I got out, I was late for work, too late. I was in shock, numb in some ways but hypersensitised in others. Mike came back, I heard him moving around for quite a while before he let me out. I was sweaty and disorientated when he opened the door and the light hurt my eyes and I didn't move out immediately." The memory of that incident came back to me as clear as the day it happened almost two years before. My tears returned and despite the offer to stop, to wait, to come back to this at another session, I continued. "He got really angry and began to shout at me, saying that as I'd enjoyed my time in the cupboard so much, I could stay there for the rest of the day and all night. I was unable to speak or move until that second because I felt sure that if I didn't find the strength to move, I'd be locked in the darkness again. When I tried to get up, my legs wouldn't cooperate, maybe because I'd been squashed into a corner on the floor so I crawled out and he laughed at me. He grabbed me by the hair until I was looking up at him and he spat in my face."

"Danni, do you need a drink or a break?"

I shook my head fiercely. I needed to do this. "I lost my baby."

"How? When?"

"For the next few days, Mike stayed at home. I lost my phone, although I found out afterwards that he'd taken it. He wouldn't let me go to work or contact the hospital. I had to sleep on the floor next to the bed, he wouldn't let me sleep next to him, but the worst thing is that I was almost glad of that, I was relieved."

"I think the relief you felt is understandable and completely natural. You must have felt a sense of calm and reassurance to know you at least had some space between you."

"I did. I had been having some cramping and spotting, had done from the start of my pregnancy so wasn't too concerned by it but then it got worse. The first day Mike left me, I still didn't have my phone and he'd locked the doors and windows so when the cramping got worse and the bleeding got heavier, I knew something was wrong. I didn't know what to do and I had no way of contacting anyone. I was beginning to think that I'd have to smash a window and call to one of the neighbours or someone passing by . . . I got as far as the big window to the front of the house when the worst pain I have ever known hit me and I don't remember anything else until I woke up in the hospital.

<u>THEN</u>

MY EYES WERE HEAVY, too heavy to open, for long minutes, maybe longer. I could hear conversations around me, some of the voices familiar, Mike, and others belonged to strangers. It was strange, the fear I had felt when the atrocious pain had struck was gone. The terror that had become common place when alone with Mike didn't coil in my gut like a poisonous snake even though I knew he was there and the nervous trepidation of treading on eggshells when in his presence with others was missing too.

With what felt like mammoth strength, I finally opened

my eyes and took in my surroundings. The first thing I noticed was the white walls and then a kind, smiling face that I quickly realised belonged to a nurse, then a doctor. I was safe. Suddenly that feeling of safety was replaced with something quite different and all too familiar when Mike's face came into view. He rushed towards me, tears clouding his eyes. His words were rushed, words of concern, relief, words I wasn't familiar with, not coming from Mike, certainly not words I'd heard since the very beginning of our relationship. Mike reached for me, pulled me to him, hugged me and cried as he spoke about our baby, how loved and wanted he or she had been and then it hit me.

The baby was no longer in the present tense.

My cries became louder and began to resemble an animalistic howl. I hadn't wanted to be pregnant, and I had decided initially that I would not have the baby, but now, it had been cruelly taken from me by mother nature. I couldn't help but wonder how the last week might have impacted on an apparently healthy pregnancy, but being shut in a cupboard and left to sleep on the floor, ignored, unless being berated, whilst not conducive to good mental health couldn't have caused a miscarriage, could it?

Hours passed and Mike seemed as reluctant to leave me as the kind nurse was to see him go. Eventually with the need to visit the bathroom, he did leave me briefly. The nurse immediately replaced his presence and sat with me, talking to me about organisations that could help me, I assumed she meant with the miscarriage but as she began to talk about domestic violence, coercion, controlling behaviour and abuse, I realised that she could see me, really see me. She spoke about starting again, having support and finding a way to move forward, and whilst she never came out and said I should do it without Mike, she did talk about me being strong, capable and having the world at my feet, if I wanted it. She even managed to get the doctor to agree to me being kept in the hospital for a couple of days and she was the one who called my mum who along with my father arrived the next day.

CHAPTER SIX

NOW

WHEN THE COUNSELLOR called me in from the waiting room, I smiled at the print of the little rowboat, still adrift, but today I noticed the slither of sunshine pushing from between the clouds. Maybe that was symbolic of me too. I was still adrift. Not like I had once been, but I still wasn't anchored, however, the sun was breaking through and I was able to see the good in the world and more than that, I wanted to be the good in the world. To smile, laugh and fulfil the dreams I'd had before Mike and the fallout from it.

Taking the seat opposite, the counsellor wasted no time in getting down to business and picking up exactly where we'd left off last time.

"So, Danni, what happened when your parents arrived at the hospital after your miscarriage?"

"The shit hit the fan!"

That description was pretty accurate.

"My mum had gone straight into protective mode and my dad into angry. Mike had tried to charm them. He had ensured they hadn't met more than necessary. Even discussing this today, hearing those facts aloud was some-what shocking. A quick glance to the counsellor revealed nothing."

"How do you feel, at that realisation?"

I'd been in counselling for a few months now and honestly, this guy seemed to be living rent free in my head and thoughts.

"It's shocking really. He had completely isolated me. Jess had gone, my family had become strangers, and through no fault of their own. My last meeting with my mother had resulted in me telling her that ultimately I would choose Mike, Mike and the baby. He had essentially ended my career before it had gotten off the ground and all I had left was him because with the baby gone, it was him."

"But your parents?"

"My mum wanted me to go home with them, and I wanted that too. I had agreed to it. My dad was ready to kill Mike and he is the most passive man you could ever meet."

"Did you go home with them?"

I shook my head an allowed a single tear to fall. "Not for another six months. Mike had invited himself along to stay with my parents and when they got wind of it, they'd issued a categorical no. I had expected Mike to be angry and kick off, but he hadn't. He had accepted their decision and as my parents were staying in a nearby hotel, he took me back to his to get some things and I was going back home the following day."

"Were you planning to stay with Mike that night?"

"I don't know, I don't think so, but I told my parents they didn't need to come back with me."

"What happened, Danni?"

THEN

WALKING through Mike's front door felt surreal. It had only been a couple of days since I had last been here and yet, everything had changed. I was no longer pregnant and although I was saddened by this, I couldn't help but think that if everything happens for a reason that it might be for the best, for me.

"I never thought your parents would leave."

I turned and came face to face with Mike who was smiling, and I was briefly reminded of the man I had met across the bar that first night.

"Leave?"

"Yeah, I know they're your parents but they a hard work. They're intent on taking you home and putting a divide between us."

"They want to take care of me." I was beginning to question if I shouldn't have gone to the hotel with my parents, or allowed them to come back here with me which they had wanted to do.

"But that's my job and by excluding me from that I can see that they want to control you, not take care of you." His tone had changed and I knew this was now going to become a bone of contention.

"Mike, I know, and I am glad you want to take care of me, but I want to go home."

My choice of word was like a red rag to a bull and suddenly Mike was pacing across the room, back and forth, the annoyance rolling off him, but he said nothing and I wasn't sure if that was worse than if he had been shouting and hurling insults. Unsure what to do, I sat on the window ledge, almost at the exact spot where I had collapsed a couple of days before. Thoughts of that day and the days before flooded my mind, not the miscarriage itself but the way Mike had treated me in the run up to it. The cupboard under the stairs. Sleeping on the floor.

"You are home!" Three words uttered and despite the anger I would have expected to hear, there was none.

Turning my attention back to the man before me, I was unprepared for the sight of him dropping to his knees before me with tears streaking his face. "Danni, please, don't leave me. I can't lose you, not you and our baby. I can do better, I promise. I know I get it wrong, but please, if you go too there is nothing left for me to live for so I might as well go to our baby."

Sinking to the floor, I joined him, hugged him, and held him close knowing that I couldn't leave him, not like this and not with threats of suicide hanging between us.

NOW

"YOU STAYED?"

"I stayed, unfortunately."

"What happened? Presumably your parents went home without you."

I nodded. "Reluctantly, but they insisted on checking in with me regularly."

"And Mike."

"He was genuinely upset about the baby."

My counsellor raised a slightly sceptical looking eyebrow that made me laugh.

"I am sure you and your eyebrows are supposed to be impartial."

His response now was a simple shrug causing another laugh from me.

"He was, I believe that. He changed, became more like

the Mike from when we first met and I honestly thought we might have a chance to make things work."

"What happened?"

"Mike, Mike happened. I think the man I first met was an illusion. That the man I had come to fear was the real version, and the nice guy was a mask. A mask that slipped after a few weeks, continued slipping until the man I feared, loathed and stood in the way of every dream I had returned." I paused, expecting a prompt of a question, but there was only silence, so, I continued. "My parents paid a surprise visit after about a month and although they still didn't like Mike, they begrudgingly accepted that I had stayed. I think he thought he was winning them over so once they left, he stopped pretending to be Mr Nice Guy. He would lock me indoors when he went out and if I objected he'd threaten me with the cupboard under the stairs. My parents sent me money and he took that from me. He never returned my phone and would answer my parents calls and vet emails and messages. He resigned my place on the foundation course, although he initially told me he had arranged a sabbatical."

"What about intimacy?"

Well, that was a curve ball I hadn't seen coming. "I was scared of getting pregnant." I heard the break in my voice. "Mike demanded sex and if I refused, he would take what he wanted anyway. Sometimes he would taunt me, saying that he hoped I didn't get pregnant as I had already killed one baby. . ."

"He accused you of killing the baby you miscarried?"

"He did." Tears flowed freely.

"You know that the miscarriage was not your fault."

I nodded. "He reminded me that I had considered an abortion and said that the baby knew I had never wanted it and that it had chosen to leave my body for those reasons. He went further than that and said that I didn't deserve to be a mother and no baby deserved me because I would be an awful mother. He listed all of the things that made me a bad person. He told me I wouldn't get pregnant anyway because I was too fat, that my body couldn't even do the one thing it had been made for and that I was stupid, incompetent."

"Danni—"

I cut him off. "I know. I do, really. I think he wanted me to get pregnant though so he would have more of a hold over me. All of the words Jess had said to me about him never letting me go and me never being rid of him would keep me awake for hours, but I was scared."

"Of losing another baby?"

If only it had been that simple. "No, I was scared that if I left, Mike would kill himself like he'd threatened."

"You know that you can't be responsible for Mike and his actions, for anyone else's actions and you can't allow your own life to be painful and abused in order to remove the risk of someone making that choice." His words were a statement more than they were a question.

"I do now, always did, I suppose, but I did feel guilty about the baby and genuinely sad, but because I believed Mike was sadder about the baby, I felt I needed to make it up to him by staying."

"But you didn't stay?"

"No. I didn't. There was a wedding. Someone Mike knew and he said we needed to go. We had never been to functions like that. I had never met his family and he never spoke of them, so it was unexpected to be told that I needed to go with him. He chose what I wore, and it was wholly inappropriate. I looked like a prostitute in a bright red dress that was too short, too low, and I felt uncomfortable. The reception was in a hotel and every time I got up or went to the bathroom or the bar, people looked at me because I was so overdressed, or underdressed. It was getting late and people were drunk. Some bloke approached me and made a pass at me, going so far as to grab my bottom. I freaked out and we ended up causing a scene. Mike was furious and rather than defend me, he apologised to the guy and then took me to one side and told me if I dressed like a whore I should expect to be treated like one."

"He said that, even though he chose the outfit for you?"

"He went so far as to make me apologise to the guy and anyone who had witnessed me *causing a scene*."

"I did it, I apologised, I didn't point out that I was wearing what he had chosen with what I suspected was the sole intention of making me stand out and embarrass me, but then, he said to the man that he'd make sure I learnt my lesson once he got me home and that naughty girls needed space and time to think about their behaviour."

"What did he mean?"

"The cupboard. He had started saying that to me before he put me in there so I knew what he meant and the last time I'd been in there he left me all night, so I had no clue how long I'd be in there for. I couldn't do it, I wouldn't. It was as though the ears of the world were listening because a song came on. It was a song that Jess and I used to belt out after a couple of drinks and we once did it at a karaoke bar in Spain when we were on holiday."

"What was the song?"

"*Stronger,* but the best line is *what doesn't kill you.*"

"Very apt."

"Yeah. At that moment I realised that Mike was killing

me, not physically but from the inside out, he was killing all I had been, all I was, and everything I ever could be."

"What did you do?"

"I excused myself to go to the ladies and snuck off to the main hotel reception and asked them to help me. I don't recall exactly what I said but there are codes you can use in clubs and bars so I think I said something about that and the receptionist took me into an office, called her manager and they helped me. They offered to call the police, but I just needed to get out of there so I gave them the only number I could remember."

"Your parents?"

"Jess."

"And did she answer?"

"She did but was out of the country so she called my parents who came to me and took me home. Mike was still there when they collected me and my dad told him if he ever came near me again he would kill him and make it look like an accident." I laughed. "My dad really wouldn't know how to kill anyone never mind make it look accidental but I appreciated the sentiment. What he actually did was to get a solicitor friend to obtain an injunction and made me report everything to the police even if I wouldn't press charges. My mum came with me and that was the worst bit, how sad she was to know what had happened to me. For the next year I hid away and then for six months I talked about what I might do but did nothing."

"What changed?"

"Kelly Clarkson."

"What?"

I laughed at the counsellor's confused expression. "She sang that song I told you about. Well, I was talking about all the things I could do for the umpteenth time and as I walked out of the room, that song came on and it was like the universe was talking to me. I contacted the university and the hospital and looked at getting on a foundation course. I had an interview and was offered a place. There was a doctor who interviewed me and at the end she suggested counselling. I hadn't told her what had happened but eluded to a bad relationship and a miscarriage being the reason as to why I hadn't already completed the course. She gave me a list of counsellors."

"And that's how you found me?"

"Yes."

"So, your course?"

"I start this week."

"Dr Danni?"

"Yeah, in fact, I may have my I.D. badge changed to that."

"I think you should."

"Thank you, for everything."

"Danni, you've come a long way and made some real progress, but I'm not sure our work here is done."

He was right. "I agree, but I might need to come less frequently with work and everything else."

"Sounds fair."

I was already on my feet and preparing to leave when he called to me.

"What happened between you and Jess?"

"She is busy and has moved away, but we're talking and trying to be friends again."

His smile was one of genuine happiness for me and my old friend. "And Mike, what happened to Mike?"

"I have no idea. Not that I have ever looked for him and we don't have mutual friends . . . it took me a long time to be able to not look over my shoulder or to sleep soundly knowing he was out there still, but as my mum says, he was a coward and a bully."

"And what does your dad say about him."

"Not much, although, he does still attempt a *Don Corleone* accent when he says things about nobody finding the body and swimming with the fishes. I have to go."

"Until next time, and Danni, don't ever let anyone make you feel less than your worth."

"That's Dr Danni to you."

A YEAR LATER

"DR DANNI, can you come and take a look at a patient for me, please?"

The biscuit that was halfway between my hand and mouth paused. I hadn't even made a drink or considered the option of sitting down when the nurse interrupted me. Placing the biscuit down, I turned and offered the lady filling the doorway of the staff room a warm smile.

"Of course."

"Sorry," she said as I passed by.

"Hey, it's fine." I meant it. This is what I wanted and for a time thought I would never manage it, but now, this was my life. I hadn't slept in almost forty-eight hours aside from a twenty minute power nap at four o'clock that morning, but I survived on adrenalin and the love I had for my work. In just a year's time my foundation would be complete and I would be a real doctor. I mean, I was already a real doctor, but I couldn't wait for the next step of no longer being in training of any kind, not that I believed I'd ever stop learning.

Heading back out into the busy emergency department where I was currently based, I followed the lead of the nurse who was now in front of me and entered the cubicle to find a young woman in obvious pain. I examined her, ordered some bloods and prescribed some pain relief and with some reassuring words, called for a consult from the on-call surgical team as I suspected this woman might have an appendicitis.

I continued with my work for the next couple of hours before the nurse from earlier called me to come back to the same patient as her blood results were back and despite pain relief, her condition was worsening. The surgical consultant had been to see her in my absence and had requested that the patient remain under observation until the blood results returned.

The woman was clearly still in pain as I began to go through the results on the tablet in front of me. She knew that the consultant she'd already seen would be coming back too and discussing next steps with her. She looked clammy and a simple touch of her forehead confirmed this. I reached for her wrist and felt her pulse hammering away far too quickly.

Looking at the nurse, I prepared to ask her to call for the consultant, fearing the patient needed reviewing sooner rather than later, but before I could speak, the curtain around us opened and the world stood still. The consultant looked at the patient and sprang into action and as he came alongside her opposite me, our eyes met. I had recognised him the second he had entered and judging by the look in his eye and the smile that followed, he remembered me too."

"Danni."

A huge smile broke out across my face. "Mr Spencer."

"You're here, an F2, a doctor." His face took on a confused expression as he read the designation on my I.D.

"You're late . . . I mean, shouldn't you be an SHO or a registrar by now?"

Not only did he remember me, he recalled the timeline of what should have been my career path and that is what made me emotional, that he remembered, or perhaps it was the reason for the delay.

"Things happened . . . life things," I explained.

"Hmm. We should catch up." He looked around and seemed to become aware of our surroundings and audience. "Arrange an appointment with my secretary and we can look at your future options, doctor."

The grin was back on my face. I was a doctor and standing before me was the man who had truly been an inspiration as a lecturer, and as a lover. Even during our short affair he had encouraged me to be all I had been capable of and had always told me that I had the means to be an amazing doctor.

All my life my parents had told me that I had the world at my feet, and I did. Everything I could ever want, all I had dreamt of was possible, and although I had wished for a time machine to change the past, I suddenly realised that those thoughts weren't real or possible, but my future was, and I could make of it whatever I wanted. I was still attending counselling and working through all that had happened and learning who the new me was.

I had survived Mike and come back stronger. That wasn't to say that I didn't still carry scars, I did, and probably always would, but it hadn't killed me. In fact, I was stronger.

THE END

ABOUT THE AUTHOR

Elle M Thomas was born in the north of England and raised near Birmingham, UK where she still lives with her family. She works in local education and writes in her spare time with dreams of becoming a full-time writer.

Whilst still at school, and with a love of writing slightly risqué tales of love and romance one of her teachers told her that she could be the next Harrold Robins. Elle didn't act on those words for many years. In February 2017, with her first book completed and a dozen others unfinished, she finally took the plunge and self-published the steamy romance, Disaster-in-Waiting.

Elle describes her books as stories filled with chemistry, sensuality, love and sex that she always wanted to read and her characters as three dimensional and flawed.

LINKS

facebook.com/ellemthomasauthor

x.com/ellemthomas24

instagram.com/authorellemthomas

goodreads.com/author/show/16429813.Elle_M_Thomas

ALSO BY ELLE M THOMAS

Disaster-in-Waiting

Revealing His Prize

Carrington Siblings Series (should be read in order)

One Night Or Forever (Mason and Olivia)

Family Affair (Declan and Anita)

Love in Vegas Series (to be read in order)

Lucky Seven (Book 1)

Pushing His Luck (Book 2)

Lucking Out (Book 3)

Love in Vegas Novellas (to be read in timeline order)

Winters Wishes (takes place during Lucking Out)

Valentine's Vows (takes place around three years after Lucking Out)

Falling Series (to be read in order)

New Beginnings (Book 1)

Still Falling (Book 2)

New Beginnings/Falling Series Novellas (to be read in timeline order)

Old Endings (prequel to New Beginnings – Eve's Story)

The Nanny Chronicles (to be read in order)
Single Dad (Gabe and Carrie)
Pinky Promise (Seb and Bea)

Erotic romance titles by Elle M Thomas:

The Revelation Series
Days of Discovery – Kate & Marcus Book 1
Events of Endeavour – Kate & Marcus Book 2

Volume 4

WILTED FLOWER

A NEW BEGINNINGS STORY

SIENNA GRANT

Meet The Team:

Cover Designer: Francessca Wingfield @ Wingfield Designs

Formatting: TBR Editing & Design

A NOTE FROM THE AUTHOR

Wilted Flower is the prequel to Saving Chains, a new Mc series and this story,

deals with domestic violence.

**This story contains scenes of domestic abuse which some readers may find distressing and cause triggers. **

So firstly, let's quickly chat about domestic violence.

It's a charity that is very close to my heart and if I can I'll always do what I can to help and raise money.

Domestic violence can happen in any home. It's real.

Physical, sexual, or mental, or even all three happens and even though we as concerned human beings don't want to think about it, it still happens. Unfortunately, no one knows what happens behind closed doors, and if we don't listen to victims when they reach out, they will never get out of that situation.

Unfortunately, it happened to me, a long time ago but I came out of the other side, I survived. It was hard to walk away. To admit I became a victim and although I didn't have really anyone to help me get out of that situation and the police didn't get involved like they do now, all it took was one person to listen to what was happening to me. I was 19, pregnant and had a 15 month old son. That day my life took another direction. I was rock bottom. I carried on for my son and the child I had on the way.

I'm putting this out there now in the hope that someone going through what I did, finds the hope and salvation that they need.

Please don't suffer in silence.

Just by reaching out to one person, they really could be your saviour.

Break the cycle.

Listen to people when they need you to.

It might just be name calling, or a slap here and there.

It's violence.

And violence shouldn't be allowed in any home. Whether it be a man, a woman, or a child. Domestic violence is abuse and it can't be tolerated.

Living in the UK? Find help here:
https://www.nhs.uk/live-well/getting-help-for-domestic-violence/

Domestic violence hotline USA: - 1-800-799-7233

BLURB

Your childhood should be the best years of your life, or at
least that's what people say.

Mine weren't.

There were so many occasions when I wished things were
different. A different father. A better life. Someone to love
my mother the way she deserved. To be nurtured by a
father the way other kids were.

But again, it wasn't for us, and some have to learn the
hard way.

My mom was the light of my life. A bright flower in such a
dark world. Unfortunately, her petals wilted along with her
will to fight. But while I tried to survive, I found a new kind
of family, a family of brothers guided by sin.

It was my time now.

CHAPTER ONE

Levi

MY FEET TRUDGE along the sidewalk, kicking up the dust as I make my way home from school. Home. It's not really a home. It's not that I want to go back there, it's because I don't have a choice. I can't leave my mom with him. As I get closer to the house, it's like my body knows; anxiety takes hold, and my stomach clenches. I take deep breaths to calm myself as I slowly make my way up the path while a shaky breath leaves my lips. One word wrong said to him, and I'll get a hiding.

Before I slip my key into the lock, I look around me, call it being careful, preparing myself for the worst. I don't see his car, and in that moment, my body sags with relief, tension rolling from my shoulders when I realize he's not here. With my spirits lifted, I push on the handle and rush into the house, dropping my bag on the floor in the hall before kicking off my sneakers.

"Levi, is that you sweetheart?" She sounds happy today, not her normal low, hushed tone. I see her appear from around the corner, and she has a smile on her face. Her eyes light up as her gaze falls on me as she dries her hands on a towel. "How was school, sweetheart?" Her arm hooks around my neck and holds me in place to leave a kiss on my head.

"Alright, I guess." I shrug and move out of her embrace to go around her and make my way to the kitchen, grabbing some snacks. There isn't much, so I grab some crackers and head into the living room, flopping down on the couch to turn the TV on, then find some cartoons to watch. When Dad is at home, the TV is out of bounds. He has his sport on and that's it. It's a luxury, so he says, and we don't deserve luxuries – his words. Asshole.

"Hey, don't eat too much junk, dinner will be on the table soon." Mom calls out.

"K, Mom." I appease her. I don't like upsetting her: I see what he puts her through. She doesn't need me being a pain in the ass too.

I'm fifteen years of age, and living in a world that I do, with an old drunk for a father who has nothing better to do than use us as his punchbag, is hard. It's hard to explain injuries at school, so now, if they're too bad that I can't hide them, I don't go. I skip school more than I'm there. I'm surprised Mom hasn't been called in. There have been times I've turned up at school with a black eye or unexplained bruises, but I don't say anything; what's the point. They won't do anything; they won't take us out of here and place us somewhere he can't find us. I can look after my mom; I do look after her, and one day, there will come a time when he will be gone.

While I'm lost inside my own head and casually flicking through the cable channels on TV, I find myself having the same thoughts. What it would be like to have a normal life.

To have a family that loves you, would do anything for you, would kill rather than let anyone hurt you. Other than my mom, I don't think I'll ever know what that's like. My mom needs to survive, too.

"Levi. Dinner's ready."

I throw the remote control onto the cushion beside me and scramble off the couch to rush into the kitchen, the smell of dinner luring me in. A pot roast sits in the middle of the table. It smells delicious. I quickly sit while mom dishes some veg and sausages onto my plate. If it wasn't for her, we'd starve. Mom can make a meal out of anything. We might not have a life where we get everything we want, and I might have a bastard for a father, but we don't starve. If she didn't have food on the table, that would be another excuse for him to hit her.

She thinks I don't hear her crying in bed at night for hours. She also thinks I don't hear how he talks to her and the names he calls her. Most nights, I sneak out of my bedroom window just to get away.

"Please bless this table and our family," Mom prays, and, on a whisper, she goes on, "and keep my boy safe." I reach across the small square table, gripping her hand tightly, pointing an encouraging smile her way. She nods, she looks sad most of the time, but even with her own shitty life and her marriage, she still smiles then sits up a little straighter. "Well, tuck in."

As I scoop some mashed potato on my fork, the front door slams shut. I pause, taking the potato from my fork just as my stomach clenches again, and suddenly, I'm not hungry. Mom keeps her eyes on me, but the smile that was there just moments ago has disappeared. Our gazes lock on each other, a silent conversation and strength passing between us as his footsteps thunder down the hall. Next, the door swings open, and when it slams off the wall, my body jolts.

"Started without me. You ungrateful fucks. It's me that allows you to eat this food, but you can't wait for us to eat together." Mom nods at me to eat. My lips close around the mashed potato on my fork and drag it into my mouth and start eating. I eat my sausages so quick I end up with a pain in my chest and hiccups. I try to block his voice out, but he's loud, so I attempt to get my mind to go back five minutes to find that somber, calm place again. I quickly eat most of my dinner, even though I'm stuffed, and place my cutlery on the plate.

"Can I leave the table please?" I ask politely, aiming it at my mom more than him.

She nods, "Of course sweetheart."

"Stop fucking coddling him. The boy needs to grow up to be a man, not a pussy." Dad sneers as he opens the beer can that Mom has placed in front of him. he takes a long swig and bangs it back on the table.

"He will be a man, but it doesn't hurt to be polite."

"Who the fuck you talking to?" His lip curls as he swings his fierce gaze toward me.

"I'm just saying," Mom replies, a shake evident in her voice. "I'm not coddling him; I'm just being nice to our son."

"Mom, it's okay." I butt in and reach across to her hand, giving her some comfort. But that just makes him even more angry.

"Did I say you can speak?" his tone is harsh and full of hatred for me. Yes, hate. I don't think I've ever felt love from him, but I don't care, the feeling is mutual, and as soon as I get the chance, I'll be out of here.

Pushing my chair back, I rise to take my plate from the

table, scraping the leftovers into the bin and pick up the left-over sausage from my plate, biting the end off as I leave the room. I snatch my school bag from the floor as I rush past the front door and head to my room.

I shove my door closed and slide the lock across. The number of times he's broken it off by kicking the door is crazy, but it doesn't stop me. It's the only power I have against him. This is for my peace of mind. I've become quite self-sufficient in the last year. I do all the fix up jobs when Dad has lost his shit, well, the jobs I can do anyway.

With the lock in place, I drag the chair across the room and lodge it under the handle. Let him try and get through that, I think as I throw myself onto my bed. I spend a minute wondering what will come of this evening. It doesn't bear thinking about, but the mood he was in sets the tone for my thoughts. A rumbling passes my house, and as I shoot up to look out of my window, I see the back of bikes passing by. It's not the first time I've seen them pass here; in fact, they pass by here a lot. Planting my forearms on the windowsill, I watch them go by in awe. The shiny chrome on the bikes has my gaze fixed on them. What it would be like to be one of them. That's what I want. I want to be one of those guys. No one will beat on me; there'll be no one that can treat me like shit. Not like he does, anyway.

After the bikers have disappeared, I drop down from my window and make a start on my homework. It's not long before I'm lost in Math, luckily, I do well with that. It's everything else I seem to struggle with.

With my eyes getting tired, I drag myself up with an exhausted sigh, rubbing my eyes before shutting my books. I throw my books to the floor and get up from the bed, removing my barricade and unlock the door, then as quietly as I can, I go into the bathroom on the landing to wash up, then brush my teeth ready for bed.

At my age, I should be out with friends, hanging around, maybe being a nuisance, but I'm not because I don't have friends. I don't have anyone to confide in. That may be my doing; I don't want to have to explain where my bruises come from, and I'm not a liar. I can't make stories up and make someone believe me; it just isn't in me. They would read right through me. And anyway, no kid in my position would admit the life they have if they were me. It's better this way.

As I come out of the bathroom, I pull the door behind me closed as quietly as I can, I don't want to piss him off further. But then I hear his loud, harsh voice insulting my mom. Unfortunately, it's the normal nightly routine. I hear his shameful words, the names he calls her. Slut, cunt. My mom is none of those things. She's good, way too good for him. I wish I could help her... I stand on the top of the stairs wondering whether I should be brave and go down there, help, try and stop him, but my thoughts are cut dead. A piercing scream from the kitchen reaches my ears, and my heart sinks as I drop down to the carpet and sit on the top step. I sit quietly, listening, wishing. One scream is followed by a wail, followed by a thud, then comes more shouting. Telling her to kill herself. To die. How he wishes that he never met her and had a bastard kid with her. Deep, ragged breaths tear through my chest as I once again wish we could escape him. But I stay where I am while the tears pour from my eyes as I lift my fingers to my face and wipe them away, my breaths shudder from the pain my mom must be in.

His heavy footsteps sound on the wooden floor, and seconds later, the front door slams. I jump from the sound echoing off the walls and wait a few minutes. If he comes back, I'll have the same, and I haven't had a bad beating for a couple of months. I peer into the kitchen as I reach the door and find Mom in the corner, curled into a ball with her hands on her head, her soft, painful cries breaking my heart.

I don't waste any time, I go in, softly closing the door and drop to my knees at her side.

"I'm here, Mom. It's okay. I wrap my arm around her shoulders and pull her against me. Her cries tear my heart out as her head falls against my chest and I hold her, telling her she'll always have me. Her arms tighten around me as I let her cry it out as she holds on to me for what feels like a lifetime.

"I'm sorry baby. I'm so sorry."

"Shhh. Don't cry." I stroke her hair the way she does to me when she tends to me after Dad has beaten me. "I love you, Mom." she lifts her head, and I see the start of a bruise forming around her eye. Her lip is bleeding, and so is her nose. "I promise one day Mom, one day we'll get away from him. I'll keep you safe."

Her chin trembles, and her head shakes, "Sweetheart I'll never get away from him, he won't let me. But you, you promise me that one day you'll get away from here and you never look back, do you hear me, Levi." The tremble in her voice scares me, "That's what I want you to do for me."

With an agreeable nod, I tighten my hold around her before dragging us from the floor and I help her to a chair. I grab the first aid kit from the cupboard and tend to her cuts, pouring my love onto her and letting her know that one person in this shitty world loves her.

CHAPTER TWO

Levi

I'VE SAT out here on this roof for hours. I couldn't listen to Mom cry anymore it was killing me. After comforting her for what seemed like hours on her bed, she kicked me out and sent me to my own bed, said it was late and I needed my sleep, not that I would anyway, so instead, I came to sit out here. This is my place, sat out here under the comfort of the stars. Most people don't like the dark, not me. Out here, everything ebbs away. It's the four walls that scare me most. No one knows what goes on behind those walls, and unless we speak out, no one ever will.

There's a cooler breeze in the air tonight, and as it wraps around my body, goosebumps prickle my skin. It's so quiet out here. Right now, you could hear a pin drop, well, that's until the shrill cry of a cat pierces the silence, and the odd dog barks at something moving around in the night, but then I hear them again, the rumble of bikes in the distance. Lifting my chin from my knees and my back straightens from my hunched position as I look out, hoping to catch a glimpse of them. I shuffle toward the edge, my fingers tightly gripping the edge of the flat roof as I look out to the end of the road, waiting for them to suddenly appear. The sound gets louder, closer, then there's three of them riding alongside each other. I don't know what it is about them, but they make me happy, feel alive.

As they pass by, the one closest to my side looks up and nods his head my way. I smile and lift my hand in a wave. when he does it back, a smile form on my lips, a real smile, something I haven't done in a long time. After watching them for a few minutes, I stand up, balancing on the edge as I look down, concentrating on the grass below as I prepare to jump.

My feet hit the ground with a dull thud, and quickly I jump back up to my feet and set off down the street, running toward their home, the compound that's situated just minutes from my house. My feet come to a sudden stop when I reach the high fences that surround it, and I look up in total awe. The sound of bikes has stopped now, and the night air is eerily silent again. As I go around the compound, I wonder what it's like inside. To be there, to be a part of something like that. Even out here, on this side of the fence, I feel safer than I do at home; it's such a strange feeling. I spend what feels like forever just staring at the inside of those fences. I can't take my eyes off the bikes sitting outside. There are guys in and out. Don't these guys sleep?

A twig snaps underfoot as I move across the front of the fence. One of the guys looks back at the sound, my stomach clenching with unnamed emotion as he looks directly at me. I'm not sure if fear or excitement has taken hold of me, but either way, I can't move or look away as the big biker makes his way toward me. "Hey kid. What are you doing there?"

My head tips back as I look up at him. His head is bald,

and his shoulders are rounded as his leather vest sits on his large frame. A long beard hangs from his face, but his eyes are kind.

"N...nothing." I stammer. "I was just looking."

"You shouldn't be out here. You should be in bed." I shrug. "Don't you have a home to go to? I'm sure your momma will be worried about you." My shoulders shrug again. "What's your name?"

"Levi," I answer stronger this time, and he nods.

"Well, Levi, you better go home. It's not safe out on these streets at this time of night." I want to say it's safer than being at home, but I don't. My teeth clamp together, and suddenly I turn mute, scared to say anything I shouldn't. I look past him to the sound of talking; the biker turns his body slightly to see what I'm looking at and smiles as he brings his gaze back to me. "You like bikes?" I nod as I carry on watching. It's just two guys talking and watching us. My fingers move through the holes in the fence, and as I grip it the wire cuts into my flesh slightly. Just then, a burst of a siren disturbs the peaceful air, and a patrol car slows down behind us. I watch as the huge biker straightens his stance and pushes his shoulders back, standing taller than he already was.

I turn to see the two cops watching us as they crawl by, and looking between them and the biker, he nods at them, and they nod back, then carry on past, still crawling by. "You better go kid, otherwise they'll be back. Do you need me to take you?"

"No thank you." I smile at the large guy, and he sniggers.

"Go on. Don't let me see you out this time of night again."

"Yes sir." I answer him politely, like I've been taught,

but I will be out again. Backing away from the fence, keeping my eyes on him, I reach the end of the grass and turn around, running back the way I came.

Once I reach my house, I find the lights are still on in the living room. I go around the side and climb back up the drainpipe, trying to make as little noise as possible, and take my place back on the roof. The wind has picked up from earlier, it's even cooler now, and as I feel the first spots of rain, I crawl back inside my window, kick off my sneakers and strip out of my clothes to slide between my sheets. My thoughts soon go back to that compound and the biker who spoke to me like I was a person, not some annoying tic. And as I close my eyes, I drift off to a world where I'm wanted, I'm tough and no one messes with me.

The next few days, I spend as much time out of the house as possible. Although I don't want my mom to hurt or to be upset, I can't stay in there. Every night, I've done the same thing, gone to the compound, watching, and wishing that I was there instead of the prison I currently live in. The sound of the bikes excites me, and the bikers make me long for a different life.

It's almost dawn by the time I return home this time. I've sat all night, hidden in a darker spot behind the fence. No one has seen me this time though, in fact, I haven't seen that guy since that first night or hardly anyone for that matter. Just as I lift my foot to the wall to secure it against the side of the house, a hand grabs my shirt. He tugs hard and I feel myself falling, then hit the ground with a sharp thud. "Caught ya, you little shit." With my shirt balled in his fist, he drags me along, back to the front door and slings me inside. As I hit the floor again, he releases me and just in that split second of freedom, I try to scramble away, my stomach churns with fright as the door closes with a loud slam.

"Leave him alone, Terry." My mom cries.

"Shut your fucking trap, bitch. He thinks he can sneak out of my house at night. I'll teach him a fucking lesson."

"Don't you touch him." Mom screams and stands in front of me, guarding me.

"No, Mom. It's okay." She launches herself at him, but he easily stops her advance. She's no match for him as his hand goes around her throat and squeezes tightly, her eyes beginning to bulge. I shift to my feet and try to get between them, my hands pushing against his chest as I use all my weight to get him to move away, but it's no good. Instead, I do something I've never been brave enough to do; I hit him, punching his stomach and chest, turn my shoulder into his body to shove him away from her, and eventually, his grip loosens, and he lets go. I push her out of the way as she gasps for air, and I stand in front of him, a tremble taking over my whole body as my bravery ebbs away, but I stand tall, just like that biker did when the cops came past. As my jaw clamps, his eyes turn black and his mouth sneers with hate. I don't see his hand pull back, not until it's covering one side of my face, my cheek feels like it's going to pop, and I hit the hard floor again.

"Noooo." I hear Mom's screams, and although it hurts, adrenaline courses through me and I jump back up, standing before him again and square my shoulders.

"Oh, think you're big enough, boy?" He sneers.

I don't answer, but I don't back down either when he grabs my face, his fingers squeezing my jaw to keep me in place but I'm defiant and don't show him my fear. I don't care anymore. He hits me again, his knuckles connecting with my cheekbone and making it feel like my face is going to break open with his fierceness.

"I hate you. I wish you'd die." I throw at him, but he laughs at me, that makes me even angrier as I hit the floor again. He rains hits on me one after the other, and by the time he's done, he leaves me on the floor, a battered heap and walks away muttering what a pussy I am.

Soft arms pull my hands from my face, and her arms go around me in a warm embrace. I let her hold me, and for the first time in a while, I let myself break down, silently crying against her chest.

One day, he won't be able to do this, he won't be able to hurt either of us, and I swear that once I'm older, and bigger I'll find a way of stopping him. Even if it's the last thing I ever do.

CHAPTER THREE

Levi

STARING BACK at another black eye and bruising on my cheeks and jaw just angers me. I'm not sad, I don't regret sneaking out, and even if I get a beating every night, he won't stop me. I do feel bad for leaving my mom at his mercy, though. If I could get us both out of here, I would.

I open her bedroom door quietly and see she's sleeping soundly on her bed. I creep inside and go around to the side she's on, kiss her cheek, stroking her hair gently and just sit with her for a little while, listening to her sleep. It's not a natural sleep; she's sedated. She's taken pills, her antidepressants to be exact. She's been taking them for a while now, she thinks I don't know about them, that I don't understand. I'm almost sixteen. I'm not a baby or a child anymore. I look after her and myself more than she looks after me now. Seeing that her eyes aren't even flickering tells me that she took more than the approved dose just so she can sleep. It makes me sad, pissed that he's brought her to this, but if it means he doesn't hurt her then I'd rather her sleep.

Kissing her head again and telling her I love her, I get back up to my feet, leave the room and close the door again behind me. When I hit the bottom of the stairs, the TV plays out loud. I peer around the door and see him still, a loud snore filling the room as his can hangs from his fingers, threatening to fall to the floor. I quickly leave before it drops and it wakes him up and he catches me, he told me I wasn't to go out other than to school but there's no way I'm going like this, this is one too many bruises to explain and although I'd love mom to get help, I doubt she'll accept it anyway.

Pulling the door closed again, I run up the street and soon find myself back at the compound, but being in broad daylight makes it seem different, bigger. I walk around the side and away from the road where people can see me and slip through the bushes. With my foot flat against the wire, I climb up, scramble over the top and jump down again. I plant my back against the fence before I see a corner I can hide in, behind some large trash units. I race across the compound and squeeze between them, crouch down and hide away, enjoying the safety the gated area can offer.

It's been a while since I got here, but the sound of bikes is like music to my ears and has my attention again. I thought about coming out of my hiding place to have a look around, but I couldn't risk that because then my safe haven would be gone. If they find me in here, they'll up their security, and I won't be able to return.

A female voice catches my attention though, and being inquisitive, I crawl out a couple of feet to investigate. As her voice gets closer, I still for a second, my body freezing before poking my head out just a little further. I soon find the girl that the voice belongs to. Her long dark hair trails down her back, she's slim and has long legs that are dancing around to some music. I watch her, smiling slightly. Her voice is soft, and she seems so carefree. What I would give to be like that. But then I hear another voice, a much deeper one this time telling her to go inside. She answers, saying she doesn't want to because it's too hot to be indoors. It's not even that hot, I don't think so anyway. The weather has turned cooler over the last few days. Her voice is sweet but defiant as she answers. "I don't want to."

"It's not safe out here for you, go back inside." The deeper voice replied.

"Dad, if it's not safe here it's not safe anywhere." She carries on dancing to the music, not caring what her dad says but in a sweet voice and a pretty smile plastered to her face. I don't know what the music is, I can't hear it properly, I'm too far away. I can only hear their voices because they're shouting. At that, she turns around and comes my way. I quickly scramble between the trash cans, watching her sail past me. I know I need to leave here and go home at some point for food, but it's not long before it goes quiet again. I guess that the girl must've been made to go back inside, so I spend some more time hiding out. I'd rather sit here behind the bins and hide than go back to a beating. I hear adults say all the time, that a person can only take so much. I've had enough of his crap. Just being inside here makes me feel safe, and I'm not about to end that feeling just yet.

I'm sure a couple of hours have passed since I saw the girl, and as I go to crawl out again and finally make my way home, I hear skipping, it's getting closer and closer. I push my back against the wall, making myself small just as I hear her singing softly. Her feet appear in the gap between the bins as she throws a bag inside. It's loud as it hits the side and drops inside the metal can, and the Converse I saw less than a minute ago, are now disappearing from my line of sight.

"Luna!" The deep voice yells, and then she calls back,

"I'm coming, Dad." She sounds annoyed, but now I know her name. It plays over and over in my head. I'd give anything to talk to her, but I can't. With her gone, I make a run for the fence and leave the way I came in, climbing back over and head home.

The next few weeks, I didn't go anywhere else. If I'm not at home hiding from Dad, I'm at the compound hiding. I've seen the pretty girl a lot over the last few days, but still she hasn't seen me. I'm there more than at home, but with every day that passes, Mom's depression worsens but then, so does his temper. He hasn't beaten her for a while now, so instead he hurts her with words, at least he does when she's awake. It's getting harder and harder to cope with these days – I wish I didn't have to. I take the brunt of his temper to spare my mom. I used to cry at night when I had a beating, now it's like a normal day. He drinks, I piss him off by breathing, and he hits me. Normal routine.

But even though I'm hiding away, I feel free.

I'VE BEEN STUCK behind this trash can for hours, my ass went numb a while ago, and my legs are hurting now from being on the cold ground, but I stay where I am anyway. I've got bruises on my back where he hit me with his shoe, and my eye being black is my usual look these days. My whole-body shakes as I wrap my arms around me, in the hope to quell the shivers that are taking hold of me. I curl tighter into a ball to keep my body warm, but it's getting harder as the days turn colder. The seasons are changing into winter, I just know if I keep hiding out here, I'll end up getting pneumonia. My teeth chatter loudly, I try to control it but it's no use, my body is cold, and it hurts even more than it did this morning. I'm not sure I can do this anymore.

"Hello. Who are you?" Her voice has my eyes popping open now, wide with fear of being caught and thrown out of the compound or worse, beaten for trespassing. I don't think my body can take another. "Are you okay?" a whole lot of questions shine in her pretty eyes. I was so lost in my head; I didn't hear her or see her appear in front of me.

My head shakes as I comfort myself some more. With a closer view, I see how pretty she is. Her dark but kind eyes match the color of her hair, and her pink lips pull into a small, sweet smile. Her cheeks blush slightly, but I don't smile back, I'm too cold and my body is aching. "Can you speak?" I nod back, "I'm Luna." She pushes her hand out in front of her, she waits as I unwrap my arms from my body to take her hand. It's so much warmer than my own as she closes her fingers around it and we shake; it makes me not want to let go.

I nod. "I'm Levi." My teeth still chatter from the coldness.

"You're freezing. Don't you have a home?" I nod again, but I don't say anything else. She pushes the bin out of the way, fills the gap it was once in and crouches beside me. "How long have you been out here?"

"All day."

She concentrates on my face as her gaze roams over my bruises, suddenly I feel embarrassed. I look away, dropping my gaze to the ground. "Have you been in a fight?"

"You ask a lot of questions." I grumble as my gaze moves back to her dark eyes, and I cock a brow.

"And you're here when you're not allowed to be, I think I win." How can I argue with that? "How old are you?"

"Sixteen in a month."

She smiles, "I've just turned fifteen. It was my birthday in August." My body shakes even more as dusk begins to fall. "Maybe I should get you a blanket."

"I'm fine."

"You don't look it." She swivels on her ass and faces me, "You know if my dad finds you hiding out here, he won't be very happy. No one's allowed inside the yard. Like no one. How did you get in anyway?"

"I jumped the fence."

"But it's huge." She replies, her eyes widen with every word. "It's like, well I don't know how high it is, but it's high."

"I climbed. I've been hiding out here for weeks."

"Oh," Just then I hear feet pounding the ground, and see boots appear in my eyeline.

"Shit," I whisper harshly, worried I'm about to be tossed out on my ass.

"It's okay. It's just Reaper. He's a good guy. I better go though I think my dad is looking for me. I'll get you a blanket and some soup. I'll be back soon."

"Luna. Where are you hiding now? Pres is looking for ya. He's pissed." With a bright smile, she crawls out of the gap she made for herself and leaves me alone, leaving me to either brave the cold for a while longer, to see if she comes through on her promise, or drag my shaky body to my feet and attempt to climb that fence, right now though, I don't think I have the energy.

CHAPTER FOUR

Levi

"LEVI." I hear my name, but the voice is unfamiliar to me. I'm not asleep just feeling drowsy, so instead, I keep my eyes closed. "Hey. Wake up." I feel a gentle hand softly rock my shoulder, and I crack my eyes open a sliver. Through my blurry vision, I see Luna crouching in front of me. "I've got you chicken soup. I had to sneak it out." A warmth settles over my legs as she covers me with the blanket that she promised me. I lift my aching head, opening my eyes wider as she passes me a travel cup. My arms hurt as I lift them to take the cup in both of my hands hoping to warm them up, my legs ache as I move them, in fact my whole-body aches. "You know you don't look too good, maybe you should go home and get into bed."

"I'm fine." I add in a croaky voice. I don't want to go home. I don't even have the energy to get off the ground.

"If you insist," Luna lifts a brow.

I take careful sips of the soup and swallow, "When I've drunk this I'll go if you want me to."

"I'm not saying you have to go, you just...well, you look sick." she shrugs, dropping her gaze into her lap, "I mean I don't want you to go."

"You don't know me." I frown.

"Will you come back?"

My shoulders lift. "Who knows." As I drink more soup, I feel myself warming up, but I still don't feel too well. I don't know how I'm going to get back over that fence.

"Lune?" The same voice from earlier calls out, I'm too tired to hide in the shadows this time. "Why the hell are you by the trash again?"

"Shit, it's Reaper again. What is his problem," she huffs, "I really need to go. I'll be back." As she stands up straight, she hesitates again, a smile twitching her lips. "It was good to meet you, Levi."

Automatically, a small smile tugs at my lips back at her. "Thanks for these."

As footsteps get closer to us, my body tenses up, "Why the hell are you hiding, Lune. You know if you've got some stray animal out here, your dad will go batshit..." His voice trails off as he appears. I push my shoulders back, placing my cup on the ground as my eyes lock with the same tall guy from earlier. "Who the fuck are you?" He asks, a scowl screwing up his face.

"Please don't tell Dad." Luna stresses. As my gaze strays to her, I see the worry settling in her eyes, and now I'm panicking. I don't want to get her into trouble, but I don't want to leave either. I attempt to get up so I can leave by myself, but I don't have the energy to move my body, I can't even lift myself from the asphalt. My legs are hurting, and my head hurts too.

"Dude, are you okay?" I shake my head as my ass lands back on the ground with a thump.

"I think he's sick." Luna replies.

"Fuck." The tall guy says. "Well, he can't stay out here. We either try and get him out of here and back to his own home or we get him inside and face, Pres. Your call."

"I can walk. My house is only like 3 blocks away." I finally get myself up onto my feet, but my legs feel shaky, and I fall against the trash can.

"There is no way he can walk." I look between the guy Reaper and Luna and see them having a stare-off. "What do you know about this kid?"

"Kid? Reap, he's a year younger than you. Dad would've helped you if you needed it, and not just because your dad was one of the brothers."

He huffs, but I can see Luna knows how to wrap him around her little finger. "Fine. Let's go see Pres then." He says, and they both look around at me and he sighs again, frowning slightly, "He does look ill." My face feels flushed, and I throw off the blanket.

"Hey, dude? I'm gonna get you help, okay?"

"No, I'm good. If they find me here and know that I've been sneaking in here, I'll get a beating. One worse than my old man can give me. Fuck that!" Forcing my feet to move, I slowly start to move past him, my weary body shifting forward until his hand wraps around my arm and stops me.

"Hey," he turns me slightly, "the brothers won't hurt ya, they may look mean as hell but they're pussycats really." He smiles, relaxing me some, "Come on let's get you inside, in the warm. You can have my bed for the night."

With an arm each around my back holding me up, they walk me across the yard. My breathing quickens, but I'm anxious with every step closer we get. What if they kick me out? What if they give me a beating, I'm not strong enough to stand up for myself. Not today anyway. "You know guys, maybe this isn't such a good idea." I attempt to release them, but neither lets me go.

"You need a warm bed, some painkillers and some sleep." Reaper says without room to argue.

"Levi," her voice is comforting and has my head turning her way, "my dad will help, I promise." My eyelids begin to droop with exhaustion, the thought of a warm bed sounds damn good. I nod back at her and let them lead me to wherever they're taking me. I guess this place can't be as bad as home, so instead of resisting, I just move my feet along with them.

We enter through a heavy door, straight into a bar. There're women in short skirts and low-cut tops with spiked shoes, and guys in biker gear drinking, smoking... I'm not sure what I expected.

"Sit him down. I'll go and see Dad."

Reaper stays with me as my body lolls back in the chair, weak from some kind of flu I seemed to have caught, and my eyes close again. If I'm honest, I'm glad I let them talk me into staying here. I'm not sure how long Luna is gone, but it's not her voice I hear first.

"Hey kid. Do I know you?" My eyes pop open at his loud, gruff voice. I look at his face as recognition hits me. It's the guy who found me outside the compound a few short weeks ago. A tiny nod just about shifts my head in reply.

"He's sick, Dad." Luna butts in.

"Where did you find him?" I hear him ask,

"By the trash, hiding." Luna replied.

"Hm. Well, I can't kick him out like that. Reaper, find him somewhere to sleep. I'll deal with it tomorrow."

"Hey, kid?" I lift my head and lock eyes with him, "Don't go running off tomorrow, we need to have a talk, and then you can tell me how you got that black eye." I don't answer, instead I let my head drop until my chin is hitting my chest as his hand splays across my forehead, "Jesus, he's burning up. Take him to lie down and get him some medicine to take."

"You take him to yours; I'll get the medicine." Luna orders Reaper.

"Can you walk?" Reaper asks. "As I nod, he helps me up, holding me firmly with his arm around my back before leading me down a hall.

Reaper opens the door and I go inside, and without even thinking about it, I drop down on the unmade bed. "Are you sure about this?" My eyelids are already closing as I think about sleep, my hands on either side of me on the mattress holding me up.

"Yeah, man." Reaper replies like it's a stupid question. "You need to rest. I'm good on the floor."

"I don't mind sleeping on the floor." A rough cough interrupts our conversation, and Reaper cocks his head.

"Yeah, I think that's how you got like this. Take the bed man, it's all good." As I lie down, a knock sounds on the door. "That'll be Luna."

Pulling open the door, she comes in and puts some hot lemon, a bottle of water and two tablets on the nightstand. "Hey, I can't stay, Dad will kick my ass. I'll check on you in the morning, kay?" I nod, unscrewing the cap and drink some water, quenching my thirst and soothing my dry, sore throat. "Take the pills, you'll feel better." I look at them like they're about to kill me or something. I'd rather not take them, but if I don't that'll be more questions, and I don't want them feeling sorry for me; no more than they already do, anyway. I pick up the pills and swallow them down with the bottled water, drinking half of it. As she's about to go back through the door, I stop her.

"Luna." I call out firmly but with a croak in my voice, she turns back and smiles, "Thank you." I say, her smile gets wider.

"See you tomorrow." She leaves the room, so it's just me and Reaper.

"She seems nice."

I try to make conversation, while Reaper nods. "She's a good kid, got a big heart." He throws blankets on the floor with a pillow on top, then settles down folding his arms behind his head and lying back. "You better get some sleep; Pres will have you answering a million and one questions tomorrow."

"Thank you for helping me." Conversation is kept short, but I prefer that. That way I don't have to delve into anything.

"No problem."

As the silence falls in the room, I quickly drink the hot lemon that Luna has made for me, and I lie back down again. My body is red hot, and the hot lemon has made me hotter, but my eyelids are already heavy. I don't fight the urge to sleep anymore, instead I let it take me under.

CHAPTER FIVE

Luna

"SO, where would you like to start," Dad asks, sitting opposite Levi. His forearms rest on the arms of the chair, and his fingers drum against the edge while he waits on an answer. "Do you want to tell me why you were hiding out on private property, or maybe you can tell me where you got that from." Dad nods his head toward Levi's face. Levi looks from Dad to me, then back to Dad again. "Or maybe if I told you I could prosecute you for trespassing then you'll give me some answers."

"Please..." His head shakes frantically, "...please don't."

"Dad," My eyes widen, and the tone in my voice goes a pitch higher at the way Dad hands out a threat, without even thinking twice about it.

His side look of 'be quiet' has my mouth closing, and he goes on, "You better start talking then."

"I'm sorry." Levi shrugs, a heavy breath filling the air as his body sags in the chair. Reaper sits one side and I the other, like we're there to support him, and we don't even know if he's worthy of our support. His hands fidget in his lap, winding his fingers around and watching as they tangle. "I loved to watch the bikes pass my house. I always wished that it was me on those bikes, that way I'd be free. The first time I sneaked into the yard was in the middle of the night, it was only meant to be one night. Have you ever wanted to run and hide away from the world and all the shit that happens in it?"

Dad and I look at Levi as Dad's brows pinch, "How old are you, Levi?"

"Sixteen soon." he glances up and locks eyes with my father.

"That's a cynical outlook on the world for a young kid, so tell me, what are you running from?" Levi shakes his head, but if I know my father, he won't leave it until he's got what he wants. "Come on, you can tell me."

"I can't, you won't believe me." Levi's head still shaking as he replies. Dad leans forward, settling his arms on his thighs.

"Try me, because if it's what I think it is, and I'm right about how you got that bruise on your face, then believe me, I'll be more than pissed, but you have to tell me." Levi locks eyes with him like neither of us are even here. "You can trust me, Levi." Dad adds to calm his nervous exterior. "You see this," Dad points to his patch, and Levi nods his head, "That's a vow of honor, brothers. When we wear that patch, we do it with pride, honor, honesty, and morals. You get that?"

On a breath, he rolls his eyes to me, then at Reaper, and we nod in unison. Eventually, he answers, "My dad." He answers in a low tone, like he's ashamed of the answer he's given.

Dad straightens up, his jaw tight like he's trying his

hardest not to lose his shit. I've seen that expression many times with the other guys in the club. "I'm guessing that's not the first black eye you've ever had then?" Levi slowly shakes his head and stands up, reaching over his head to pull his t-shirt up his back. I'm shocked at what's staring back at me. Considering I've been brought up in a club, I've never been allowed to see what goes on. I know violence happens, but I'm sheltered. I don't have another choice other than to be here, my mother left a couple of years back, and we never knew where she went, and no relatives would dare question the mighty Thomas Scott.

Dark bruises and red welts cover his back, and thoughts of my mother are gone instantly as a lump forms in my throat. I put my hand to my mouth to muffle the shocked gasp that falls from it. Dad lifts Levi's arm up slightly so he can look at his ribs. A mix of purple, black and yellowing skin shines back at me. "Okay kid, put your t-shirt down."

With his shirt back in place, Levi sits back down, but doesn't look any of us in the eye. Reaper and I share a look before we both look at Dad. "You're safe here, Levi." he lifts his head slightly and eyes my dad, relief filling his gaze. "So, you like the clubhouse, huh?" Levi nods. "Okay, from here on out this is shelter, but you come through that gate, not over the fence. No more hiding."

Levi smiles. "What about my dad. What if he finds out I've been coming here?"

Dad ponders on something; I can see him thinking. "Then he'll meet his match, kid. Have you got a cell?"

"No, sir."

"Okay, leave that with me. But once you've got it, any problems, I want you to call me or call Reaper. You got that. Any problems at home, you call. I don't care what time of day it is; you make sure you make that call."

His lips spread into a smile across his face.

"Do you go to school?"

"Not often."

"Alright. You can work here. I can find you something to do. Would you like that?"

"Yes," He quickly answers, still smiling like his Christmases have come all at once.

"And I want you to make me a promise," Dad hesitates for a second. "I want you to tell me every little detail about your father. I don't like abusers, especially child abusers." Levi chews on his lip, but nods. "You can trust me, Levi. I don't break promises, but you need to give me the same trust. Everything else will work itself out." Dad stands, and as Levi stands with him, he slides his arm around his shoulders and pulls him in. "Stick by Reaper, he'll teach ya, kid."

Dad's large hand messes Levi's hair as he rubs it. Dad might be this mean and moody president leading a motorcycle club, but he's a teddy bear sometimes. He goes to walk away but Levi calls out, "Sir?" Dad turns back, "Aren't you angry that I kept sneaking into your yard?"

He sighs, "Maybe a little, but there've been lots of guys in and out of here over the years that have needed shelter, or guidance of some kind," Dad grins, "I know a cry for help when I see one."

"Thank you." Levi says a little louder, his shoulders squaring as he stands taller.

Dad nods at him and turns away again, his footsteps loud as he begins to stomp away then stops, "Oh, and Levi,"

"Yes, sir?"

"It's Pres," As Levi sits back down Dad's footsteps echo, even after the door has closed.

I was awake early this morning because I was worried

about Levi. He has a tough exterior, I can see that, but I don't think he's as tough as he thinks he is, and I was hoping that Reaper wouldn't give him a hard time once I left them alone. Reaper can be very protective, like a big brother kind of protective. He's a pain in my butt at times, but it's nice to know that he has my back. Reaper is reliable, dependable, and my brother from another mother.

"Right then," Reaper pipes up, "what you want to do first?"

"I don't know." Levi shrugs. "What do you usually do?"

"How are you feeling today?" I interrupt, my gaze roaming his face, concerned that last night he was coming down with a virus.

"I'm good..." his brow lifts, cocking the corner of his mouth up with it. "Thanks." He adds, remembering his manners. "I feel much better."

"Good. I'm glad."

"Well," Reaper pipes up, "you can't start the day without food, and Kerry, the cook, she makes a damn good breakfast." I snigger, shaking my head at Reaper.

"What's funny?" Levi looks between us, confused.

"Him," I nod at the idiot walking toward the door. "He always thinks of his belly first. Come on." I start to walk then spin back on my heel. "He is right about Kerry though, her cooking is amazing." I walk backwards, enticing him with the lure of food and he smiles. He has such a cute smile. "Bacon, eggs, whatever you want." His eyes widen, "and however you want them cooking." I add, spinning back around and waltzing through the open door.

I hear him right behind me but don't stop, then his hand is on my arm, "Luna?" I turn to face him, "Thank you." He stands an inch or two taller than me and as I smile, I look up into his brown eyes to see specks of gold. His cute smirk has me smiling back, the worry lines that have been set in his forehead have lessened, and right now, I can see something more than a guy treating me like a sister, like Reaper does. No, the unfamiliar feeling in my chest tells me he could be so much more than that.

CHAPTER SIX

Levi

LUNA WAS right about the food. I had a plate full of scrambled eggs and bacon, then washed it down with juice. I was like a homeless person who hadn't eaten for days, but I was starving, since I hadn't eaten or slept properly for two days. Other than the soup Luna had given me last night. Today though, I feel much better, the full night's sleep and hot lemon must've worked.

After eating, Reaper took me on a tour of the clubhouse. The place is amazing. He showed me his bike, and Pres showed me his. I was in awe of all the shiny chrome and black, and I can't believe how big they are. He then introduced me to some of the older bikers. He introduced me to a guy named Popeye. He had muscles popping all over the place, I could see why he got that name. He wore a tank with his leather cut. It had the same symbol on the right side as Pres', then another in a bigger version on the back, saying Brothers of Sin. Then, I met another guy named Snake. A tattoo of a snake etched to his bald head leads around his neck, and the tail disappears under his shirt. These guys are a little intimidating at first, but they seem friendly, and they welcomed me. A couple of them looked a little wary, but I couldn't expect everyone to accept me with open arms. I'm an outsider until I prove myself, even I know that. After shaking my hand, they asked my name and asked if I was sticking around, then said if I wanted to be a real biker, and a real part of the club, then I needed a road name. In that moment, I knew that I wanted that more than anything.

Then we hung out with Luna. She told me some of the things the guys do, apparently, they have parties for everything. But most of all they were a family. I've never known a real family other than my mom, and I was excited to get to know them all.

As the rest of the day passed, I was getting more and more anxious, and I knew it was because I had to go home at some point today. If Mom wasn't too out of it, she'd be worried about me. Dad, he couldn't give a shit, and to be honest the feeling is mutual. I don't care what he does or if he drinks himself to death. I only want to go home to check on Mom. I don't want to leave here at all, but I need to.

"What's wrong?" Luna asks from her place at my side, while we sit eating fries outside in the yard. She could probably feel the anxiety rolling from me.

"It's time to go home soon. I have to check on my mom."

"Is she poorly?"

"Only from the way he's made her. She uses pills to numb the pain. I've looked after her for a while, but she's lost her spark..." I breathe, closing my eyes tightly as the description of my mom makes my heart hurt. "I hate seeing her like it, and I wish I could get us both out of there." Staring into the distance, I place one fry after the other in my mouth, numb as I watch Reaper washing the guy's bikes. He said it's one of his jobs as a prospect. I have no idea what a prospect is, but it sounds good. I hope I get the chance to be one.

"I'm so sorry, Levi." Luna's quiet tone breaks my concentration on Reaper, it's full of emotion as she moves her head to rest on my shoulder. The strawberry scent of her hair drifts up my nose, distracting me from my thoughts. Damn, she smells so good.

"I don't tell anyone what goes on at home." I admit quietly.

"Not even friends?" A confused look appears in her eyes as I shake my head.

"I don't have friends. Maybe the odd one or two at school, but I'm never there so you can't class them as friends. They don't check up on me, or ask why I haven't been…" I shrug.

"That's awful, Levi."

"I'm used to having no one. It's not a big deal."

"Yes, it is. Everyone should have someone they can turn to, even if it's just one person." Her face turns sad, but I don't want her to feel sorry for me.

"Hey, I survive." I shrug again before I reach between us and find her hand. My fingers slide between hers and I hold on, loosely at first. I hold my breath thinking she's going to reject me, but to my surprise she tightens her fingers around my hand.

"Well, you have us now," our gaze's clash. "You have me." The thought of having Luna as a friend makes me feel something other than the normal feelings of wanting a friend, and we smile at each other.

"I'd like that." A cute blush appears in Luna's cheeks.

"Thank you." She sighs and shifts her gaze into her lap where our hands are still joined.

Enjoying her comfort, I release her hand to put my arm around her shoulders. She inches closer until there's no gap between us, and we sit for what feels like hours just watching, not saying anything to each other, and the only sounds around are in the distance.

But the time to leave comes around way too quickly. I almost pussy out and decide not to, but I know I need to go. If I don't, I'll never go and I'll be leaving my mom at his mercy, but even with that thought bouncing around in my mind, I still don't move.

We've been sat here for around an hour. It's not until I hear my name that I take my arm from around Luna, and I look up. Luna's dad is leaning against the wall of the clubhouse smoking a cigarette, watching us. I jump to my feet as he motions with his hand, calling me over. Our quiet time is over. I run over to the club President to see what he wants. If I want to be like one of these guys, I need to get used to answering to him.

DUSK IS FALLING as I make my way home, and everything runs over in my mind. The way I told them so easily about my home life, the way Luna, someone I've literally just met, made me feel so different to anyone else I've ever met. I've never connected to another person the way I do her.

We live in the second house along, so as I turn onto my block, I can see our house, but my steps falter at the sound of shouting, a woman screaming so loud it sounds like she's being murdered or something. My feet begin to move quicker when I realize it's my mom screaming, I break into a sprint until I reach the door and push down on the handle, barging through it. But I stop dead when I see her in a heap. "Mom?"

"Where the fuck have you been?" Dad roars, stopping me in my tracks. Before I can help her, he's grabbing me by the shirt and dragging me up until his face is in mine. His whisky smelling breath stings my nose, and I turn my face away, swallowing and gritting my teeth as hard as I can to try to be brave. "I asked you a fucking question!"

"Nothing to do with you." I fire back, so much hate staring back at the man that helped to put me on this earth. I don't want to be weak against him, I want to be strong. Why can't I just stand up to him, that's what you have to do with bullies, right? If you stand up to them, they back down. My back slams against the wall and my breath leaves my body in a sharp gasp. As he releases me, I slide down the wall and drop to the ground with a thud, urging my lungs to work. As the breath begins to filter through my organs, I scramble onto my knees, hoping to get to Mom before he can stop me, but his fingers wrap around my foot and he tugs hard, yanking me back. My palms plant to the carpet, hoping to get something to grip to but it's useless. He flips me over. My teeth grit as I wait for the impact of the first punch coming towards me, and I take it. My face feels like it's about to cave in on itself, my eye feeling like it's going pop, and with my eyes shut tightly, I don't see the one after.

"Where the fuck have you been." He shouts, thinking I'm going to tell him now. "Tell me or I'm going to beat you so fucking bad, you'll be drinking through a straw." He screams in my face.

My eyes open, and I look directly into his, seeing the

hatred that simmers there, then I think fuck him, and say it slowly. "I hid at the biker yard."

He rears back slightly then narrows his eyes. "You think those pussies can protect you?" I don't answer, I can't because as much as they said to tell them, I don't know if they will. "I'm your father, I can do whatever the fuck I like. If I want to punish you, I will." With my shirt tightened in his fist, he drags the top half of my body up.

"Then do it, I'm not scared of you anymore." I fire back in a quiet tone. He laughs, but it's not a good laugh, it's one of those that speaks so many words. His fist connects with my nose, wetness building inside, my nose immediately blocking, and unable to breathe through it. It's then I feel the trickle of blood that leaks from my nostril. Dad sneers but I don't say or do anything as he hits me again. He rains punches down on my face and body. I'm numb, I hear Mom screaming at him to leave me alone, but he doesn't listen. He never listens. One blunt strike leads into another, and by the time he's done, I'm in too much pain to move.

I don't remember making the way to my room. I don't even remember getting into my bed but as I wake up, Mom is lying next to me, asleep. She probably took more than the recommended dose to numb the pain after she crawled to my room. Her face is puffy with cuts, her eyes black and her lip split. Tears fill my eyes but I'm too weak to stop them.

Why can't I be stronger.

Why can't I be like those bikers.

I just want to protect my mom.

With that thought, I drag my aching body up to sit in the bed, careful not to wake her, and move my hand to cradle my ribs as I gently leave my bed.

I refuse to be weak anymore.

CHAPTER SEVEN

Levi

IT'S BEEN a week since I left Luna and the clubhouse, but every time that I look in the mirror, I'm reminded of the promise I made about letting them know when he hurt me again, only I couldn't. I couldn't shake off the feeling that I was weak, that I let him beat me again. I let him hurt the woman that gave birth to me, the one who has tried to keep me safe all these years. Dad's right when he tells me that I'm not big enough, but one day I will be, and when that day comes, he'll need to watch his back.

The swelling on my face has started to go down, but there is still some bruising around my eyes and a cut across my nose, but honestly, my body hurts more than my face. It aches, it hurts to breathe and every time I move, I'm in agony. On top of that, my ribs are still black. If I'd gone to the emergency department, I think they would have told me that I may have broken something, but I couldn't risk that, they'd investigate and would take me away from my mother, so instead I've stayed hidden away, either in my room, or in Mom's room tending to her.

That piece of shit hasn't been here much for the last few days, so Mom and I have had a reprieve. When he is here, we don't speak, and Mom doesn't get out of bed. We've managed to look after ourselves and each other. I wished he'd leave for good, but we're not that lucky.

After a week of not seeing Luna, I kind of miss her. I don't know how I got so attached to her in such a short space of time, but I have. I've never got close to anyone, or wanted to, never told them my deepest, darkest secret either.

"You alright, Mom?" I ask from the doorway of her bedroom. She barely wants to get out of bed now, she's a shell.

"Oh, my boy, come here." Her head rolls my way as she reaches out for me, she tries to smile but there's nothing to smile for. I get that. I push from the doorway to cross the room and perch myself on the edge of the bed. Her hand holds mine as I look into eyes that are so like my own and every feeling, every emotion finds its way into my soul. I'm angry he can do this. I'm sad that my mother has come to be this person because of one man, she used to be so full of energy and life, and I'm hurt that I have to watch it happen, time and time again. "I love you, Levi."

"I love you, Mom." My brows pull together, but I don't question it.

"Are you feeling, okay?" She asks, causing me to frown.

"Don't worry about me, I'm good."

"Oh baby, you're so strong. You know I'm proud of you, right?" I nod but I don't feel much like I deserve it right now. "I am. You will always make me proud, no matter where you are or what you do, but remember you'll always be my baby. My boy."

"I know, Mom. How are you, are you still hurting?"

She nods, "Yeah, could you pass me those pills, sweetheart." I reach across and grab the bottle, her antidepressants. I wish I could get her to come off them, but I know she won't. She's hooked on them now; I don't think she could stop if she wanted to.

Sighing, I pass them to her, "You know Mom, maybe you should try and cut down on these. For me?"

My gaze finds hers, and her sadness is clear when a tear rolls down her cheek. I gently brush it away, "I'll try, sweetheart." I get the water so she can take her pills then place it back on the nightstand when she's done. I move around to the other side of the bed and lie beside her; she reaches out for me and lays her head on my shoulder and gets herself comfy. We lie there in silence, just the sound of our breathing filling the emptiness of the cold room. Once I know she's fast asleep, I take the duvet in my tight grip and drag it up to her chin, carefully cradling her head and lay it on the pillow.

Before I leave, I pause at her bedside. It's my birthday tomorrow. I'll be sixteen, but as I look at her, I wonder to myself if she'll be alert enough to even remember the day, let alone the actual date. The day she brought me into the world. The day when I had no idea what kind of person I was being born to. I swipe angrily at the wetness that has collected beneath my eyes, unshed tears blurring my visions and breathe.

With one last look at my mom, and a kiss on her cheek, I tell her I love her one more time, hoping she can hear me. Once I know she's warm and covered up, I leave her side and make my way out.

—————

I'M a little apprehensive by the time I reach the club gates, my stomach is churning with nerves. I wasn't sure if they'd still welcome me since I haven't been around for the last week, and when they see my face they'll know why, then they'll realize that I didn't trust them enough to tell them. Shit is fucked up.

The padlock on the gate is locked when I try to open it. I promised I wouldn't climb the fence again, and with no way of getting in touch with the guys or even Luna, I guess I'll just have to stand here and wait. I drop my ass to the ground and lean my back against the wire fence, waiting patiently.

I'm not sure how long I've waited, but when the fence rattles behind me. My head twists around to see Reaper standing behind me.

"Fuck, look at your face man." I move to my feet as he unlocks the gate and opens it for me to go in.

"Thanks," I reply sarcastically with a smirk, and enter the compound.

"Do you want to talk about it?" Reaper asks after locking the gate again and catching up with me.

"Nope." I reply curtly, but I don't mean to. His side eye burns away like a laser aimed at my face; I know he has questions. I know I'll have to tell them eventually, but right now I don't want to talk about it. Silence falls between us as he leads me through the compound, his fingers flying over the keyboard on his cell as he messages someone. I stop as I reach the door of the clubhouse to wait for him. I'm not courageous enough to go in by myself yet. I don't know them all.

"Come on," he says passing me and leading me inside. "let's get the Doc to take a look at ya."

"I'm good." My feet stop dead, and I refuse to go any further.

Reaper spins around to me and snorts, "You're not good. I saw the way you got up from the ground." he huffs, "Look, I've had a beating. I know how your body feels after one, so you can either come with me to see Doc, or we can go to Pres, and then you won't have a choice." He drops the ultimatum on me, knowing I'll follow him, fuck.

We pass the bar and head through to the hall and start down it, passing rooms as we go. Turning the corner, we walk further on until we reach the end and Reaper knocks on the last door. As a voice comes from the other side, Reaper opens it up letting me go in first. A guy sporting a well-trimmed beard, and well-kept short hair is in the room, but when I see him wearing a cut, I'm a little confused. "The doctor is a biker." I ask.

"He's one of the brothers." Reaper answers as the doctor answers at the same time.

"I am indeed. What can I do for you?"

Reaper glances at me before turning back to Doc. "He's had a beating. Can you look at him for me?"

"Yeah," There's hesitation in his voice. "Sit down, mate. Reaper, does Pres know you're bringing strays into the club?"

"Yes. Pres knows him."

"Okay then... so little buddy, do you want to tell me where you got these cuts and nice shiny bruises from." I'm so done with hiding what happens to me that I blurt it right out.

"Yeah, my dad is a piece of shit."

"Jesus, fuck," He curses, a more solemn tone to his voice now, "Okay, tip your head back." His hands are firm on my face as he looks at my injuries pressing his thumbs lightly to the bridge of my nose. It hurts and my teeth grit, "Yeah, all this bruising should go eventually, there's a nasty cut across your nose, and from the feel of it, it's broken. Do you want me to try and straighten it? I'm not sure it'll be perfect, but I can try." I don't hesitate as I answer yes. He gets a firmer grip and presses hard, the bone crunching beneath his fingers. The pain sears through my face as I bare down on my teeth again and tense, with a growl coming from the back of my throat. My hands ball into fists as I squeeze tightly and swallow down the pain. Pain is my friend. It's familiar. As he releases me, sharp pain shoots back through my nose and face, making the breath heave from my chest. "You alright?" I nod, closing my eyes, "Okay, I want you to take these, they'll help." He drops two tablets into my hand, I look at them like they're foreign.

"I don't want them."

"Your face is going to ache and hurt without them, buddy."

"I can take it. I've taken worse. I don't do pills."

"Okay." Doc soothes, I give them him back and pull off my shirt.

"Can you take a look at these though for me?"

"Fuck man, I thought your face was bad." Doc exclaims, sucking sharply through his teeth. His fingers trail over my ribs, then he turns me around tracing his rough hands over my back and kidneys. "Right, sit back down." I do as he asks, Reaper has been quiet through all of this, and if I hadn't seen him leaning against the wall, I would think he had already left. The doc presses his fingers against my ribs, and

I shout out, biting down again on my teeth. My fingers gripping the edge of the chair every time he touches them. "It looks to me like you have a couple of broken ribs, but I'd say you got off pretty lucky."

"Thanks," My sarcasm really is out there today. "I don't feel too lucky."

"What's your name, dude?"

"Levi," I reply, still breathing through the pain he's put me in,

"Well, Levi, I'd say you're made of strong stuff. There are guys that would've been in hospital with this. When did it happen?"

"Last week." I answer sheepishly, knowing Reaper is behind me.

"Last week?" the doc repeats,

"Yeah, six or seven days ago," I say quite blasé about it all.

"Right, hold your shirt up if you can." With my good arm I inch it up further, but I struggle to grip it with the pain in my side. "Reap, come help." He comes over and holds my tee up while Doc goes to fetch something. When he turns back to us, I see bandages in his hand. "Right then, I can't do much for broken ribs, they need to heal on their own, but I can help them on their way. I'm going to strap up your ribs, but it needs to be kept tight, and you need to keep it on, and we'll check them again in two weeks." I thank him for his help. In fact, I'm so thankful to all these guys for welcoming me into their club and treating me like one of their own. He wipes an anti-bacterial wipe across my nose to clean up the scab that has already formed and then sticks some tape across it. "Okay, you're done. You need to rest those ribs."

"Thank you."

"No problem, bud." He smiles at me, and with a half a smile back, I turn for the door.

Just as Reaper and I are leaving, I see the darkness of Luna's hair swish at the end of the hall. "You, okay?" Reaper asks and I answer quietly, Luna spins on her heels and her eyes widen when she sees me, making her way quickly toward me.

"You came back. Oh, my goodness I didn't think you would." She stops dead in front of me when she sees my face. "What the hell?" She exclaims, her hand covering her mouth in shock.

"I'm good." I guess I can say that until I'm blue in the face, but I bet they won't believe me.

"Lune, he's been to see Doc. He'll be alright. He patched him up."

"I've been so worried. When you didn't come back, I thought that was it, and after what you said about your scumbag dad, I didn't know what to think." She throws her arms around my neck, her head resting against mine as she sighs softly. She takes her arms from around my neck and puts a gap between us and as she does. I see the worry lines creasing her forehead. "So can you hang out?"

Answering her question, a little too quickly she smiles. I've missed that smile. She takes my hand and leads me away, with a small tug on her hand she stops, and I turn around to Reaper. "Thanks for helping me," he lifts his chin, appraising me, "catch you later?"

"Sure, dude." He gives me a chin lift and I smirk before turning back to Luna and let her lead me out into the club-house. With a diversion to the kitchen for food and a soda, we head outside of the compound, back to where we were the last time I was here.

"Were you really worried?" I ask her as we finish our sandwich.

"Yes. I kept asking Reaper if you'd been by, I've pissed my dad off by asking questions, thinking you had and none of them were telling me the truth."

"Why did it piss off your old man?"

"Because Levi, I'm the president's daughter. I'm off limits. And honestly, the only other guy around my age is Reaper, and he's like an irritating brother." Her eyes find mine as I turn my head to face her, looking directly into the luxury of her brown eyes, but something tells me she doesn't want to think of me as a brother. And I guess since I'm not really a part of the club those rules don't apply to me.

Taking her hand in mine, I rub my thumb across her knuckles and breathe as her teeth capture her lip. My gaze roams over her pretty face, "What if I said I liked you, Luna?"

She lifts her shoulder and lets it drop, "How about if I said I liked you back?"

Smiling I lick my lips, "So what if I said I'd like to kiss you."

She looks around us and brings her gaze back to mine, and something sparks in her eyes. I can't decipher what though. "I'd say, go on then."

My heartbeat quickens in my chest, my mouth dries as I swallow. Before I can change my mind, or talk myself out of it, I take her chin between my finger and thumb in a soft grasp, pulling her lip from her teeth and hesitantly, I press my lips to hers. Confidence isn't my strongest point, but I let my feelings do the talking. As my lips press firmer to hers, she moves her hands to my shoulders and mine cup her face, then I kiss her.

Heavy gasps leave both our lips as we part, but we don't

look away. "It's my birthday tomorrow, will you spend the day with me?"

"I'd love to." She smiles wide and joins our fingers as we sit in silence again. Just enjoying each other's company.

CHAPTER EIGHT

Levi

THE HOUSE IS quiet when I get up. I don't think Dad came home, because I can't hear his resonating snore that thunders through the house after a drunken session. That means I don't have to tiptoe around the house, worried I'll wake him up, which then leads to another caning. Even that couldn't ruin my mood today though. It's my sixteenth birthday, and I get to spend it with Luna.

All I've thought about all night is her.

I wash as quickly as possible since I can't shower because of my bandages, I need someone else to put them back on for me, and I don't have anyone to do that. Then I dress as quickly as I'm able in some dark jeans and a white tee.

Once I'm ready, I splash some cologne on my face that Mom bought me at Christmas and go into her room. I tap softly on her door, my hand wraps around the doorknob and I hear her, "Come in." My brows pinch at the sound of her voice, and I peer around the door as I open it. She's sitting up in bed looking toward the door. "Ah sweetheart, are you alright?"

"Are you?" I ask hesitantly, I'm confused. For weeks she's either been crying or out cold on her antidepressants, sleeping like she's in a coma.

"Oh, don't worry about me. I have something for you, though." A nervous smile tips her lips, and she goes into the drawer in the nightstand. Whatever it is, it's in a small gift bag. "Happy birthday, sweetheart."

"You remembered," I say as I take the bag from her, scared to even be happy.

"Oh, my boy, of course I remembered. You're only sixteen once. I know…" tears fill her eyes, and she licks her lips, "I know I've been a little out of it, but I'm alright." Her head nods reassuring me, "Open your present."

Looking between her eager eyes and her shaky hands, I look inside. "What's this?"

"It was your grandfathers. He always wanted you to have it when you were old enough." my gaze lifts to the smile on her face. "It was his grandfathers before him. He met you when you were a baby. I think you were six months old when he died. He had cancer."

"How come you've never told me about him."

"Your father and him didn't get along. But this is yours. Treasure it." I look at the tarnished gold pocket watch, then turn it over and see the back engraved with words. "Love Pops."

As I look back up, I smile at her. She seems so with it considering she's been so out of it on her meds. I'm still confused, but I'm rolling with it. "I love you, Mom." I lean forward and pull her into a hug.

"Oh, baby I love you. But please go and enjoy your day, and don't let anyone or anything ruin it for you. Do you hear?" I nod into her neck, unshed tears in my eyes threaten to fall, but I blink them back.

"Okay." I agree smiling wide. Happy she's coherent, and even happier that she's remembered what today is. Seeing her like this tells me that no matter how much he's tried to break her spirit, my mom is stronger. Moving my arms around her neck, I hug her tightly, holding on to her like she's going to disappear from my grasp. Her arms slide around my sore ribs, but I bite back my pain for this. I could never hurt when my mom is like this.

"So," she rears back slightly, "how are you spending your birthday?" As my arms fall from around her neck, we sit side by side on the edge of the bed.

"I've met a girl."

"Really," she smiles through the tears in her eyes and slowly they trickle down her face.

"Yeah, her name is Luna. We're spending the day together."

"Oh, is she pretty?" Feeling a little embarrassed, my head dips but I nod my answer. "You deserve the best, sweetheart. Now give me a kiss and get going." Smiling, I lift my head and kiss her cheek like she asks. "Be a gentleman and don't keep her waiting."

A smile tugs at my lips, "Get some rest, Mom. I'll be back later." She rests her head on her pillow.

"Enjoy yourself, that's all I want you to do." As I head for the door, I look back over my shoulder, squeezing the pocket watch in the palm of my hand and smile, kissing my fingers and blowing it to her. "Love you."

"Love you, too." With a small wave I turn and leave her

bedroom, and rush down the stairs, through the house, before shoving my feet into my trainers. I pick up my house keys from the table, then tug open the front door. My elation soon turns to anger though when I see his car pulling up outside.

As the engine turns off my body turns to stone, I can't make my feet move. My pulse picks up, but I can't be scared anymore. I square my shoulders and stare back at him, no fidgeting of my hands or twitching in my eye. I pull in a breath and move from the step as he gets out of the car. `As the door slams, I flinch slightly. He sniggers as he makes his way up the path. I cut across the path away from him, "Where the fuck you are going?" He asks bluntly.

"Out." My answer is sharp, but I don't give a shit.

"Where's out?"

"To spend time with someone that cares about me. Someone who knows it's my fucking birthday, so screw you." I sneer, shoving my hands into my pockets, making my way down the sidewalk. I'm not answering to that piece of shit anymore. I walk a little faster to get where I need to be, my walking pace soon turning to a jog until I'm just meters away from the clubhouse. I stop when I see Luna on the other side of the fence. I smile and jog the rest of the way to her. She looks happy as she opens the gate, welcoming me, and we walk in together. "Hey," I greet her.

"Hey, to you." She answers as she turns to stand in front of me. "Happy birthday, Levi." As I smile, I feel my whole face do the same, she makes me feel happy, something I've never fully felt. Her lips brush my cheek tenderly, but she takes them away as quickly as she put them there, but I'll feel that small kiss for hours as my cheek tingles. She links her arm around mine and we start walking through the compound. "I've got something for you."

"You didn't have to do that." She spins and places her back against the door of the clubhouse.

"It's your sixteenth," she shrugs and smirks, licking her lips, "you deserve something."

"Spending it with you, is more than I could ever ask for."

"You're sweet." A blush fills her cheeks, I realize then that I can't get enough of that look. "Come on. You're going to love it." Before she turns back to the door, she grips my hand tightly and pulls me inside behind her. As I step inside though the place has been decorated with banners and balloons. I get a little choked up inside. No one, and I mean no one, has ever done this for me.

"Wow. You did his for me?" I ask, looking directly into her big brown eyes.

"Of course, I did. I don't see anyone else here that's sixteen today."

I get a handle on myself before I look like a pussy and start crying in front of Luna and big bad bikers, then with my hands on her shoulders, I smile, "Thank you, Luna." I tug her against my body and hold her tight, expressing my gratitude the best way I can in front of all these guys. The guys I've already met are here, Snake, Popeye and Doc. Reaper is here and then Pres walks in, a box wrapped up in his hand.

"Happy birthday, kid." He hands the box over and nods as I smile at him.

"Thanks, Pres." His eyes light up when I call him by his title. It feels so good, like I'm part of something. Even though I have no real place here, in my own mind, I've found it.

"Well, open it then." He exclaims with a smirk. "Damn kid, Luna would have had that torn open already, what you are waiting for?" My eyes roll as I tear the paper from the rectangle box. A picture of an iPhone stares back at me.

"Seriously?" I lift my gaze from the cell to Pres, "this is for me?"

"Yeah, seriously. Now there's no worrying about that bastard you call dad. If he lays another finger on you, you ring one of us. If you don't know how to use it, I'm sure Reaper or Luna will help."

"I don't know what to say. I guess, thank you." A booming laugh comes from Pres. I open the box and take out the shiny black, brand-new iPhone and turn it on.

"You can have all of our numbers just in case, now come talk to me." Pres says. He walks over to the corner of the room; I follow him, and I stop in front of him.

"Pres?" I question as he tips my head back, paying close attention to my face.

"How is it?" He's talking about my nose.

"It's not too bad."

"And your ribs." Pres asks, eyeing me carefully.

"Hurting, but Doc said they would."

"If you need him to check you over, you go, alright." I agree with him in an instant, "now let's get this party started." He slides an arm around me, "I mean it's not the normal kind of party we have here, but I guess I can make allowances," he cocks his head smirking as I lift a brow, "since it's your birthday and all." He smirks back at me and leads me back toward the others.

"Now give the birthday boy a beer." Pres shouts.

After Popeye brings the beer over to me, I argue with myself over whether I should drink it. I don't want to turn into my dad. If I start drinking, will I be like him? I toy with the bottle, picking at the label that wraps around it. "What's wrong?" Reaper asks, which gets Pres's attention.

"I don't want it." I shrug.

"Drink it, it's your birthday, it's just a beer." Pres reassures me.

I sigh and place it on the table. "I don't want to turn into him. What if I turn into him?"

"Hey, kid. One beer doesn't turn you into an abusive cunt. That's something that's already there, it just takes a trigger. You'll never be like him, I promise." I nod at Pres, but still, I'm not too sure. "I promise you Levi, I won't let you turn into a bag of shit like him. You have us now."

My shoulders sag, and lifting the bottle to my mouth, I take a sip, the tangy, wheat taste is foreign on my tongue, but I swallow it down anyway. "We'll teach you how to be a man, we've got your back, kid."

Luna doesn't leave my side all day. We eat, sit and talk; we laugh watching the guys drinking and having fun. There's a couple of women hanging around in short skirts and low-cut tops, not my type, but I don't even know my type. As I look at Luna though, something tells me that she is my type. She's the only girl I want to look at. And when her dad has left the room with one of those women on his arm, I take her face in my hand and kiss her, she kisses me back with as much gentleness as I give her. God, this girl.

I have another couple of beers as the day goes on but nothing too much. As much as I believed what Pres said to me earlier, I don't think I could drink much more of it. I ended up sleeping in Reapers room, only this time I took the floor, well after a solid discussion with him anyway.

Banging on the door the next morning wakes me. The sun is shining through the window, right onto my face. As my eyes open, they squint at the sunbeams, and I lift my aching and still sore body from the makeshift bed to open the door. I smile at Luna's fresh face as she stands before me. "Morning." I don't answer, I just nod my head. "Fancy some breakfast?" she asks as I smile back. If you're going to get me to do anything, use food.

"Yeah, I'm starving."

"Reaper?" Luna calls out and a grunt comes from under the bedding. "Ugh, Let's leave him." She says, 'he'll find us," and turns back to go out of the room. Grabbing my new cell, I slide it into my pocket, and we go through to the main room and into the kitchen, asking Kerry to cook us something.

Once we've finished, I push the plate away from me and drink my soda before looking across at Luna. "I'll have to go home soon. I need to check up on my mom."

"Can I come with you?" she asks quietly.

I breathe softly, noting the desperation in her eyes, "I don't think that's the best idea. If he's there and he kicks off it's not going to be pretty."

"Dude. I'm a biker's daughter. Do you not know that I'm badass?"

Holding her hand in her lap, I chuckle. "I know you're a badass, but if he hurts you as well, I can't protect you." The pretty smile falls from her face then her head dips. I lift it back up with my fingers beneath her chin, "Thank you, but I can't risk it." She nods in agreement, thank goodness, but looks like she's about to say something else. "What?"

"Take Reaper with you then. You can't go on your own." Just to appease her I agree. Maybe I have found my place after all.

REAPER WALKS by my side as we make the journey here. We've talked about everything, his job as a prospect, and what that means. My parents, and the piece of shit that is my flesh and blood. Pres... But then I did something completely out of character; I told him about Mom. How she's addicted to meds, how he beats the shit out of her too. He bit back the anger he felt. I could see it swimming in his eyes. Then, with a rare smile, when I think of her, I also told him about yesterday, how she remembered it was my birthday, and I showed him the watch she gave me. In fact, I can still see her smiling face in my head.

The house soon comes into view and my whole attitude changes. My body tenses when I see his car sitting at the curbside as we reach the house, but I take a deep breath and carry on. I'm just here to see my mom, check on her and leave. If I keep using that mantra, maybe I can get in and out of here without ending up with another beating and more bruises.

"You okay, dude?"

"I'm good," I look at Reaper. He's fast become a friend, someone who will stand beside me, "Thanks." I leave him at the bottom of the path and push my key into the door. "I won't be long." I try the handle and the door opens. The house is quiet, so I walk in quietly. Maybe he's pissed again and asleep. The number of times he's been pissed and fast asleep, any shithead could've walked into this house and burgled it while he was out of his head. He didn't give a shit.

I peer around door of the living room to see him in his chair, his upper body leaning forward with a cigarette in one hand and as I look around him, I find a bottle of scotch hanging from his fingers. My teeth clench together as I wonder what I'm about to walk into, but he doesn't say anything. He turns his head slightly to glance over his shoulder at me. I stand firm, ready for whatever he's about to throw at me, but nothing comes. Without saying a word to him, I back out of the door and take the stairs two at a time.

Her back is to me when I open the door. "Mom." I call out, but nothing. When I left her yesterday and she was talking to me, I guess I thought she would still be like that today. My heart sinks when I realize she's out of it. So instead, I cross the room, move her hair from her face and lean over to kiss her head. Snatching my head back I look more closely, "Mom?" She doesn't even a twitch at the sound of my voice. My heart beats like crazy in my chest, pumping blood quickly around my body until my ears feel like they're going to burst. My gaze darts from the bed to the nightstand, my fingers itching to shake her, but the lack of movement has me scared to touch her. Water fills my eyes when I see the pill bottle...empty.

My breath comes in spurts, fast, irregular. I can't control it. my heart pounding as I reach for the bottle and lift it up, I want to prove to myself that there's nothing in there. My chin trembles before I let out a cry, squeezing the bottle hard in my fingers, and clutching it in my fist. With rough spurts of breath filtering in through my nose and my jaw tight, I reach for the bedding. I'm hesitant to see what I already know I'm going to find. My mouth is as dry as a bone, I barely have any saliva to spit, let alone to swallow past the huge boulder that's formed in my throat. I attempt to steady my breathing, grip the sheet in my fingers and with a shaky hand, I inch it back slowly.

My stomach churns. I feel sick as tears finally slide down my face. Lifting my fingers to her face, her lips are blue and she's as pale as the white sheets on the bed, her skin cold to the touch. Eventually, as it hits home fully, I break. A strangled cry pouring from me as I grieve for the person that loved me so unconditionally, nurtured me, loved me... leaning over her, I hug her but there's nothing. She doesn't hug me back; she isn't able to tell me she loves me. I cry for her, call her name... nothing.

I just want to see her smile, but I'll never see that again.

My mom has gone.

She's left me, but what's more, she's left this shitty place to be in a better one. How can I deny her of that after everything she did for me?

She wasn't so strong after all, is all I can think...he broke her.

I'm not sure how long I've been up here, sitting on the bed, my knees pulled into my chest just watching her. It's crazy how a person can look so peaceful in death, that makes me cry even harder. Stuttered breaths heave from my lungs when I realize my cell is ringing in my pocket. I pull it out to see Reaper's name flashing up on my screen but push it back in my pocket again. I kiss Mom's head one last time and get up. Anger sears through my blood as my hands curl into fists. That bastard has been sitting downstairs while my mother has lay dead in her bed. My lip curls and my body shakes. I'll fucking kill him.

I take the stairs quickly and jump down the last few before barging into the living room. He's still clutching that fucking bottle of Whisky in his hand. "What have you done? You fucking killed her!" I kick the bottle from his fingers.

"I didn't do anything, she killed her fucking self!" he stands up, slightly unsteady on his feet, so I take advantage and kick him. He drops into the chair before springing back up, a little too quickly for an alcoholic that's probably been swigging Whisky for fuck knows how long.

"You fucking did this. Did you know she was dead. Did

you know? Did you help her. Did you feed them to her?" I fire questions but I don't give him time to answer them. "I should kill you where you fucking stand. You took her from me." I'm so incensed and filled with rage I don't see his hand fly towards me, he smacks me up the face and grabs me around my throat.

"You haven't got her to rescue you now, you little cunt." His fingers are tight, squeezing me, "What you got to say now?"

"I'm going to fucking kill you one day." I snarl in his face.

A door slams off the wall, "Fuck." I look over my father's shoulder to see Reaper. He puts his cell to his ear and relays my address down the receiver. "Put him down."

I scratch at his fingers to get him to release me. "Your little friend isn't going to help you." He sneers, throwing me to the floor. I cry out in pain as my back hits the ground, the pain doubling from my already broken ribs and bruises. "You're just fucking weak. You're not even worth the fucking effort."

Suddenly, and in no time whatsoever, the sound of bikes reaches my ears, it's so familiar to me now, it's like a comfort. The engines quieten, and before I know it five or six bikers are filling the room. Pres shouting to get me out of there. Doc comes over and helps me up. "Come on, bud, let's get you out of here."

As we make our way to the door I stop and look at Pres. "My mom's dead." I tell Doc but then say it louder for everyone to hear. "He let her die." I swipe the wetness from my face, "he took her away from me." I stay long enough to see Pres throw a punch toward him, it connects with his nose, and it explodes across his face. A small amount of satisfaction seeps into my body, and I smile.

"Take him out, Doc." Pres bellows.

Once I'm outside, I break, my knees buckle, and I hit the grass beneath me and cry for everything he put us through. I cry because finally she's at peace and out of this shit fucking life.

CHAPTER NINE

Levi
<u>One year later</u>

I'VE THOUGHT a lot about my mom over the last year. I have so many things I want to tell her and there's so many things that she's missed in my life, I just hope she's happier where she is now. I miss her with all my heart, but honestly, she's better off. It's taken a lot for me to admit that.

I don't think I'll ever get the sound of sirens out of my head; they rang in my ears for days after. Paramedics and police rushed in and out of the house after Doc checked her and rang the emergency services. Reaper stayed with me as they took her out, a sheet placed strategically over her body and face so I couldn't see. The cops questioned Pres, Doc, Reaper, and me. Eventually, they determined it was suicide, no matter how many times I told them he drove her to it, there was no foul play. My trust in the justice system was gone. I was failed. Instead, they allowed him to walk free. One day, karma will find that son of a bitch.

It was only a few days after finding her that we held her

funeral. The MC footed the bill, said it was their responsibility now. Pres might not have been my legal guardian, but he said she deserved something special. I'll admit that it made me cry. It was all I ever wanted, but I didn't allow Dad to come to the funeral, and two of the guys stood guard to make sure he didn't try and get in on it. It took me a while to come to terms with the knowledge that she's gone, and that I couldn't save her. I couldn't help her no matter what I did or even tried to do. It was hard. What was harder was that, on the day of my birthday, she seemed so much more put together. Should I have stayed at home that day? Maybe, maybe not. But it'll be something I'll always question.

Luna and the MC have been so good for me. They've stood by me, and they've taught me so much. I know I'm a stronger person now than I ever was back then, I'm not so quiet either, you could say I've come out of my shell, and I've bulked up a bit. I've been working out with Reaper and Popeye. Pres has even taught me how to ride.

While I'm stuck inside my head, thinking about my life, I didn't realize the brothers had started coming out into the yard, at least not until I see Luna jogging excitedly toward me.

"What's got you looking so happy?" My chin lifts at the girl who saved me. She greets me with a wide smile before nibbling on her lip. "What's going on?"

"It's a surprise, you need to cover your eyes." After my upbringing I'm a little wary but I look into her eyes and relent. I have a strong urge to kiss her right out here on the compound, Pres would kick my ass, but I don't care. It's no secret that we like each other, we have done since we met, but her words always come back to me, *"I'm the president's daughter, I'm off limits to everyone."* I always thought that didn't apply to me, but I've never tested the theory, well apart from a kiss, but we were only fifteen. Breathing softly, I capture her chin between my fingers and tip her head back slightly, an adorable blush fills her cheeks as she licks her lips, and I smile just about to test the waters... "One day Lu, one day."

"Luna," Pres shouts, and she jumps away from me suddenly. "Cover his eyes."

"Not a fucking chance." I shout back, but Pres just chuckles and nods at Luna. Within seconds, she's jumping on my back and covering my eyes with her hands.

"Don't let go of him."

"You need to turn around." Luna whispers against my ear, so I do as she asks and hold on to her sliding my hands up her bare thighs, wanting to go even further. It is my birthday after all.

My head turns to the side, my cheek softly resting against the softness of hers and I whisper, "I've always wanted to know what it feels like to have your legs wrapped around me." I hear the sharp gasp she makes, and a smirk tugs one side of my mouth up. Bringing her long legs higher around my waist, my hips in a vice-like grip between her thighs. It feels fucking good, though. If nothing else happens for my birthday, this will be at the front of my memory. I squeeze her thighs slightly and rub my thumbs across her skin. "One day Lulu, you'll be mine."

"You wish." She giggles.

"No, that's a promise."

An engine rumbling lowly pricks my ears up, but it's nothing new so I take no notice, only of the girl wrapped around me, but then heightening sound of chatter gets my attention. The brothers are like women, gossiping when they get the chance. Pussies.

"Come here, kid." I hear Pres as Luna jumps down from my back. I feel the loss of her instantly and as Luna comes around me, she nods her head. All the brothers are standing in a crowd, I high five each of them and as I push through, I see Reaper standing by a Harley. I look from Reaper to Pres.

"What's this?"

Pres looks amused. "Well, I know you had a hard childhood, but I don't think I need to tell you what it is."

"You know what I mean."

Pres slips an arm around my shoulder. "Happy birthday, kid," he smiles, "annnd..." he says, and turns around to someone behind him. Luna pops her head through to the front, smiling excitedly. As he turns around again my gaze falls on a cut in his hands, just like the others. He then shows me the back, the brothers of Sin logo is there along with the word Prospect. My eyes go wide, I can't seem to shift the stupid grin from my face. In the middle of my shock, I shake Pres' hand like the man I've been taught to be, but then emotion overcomes me, and I pull him against me, slapping his back in a hug. I just can't believe it.

All the brothers shake my hand and say happy birthday, congratulating me on making Prospect, then I turn back to Pres to thank him again. Promising him that I won't let him down. Reaper looks as happy as me as he comes over, the last to congratulate me, and the one brother to hug me. If I ever had a biological brother, I'd want him to be like Reaper. Before I know it, Luna is throwing herself at me. I catch her as she falls against me and flings her arms around my neck, "I'm so happy for you. Happy birthday." She squeals.

Here arms are tight around my neck, and with my lips at her ear, I make her a promise, "No one will ever hurt you while I'm around." I leave a tender kiss on her cheek. My lips linger longer than they should before she breaks our embrace. I shake off the heat of Pres's stare and turn to my bike, throwing my leg over and sitting on the seat, then slip on my cut admiring the beauty beneath me.

I HAVEN'T THOUGHT of my shithead father for months, I've tried to forget he even existed, but every now and then, that day comes back to me like a movie still. The day he had his comeuppance still gives me a flutter of satisfaction, but it's still not enough. I felt good knowing that I never have to go back there, never see his fucking face again if I don't have to or suffer at his hands again. That's something I didn't think would ever happen soon.

That day, I might have felt satisfaction at seeing him hurt from the beating the brothers gave him, but I also lost something. I lost a piece of my heart. My precious mother couldn't take anymore, and that kills me more than anything. That morsel of emotion chips away in my head. But my brothers and Luna keep me levelheaded and that's something I can be thankful for.

NO ONE UNDERSTANDS the meaning of family until they've been through something. Walking on eggshells isn't a normal, everyday thing, hoping you don't piss them off in case you get another beating, that's not a home. Who says that it's only people that share the same blood who are family? Sometimes, blood relatives are the worst ones. My blood took away the one person from this world who was kind and loving. No, my family are the ones that chose me for who I am.

He never loved us, he hurt and abused us, and maybe one day karma will catch up with him, but patience is a virtue, or so mom used to tell me. Maybe, maybe not. But I've finally found my place. I found a new family.

My home.

My brothers.

No one will ever hurt me again.

THE END

ACKNOWLEDGMENTS

Right then, this isn't going to be long but just a few words to thank Francessca Wingfield for everything she does for me. I joined her Creative Writing Corner back in December/January time, since then Fran and the rest of the writing corner ladies have been such a big help, they're an amazing bunch and help to inspire me every single day.

Seriously if you're an author and reading this, and you need some positivity and guidance in your life then join the group, you'd be surprised how much it helps.

Quickly, I want to thank my team and editor for everything. They're always there ready and willing to read for me, I love you guys, thank you so much!

Lastly, you the readers.

Thank you so much for picking this series up, spreading the word and donating to such an important cause. You're a beacon of hope to those impacted by domestic violence. You make a difference.

Thank you so much for your unending support, it means so much to us all. <3

Lots of love,
Sienna xx

ABOUT THE AUTHOR

Welcome to the world of Sienna Grant…
Where love isn't meant to be easy.

Sienna Grant is a British writer from the West Midlands in the UK, who decided to step into the world of writing and has since never looked back.

She started her journey with contemporary romance as she loves a happy ever after but has since sampled different genres and has pushed every boundary that she has set herself. From contemporary romance to suspense, teen and young adult but also stepping into the darker world of Mafia and women's fiction.

When she's not writing, she's a wife and mother to three grown up kids and a nanny to two gorgeous grandchildren.

Sienna loves to read most romance when she can, but always with a hint of realism.

LINKS

facebook.com/AuthorSiennaGrant

instagram.com/author_sienna_grant?igshid=
NTc4MTIwNjQ2YQ==

goodreads.com/author/show/15613594.Sienna_Grant

tiktok.com/@author_sienna_grant

ALSO BY SIENNA GRANT

This is the start of a new MC series:

Brothers of Sin MC

This is the first book – Saving Chains

If you enjoyed Wilted Flower, then join Levi on his rise from prospect to patched member and meet the rest of the brothers of sin.

Also find out what happens with Levi and Luna...

ADD TO GOODREADS TBR: https://www. goodreads.com/book/show/63189459-saving-chains

PRE ORDER YOUR COPY HERE: https:// books2read.com/SavingChains

BLURB

I'm Levi 'Chains' Brown, Sergeant at Arms for Brothers of Sin MC.

My problem is, I take sin to the next level.

I haven't had a normal life. It's been fraught with survival and finding an escape.

Brothers of Sin were my salvation.

They took me in, fed me, clothed me, and taught me how to be a man. Something my own father should have done, but he used me as a punch bag.

It was when I found shelter that I met Luna Scott. She was my savior and the President's daughter but also my best friend.

The girl I'd die for.

She rescued me in more ways than one. Until one night changed everything.

Now I need to find my way back.

SNEAK PEEK

Saving chains

Prologue

MY HARLEY stops at the curb outside the house I used to call home. Only it's never really been a home, it was a place of torture. It was only a home when my mom was here and alive. When she was here to protect me, to love me like a mother should. Only he beat her too, tortured her even more than me.

Broke her body and her spirit, until she had no other choice but to leave me and this world.

Death was a better option.

I kick the stand down, and my foot hits the tarmac. I spend a few minutes just staring at the dirty, darkened front window. My hand dips into my cut to take out a smoke, and I lodge it between my lips and light it up, inhaling a long drag into my lungs then puff the smoke from my lips in a heavy breath. The grass on the front is long I notice; the porch swing hangs broken at one end and the screen door also stands lopsided. All I'm waiting for is some movement to let me know he's still in there, still breathing his sad, pathetic, and useless drug and alcohol induced, fucking life. I've thought about this for the past three years. From the day I escaped this shithole until now, I've thought about coming here and taking his last breath from him. Watching as life drains from him.

Watch him suffer the way he made my mom and me suffer.

Lifting my hand to my face I find moisture, but I'm not crying for what I'm about to do, no, my emotions are for the woman that gave me so much. Right up to the moment that she couldn't anymore. I don't blame her for taking her own life. I blame him.

I swipe my hand across my face, I take a moment of weakness to remember a woman that stood in front of a fist to protect me. For a life I was never allowed to have, all because of that cunt. As a shaky breath leaves my lips, I suck in some more nicotine as the toe of my boot taps the ground. My nerves are shot. I take in another long drag as the smoke billows from my nose, and curling the tip of my finger, I flick the butt to the grass. I drag my other leg from my bike and walk the path, climbing the few steps onto the porch. The screen door creaks from rusty broken hinges as I pull it open and try the handle of the front door. It turns and soon opens. Glancing behind me I look out for people that could be around but it's past midnight. As I push the door, a shit ton of unopened mail scatters the floor. I wonder to myself if he is alive or even here. Still, I go on and reach the living room, it's empty other than dirty, yet ripped furniture. In fact, it's the same furniture that was here before I left. Swallowing hard at the memory of Mom being here, I push it back down as quickly as it came and walk around the furniture. I try to quieten my heavy boots on the floor, but it's no good. My body is heavy, like I'm walking to my fate. It's then I see the TV on, and some old western plays out on the screen. The nicotine-stained armchair is situated in front of it and with a few more steps, I'm standing alongside it. Peering around the piece of furniture, I find him. His eyes are closed with one hand shoved under the waistband of his pants. I pull my gun from the back of my trousers and aim it at his head.

"Well, well, well. if it isn't my beloved son?" I wondered when you'd eventually show your fucking face." His eyes open and fall on me, but I don't waiver. I'm not scared of this piece of shit anymore and if I must, I'll blow a hole in his fucking face.

My breaths heave in quick succession as I tighten my fingers around the handle, my finger strategically placed loosely over the trigger, ready to squeeze it and blow his fucking brains out the back of his head, and onto the dirty cushion behind it.

"Do it," he taunts. "You ain't got the fucking balls to pull that trigger, or is it because you ride a Harley now, and that fucking motorcycle club that you think your Billy big balls?"

"If you want to stay alive, you'll do well not to taunt me."

"You'll never be big enough." I cock my gun ready to fire as a sneer curls his top lip. "If you kill me, you'll go to prison. Do you think you can handle prison?"

"Prison will be a walk in the fucking park after living with you, you sadistic fuck." He reaches forward and pulls a smoke from the packet, then drops the box back down with a smirk. He thinks I won't do it. Lighting it up he casually takes a drag, and stares at me. I push my hand forward until the barrel of my gun is resting softly against his forehead.

"Do you think I fucking care about dying? Do it. His head thrusts forward now, with the barrel pressing hard against it. "Go back to your fucking little club. I was fucking glad the day you left, you did me a favor, you and your mother were weak."

My pulse races as my temper begins to get the better of me. Swiftly shoving my gun back into my pants, my hand balls into a fist, and before I can stop myself, it's hammering into his face and connecting with his nose. I don't give a fuck anymore. I hit him and hit him as hard as I can. His nose bursts as it breaks, his eye begins to bloom with color just as his mouth fills with red, and that's only just breaking the surface of what I want to do to the cunt. I want to break him like he did my mom. I want to make him cry and shake with fear as he curls into a ball to shield the hits, and then I want to pull the trigger and watch the life leave his sadistic body.

I'm so lost in the moment with my fingers around his throat that I don't realize the cigarette he was holding has dropped from his fingers, not until the smell of burning hits my nostrils. I look down the side of the chair to see the cigarette burning away into the carpet, and a thought crosses my mind. While he's knocked out, I grab my lighter from my pocket and add a flame to the now smoking carpet until it spreads to the armchair. The side of the chair goes up and as much as I want to stay here and watch it happen, I need to get out of here. There's no way he'll get out of this. As I stand, flames multiply and begin to spread, and when they put out the fire, the fire department will see it was started from a cigarette. Accident.

"Burn in fucking hell, you piece of fucking shit." I hesitate for a second with my words and look around me. "Even this is too good for you."

His cries have already started before I've reached the door, and I smile.

Nothing tastes as sweet as karma. Die, you son of a bitch!

Volume 5

SINS

OF THE

FATHER

A NEW BEGINNINGS STORY

KATE BONHAM

Meet The Team:

Cover Designer: Francessca Wingfield @ Wingfield Designs

Formatting: TBR Editing & Design

This book is dedicated to my mother.
She taught me that "you need to learn to save yourself, there isn't always going to be a knight in shining armour to help you."

This book is based in Australia and as such is written in Australian English.

TRIGGER WARNING

Domestic Abuse

Violent Scenes

CHAPTER ONE

JUDD WAS LAUGHING with two women on either side
of him as well as his men all lounging around in the back of
the restaurant, where they always were. I'd had just about
enough of this bullshit. I stood across from the guard
keeping me out of the VIP area.

"Move, Kristoff," I said to him. "I'm in no mood to play."

"It's best you return home," he said in his rich accent.
"Mr. Gallo is busy."

"Fair warning, I'm not going anywhere and I'm not going
to ask again," I told him, as I looked up into deep blue eyes.
He knew I was serious too, but this guy hadn't come across
angry Brielle yet. I'd only ever been cordial with him before.

"Go home, Callie."

He turned his head back to focus on anyone behind me
and I felt my anger rise. Without further warning, I shifted
my weight to my other leg so I could bring my knee up and
crush his dick and balls against my patella.

Kristoff tried to remain upright but instead he fell to his
knees, a pained look on his face as he clutched at his crown
jewels. I moved past him just as someone else came to stop

me. Judd was no longer laughing and enjoying his time. He had dismissed his bitches and looked over at me with a thunderous look that sent chills down my spine. I'd seen him like this before.

And that had been the last time I'd seen him before I woke up in my bed with fractured ribs and a black eye. I knew I should back up and run but something in me couldn't do that. I didn't want to end up like my mother and be pushed aside while Judd's new woman raised my child.

No way in hell I would allow that.

"What the hell are you doing here?" he asked me, his fists already balling at his sides as he pushed up from the booth.

"Come home," I told him. "Christa is asking for you."

"Isn't that your job to look after her?" Judd asked me. If he'd never taken over the Gallo crime family, and he had been able to be the man he was when I met him, he never would have said that. "You don't tell me what to do, woman. Now get home. I will be home when I choose to come."

"Judd, please," I said. The women who had been lounging over him were all waiting on the side, waiting for me to go. But I didn't want him to resume whatever he had been doing with them. I wanted him to come home with me. I was no fool, the long nights, the days where he would be gone with no contact, I knew he was running around behind my back, but I didn't want to be that woman. I didn't want to bow down and lose my husband because I didn't fight for him.

"Get in the goddamn car," he said through gritted teeth. I turned and followed him out of the restaurant, smirking at Kristoff just getting up and standing gingerly. As we neared the front door, I felt Judd grab my arm and haul me up against the wall. His hand wrapped around my throat and squeezed. I could feel myself start to panic as breathing became hard. Judd's fierce eyes looked directly into mine.

"You will *not* embarrass me, Callie. You do as I say, and you will respect what I say."

I tried to nod, so he would release me, but his fingers were pushing into my neck. My lungs were burning, my fingers trying to pry his hand off me so I could breathe. I was slowly becoming weaker than I liked and had no idea how much longer I would be conscious. I couldn't speak, I couldn't beg.

Was this it? Would I die here and now?

Finally, Judd removed his hand from my neck, and I fell to my knees, sucking in air until it stopped burning. The skin around my throat was burning from his squeezing, I would have a mark there. Luckily, it was cold out. I could hide the bruises behind a scarf or turtleneck.

Kristoff picked me up from the floor and pushed me out the door and into the cool night air. He took joy in having me weak and hanging off him for leverage.

"Put her in the boot," Judd said. I could only just barely understand what was happening when I felt Kristoff push me backward. I hit my head on the side of the boot, my entire body feeling sluggish as he closed the boot door, and I was in complete darkness.

I tried to push my hands against the roof, but I was weak. The car started and sped out of the carpark. This wasn't good.

He rarely took this kind of violence publicly which is why I had decided to come here tonight. Something had pushed him over the edge. Something that may just mean I'd not see the sunrise again.

I FELT my stomach burning with nausea as the car came to a stop. I tried everything to stay awake. I knew I had to have had a concussion. The back of my head throbbed where I hit it, and the skin of my throat burned from where Judd's hand had squeezed. I heard the boot door open, and Judd's face hovered over mine.

"Get out," he ordered. I struggled to move, but my entire body felt like it was weighed down with concrete. Judd was impatient, I knew this was going to end bad. I just prayed Christa stayed in her room.

Judd's hand reached out and grabbed my hair. Pulling, I felt my scalp burn as he tried to pull me out. My body magically moved, and I tumbled over the edge of the boot and onto the hard gravel at his feet. He pulled me along the driveway, by my hair. I reached up, screaming, trying to remove my hair from his grip as he pulled me up the stairs to the front door. No one would come to my aid. They knew better than to do anything to anger Judd Gallo.

He finally let my hair go so he could open the door. Once he did, he moved to grab me again, but I crawled inside with every ounce of energy I had left. I was crawling for my life as I tried to get down the hall to the closest room, I could lock him out of.

He closed the distance between us just as I got to the doorway. I grabbed the doorway and tried to stop him from getting me. He pulled me so hard, I thought he may pull my leg off my body. My grip lifted and I was being dragged through the house, toward the dining area. We kept knives in there and given his mood, there was a high likelihood I'd end up stabbed.

I had to keep him away from me. He dropped my leg and grabbed my arm, hauling me to my feet. I was unsteady, but when I saw the darkness in his eyes, I felt a chill run down my spine. I couldn't let him kill me, I couldn't leave Christa in his care.

I had to stay alive for my baby girl.

"Judd, please," I begged. "I'm sorry I embarrassed you. I'm sorry."

"Sorry?" Judd spat back, angrily. "You're never sorry, bitch. Why can't you just do as you're fucking told? I could have any woman I wanted, and they would drop to their knees when I want them to."

"You fell in love with me, Judd. You knew I wasn't like that."

"I am a fucking God, Callie. You will bow down to me and be the wife you need to be. You stay hidden, in the house, look after my kid, and when I want that pussy, you will gladly open those legs and I will fuck you senseless. *That* is your job."

I wanted to slap him. Everything inside of me wanted to reach over to the side bureau and grab a knife and stab him to death but I knew I'd never see Christa again if I did.

He grabbed my hair in his hand again and forced me into nodding, acknowledging what he had just told me. He pushed me back, so I fell onto the table. I righted myself and he turned around, but not before he backhanded me. He walked away, heading upstairs. I could taste blood in my mouth, finally allowing myself to cry.

That's when I saw her.

Christa.

Cowering in the doorway to the kitchen. I hadn't noticed her before. She must have seen the entire thing.

My heart hurt.

"Baby," I said. "Come here."

She ran over to me and hugged my legs. I'd always sworn, since Judd had started to beat on me, that she would never see this. My father had never let me see what he did to my mother, but I knew, somehow, I knew what he did to her for her to run away from us.

I took her up the stairs, making sure that we didn't make a sound to annoy Judd. I had no choice but to believe he would hurt Christa if she were in the way.

Taking her into her bedroom, I closed her door, and pushed a chest of drawers behind it. I doubted Judd would come in here, but I didn't want to risk it. Sitting down on the floor, leaning against her bed, I opened my arms for her. She sat down in my lap and cuddled into my neck.

"Mummy, why does Daddy hurt you?"

I felt my chest squeeze uncomfortably. She'd known. We hadn't hidden it well enough. Christa was only seven. I hated that she knew or had seen what he did to me.

I didn't want her to think this was normal. I had every bone in my body telling me that my father had made me feel like this was normal, especially within a crime family. After all, my father was the head of the Bianchi crime family. The number one enemy of the Gallo's. It was why Judd had been so appealing, never did I think he would be the one to take over and become his father.

"Daddy has problems," I said, soothing her hair with my fingers. "I'm sorry you had to see that, baby, but it's not going to happen again."

"Are you okay, mama?"

I loved this baby girl with all my heart. I had to do everything to protect her and show her that real men didn't treat women this way.

"I need you to promise me something, okay?" I said to her, the exhaustion hitting me hard. "Mama hit her head, and she can't go to sleep okay. I need you to make sure I don't fall asleep. Can you do that for me?"

Christa nodded. "Okay, mama."

"If I do, you shake me awake and if I don't wake up, you take my phone and you call Uncle Indi, okay?"

Christa nodded, taking my proffered phone. I hoped I could stay awake, but I could already feel how weak I was becoming. I just hoped I didn't fall asleep and die with my daughter in my arms.

CHAPTER TWO

MY WHOLE BODY SHOOK. My eyes shot open to see my brother Indigo staring down at me, concerned.

"Indi?"

"Where the fuck is he?" Indigo growled. "I'll kill that motherfucker."

"Where's Christa?"

"She's just here."

"Don't swear in front of her."

"I think I've earned the right, Cal. Where is he?"

"If he's not here, I don't know," I told him. "What time is it?"

Indigo helped me up from the floor. I moved my hand to the back of my head where my bump was and groaned. It still hurt.

"You need to go to the hospital."

"Yeah, well, I didn't really think the guards were going to allow an ambulance to come in here last night."

Indigo sighed, his hands on his hips. I could see the disapproval on his face. When I left the safety of my family, and the confines of the Bianchi crime family walls, I knew I'd be alone. Indigo had reached out to me when Christa was born to tell me I could call him anytime. He would be there for me. It had been a comfort I didn't realize I needed.

"Let's go," he said. "Get your shit. I'll put Christa in the car."

"Don't let her out of your sight. Did anyone stop you from coming in here?"

"Nope, but it won't be long. I constructed a diversion, but it won't work forever."

I knew what that meant. The Bianchi's had started something with some of the Gallo's. Judd would realize it was a ruse soon enough. I moved to our closet and grabbed as many clothes as I could. Packing for Christa was easier, I knew what toys she loved the most. My head was fuzzy, and I knew I needed to be seen by a doctor, but I needed to get Christa safe first.

My anger was rising. Anger at Judd for being who he was, and anger at myself, for letting it happen. I never thought I would be this woman, one who was stuck in a position that she couldn't get out of. A woman who allowed a man to hurt her but when you're trapped, you realize your captor has all the power.

Not anymore.

I knew what I was going to have to do. To keep my baby girl safe.

Forever.

Pulling the bags down the hall, I took the stairs as fast as I could and ran to the car. Indigo put the bags in the boot, and my mind shot back to the night before when I was hauled out of it by my hair. The pain from last night, came shooting back and I felt a headache forming.

"Take me to the hospital," I told him when we got in the

car. Indigo nodded. I could see the concern in his eyes, but I couldn't reassure him. Not right now.

———

I KEPT my hands on Christa's shoulders as I waited for the door to be opened. I was nervous about being back here. If I hadn't put my hands on Christa's shoulders, they'd be shaking. My heart hammered in my chest as I waited.

The door opened and I saw her.

My stepmother Clare looked down at me, and then at Christa. Her scorn was replaced with a sweet smile when she bent down to speak to Christa.

"Hello, darlin'," she said, sweetly. "Do you like chocolate milk?"

Christa looked up at me. I nodded at her to let her know it was okay. She turned back to Clare and nodded. Clare stood back up and held her hand out to her. Christa took it and I watched as she was taken into the kitchen.

Clare looked back at me before she disappeared. "He's expecting you in his den."

Great.

Clare liked me as much as I liked her, but I knew she wasn't an evil woman. She would take care of Christa. I'd seen firsthand how sweet she had been to my younger half siblings. I pushed through my nervousness and headed down the long hall that would lead into my father's den. It was bigger than his office and where he usually entertained his guests or on occasion his enemies. The hall was dark and reminded me of a prisoner walking to the death chamber. My overactive imagination was at work once again.

I knocked on the door and heard my father call out that it was open. Pushing the door handle down, the door budged open. My father was sitting in his large throne-like chair, sitting close to the fireplace with a whiskey in his hand.

"Hello Calliope," he said.

"I prefer Callie."

"It's nice to live in a world where preferences matter. I would have preferred my daughter didn't run off with the enemy's son."

Taking a deep breath, I suppressed the sarcastic remark that was bubbling to the surface. Now was not the time to give him lip. I was no longer that bratty teen girl who wanted to stick it to her father.

"Is that what he did to you?" he asked, pointing to my face. I'd caught a glimpse of what I had looked like in the hospital and had no idea how Christa had been able to look at me without wincing. I was barely able to recognise my own face.

"Yes."

"How long?"

"Too long. I knew better."

"Was he always that way?"

"No, only after he became head of the family."

"Did he ever touch that beautiful child of yours?" he asked me, looking down at the liquid in his glass rather than at me.

"No, I would never allow that."

He finally looked up at me again. I saw something in his eyes, but I couldn't place the emotion. He downed the rest of his drink and stood up, coming over to me. I wasn't sure how to react when he pulled me into his arms and hugged me. I felt the tears threaten, my eye throbbing from the pain of the bruise. I wrapped my arms around his waist, and we stood there for a few minutes.

When I pulled my hands back, he did the same and looked me in the eyes. "We'll take care of this."

"No," I said quickly. "I need to do it."

He was shocked, I could tell by the way he stepped back a bit, but I also saw the pride in his eyes. "Okay. Whatever you need."

"I need someone to help me," I said. "Just one."

"Indigo?"

"He's going to take Christa so she's away from all this. I can't let her get involved and Judd will try to use her against me. He's the only one that can protect her and that I know can't be bought."

My father nodded. "Agreed. You can have Caleb."

I was confused. "He's your head enforcer, dad. I can use anyone, even someone from the lower rung."

"No," he said quickly, pouring us both a drink. "I have others who can help me. You need someone you can trust, and I trust Caleb with my life which means he is someone I can trust to have your back."

I nodded. "Okay. Thank you and thank you for letting me come back."

"Calliope, you have always got a place here. You are my daughter," he said, handing me the glass. "Anything you need."

"I got this, dad. I need to show my little girl that men can't do this to their women."

He looked guiltily at me. He'd beat my mum once or twice while I was growing up, I knew it, but I'd never heard him beat Clare once. I didn't know if I was ever going to forgive him for that, but he'd never hurt me. Not once.

My father nodded, probably realising what I was thinking about, and he sat back down. "Callie."

He never used my preferred name. I was so surprised I

didn't know what to do.

"This path you're going down, it's a dark one. It's one that will change you. Are you sure you want to do this?" he asked.

It's not the first time I questioned myself on what I knew I needed to do, but I was resolute.

"Yes," I said, tossing the whiskey down my throat and putting the glass down on a cabinet by the door. "I'm sure."

My father nodded again. "Okay. Get some rest. I'll have Caleb come and get you in the morning."

I left his den and headed back down the hall to the kitchen. Christa had a chocolate milkshake moustache and a smile on her face. I hadn't seen her smile in so long.

Clare looked at me, her own smile disappearing. "Your room is still up the stairs. We haven't touched it."

That surprised me. I would have assumed she'd take every pleasure in turning it into something she wanted.

"Thank you for watching Christa."

Clare softened a little. "Of course."

Christa jumped off the stool and took my hand as I led her up the stairs to my old bedroom. It was like opening the door to a time capsule. Nothing had changed. Not a damn thing.

"Is this your bedroom, Mum?"

"Yeah, baby, it is."

She let go of my hand and moved over to the bed, laying down on it. She must have been exhausted. Just like I was. I sat down with her and wrapped my arms around her as we laid down on the soft pillows. There was no fear of being dragged out of bed and hurled against a wall or being yelled at. We were safe here.

Finally.

We were safe.

CHAPTER THREE

I PUT the car in park and looked over to the house that looked like every other house on the street. It was a modest home, not at all like the two I'd lived in my entire life and definitely not one I would think she would live in.

"Are you sure about this?" Caleb asked me from the passenger seat.

"Yeah, she has exactly what I need," I told him. "Don't worry, she's not going to hurt me."

"I ain't leaving you unguarded, Cal. I'm not stupid."

I rolled my eyes and opened the car door, and swiftly crossed the street. Caleb followed behind me. I knocked on the door and waited. My heart was in my throat, but without her, I wouldn't be able to execute the plan to kill Judd.

Slowly, the door opened, and she appeared before me. Her smile disappeared and she looked at me like I was a stranger before faint recognition hit her.

"I was wondering when you would darken my doorstep," she said. Her eyes briefly flicked up to see Caleb standing behind me before coming back to me.

"Hi Mum," I said. "Mind if we have a word?"

"Did Cole send you?"

"No, Dad doesn't know I'm here," I said.

She looked back at Caleb and smirked. "Yes, he does. That kid wouldn't dare keep him out of the loop."

Caleb had been with my father since I was fourteen. I'd even had a crush on him before I met Judd, when he'd been a hot 17-year-old looking for a job and I'd been a young and head in the cloud's teenage girl hit with all sorts of hormones I didn't know how to deal with. He was his head enforcer because he was damn good at his job but also because he'd never let anything happen to my dad. He protected him like he was his own father, and in a way, he was a father to him.

"Can I come in?"

"You can, he can't."

"Hell no," Caleb said. "I go where she goes."

I turned around to face him. "It's okay. I'm right here, you wait in the car."

He didn't want to, but after a brief moment of silence, he finally stepped back and headed back to the car. My mother opened the door and let me inside. The house was light and airy, not at all like the house I grew up in. She had paintings on the walls of plants and a vase full of flowers on her dining table.

"Do you want something to drink?" she asked me.

"No, I was hoping I could talk to you about your garden."

"My garden?" she repeated, cocking her head to the side. "Now why would you need to see my garden, Calliope?"

"Callie."

She rolled her eyes, annoyed that I had never liked the name she'd picked out for me.

"Callie, I won't be asking the same question again."

"I just ... want to see your garden."

"To steal some flowers, perhaps?" she asked. "You could just ask for the deadly ones. No need to steal them."

"You're okay with me wanting them?" I asked her. "You don't know what it's for."

"I'm no fool, I still have spies, Callie. I know you left your husband and judging by the weathered bruise around your eye, I suspect he's been hurting you for a while. Why would I, as a responsible mother, care if you were to kill your husband?"

"Because that's a crime," I said. "You've grown poisonous plants all your life, and yet you never thought to do it to my father."

I followed my mother out the back door and into her garden. Her entire backyard was full of green lushness with assorted colours peeking through. It was as I remembered it when she had one at the old house.

"Do you love Judd?" she asked me.

"I did," I said. "That's why I married him."

"But do you still?" she replied.

"No, I don't. He's not the man I married."

"Then you never loved him," she told me. "You just wanted to escape, and he was the one you could do that with."

"How can you be so sure?" I asked her, genuinely curious.

"You asked me why I didn't poison your father when I had the means to," she stated, walking me through the path around your garden. "The answer is simple. I loved him. I still do to this day, but we can't be together. He's happy with his new wife, and I'm happy in my life. We love each other, but from afar. It's the only way we can do that."

"Because I want to kill Judd is why you think I don't love him?" I asked.

"No, because you so easily want to kill him. You're not using your father's men to do it, you want to do it. That's personal. I think you did love him, but he betrayed you. You're letting your anger do the thinking."

"I'm not doing it for me. I'm doing it for my daughter."

My mother turned around and I saw a glimmer of what I could tell was surprise.

"I thought you would have known since you have spies and all."

"Not on you," she said. "What's her name?"

"Christa."

"And she's the reason you're going to kill Judd?"

I nodded. "I have to. He'll take her away if I don't and he won't treat her right."

This changed the way my mother was looking at me. I could see real sadness.

"The choice you're making is a personal one. Poison isn't easy to pull off, you'll have to get really close to him. You do know that, right?"

I nodded. "Yes. But it'll also be slow. He'll know it's me before he dies."

She came to a stop in front of a familiar plant with white petals. It smelled like vanilla. I knew what it was just by the look alone.

White Oleander.

"This is what you're looking for," she said. "I'll cut some of them off and put them in a jar for you. Go inside and wait."

I did as she requested and waited in her living area. She didn't have photos out, like most mothers would, but she did seem to favour bright colours and sunlight. I could see

Caleb sitting in the car, waiting for me. He was tense, probably because I'd made him sit outside.

My mother came in not long after I had and handed me a jar. I could see the cuttings of the Oleander and some berries in the bottom.

"What are the berries?"

"It is the fruit from the belladonna plant," she said. "The most toxic plant I can give you. The berries are easy to grind up, but make sure to use gloves."

"Belladonna?" I asked as I looked at the plump little black berries.

She nodded. "Let me know if you need help. Oh, and just so you know, the poison can be bitter, so you need to mask it well."

I nodded and she walked off, back to her house, and closed the door.

"You okay?" Caleb asked me.

"Yeah, let's go."

I put the jar in my backpack that was on the back seat and zipped it up. Caleb took off and headed back home. It felt weird to be in a car with him again. He wasn't at all like the hot guy from my girlhood dreams, he was hotter. He was tatted up now, a large tattoo on the side of his neck gave off dangerous vibes but I could tell he was still a gentleman. He'd always been the one to open doors for me when I was younger, the knight I'd always needed.

"What?" he asked. I hadn't realised I'd been staring at him until just now.

"Sorry," I laughed at myself. "You grew up. I was admiring your neck tatt."

He smirked over at me. "You like tatts, huh?"

"Sure," I said. "What girl doesn't?"

"You have any?" he asked me.

"Nope," I replied. "Judd didn't like them on women."

The tension in the car rose and we both sat in silence.

"I can do this for you, Cal. You don't have to get your hands dirty. Take that girl of yours and disappear."

It was tempting to be sure, but I knew this had to be me. I didn't want to tell my daughter one day that I let someone else, a man, take care of my problems. I had to do this myself.

"No, I've got it handled."

"How? How are you going to get close enough to get poison him?" he asked. "Doesn't it take longer to die, so you need to keep doing it?"

"I have a plan," I told him.

"Tell me."

"My friend Scarlett, she's the only solace I had in that place. She used to be married to Judd's cousin, but he died, so we kind of adopted her as the aunt to Christa when Judd wanted me alone. I've known for a while now that Judd has wanted her for himself. In fact, the day I left, he made a move on her. She's going to slip it to him for me."

"You're trusting her to do this for you?" Caleb asked. "She's always been team Gallo, why would she help you when she can be his Queen now?"

He seemed genuinely concerned for me, and it was so sweet. I wasn't used to being treated like this, especially not by Judd, not lately anyway.

"Caleb, you gotta trust me here. I can trust in her. Women have a bond."

"And they also betray you at the drop of a hat," he said, almost under his breath but it was loud enough for me to hear. Who the hell hurt him?

"I trust she will do this because she hates Judd. He's the one who ordered her husband killed."

"Fuck me, the Gallo's are a seriously fucked up family," he uttered. "I can't believe you left us for them."

He realised what he said as soon as it was out, and he looked at me apologetically.

"I know, but at the time, it was better than the alternative. I didn't think he would become his father in a matter of a year. He always swore to me that he hated who his father was."

"I guess we never really know who someone is," he said. It made me think someone had hurt him and hurt him bad. That made me so angry that someone could hurt Caleb. He was the kindest soul I'd ever encountered, unless you had made my father want to hurt you then he never missed.

Caleb pulled into the Bianchi compound and pulled into the garage. I grabbed my backpack and headed inside. Caleb hung back, probably to tell my father where we were. I was just waiting for him to come and give me a lecture, but this had to be done and she was the only person I would be able to get that shit off and not have it traced back to me.

Heading down the hall to the outside doors that would lead down into the gardens that Clare had replaced all my mother's flowers with her own. The greenhouse sat unused because Clare really didn't care about gardening like my mother did. It was partially overgrown, and weathered due to lack of use, and it would be perfect to set up my little experiments. I had already hidden mortar and pestles out here, mixing bowls and my old lab chem kit from high school so I could brew the concoctions with ease. Clare wouldn't come out here, and I definitely knew my father wouldn't. I pulled the jar out and the printout I'd gotten from the library yesterday afternoon after I used their computer to find a recipe for hiding the bitter taste, and I got to work.

THE SUN SHONE through the glass of the greenhouse and turned it into a near furnace, but I was almost done with my first concoction. It smelled bitter with just a little bit of sweetness. I'd combined both the belladonna and the oleander into this one. It was going to be potent as all get out. As I let it stew, I went outside for fresh air, removing my mask and hanging it on the back of the door. Caleb was sitting up on the back porch, probably watching to make sure I wasn't going to blow myself up.

I headed toward the house and sat down next to him on the porch.

"How are you going in there?" he asked me.

"It seems to be cooking along quite nicely," I replied. "Do you really care or are you worried I'll poison myself?"

He chuckled, and it let the tension lift from his shoulders. "The offer is always there. No one is going to know it was you if you let me take him out."

"I got to do this, Caleb. I don't want my kid to think you need a man to take care of all your problems."

"Makes sense," he said. "I didn't think you would want your kid to know you're going to murder her dad though."

"She saw him, Caleb. She saw what he was doing to me. That was the last straw. I can't let her know that it's okay for a man to abuse his wife. I witnessed it myself. I saw what my dad did to my mum, the after effect, btu I heard the screaming. I heard the walls being punched in. It's traumatic for kids."

"I didn't know your dad did that," Caleb said. "He's never touched Clare in anger."

I sighed. I'd come to the realisation a while ago, that

they had just been so mismatched and both hotheads. It didn't make it right, but I knew Clare was good for him.

"I asked my mum why she never tried to poison my dad. She had the means to, but she never did. She told me she still loved him. Sometimes love isn't enough to keep you together and the best thing is to part. I don't understand that kind of love, but she didn't have any mean things to say about him even though he hit her."

"It kind of sounds like he hit the wall more than he hit her," Caleb said. "You heard walls being punched, right?"

"Well, yeah."

"He probably punched the wall, so he didn't have to punch your mum. He tried to stop himself because he knew it was wrong. That's where your dad and Judd differ. He punched you and for that, he should be fucking drawn and quartered."

I smiled at his reply. "And you think my poison is medieval."

"I never said that," he answered. "I just don't think you should need to bloody your own hands."

"Nor should you."

"Mine are plenty bloody," he replied. "There's no way I can replenish my soul before judgment day."

"You're a good guy, Caleb. One of the best. You've nothing to fear, believe me."

"There's a lot you don't know about me, Callie."

"You made yourself so gruff then. It was kind of a turn on. Too bad I didn't run away with you back then, hey?"

It was a joke, but I knew in my heart that I meant it. My life could have been so different if only I had fallen for Caleb, but we couldn't live a life full of what if's.

"I had the biggest crush on you back then," he blurted out.

"You?" I replied, surprised. "On me?"

"Yeah, but I knew I couldn't go there. You were the boss's daughter, *and* you were too young for me, but I made any excuse I could to be around you."

I giggled like a schoolgirl at the admission. "I had a crush on you too. That's so crazy, I thought you had a bevy of girls who threw themselves at you."

"Oh, I did," he laughed. "But there was just something about you."

"So, by running off, you avoided temptation," I said. "I did you a favour."

"I guess you did," Caleb replied, a smirk playing at his lips. "Thanks for that."

We both laughed, but then the gravity of it hit us both and we sat in silence. Why couldn't I have fallen for Caleb? Why couldn't I have had the boy who I knew would never lay a hand on me?

Fuck. Stop thinking about this, *Callie*. I never would have thought Judd would be capable either. He was as sweet as pie when I met him and now, he was the monster he had been trying to get away from all his life.

I guess you never really knew what lurked beneath the surface. I sure as hell didn't think I would imagine myself capable of poisoning someone I thought I had once loved.

CHAPTER FOUR

"HOW IS SHE?" I asked my brother as he looked at me with weary eyes.

"She never stops talking," Indigo said, exhausted.

I could barely contain my amusement. "She's seven, she has a lot to say."

"Clearly," he replied. "She's asleep now, though, finally."

"Good. Hopefully not too long and I can come and grab her."

"Are you sure about this plan, Cal?" he asked. "If you get caught...she's going to have no one."

"She'll have you," I replied.

He nodded. "Yeah, she will. How will you contact Scarlette?"

"I put the poison in a locker at the bank. She has a safety deposit box there too, and we both know each other's combinations. So, I'll deposit it in there and the next day, she's going to grab it. She told me she has already gotten in, he's basically walking into his own death trap."

"Can we be sure about this?" he asked. There was real

concern in his eyes. "Maybe I should come back and help you."

"Don't you dare leave my little girl," I said. "I have Caleb here. He's been helping me a lot, actually."

Indigo's smirk was hard to miss. "I bet he has."

He knew about my crush on him when I was younger, and he'd made fun of me mercilessly. "Don't even think about saying it, dick."

His laughter was loud and genuine before he said goodbye and hung up. I could punch his little giggling face so hard right now, but he was doing me a favour, so I had to be thankful for that. I missed Christa, which only made me want to get the job done and now.

"All good?" Caleb asked. I jumped at his voice which made him smile.

"Yeah, let me grab the vial and we can head into town."

I made a move out to the greenhouse and grabbed my bag and the vial and carefully placed it into a box so it could be hidden in the safety deposit box. I put my bag on my back and headed out to the car. Clare eyed me suspiciously but kept her mouth shut. She'd been keeping herself away from me, probably because she knew I was into shady dealings since Caleb was with me. She had never wanted to be part of the criminal aspect of the family, which I kind of admired about her. I was too much like my mother and took a huge interest in Judd's business.

Caleb was quiet on the way into town, and I couldn't help but wonder what he was thinking about. Did he agree with my methods, or did he just want to swoop in and save the day?

"Have you had a serious girlfriend?" I asked him. I had no idea where the thought had even come from, but it was out in the open now.

"Yeah, one."

"Just one?"

"One serious one, yeah."

"What happened?"

"She didn't like this lifestyle," he replied. I could see it wasn't exactly a subject he liked to discuss.

"Well, I'm sorry, Caleb. That sucks."

He shrugged his shoulders, but when he looked out the window, I could see it still pained him. I wondered what she had done to him for him to still pine for her.

We remained in silence until we got to the bank. Caleb accompanied me inside as I showed my ID and asked to see the box I shared with Scarlette. The bank teller looked at Caleb behind me, and I could see he didn't approve. It was probably the neck tattoos, but I didn't care. This wasn't about who I was with, this was about the box.

"Do you have an issue?" I asked him, feeling somewhat annoyed.

"No, of course not, ma'am," he said with a fake smile. "Follow me."

I told Caleb to come with me, because I needed the backup, and we followed the asshole down a narrow hallway. He opened a vault door, and we stepped through. I used my key and opened the box labelled 436. The asshole had to turn his key too in order for it to unlock. We needed the most secure box possible otherwise this never would have worked.

"Anything else, ma'am?" he asked. I shook my head, and he left the vault. Caleb came over to me and handed me the backpack he'd taken from the back seat.

"How do you know she will come here to get it? How are you communicating with her?"

"We have a code," I told him. "She knows about this plan

because she came up with it years ago when Judd started to become violent. She's been trying to get me to leave for years."

"I hate that you didn't tell us what was happening," he said. "I would have gladly helped you."

"I was thinking it was best for Christa to have her daddy around," I said as I lifted the lid of the box and looked inside. Scarlette had left me a letter. I grabbed it out and flipped it open. "But I don't want her to think that a man should treat her that way and I don't want him to take her from me. That's the reason for the drastic measures."

I started to read Scarlette's letter:

Callie,

If you're reading this message, it means it came to our plan. I have a phone code for you to use. Text me on the number below with the following code:

XoX – You want to disappear and need me to distract Judd.

XX – You plan to kill him and need my help.

I will do whatever I can for you, babe.

Scar

"How much can you trust this Scar?" Caleb asked.

"With my life," I said. "I need to use your phone though. I got rid of my phone when Indigo left because I knew Judd would have tracked it."

"Anything."

I pulled the poison out and placed the vial in the box. Once it was inside, I closed the lid and hid the letter in my bag before I locked it and Caleb put it back in the hole in the wall. A lock clicked once it was inside, and I zipped up my bag again. Caleb took it off me and hung it over his shoulder as we left the vault. We passed the asshole, and he came out from his desk and smiled at us.

"Do you have everything you need?"

"I do."

"And your bag?" he asked. "We do reserve the right to check it upon departure."

I felt myself freeze. Caleb moved forward.

"Just try and take it from me, mate."

I could see the asshole shrink back. "I suppose we can make an exception this time around."

He moved back to his desk and picked up his phone. Caleb took my arm and led me out the door.

"He's working for Judd. He probably couldn't get into your box, but he knows it exists. We need to go now."

I felt my heart race as we ran to the car and Caleb took off.

"Do you think Scarlette is safe?" I asked him as we neared the house.

"By the sound of that letter, she's thought of all the risks, so she is safe. But I can take her out of the equation. Just give me the word."

It would be faster, and I could get away with a lot. I know he was a professional, I know he would be able to do it quicker than poison, but I didn't want to put that on him. This was my mess.

"You know I need to do this myself," I said. "But thank you."

He smiled over at me as he pulled into the driveway to my father's compound. "You know where to find me if you need to."

"Thank you, Caleb."

I meant it too. He'd always been there for my father, for me, even when my stepmother had brought me to tears when I was fifteen. He'd put his strong arm around me and comforted me when I'd felt the most alone. If only I had fallen for Caleb.

My life would be so different now and I probably wouldn't be needing to poison someone. What was I doing to my soul? I was acting like it was easy. Just like my father thought it was that easy to take someone's life.

The sins of my father were going to haunt me through the rest of my life, especially if I were successful.

But I had to do this. Otherwise, he'd take Christa and I would lose the only reason for my breathing. She deserved a life away from this.

She deserved everything.

CHAPTER FIVE

Days Later

CLARE CAME into the room as I finished my breakfast. My daily call from Christa had lifted my spirits some and I was able to finish my breakfasts now. It would be over in a few days, and then I could disappear with her. We would be able to live our lives with freedom.

"This came for you, Callie."

I looked over at the box she was carrying. It was larger than what I would expect. A bigger fear rushed over me though. No one should know I was here. Only Scarlette knew and truthfully, she'd never risk sending me something.

Caleb sensed my unease, and he jumped up from the couch and rushed over.

"Wait," he said, holding my hands back. "Who knows you're here?"

"Scarlette but she'd never send something here."

He looked at the label.

"What did the courier look like?" he asked Clare.

"No courier, it was on the doorstep."

"Get the security tapes from the cameras out front," he barked at the guys who were standing around. "Where's Lou? He should be guarding the gate."

Immediately, I felt my curiosity get the best of me. I needed to know what was in the box. Clare was starting to look fearful, but she stayed put.

"Callie, I got this," he said.

"No, it's okay. It's for me."

Caleb didn't argue, instead he stayed next to me, but I could see the fear in his eyes. Someone had breached our perimeter. I pulled the tape off the box and started to lift the lid just as one of the guys who went to check on Lou came into the room.

"Lou's dead, bullet through the temple."

I looked down at the contents of the box, shrieking as I almost fell of the kitchen stool. Caleb caught me before I could fall and pushed the lid back down on the box. But I'd seen it enough.

I should have known this would happen.

This was all my fault.

Caleb took the box off the kitchen table and moved it away from me as I struggled to breathe. Tears fell down my face as I realised what I had done.

Clare ran to my side. "What was it?"

She pulled me into her arms and gave me a hug. I never expected her to be so kind. Before I could answer, Caleb came back and took me away from her. She asked again but no one answered her.

It was too gruesome.

"This is my fault," I said.

Caleb took me to my room and sat me down on the bed. He waited for my sobbing to ease before he asked me, "Was that Scarlette's head in the box?"

I nodded. "She died for me."

"It's not your fault. This is on Judd."

I got off the bed and started to pace, it helped me a little. Yet, I did feel as if I were completely helpless, just like the first time he'd beaten me. I'd sworn I would leave him then, but I stayed because he had sent me flowers the next day and taken me on a holiday to France. I told myself it had been a once off, even though I knew that wasn't true.

"She was my only friend that I had left and now she's dead because of me."

I wanted to run, run over to the house and murder him with my bare fists, but Caleb caught my arm as I headed for the door and wheeled me back. I slammed against his chest and looked up in his eyes.

"She wasn't your only friend. You have me."

I don't know what it was that passed through me, but I felt the intensity of his fingers digging into my elbow. His eyes were dark, darker than I had ever seen them before. His eyes moved to my lips, and I licked them only to see his eyes shoot back to mine, and a darker still intensity shot through him.

Before I could stop myself, I pulled his head down so I could kiss those delectable lips. He groaned into my mouth as he pushed me against the wall. The heat from under his shirt melded against my own tummy and had sparks shooting down my veins, all the way to my toes and back up to my pussy.

He leaned back, looking me in the eyes as he pulled his holster off, the guns clunking to the ground. Next, his shirt came off and I saw the ripples of muscle on his abdomen, covered in tattoos, as he stood before me. My pussy was begging for him to continue. I needed to see what was beneath those pants, and urgently.

No words were needed.

Caleb reached over and shut the door with a flick of the wrist before he carried me over to the bed. I needed this. I needed it more than I ever thought I ever needed anything. And Caleb sure did look like he knew what to do.

"WHAT ARE YOU DOING?" I heard Caleb's husky voice from the door. I hadn't even heard him coming which only proved that I needed to be more careful and aware. Especially given one of the Gallo's had crept up on us without anyone noticing. I turned in the stool I'd brought out here to the greenhouse and looked over at him. He'd put a white tank top on, but I could still see those muscles and those tatts peeking out.

"I'm seeing how much poison I have left," I told him. He came into the greenhouse and closed the door behind him. As he got closer, I could smell that masculine scent on him which did things to my legs and my tummy. The sex with him had been amazing. If I'd been wearing socks, they would have shot off the second his cock entered me.

"Let me take care of it for you," he begged. "I can have it done by the end of the day and you and Christa can be together."

"I can't lose another friend because of him," I said. "But I appreciate it."

"He won't know what hit him. I'm a trained sniper," he said. "It will be over in the blink of an eye."

"I appreciate it, Caleb, I do, but you know I need to do this myself now. I need to make it right for Christa. He will take her from me, if not by force, then definitely by law."

"Don't do it now," he said. "I can get you a new identity,

get you out of the country. You can start a new life with Christa."

I put my hand on his cheek. He was doing everything for me, even risking himself in the process.

"I appreciate it, Caleb, I do, but you know I have to do this. I am, however, going to take a break from trying to wreak havoc on him. I want him to let his guard down."

Caleb nodded. "Why don't I take you up to see Christa?"

"We can't. He'll have people on us."

"Not if we start some shit in the middle of the city. We know where they are during the day. If they get the call that we started a beef, they'll all run to help."

"No, we can't do that."

"They killed one of our own," Caleb said. "Judd ain't stupid. He knows what's coming, so they won't think it's a diversion. They will know it's for Lou."

He had a point.

"Can you be sure they won't know it's for me?"

"Yes," he said. "Let me go get changed and tell the boys to go into town. Then we'll go."

I could barely contain my excitement at seeing Christa again. I had hoped it would be all over by now, and I could be with her, but Judd had outsmarted me, and that really pissed me off. I put my poisons away and headed inside.

"Caleb tells me you're going to see Christa," my father said. I almost jumped at his voice. Turning around, I saw him standing at the doorway, with a car part in his hands, his face dirty and his hands greasy. When he needed to think, he had always gone to work on his classic cars.

"You don't agree with that?"

"You just received your best friend's head in a box," he

said. "I think you need to take some time and come to terms with that loss."

"If I waited around to grieve for everything I have lost since I met Judd, I'd never do anything ever again."

He straightened and I could see he didn't like what I'd just said. "You went to see your mother a few days ago. Any particular reason?"

"I thought it time to say hello, it's been a while."

"It didn't have anything to do with the fact she had a garden full of poisonous plants?" he enquired.

"She told you?" I asked. "I didn't think you still spoke."

"Of course, we do," he said, exhaustedly. "We have children together."

"Only two and we're both grown," I replied. He was growing tired of my sass, but I wanted to know if what my mother had said was true. Did they still love each other? Suddenly, I felt bad for Clare. "What about Clare?"

"Clare is aware I have children with your mother," he said, angrily. "Now grow up. Going to see Christa is dangerous, for you and for her. Indigo has her, and she's safe. We can get you a new identity, so you and her can go and be free."

"I don't want to be someone else," I replied. "I shouldn't have to change my name and disappear. I shouldn't have to run with my daughter and change everything she knows."

"You're right, you shouldn't have to, but life is hard. We need to do things that aren't fair."

"I thought you would be all for me taking a hard stance, for doing what needs to be done."

"You never wanted this life, Calliope. I only ever wanted for you to achieve what you wanted to achieve, not just what Judd wanted."

"My mind is made up, Dad."

He nodded, looking down at the part in his hand. "Okay, as long as you understand what it could mean for you."

I had.

I knew exactly what was going to happen. The Gallo family would falter, probably act recklessly, and take out my own family but without Judd, they wouldn't know their left from their right hand, and they'd all die.

Long live the Gallo's.

CHAPTER SIX

CHRISTA SWUNG on the large tire that had been made into a swing that hung off a large tree branch and laughed. Indigo handed me a cup of coffee and sat down on the doorstep with me. Caleb was pushing Christa on the swing, causing her to scream with delight.

"Any issues?" I asked him.

"No. We're safe here. I told you I would protect her with my life."

"Is that why I can smell whiskey in your coffee?"

Indigo chuckled. "If I don't, then the multiple episodes of Paw Patrol will actually make me want to shoot the TV."

I couldn't help but laugh. "Everything else okay?"

"She's pretty smart," he said. "She's asked if you're okay a lot, and somehow, she knows when I'm lying."

"Unfortunately, she's seen a lot. She had to keep me awake the night you rescued me. I don't want her to keep living this life. Judd needs to die."

"No doubt," Indigo replied. "But let me or Caleb do it. You can take her, run from here, start a new life and be happy."

"Everyone wants me to do that, but I just can't. I need to show him...I need to take back my freedom."

Indigo nodded, finishing off his drink and getting up to head over to Christa and Caleb. Christa ran over to me and tackled me to the ground. I hugged her tightly as I righted us on the porch.

"Are you sad, mama?" she asked me. I looked down into those beautiful blue eyes that held all the innocence in the world, and I realised in that moment I would do anything to protect this little girl. I would lay down my own life for her to be happy.

"Why would you ask that, baby?"

"I can see it," she said. "You have red eyes just like when we had to lock ourselves in the bathroom."

My chest seized as I realised just how much she knew at such a young age. I'd done that. I had made it so she knew pain and anguish when she shouldn't be able to tell if I'd been crying or not.

"Baby, you don't need to worry about me. I worry about you."

"Was it Daddy?" she asked me, the sadness was evident in her eyes. I didn't want to tell her what I intended to do, it was her father after all, but she had to know he wasn't a good man.

"I lost a friend today," I told her. "That made me sad."

Christa hugged me tightly, and I felt the tears begin to well in my eyes. I fought them off, not wanting to show how weak I really was over Scarlette's death.

"We should go," Caleb said as he came over to us. "It's getting late."

I nodded and stood up as Christa hung off me. "I may need some help with this big bag of bones."

Indigo wrestled Christa off me, and she giggled and

screamed in joy.

"Say bye to mama," Indigo said to Christa. She blew me kisses as Indigo took her inside. I needed to get Judd out of the way so I could get Christa and we could live a happy life together. I owed this to her.

Anything for her.

Caleb led me back to the car. Once we were on our way, he looked over at me. I could see it from the side of my eye. "What?"

"What do you want to do now?"

"I need to brew more poison and I'll take the fight to him."

"How?"

"I can't tell you and run the risk you'll thwart me."

Caleb slammed on the brakes, sending the car skidding across the road and toward the side. He looked absolutely fucking annoyed at me, but he didn't look at me. Instead, he sat there, looking out at the road, his chest rising and falling in anger.

"I'm here to help you," he said, finally. "Why are you so hellbent on having to do it all alone?"

"Because I have been alone," I yelled at him. He finally looked at me. "I've been alone since he took over for his father. I have to do this. I have to make things right for Christa."

He seemed to understand. Caleb started up the car without another word and took off, faster than before and headed back to the compound. I could feel the tension between us, and I knew I had probably blown whatever friend I'd had in him, but he had to understand that he couldn't be my priority. Christa had to be.

We were so close to being free.

I couldn't stop now.

CHAPTER SEVEN

Three Days Later

THE ANNUAL PARTY was in full swing when I snuck into the Gallo compound. Even the guys he had on security were getting on the drink in their little box at the gate. It had been child's play to run past them and climb over the wall. I was hidden by the side of the main house, waiting for my moment. I could see Judd's second in charge and best friend, Mark, standing at the door, smoking. He was surrounded by some of the men I knew were vying for Judd's attention.

I couldn't get caught when I was so close already.

This was for Christa.

I felt for the vial of poison in my backpack as I ran down the side of the house and headed toward the only window, I knew I could budge open. Judd had never fixed it from when he smashed my hand through it. I'd had six stitches along my palm from that. I closed my eyes and tried to block out the painful memory.

I grabbed the window and shoved my weight behind it.

As I pushed it open, I hoisted myself up and swung my legs over the sill and edged my way down to the ground. This room was usually off limits so I knew I could gain my composure before I'd be found. Taking a deep breath and grounding myself, I moved to the door and opened it slightly to check for anyone outside before I made my way down the hall and into his office. It was empty, which was surprising, but I wasn't going to look a gift horse in the mouth. Pulling my bag off my shoulders, I rested it against the desk. I pulled out the vial and looked around for the bar cart, I knew he always had a drink when he came in here. I poured a little of it in the decanter and wiped the glasses with some of it before I moved over to the safe behind the fake painting. I knew this was risky, but I had to try, right? I keyed in the code he'd always used, even though he thought I didn't know it.

6969.

How fucking original, right?

To my surprise, the door opened, and I gained access. I wasn't stupid, I knew this would have triggered a silent alarm somewhere. I had to work fast. I grabbed all the documents, finding my passport and Christa's and put them in my bag. I closed it again, making sure to pour the last of my poison over the handle of the gun. Before I closed the safe door just enough that it wasn't clearly locked but it wasn't obvious that it was open, I put the painting back up just as I heard Judd's obnoxious voice coming down the hall. I grabbed my bag and moved over to the corner of the room, hidden by the filing cabinet. Crouching down, I waited for his guards to grab me.

But a part of me knew he wanted to see me, and he wouldn't let them take his fun. My heart hammered as the door opened and I saw him.

I looked upon the man I married, and the man I left my own family for, and wondered what the hell had I seen in him. He was a puny man. A man made popular by his status, not at all by his looks or his build. It's funny how you form rose coloured glasses when you think you're in love. He moved over to the painting, removed it, and wedged the safe door open. He could see what was missing.

He knew it was me.

He knew I was still here.

I smiled when he grabbed the gun in there and looked over to his guards. "Leave me."

"But Judd—"

"Go," he barked at them. I could see they didn't want to, but they started to back out. "Check the grounds. She can't have gone far."

They ran to follow his order and left me alone with him.

"I know you're still in here," he said. "Are you going to be a coward?"

I moved out from the corner, keeping the bag stowed away, and confronted the bastard who beat me into submission for far too long.

"What are you waiting for?" he asked. "Pour me a drink."

I hid the smirk that was about to pop up.

"Pour yourself a drink."

"Oh, you have sass now?" he enquired, sitting down in his chair. He kept the gun trained on me. "Where's my daughter?"

"*My* daughter is safe."

"You can't possibly think you'll win here. I have more power than your father ever had."

"And yet, I have my daughter and you haven't a clue where she is. In fact, I managed to sneak on the compound unnoticed."

"Perhaps," he replied, nonchalantly. "But you won't leave unnoticed."

"We'll see."

He put the gun down on the desk, the nozzle still aimed at me, and leaned back in his chair. He looked over at the decanter of whisky and smirked back at me.

"You poisoned it, didn't you?"

"If I did that, wouldn't I want to eagerly pour you one?"

"You think you can outsmart me, Callie?" he asked. "Think again. What do you hope to accomplish here?"

I had thought that same question before I'd climbed the wall and snuck in.

Simply put, I wanted a life.

A life where Christa didn't see men beating women and think it's okay. A life where she would question whether violence was normal or not.

I wanted her to live happily.

Judd would never let me have Christa, and I knew that. That was why this was the only option I could take. I just knew I couldn't leave her in this maniac's psychotic hands.

"I have what I came for."

"The passports?"

"I'll be on my way now."

Judd smirked. An unnerving smirk that would be my undoing if I weren't so in control right now. He was utterly amused. He brushed his fingers over his lips as he thought of his next move. I had to hold back the victory I was feeling. The poison I'd dipped his gun in would now be making its way through his lips. Soon, he'd feel a burning and I knew he would flick his tongue out to wet his lips, sealing his fate.

He was doing exactly what I thought he would do.

I could leave now, and get away, but I knew I had to see

it. I had to watch him writhe in pain as he died, and I needed to see his eyes when he realised, I had bested him.

He picked the gun up and stood. "What makes you think I'll allow that."

"You can't control me anymore, Judd."

Just as I suspected, Judd's tongue flicked out over his bottom lip and circled up to his top lip, wetting them. I could see his lips were becoming swollen, and sweat was slowly starting to beat on his forehead. His eyes widened, as if he knew what I'd done. I felt a sense of jubilation bubble over me at what I would soon witness.

Judd.

Crumbling.

"What did you do?" he asked, his voice strangled in pain.

I could see those lips, red and gross, turning blue as he spluttered, and gasped for air. I took a step back to avoid getting him too close. He stumbled, clutching at his desk as he tried to move around it, possibly for help.

This man who I had loved, who I had given everything up for, was falling.

And I couldn't be happier.

Did that make me sadistic?

Maybe, but I couldn't care less right now.

His eyes watered, pink tears, filled with blood, as he fell to his knees. Papers from his desk flew to the ground as he struggled to stay upright. Blood poured from his eyes, his nose, and ears as he fell onto his back with a thud.

I stepped closer, making sure he could see me as I leant down.

"Who's the one in control now?" I asked him. He was turning red, as red as a tomato, and his neck was swollen. His eyes were red masses as he looked up at me, realising it was me, the one he beat every time he had a difficult day, who beat him.

"Goodbye, Judd."

As I watched him take his final breath, I got up and grabbed the bag before I headed out the window I'd come in and down the sidewalk toward the wall I could climb over. Instead, I continued walking, in direct sight of everyone.

Especially Mark.

He stopped his conversation and dropped his cigarette on the ground. His mouth was half open as he considered what to do next. I continued walking toward the exit. He could quite easily put a bullet in the back of my head, but I had to hope he had a conscience.

"Judd's dead!" someone yelled. Everyone jumped to attention. I turned back to see what they were going to do. Mark had his gun trained on me.

"Stop!" he called out to me, but he didn't pull the trigger.

Shit.

My heart was hammering as I stood there, waiting for someone to shoot me.

But when Mark fell to his knees, his gun clattering to the ground, I couldn't believe my luck. That's when I saw Caleb coming from out of the shadows, two guns trained on everyone who had started to surround me. He shot off bullets, left right and centre, as men fell to the ground, dead.

He moved in front of me as he continued to finish off the surrounding men. He dropped two guns and grabbed another two from his belt and continued to shoot up the house. No one was returning fire.

"I had this," I said to him.

"Clearly."

I wanted to argue but now really wasn't the time. I backed up, holding onto him to guide him back as he continued to shoot at anyone stupid enough to show their face.

As we got out the gates, I ran for the car that he'd parked on the street and opened the door. He put the guns away and tore away, heading for home.

We sat in silence, as the joy of what I had accomplished wore down. Judd was dead.

I was free.

EPILOGUE

"CALEB!" Christa screamed as she ran out of the car and toward him. He smiled at her as she launched into his arms. I'd never seen her do that to anyone but Indigo before. "Did you know we went on a holiday!"

"I heard," he said. "Did you have fun?"

She nodded her head, just as a yawn escaped her.

"Looks like you need a big nap," Caleb said. "Come on, I got the best bed in the whole house."

He disappeared inside with her as I pulled my bag from the car. Indigo emerged with my father from the garage.

"How was it?"

"Exhausting, but I think I found a place. I did hear that the Gallo's are officially no longer a problem."

"Well, yeah, Caleb shot them all."

Indigo smirked at me, and it annoyed the hell out of me.

"When are you going?" My father asked.

"Today, after Christa wakes up."

He nodded, and looked down at the rag he was wiping his greasy hands on. I could never read him, but I knew he hadn't been happy about what I'd done to Judd. He'd never say it though. I think he was glad the dick was dead.

"Clare's putting on a lunch for everyone," Indigo said. "Stay for that and then you can head up home."

I nodded. "Sounds good."

Indigo took the bag and headed inside with me. My father went back to the garage without another word.

"Is he okay?"

"Yeah, he's just...upset that you got your hands dirty."

Indigo moved off and left me on the back patio with Clare. She was on the phone, organising her lunch with everyone. I was glad my dad had her. She wasn't chaotic like my mother was. They may still love each other but Clare was good for him. I could see that now. She offered a brief smile over at me before she went back to talking. I sat down on the love seat and started to rock it as I looked down at my phone.

CHRISTA WAS BUBBLING from the massive lunch Clare had put on. I had seen her sneak Christa a few donuts under the table when they thought I wasn't looking which meant she was going to be a chatterbox the entire way back to the little piece of paradise I had scored for us. It was out of the city limits and close to a lake, enough of a distance that I couldn't be dragged back down into the Gallo mess but close enough that I could still see the family when I needed to.

Caleb put her in the back and handed her an iPad. She was glued to the damn thing, but I was also grateful for it. Indigo came to stand at the door, as I sat down behind the wheel of the car.

Just as I was about to start the car, Indigo smirked at me as he leaned down.

"What?" I barked. "Why are you so fucking smirky?"

The passenger side door opened, and Caleb jumped in, closing the door, and putting his seatbelt on.

"What the fuck are you doing?" I asked him.

"You think I'm letting you go off on your own?" Caleb asked me. "Hell no. You need someone to watch your back."

"Yeah," Indigo piped up. "Her back. Sure."

I turned back to Indigo to slap him, but he backed away, laughing.

"Caleb..."

"Look, you may think that you need to do this alone, but that girl needs someone in her life as a father figure, one she can trust. I'm not her dad, but I can help you. You don't want to be a single mum."

"I can't be in a relationship, not yet," I told him.

"I didn't say I wanted a relationship," Caleb replied, a smile on his face. "Look at you, thinking you're hot shit and all that. I'm just coming to make sure this girl stays away from the donuts."

"Hey!" Christa exclaimed. "I like donuts."

"I'm very aware," Caleb replied.

"Can we keep him, Mama?" Christa asked. "I like when he pushes me on the swings."

"Yeah, Mama," Caleb said, a huge smile on his face, knowing he'd won the kid over. "Can you keep me?"

I rolled my eyes and looked in the rear-view mirror. Christa's big eyes had sold it for me. Not that it was hard. Caleb was a hunk of a man, and I knew I could trust him implicitly. I hadn't really wanted to do it alone, so this was perfect, but could it be too perfect?

"Put the car in drive, Callie."

I started the car, pulled out of the driveway, and headed toward our new place. Just me, Christa, and Caleb.

ABOUT THE AUTHOR

Kate grew up in Western Sydney, in Australia, and remains there today. She has always loved the written word, being influenced by the likes of Edgar Allan Poe, JR Ward and Anne Rice, she ventured into writing at a young age.

Finally taking the plunge in 2016 and publishing for the first time. Ever since, she's been trying to bring the worlds she's created in her head to the page for everyone else to enjoy as much as she does. When she's not writing, she's looking after her bevvy of pets including snakes, lizards, axolotls, birds, a turtle and a dog with her husband Kyle.

LINKS

Facebook Author Page:
   www.facebook.com/AuthorKateBonham

Instagram:
   www.instagram.com/kbonhamauthor

Tiktok:
   www.tiktok.com/@kbonhamauthor

Bookbub:
   www.bookbub.com/profile/kate-bonham

Printed in Great Britain
by Amazon

WELCOME

Take a look at your wine rack – how many are bottles that you've been buying for years? It's all too easy to fall into the habit of staying 'safe'. We know what we like, so why waste time and money on trying something that might serve us better simmered beyond recognition in a stew? For experts and enthusiasts alike, The Wine Lover's Handbook is the essential companion to help broaden your wine horizons.

Brought to you by the team behind Decanter magazine, our connoisseurs will guide you through the wine world, from recommending the finest wines you can buy to drink now or to age, to exploring the regions and destinations ideal for the amateur sommelier. Elsewhere, meet the producers who are making waves in the industry, and find out what our judges make of some of the world's most popular wines in our panel tastings.

FUTURE

THE WINE LOVER'S HANDBOOK

Future PLC Quay House, The Ambury, Bath, BA1 1UA

Bookazine Editorial
Group Editor **Philippa Grafton**
Senior Designer **Perry Wardell-Wicks**
Senior Art Editor **Andy Downes**
Head of Art & Design **Greg Whitaker**
Editorial Director **Jon White**

Decanter Editorial
Editor-in-Chief **Chris Maillard**
Magazine Editor **Amy Wislocki**
Content Manager & Regional Editor
(US, Canada, Australia, NZ, South Africa) **Tina Gellie**
Editor, Decanter Premium & Regional Editor
(Bordeaux & Burgundy) **Georgina Hindle**
Editor, Decanter China & Regional Editor
(Asia, Northern & Eastern Europe) **Sylvia Wu**
Regional Editor (Spain, Portugal, South America) **Julie Sheppard**
Regional Editor (Italy) **James Button**
Regional Editor (France excl Bordeaux & Burgundy) **Natalie Earl**
Production Editor **David Longfield**
Art Editor **Patrick Grabham**
Editorial Assistant **Elie Lloyd Ellis**

Cover images
Getty Images

Photography
All copyrights and trademarks are recognised and respected

Sales & Marketing
Commercial Director **Clare Dove**
Events & Awards Director **Victoria Stanage**
Head of Sales **Sonja van Praag**
Head of Marketing **Alex Layton**

International
Head of Print Licensing **Rachel Shaw**
licensing@futurenet.com
www.futurecontenthub.com

Circulation
Head of Newstrade **Tim Mathers**

Production
Head of Production **Mark Constance**
Production Project Manager **Matthew Eglinton**
Advertising Production Manager **Joanne Crosby**
Digital Editions Controller **Jason Hudson**
Production Managers **Keely Miller, Nola Cokely,
Vivienne Calvert, Fran Twentyman**

Printed in the UK

Distributed by Marketforce, 5 Churchill Place, Canary Wharf, London, E14 5HU
www.marketforce.co.uk Tel: 0203 787 9001

The Wine Lover's Handbook Volume Three (DBZ4869)
© 2022 Future Publishing Limited

Future plc is a public company quoted on the London Stock Exchange (symbol: FUTR)
www.futureplc.com

Chief executive **Zillah Byng-Thorne**
Non-executive chairman **Richard Huntingford**
Chief financial officer **Penny Ladkin-Brand**

Tel +44 (0)1225 442 244

Part of the

Decanter

bookazine series

Widely Recycled

ipso. For press freedom with responsibility

Contents

28

88

64

Pink
and proud of it

Darker-coloured, fuller-bodied rosé styles may have slipped out of the spotlight, but they offer a useful combination of summery style and versatility in pairing with foods. Here are 25 top pink (some almost red) choices to explore

STORY & SELECTION ELIZABETH GABAY MW

Pale pink Provence rosés seem to be everywhere, but 20 years ago the majority of rosés on sale were relatively dark and full-bodied, and many of them lacked freshness and finesse. The evolution of rosé led to the rise of lighter, more elegant wines, along with the idea that the paler the rosé, the better the wine. True or not, this has had the effect of reducing the popularity of darker rosés.

Producers of these styles often have a long history of fuller-bodied rosés, and are today often fighting against the tide of international trends. The fightback has resulted in renewed pride in these historic styles and brought fresher, more modern interpretations of these wines, which are worth looking out for, despite the pressure for 'paler is better'.

Most darker rosés were originally made from juice 'bled off' (by the saignée method) from red wines as a by-product, which would result in wines that often lacked acidity and were slightly tannic. Typical regions where you'll still find this approach today include northern Spain and its Garnacha-based rosados and, in central-eastern Italy, Cerasuolo d'Abruzzo rosato wines made with the Montepulciano variety. However, producers are now choosing to make these wines separately from the red wines, harvesting earlier to maintain freshness and reducing the temperature during skin contact and maceration, so that their saignée method wines now have both full-bodied freshness and darker colour, but without the heavy, clumsy structure of old. In the New World, darker rosés are often produced in this fruitier style, but often lack the structure found in European wines.

Some varieties lend themselves to the fuller-bodied structure, often with

> ## 'Full-bodied freshness and darker colour, but without the heavy, clumsy structure of old'

darker fruit flavours, and these typically include Mourvèdre, Syrah, Cabernet Sauvignon, Sangiovese and Petit Verdot.

TIME WELL SPENT

Another traditional style of winemaking which can result in full-bodied rosés in both pale and darker hues is the use of black and white grape varieties blended together. Depending on the vintage, the depth of colour in such styles can be determined by the relative proportions of black or white grapes used. Today, a tendency for higher percentages of white grapes, such as Rolle or Macabeu, allows for greater extraction of fruit without leading to such a deep colour in the final wine. Examples include the clarets of

Cigales in northern Spain, the clairets of Bordeaux and German Schillerwein, as well as the rosés of Tavel and Provence.

These styles' extended skin maceration, ranging from 12 hours to a week, means the wines can fall between full-bodied rosé and light red, accompanied by great ageing potential. Rosés made with paler grapes or with more white grapes in the blend can be deceptive, their pale colour hiding the fuller body coming from the extended maceration. Time spent in oak is another invisible factor that can contribute to weighty, paler rosés, although this is still more of an Old World style (see 'Can rosé really age?', p16).

While some producers have abandoned traditional styles, and seen sales increase with modern paler wines, others have introduced the pale rosé style alongside their traditional darker wines. For some, the traditional dark wines are perceived as the wines drunk by the grandparents; for others they are seen as an act of defiance to the increasing dominance of pale rosé. Among natural wines, rosés are often darker, too, with many producers rejecting the 'rosé' term altogether and declaring their wines to be 'pale reds'.

These fuller-bodied rosés are both more suited to being matched with a range of foods and less restricted to the summer season – and they usually find favour with a broader range of consumers' wine preferences.

1 Domaine d'Ansignan, Les Grenadines, Côtes Catalanes, Roussillon, France 2021 95

£14.99 **The Real Wine Co**

Roussillon négociant Jeff Carrel makes this wine at his own estate with a blend of local varieties – Carignan, Grenache, the white Macabeu, Syrah and the very local Pellut (Hairy Grenache). Presented in a dark bottle, the light red colour is hidden.

Labelled as 'red', the wine is vinified 80% as a rosé, 20% by carbonic maceration. If you like Burgundy, this could be the rosé for you. Smooth, silky texture with intense wild red berry fruit, crunchy cranberries, blue flowers, a hint of tropical creamy peachiness and long, fresh, almost saline acidity, the beautifully integrated weighty fruit slips down easily. A steal at the price. Stunning. **Drink** 2022-2030 **Alcohol** 13%

2 Johannes Zillinger, Numen Rosé, Weinviertel, Austria 2020 94

£42 **Roland Wines**

From old St Laurent vines planted in 1982, which produce good fruit even in poor vintages. Zillinger likes to stretch the potential of his rosé wines and this is no exception. Fermented in amphorae, this has a vibrancy and energy: sour cherry, rosehip, sage, thyme and floral notes, crisp freshness on the palate, silky but slightly grainy texture. It exudes both ripeness and an angular, structured acidity and body which opens and develops in the glass. Biodynamic. **Drink** 2022-2027 **Alc** 12%

3 Pierre Amadieu, Romane Machotte Rosé, Gigondas, Rhône, France 2021 94

pierre-amadieu.com

A combination of maceration and direct press are used to achieve a fresh wine with enough fruit to carry the oak, used for both fermentation and ageing, to create a serious wine. Old vines grown at altitude add further intensity and freshness. Full-bodied wild cherry fruit (neighbouring Ventoux is famed for its cherry orchards), a saline edge, long mouthwatering acidity: the whole is beautifully balanced. The toasty oak notes are evident, adding an umami twist to the saline finish. The intensity of weight and structure make this rosé a fitting companion to the red wines from this region. **Drink** 2022-2030 **Alc** 14.5%

4 Domaine Maby, Libiamo, Tavel, Rhône, France 2019 93

£18 **The Wine Society**

From grapes grown on the hotter galet roulé soils, the use of Cinsault and white Grenache keeps this wine at the paler end of the Tavel spectrum, while fermentation and ageing in barrel gives added weight – Maby aims for flavour rather than colour. A deep golden amber colour with delicate smoky chestnut aromas, the wine opens up to rich white chocolate, bitter orange and honeyed red fruits. It is powerful, complex, atypical, and rather gorgeous. The tannins are delicately integrated and sweet. **Drink** 2022-2035 **Alc** 14%

5 Rozès, Terras do Grifo Rosé, Douro, Portugal 2020 93

POA **Nicolas**

I hate to say this, Port lovers, but the Douro makes some stunning rosé! Medium-dark copper-pink with buttery, leesy, slightly oxidative aromas, results in a delightful joyousness with opulent, intensely ripe juicy cherries and mouthwatering freshness. But just as you think this is all, notes of sour cherries and salinity emerge with an almost sharp pomelo freshness building up on the finish when you least expect it. Structured and full of energy, this wine continues to develop in the glass. **Drink** 2022-2030 **Alc** 13%

6 Cume do Avia, Ni Rosado Ni Clarete Rosete, Ribeiro, Spain 2019 92

£16-£19.33 Iconic Wines, North & South, Wanderlust Wine

This Galician rosé from Spain's northwest Atlantic coast is made with a blend of six local varieties: Caiño Longo, Mencía, Carabuñeira, Merenzao, Brancellao and Treixadura. Initially restrained with cool-climate freshness and notes of sour berries, the wine opens up to blackcurrants, rosehips and intense dark fruit. Long, fresh crunchy acidity with a saline bite, a chalky texture and a firm red fruit tannic grip give this wine structure but overall it is charmingly delicate and supple rather than powerful and opulent, and very much a rosé for red wine drinkers. **Drink** 2022-2025 **Alc** 10%

7 Domaine de la Bégude, L'Irréductible, Bandol, Provence, France 2020 92

£32.50 Connaught Cellars

Guillaume Tari aims to give his two rosés maximum Mourvèdre expression, and while his estate wine has fresh, youthful floral, fruity charm, L'Irréductible takes the complexity a notch higher. Both are among the darkest Bandol rosés. From aromas of red berries and forest floor, the wine opens out to an explosion of cherries, strawberries, tart cranberries and crunchy red apples. A slightly sour, pithy finish and crisp acidity give the wine a long, mouthwatering freshness with the power and structure one expects from a Bandol rosé, while hinting at its beautiful ageing potential. Organic. **Drink** 2022-2030 **Alc** 13%

8 Mas Foulaquier, Pierre de Rosette, Gard, Languedoc, France 2021 92

masfoulaquier.fr

Always a brave move to make a rosé with Alicante Bouschet: a defiant move against the sea of pale. The colour is a pale red, with aromas reminiscent of a red wine: red fruits, hints of coffee, cocoa and savoury notes. Lovely depth of structure with rich, almost jammy blackberry and mulberry fruit while still keeping all the instant freshness and gentle red fruit of a direct-press wine. Nine months in amphorae adds to the complexity with herbal notes and some evident structural tannins pointing this towards a light red wine style. Very much a gastronomic wine with freshness, fruit and body that will keep light red drinkers happy, rosé drinkers happy, and natural wine aficionados ecstatic. **Drink** 2022-2025 **Alc** 13%

9 Cathar(tic) Wines, Fingers Crossed, Côtes Catalanes, Roussillon, France 2020 91

POA GB Wine Shippers

This wine, normally known as By Any Other Name, was given the name Fingers Crossed due to the strangeness of the year and the extra-long barrel ageing due to Covid. The resulting wine is still a success and one of the few dark Mourvèdre rosés in southern France. Pale red-pink. Abundant cherries, with intense cooked red fruit, black tea, a gentle yeastiness and a touch of oak – a perfect balance of crunchy berries, summer-ripe red fruit and the sweet vanilla spice of the oak. Vibrant, fresh acidity, lively and moreish, and it has some saline minerality on the finish. **Drink** 2022-2025 **Alc** 13%

10 Contesa, Caparrone, Cerasuolo d'Abruzzo, Abruzzo, Italy 2021 91

£9.19-£10.50 (2020) All About Wine, Field & Fawcett, Five O'Clock Somewhere, Kwoff, ND John, North & South

With a name like Cerasuolo, meaning cherry, it comes as no surprise that this wine is a bright cherry-pink colour and that cherries are a typical fruit profile of the wine. Aromas of fresh red cherries and the bittersweet notes of almond kernels lead onto rich, ripe sour cherry fruit, almost intense and jammy, with restrained fine mineral structure, a hint of chalky texture, delicate tannins on the finish and lifted by a vibrant, fresh leafy acidity. Beautiful and unapologetically intense, ripe fruit with mouthwatering freshness. **Drink** 2022-2027 **Alc** 13.5% ▶

11 Domaine de la Rectorie, Côté Mer Rosé, Collioure, Roussillon, France 2021 91

rectorie.com

This wine is distinctly non-Provençal with its wonderfully bold Roussillon character. Copper-pink. Delicately peach floral notes on the nose, the palate continues with an amazing intensity of yellow stone fruits, bitter oranges, candied citrus peel. Concentrated and rich with a weighty, firm structure and lifted by youthful sherbet acidity. More in keeping with a skin-contact white wine, with its sour phenolics, than a traditional rosé. Big, bold, unapologetic, and delightfully gastronomic, this wine opens up even more if you allow it to breathe in the glass. **Drink** 2022-2030 **Alc** 14%

12 Bird in Hand, Rosé, South Australia 2020 90

£13.99 **Waitrose**

Proof, if it were needed, that colour does not always determine whether a rosé is fuller-bodied. This delicately pale Pinot Noir rosé has the fuller fruit you'd expect from an Australian wine. It has lovely, vibrant dark cherries and blackcurrants with pretty cherry blossom and summer garden freshness and crisp, cool-climate (Adelaide Hills) acidity. Such a pretty wine with the depth and weight of ripe black fruit, even a hint of wine gums, giving serious structure. Punches way above its price point. **Drink** 2022-2024 **Alc** 12%

13 Cramele Recas, Solo Quinta Roze, Romania 2021 90

cramelerecas.ro

Despite a rather eccentric blend of Romanian variety Feteasca Neagra with classic varieties Merlot, Cabernet Sauvignon and Pinot Noir plus Alicante Bouschet, this wine works really well. A darker pink with blue tints, which leads to the typical Feteasca Neagra aromas of blue flowers and red fruits. On the palate, juicy, ripe red fruit with almost jammy richness stops short of overly ripe softness, with mouthwateringly crunchy red berry acidity, a fine powdery texture and well-integrated, delicate tannins on the finish. A lovely, joyous wine. **Drink** 2022-2023 **Alc** 12.5%

14 Celler Alimara, Llumí Rosat, Terra Alta, Catalonia, Spain 2020 90

£11-£13.95 **Waddesdon Wine, WoodWinters**
A prime example of how some of these more full-bodied rosés shine if served at 12°C rather than straight from the fridge, and are even better if decanted. A pretty copper-pink colour, this Grenache rosé was initially very closed, but opened up on decanting to reveal intense ripe rosehips, pomegranates and sour cherry fruit balancing the acidity, saline minerality and hint of tannins. Grippy and structural, this is a distinctly gastronomic rosé with its intriguing blend of minerality and ripeness. **Drink** 2022-2024 **Alc** 13.5%

15 Château Penin, Natur, Bordeaux Clairet, France 2020 90

£12.50 **WoodWinters**
Harking back to the days when luncheon claret was the perfect wine for lunch, this clairet is the result of deep-rooted traditional winemaking. A dark pink, it looks like a pale red. A Merlot-expressive nose of black cherries and violets leads into ripe cherry, raspberry and redcurrant fruit with a sour, wild berry saline finish and vibrant leafy acidity. A hint of tannin gives a firm, gravel-like grip; this wine knows where it is going and says it firmly, but without shouting and screaming. A style that needs love before it disappears. Organic. **Drink** 2022-2025 **Alc** 12.5%

16 Domaine d'Arbousset, Tavel, Rhône, France 2021 90

£12 **Tesco**

This is a great introduction to the wines of Tavel, with lashings of ripe strawberry, a touch of raspberry jam and that tell-tale twist of spicy tannins on the finish. This is a full-bodied, fruity rosé par excellence with the abundance of fruit and body that is so appealing in Tavel, combined with lovely freshness. It's not dissimilar in style to the rosés of Navarra in northern Spain, which are also Grenache-based with extended maceration. **Drink** 2022-2024 **Alc** 13.5%

17 Les Vignerons Catalans, Trémoine de Rasiguères, Côtes du Roussillon, France 2020 90

tremoine.com

Copper red-pink, this rosé is all about juicy dark cherries and silky-smooth velvet acidity. Soft and supple with almost jammy weightiness, the acidity, while not as vibrant as some, has a mouthwatering minerality. With an intensity of rich fruit, some weighty tannins and extraction, this rosé is grippy and structural in a traditional bold, tannic, somewhat old-fashioned style but it does exactly what I would ask from a dark rosé. **Drink** 2022-2023 **Alc** 13.5%

18 Señorío de Sarría, Viñedo No5 Rosado, Navarra, Spain 2021 90

£9-£13.33 **All About Wine, Five O'Clock Somewhere, North & South**

While most modern rosé producers chase the pale pink wines made by direct press, those of Navarra (as in Tavel) rely on maceration to extract weighty and full-bodied wines. This old-vine Garnacha is a pale cherry red and strikingly fruity and well-extracted. The trick with these wines is to balance the heftier fruit with freshness and acidity and this wine strikes the balance perfectly. Smooth, round, rich strawberries and raspberries, gentle pippy tannic structure and delicately leafy acidity with a touch of juicy, crunchy redcurrant and a hint of blood orange. **Drink** 2022-2027 **Alc** 14%

19 Trimboli, Pink Duck, New South Wales Australia 2021 90

£10.99 **Laithwaites**

This could be a rosé that divides opinions, but love it or hate it, it has some intriguing character which I loved. Not as full-bodied as many, it has a range of complex notes that make it different from so many other more neutral styles. Pale salmon-pink, this classic-toned rosé surprises with notes of orange blossom and Lapsang Souchong tea on the nose. On the palate it has creamy weight with notes of jasmine, violet, lemongrass and lime acidity with some saline notes, dark fruit and firm minerality giving structure. Plus the added curiosity of using the red variety Montepulciano (with 'a splash' of Vermentino), which is also used in the very different Cerasuolo d'Abruzzo in Italy. **Drink** 2022-2023 **Alc** 12.5%

20 Villa Calicantus, Chiar'otto Chiaretto, Bardolino Classico, Veneto, Italy 2019 90

£20 **Wanderlust Wine**

Made with the classic Bardolino grapes, this is one of the rare Chiarettos that has not followed the very pale pink path. A pure expression of Corvina's fresh, juicy cherry fruit (often similar to Gamay), it has extra depth with intense blackcurrant notes, crunchy cranberry acidity and a lean, saline minerality which gives a mouthwatering length and finish, ending with a slight natural apple and savoury twang. Delicate, fresh and youthful, this is a wine that's showing elegant potential for further ageing. Biodynamic. **Drink** 2022-2024 **Alc** 12%

▶

21 Domaine des Trinités, Le Pioch Rosé, Faugères, Languedoc, France 2019 89

£13.99 **Cambridge Wine Merchants**

Made by Englishman Simon Coulshaw, this wine could be described as either old-fashioned or avant garde. It's made using the thoroughly unfashionable saignée method, bleeding the juice off the red wine. Dark pink with intense cherry fruit and floral aromas, the wine has weighty strawberry jam and kirsch fruit with herbal notes on the finish. Elegant structure, ageing well, although like many rosés made using this method, the acidity lacks the vibrancy of more modern methods. One for those who reminisce about past summers and enjoy rosé with a charming touch of maturity. Organic. **Drink** 2022-2023 **Alc** 13%

22 Charles Melton, Rose of Virginia, Barossa Valley, South Australia 2021 88

£29.99 **The Wine Reserve**

Charles Melton is well known for his flamboyant wine styles, and this is no exception. Confidently dark pink, almost a red, this wine is opulently full of ripe cherry and raspberry jam, suggesting a touch of residual sugar with ripe redcurrant fruit leading to some vibrant and crunchy acidity (could do with a touch more) and finishing with a hint of salt and pepper on the finish. It very much fits in the league of the fuller-bodied rosés of Tavel and Navarra. **Drink** 2022-2023 **Alc** 13.5%

23 Nelson Family Vineyards, Rosé, Paarl, South Africa 2021 88

£11.25 **Corney & Barrow**

There aren't many rosés made from Petit Verdot (here 85%, with Syrah), which gives more colour than is fashionable, but it is a variety that makes attractive, full-bodied fruity pinks in a style made popular a few years ago by fellow South African producer Rustenberg. Pale red in colour, and shouting out varietal character with notes of strawberry sorbet and a hint of ripe raspberries. This version is quite delicate and charming with crunchy acidity and a lovely note of pepper and herbs on the finish. **Drink** 2022-2023 **Alc** 13%

24 Viña Nava, Garnacha Rosé, Navarra, Spain 2020 88

£8.99 **Laithwaites**

One of the joys of this style of wine is that it is exactly that – joyous. While it's not for those seeking sophisticated elegance, this dark-ruby pink shouts out cherry fruit on the nose, opening up to classic concentrated raspberry-Grenache fruit on the palate. Full-bodied dark fruit, easy-drinking, no-nonsense for a relaxed evening with friends or around the barbecue. **Drink** 2022-2023 **Alc** 13.5%

25 Domaine La Soumade, Hors d'Age Rasteau Vin Doux Naturel, Rhône, France 2014 94

£17/50cl **Thorman Hunt**

It is easy to forget that many of the vin doux naturel wines of Rasteau are actually at their base made as a rosé wine before being fortified – so a good excuse here to include this amazing tawny Rasteau. Age in oak has turned it a tawny brown-orange. On the nose, notes of desiccated coconut and toasted nuts open up to the smooth, mellow fruit of bitter oranges, red cherries and raspberry jam before diving into complex notes of digestive biscuits and sun-kissed garrigue herbs. Stunning acidity, structure, perfect fruit with gentle tannins keeping things up. Beautifully balanced. **Drink** 2022-2040 **Alc** 16.5% **D**

Can rosé really age?

Yes, there's an ocean of young, pink wines to choose from. But why not offer a bottle-aged, more food-friendly alternative? A niche set of southern French producers do just that – though their approach divides opinion

STORY ELIZABETH GABAY MW

The subject of ageing rosé elicits passionate debate. For many, 'aged rosé' or rosé de garde, still means rosé with only two to three years of age; but with the increase in quality inherent in wines of this type that have a capacity to age, these rosés are still youthful. The big question is: 'How do rosés continue to age?' What are their secondary and tertiary profile evolutions as they shift from fresh fruit to other flavours?

'Rosé should be drunk young and fresh' is the prevailing mantra of producers and critics, who cite its simplicity and fun-loving style as one of the many reasons for the rosé boom. Vintage charts and extra wine knowledge are not required.

In southern France, rosé regarded as good for the season has meant traditionally that winemakers rush to bottle their wine by January/February to be tasted in time for reviews and new listings from Easter. By the following spring, any wines left over are relegated as old stock to dispose of by the time the new wines come in.

Many believe rosé does not age well beyond a few years because older vintages have never been tasted, yet very few producers retain a library of older vintages to taste or show to those who are interested – let alone to sell! It makes it difficult

Daniel Ravier of Domaine Tempier in Bandol, where ageing rosés show salinity to evaluate and assess the ageing potential of rosés, requiring great effort to locate old vintages.

Near Narbonne in Languedoc, Gérard Bertrand is keeping back examples of his Clos du Temple to be able to offer vertical tastings, and Château du Galoupet in Provence, now in the LVMH stable, is considering the same policy.

STAYING POWER

Various winemaking techniques are used to help rosé age. Because rosé is halfway between white wine (avoiding extractions of phenol compounds at the tannin level) and red wine (with potential problems in colour extraction and structure), producing rosé wine that ages means developing ways to help the wine age within the style. Philippe Bru, winemaker at Château Vignelaure in Provence, sees complex reasons why a rosé can age. 'Maceration adds to concentration and rich fruits, wood adds tannins and structure; and although malolactic fermentation does not in itself contribute to ageing potential, as it reduces vital acidity, if the wine has naturally high enough acidity to allow for malo, it has ageing potential.'

Mireille Conrath, consultant winemaker for the Syndicat des Vins Côtes de Provence, feels that the techniques used for creating a rosé that will age are hit and miss. Over the past 10-15 years there has been an extensive modernisation in rosé winemaking, which could impact on how current and future rosés will age.

Aged Provence rosés tend to have spent time in oak, and they usually age quite gently, taking on soft ripe fruit character. However, with fewer older vintages around to taste, it's not always easy to evaluate such wines' ageing potential. On the south coast, St-Tropez cooperative Torpez's Ultimum 2015 (40% Grenache, 40% Mourvèdre, 15% Tibouren, 5% Syrah, aged 18 months in foudres) has oranges, juicy raspberries, white peach, saline freshness and sweet, gentle oak.

Château Vignelaure 2014 (Grenache, Syrah, Cabernet Sauvignon) is from one of the most northerly Provence vineyards – at up to 400m between Rians and Jouques– and has ripe, sweet red fruit, quince, sweet apples, peaches and apricots, with long, fresh vibrant acidity.

Also on the coast, Bandol's direct-press wines take on golden salmon hues and nutty quince and bruised apple notes quite quickly, while remaining fairly concentrated, with saline notes a commonly used descriptor as the wines age, defining the freshness.

Domaine Dupuy de Lôme 2015 (70% Mourvèdre on north-facing clay and limestone) has powerful structure and ageing potential, with youthful peaches and apricots and an underlying darker fruit power. And Domaine Tempier's 2011 (55%

Mourvèdre on limestone) has saline, rich orange and apricot fruit, caramelised bitter almonds and long pomelo freshness. Domaine de Terrebrune's 2010 (60% Mourvèdre on brown clay), meanwhile, has fresh, bitter orange, hints of blackcurrant fruit, saline molasses and citrus vivacity with honeyed concentration.

TAVEL TOO

Up in the Rhône valley to the north, Tavel producers use lengthy maceration ranging from 12 to 72 hours, and they attribute the ageworthiness of their full-bodied rosés precisely to this maceration and the weight and tannic structure it provides. Tavel can develop notes of chocolate, orange and floral delicacy with tannins giving freshness, while some of the wines that have had longer maceration can develop notes of dark cherries and kirsch, but very rarely the saline notes found in Bandol.

Domaine Maby's Libiamo 2015 (50% Grenache Blanc, 50% Cinsault on the hot galets roulés terroir, fermented and aged in new demi-muids) has notes of marmalade, black chocolate and honey, with firm tannins.

Château Trinquevedel's Les Vignes d'Eugène 2011 (Grenache, Clairette and Cinsault on sandy soils and 24 hours' maceration), has ripe cherry fruit, floral notes, hints of bitter almonds and blood orange acidity. Château Manissy's Tête de Cuvée 1976 (sandy clay soils, fermented in concrete, aged in foudres), has dried apricots, honey, Lapsang Souchong tea notes and amazing freshness and length.

'Producing rosé wine that ages means developing ways to help the wine age within the style'

Domaine Maby, Tavel

Oak ageing is another hot topic in the rosé world, with many arguing that extra care during winemaking and the use of oak helps rosé to age longer, especially if backed up with greater weight and extraction in the wine.

THE BENEFITS OF OAK

Allowing the must to interact with a little oxygen before, during and shortly after fermentation can protect wine from subsequent oxidation in the bottle. Oak, which is naturally slightly porous, is an easy way to let in this small amount of oxygen – too much and the wine will oxidise.

Ageing in oak (and extended skin maceration) will also provide tannins, which can protect rosé from the negative effects of oxygen, just as they can in reds. For many winemakers, this use of oak is a statement of serious, ageworthy rosés that justifies waiting a year before release.

Even if a rosé is made to age well, its ageing potential can still be jeopardised by lightstrike. While its colour is flaunted in clear bottles, there's a risk it will be exposed to harmful UV light. Nevertheless, only a few producers put their rosé in dark or recycled glass. Château Trinquevedel's Guillaume Demoulin, who is also the current president of the Tavel producers, is working towards the syndicat having a dark glass bottle to use for the premium wines intended for ageing.

The question now is no longer whether rosé can age, but rather what the impact is of the different varieties, terroirs, vintages and vinification techniques in creating different styles we can enjoy in five, 10 or 20 years. **D**

Benefits of age: Gabay's half-dozen rosés to tuck away

① Domaine La Grande Bauquière, Moment Singulier, Côtes de Provence 2021 93

POA **Alliance Wine**

New oak on the nose almost dominates the aromas, but exotic flower notes peek round the edges. Charmingly juicy white peach, lychees and creamy (reflecting the chalky limestone of Ste-Victoire) and sweet nutty new oak up front, with some hidden depth of dark berry and cherry fruit developing on the palate. Beautiful structure, with some gentle tannins and lime acidity. A serious gastronomic wine with ageing potential. **Drink** 2022-2028 **Alcohol** 13%

② Moulin-La-Viguerie, La Combe des Rieu, Tavel, Rhône 2020 93

£29-£29.50 (2019) **Natty Boy Wines, Salusbury Winestore**

Even with a good amount of white grape varieties in the blend, this wine is full of juicy raspberries, cherries and strawberries, with supple, intense black tannins and sour red berry acidity, complex notes from the oak of toast and coffee coming through on the finish. Lovely balance, building in complexity and concentration. Promises great ageing potential. **Drink** 2022-2035 **Alc** 14.5%

③ Château Les Mesclances, Faustine, Côtes de Provence La Londe 2021 92

£19.95 (2020) **Davy's**

Extended maceration to emphasise the ageing potential also serves to heighten the saline minerality of the coastal schist terroir. Silky soft, velvet texture with intense, long, mouthwatering minerality. Full-bodied with ripe, dark berry fruit, crunchy salinity and long, linear, direct attack. Combines both restrained elegance and powerful structure, hidden fruit pushing beneath the surface to appear with age. **Drink** 2022-2028 **Alc** 13.5%

Domaine la Suffrène, Tradition, Bandol, Provence 2020 90

£19.50-£22.49 **Deliciously French, Joseph Barnes, L'Art du Vin, Les Caves de Pyrene, S&J Cellars, Sip Wines**

This is on the cusp of moving from youthful freshness to slightly more mature fruit. The dark cherry and full structure plays with the more exotic fruit and creamy notes and is balanced by youthful, crunchy wild berries with their delicate length and fresh acidity. The weighty structure finishes with textural phenolics. Drinking well now, and the fruit will continue to integrate into a seamless, complex wine. **Drink** 2022-2032 **Alc** 13.5%

Domaine Lafond Roc-Epine, Tavel, Rhône 2021 89

£17.95 **Brompton Wine, Fraziers, Latitude Wine, Le Bon Vin, Montrachet, The VIneking, Vindinista**

The perfumed florals of the Cinsault and Clairette in the blend give pretty aromatics of sweet spice, jasmine tea, dried apricots, opening up to creamy peaches, apricots and fresh raspberries. Long, crisp acidity with some fine tea tannins. Fresh elegance reflecting the newness of the vintage and the wine's potential for ageing. The fresh fruit will develop more intense dried fruit character, with the spice notes adding to the complexity. **Drink** 2022-2035 **Alc** 13.5%

Domaine Tempier, Bandol, Provence 2021 88

£29.99 (2020) **Lea & Sandeman, Noble Grape**

A youthful, fruit-forward wine with almost red jam richness on the nose. On the palate, crunchy red fruit and green leafy-fresh acidity, not dissimilar to the typical Provence rosé style, but with more powerful, strong phenolic extraction. Quite restrained at first, slowly opening up to reveal quite a powerful structure and riper fruit. Drinkable now, but seems a shame to open it while so young and before its potential (hence lower score) is reached with a few years of age. **Drink** 2023-2032 **Alc** 13% **D**

① ② ③

CREATE YOUR DREAM OUTDOOR SPACE WITH OUR BRAND-NEW TITLE!

As the warmer weather brings with it the opportunity for outdoor entertaining, why not get a headstart on building the garden of your dreams? From design ideas to planting tips, we've got you covered!

My life as a personal wine consultant

It isn't a job you'll see advertised, so what does it take to become one? Right place, right time?
Experience, qualifications, hard work, connections? All of those and more, it turns out

STORY CHARLES CURTIS MW

Tongue firmly in cheek, I sometimes define 'wine consultant' as 'someone lacking employment who will work for whoever pays them'. Although meant in jest, the implied question is valid: just what does a wine consultant do? More importantly, in this age, when every assistant in a retail shop styles him- or herself a sales consultant, who would hire one?

The short answer is this: a wine consultant is someone who advises wine lovers about their passion. He or she advises buyers on what to buy (and at what price, and from whom); and advises sellers on how and where to sell in order to realise the best return. It involves inspecting a collector's purchases and advising on issues of condition, provenance and authenticity; and advising on storing, shipping, insuring and, eventually, on serving and enjoying one's purchases.

If I did not begin my working life at 17 with the ambition to become a wine consultant, it was solely due to a lack of imagination. I loved food and cooking, and started out as a chef, which took me to Paris in 1981 and the Le Cordon Bleu culinary school. Back in the States from 1994, I began a career in the wine trade that included seven years in wholesale, a further seven at Moët Hennessy USA, and four as head of department at Christie's auction house.

In 2012, however, I then found myself living in Hong Kong and needing a change. I still kept an apartment in New York, where I had worked from 2008 as head of Christie's wine department at under my mentor, the late Michael Broadbent

MW. But how would I pay the rent? I reasoned that the skill set I had developed at Christie's was sufficiently advanced to offer value to the right buyers. My first qualification was that I knew all the tricks of an auction house, and could help those on the other side to navigate the tricky shoals of the secondary wine market. Buy three cases of great wine at the right price, and in principle you can drink one for free if you sell the other two at the right time.

I mentioned my thoughts to a client at a pre-sale dinner one evening at One Harbour Road restaurant in Hong Kong. 'Let me be your first client!' was his immediate response. The die was cast – I had decided to open my own shop, and said buyer did indeed become my first client.

PAINSTAKING DETAIL

My first step was to complete the qualification to perform valuations of wine collections that would stand up to the scrutiny of insurers, lawyers and banks. The process is far more complicated than pulling a number out of a hat, since detailed standards have been established for valuation professionals. This aspect of the consultancy is far from the allure of the image many have of the globe-trotting wine expert, yet it is the essential underpinning to this line of work.

A proper valuation begins with inspecting and photographing a collection and describing the condition of each bottle in detail. After spending a week or more in a cold cellar evaluating a wine collection, the riveting process of seeking out

'A wine consultant is someone who advises wine lovers about their passion'

comparable sales begins. Weeks of research in front of the computer are followed by days of writing up and justifying conclusions.

The work is dry, detail-oriented, and not at all suited to pairing with a nice glass of claret. The results, however, can be enormously helpful. A properly prepared appraisal can be beneficial, whether it is used to submit an insurance claim for damaged wine or to bring top dollar for a collection being sold at auction. One client even secured a loan of £20 million using his wine collection as collateral.

The inspection process can have other uses as well. As wine prices have continued their steady rise, nefarious actors occasionally attempt to counterfeit sought-after bottles. Through long years of looking at rare bottles of wine, it is possible to learn the 'tells' – mistakes made by counterfeiters as they prepare their forgeries. Some are obvious, such as misspellings or anachronistic labels. These days, though, counterfeiters are more sophisticated than they were in the past, and problematic bottles are more difficult to spot.

Above: close inspection of wine label details helps to avoid the purchase of counterfeit bottles

Wine consultant: services rendered

Some clients want to be told what to buy and what to pay for it, while others love the thrill of the chase and make their own purchases. Most clients are somewhere on the spectrum between buying only to drink and buying only for investment – very few are purely motivated by one or the other.

Work can include vetting stock prior to purchase, liaising with vendors on fulfilment, shipment and storage of wine and subsequent inspection, as well as negotiating returns if required.

Many clients are more interested in selling than in buying, and I assist by negotiating the terms and conditions of the contract, the marketing of the sale, and the settlement of funds. Other clients are more interested in visiting wine regions and meeting producers. Clients who don't have time to travel often want to meet in restaurants to enjoy top bottles. The unifying theme is that they want the best from each region, and are seldom intrigued by wine-world fashions such as natural wine or orange wine.

One ends up choosing wine for every occasion. Often, they will be for cellaring, but sometimes they'll be wines for a business dinner, a family gathering, or provisioning a yacht in the Mediterranean for a month of cruising.

Fees vary with the level of service required, but are invariably in the form of a retainer paid quarterly, to avoid suspicion that I am driving up purchases to enhance my compensation.

'Don't chase the unicorn – wines that seldom come up for sale, precisely the sort of wine that is most liable to be counterfeit'

With experience, one develops a sense of when something is not quite right. However, it is far more challenging to articulate clearly why this is the case. A well-written inspection report that sets out the reasons clearly and backs up the assertions with photographs has more than once garnered a refund for a doubtful client.

CAVEAT EMPTOR

Ultimately it is much easier not to purchase dubious wine in the first place. Performing due diligence before purchase is one of the primary services that a competent wine advisor can offer. The process begins with an essential injunction – know the vendor and the provenance of the wine. If either seems opaque, it is best to forgo the purchase. Although it may seem like a lost opportunity, it is usually the case that if it seems too good to be true, it probably is.

Dealing with a reputable merchant that is straightforward about its sourcing processes or an auction house that has examined the provenance of the wines it is selling will go a long way in the quest to avoid the questionable.

The other injunction that I often invoke is 'Don't chase the unicorn'. Unicorns are rare wines that seldom come up for sale. It is precisely this sort of wine that is most liable to be counterfeit. The trick is to identify wines a client will love (rather than those you would have for yourself), and how much to pay to secure them without overpaying.

Sometimes truth can be stranger than fiction. A client once sent me to Burgundy to look at a collection of large-format bottles of older vintages from a very renowned domaine. The labels indicated that they had been exported to Italy. The labels looked correct, but something was wrong – the wax at the top of the bottles was the wrong colour, and it was not neatly applied. It looked as if someone had dribbled candle wax on the top of the bottle.

I mentioned my reservations to the vendor, who produced a receipt. The asking price was more than €1 million; I wanted to be sure. As it happened, I knew the Italian importer personally. Later that day, we spoke on the telephone. 'Charles, the wax was all broken when the bottles arrived, so we fixed it,' he said. 'You fixed it

Biography of a wine consultant

1963 Born, St Paul, Minnesota, USA

1981 Worked in kitchens in San Francisco and St-Thomas in the US Virgin Islands, before attending Le Cordon Bleu in Paris and apprenticing at the Hôtel de Crillon and La Grande Cascade, Bois de Boulogne

1994 Wine distributor salesman

2001 Sales at Clicquot Inc (Veuve Clicquot importer for the US)

2004 Passed Master of Wine exam; founded educational programme for Moët Hennessy USA

2008 Head of Department, Christie's auction house (New York & Hong Kong)

2011 Columnist, *La Revue du Vin de France*, China

2012 Founded a fine wine advisory called WineAlpha, focused on private clients and appraisals

2014 Published *The Original Grand Crus of Burgundy*

2015 Senior editor *Le Pan* magazine, Hong Kong

2020 Published *Vintage Champagne 1899-2019*

yourself, at your warehouse?' I queried. 'Yes, Charles, we fixed it ourselves.'

This was 1985. Times were different then. I advised my client that I believed the bottles appeared to be correct but that they would be unsaleable since no one would believe that story secondhand. The client bought the bottles. To the best of my knowledge, he has drunk most of them with his friends.

DINING OUT

Unfortunately, he did not invite me. Often enough, however, I am included. I was recently invited to a two-star Michelin restaurant for lunch by an old friend I mentored in the Master of Wine programme a decade or more ago. He asked me to order wine: 'I was thinking Bordeaux, and I want something nice. My treat.'

I suggested a St-Emilion, Château Magdelaine from the 1980s. 'Good, but I want something nicer. What do you think of this?' He pointed at the Mouton Rothschild 1993. I explained that if he really wanted to splash out at lunch, the Mouton '89 was only $50 more on the wine list, and it was a much better wine. He agreed, and it went down a treat.

We enjoyed this charming luncheon wine as he explained that the start-up he helped found had just sold for $1.2 billion. Apparently, he now had everything he wanted in life... except someone with whom he could enjoy great wine.

I have, in fact, learned many valuable lessons over lunch. One of them was at Scott's in Mayfair. After inspecting wine for a week with a client at Octavian's cellar storage in Wiltshire, we returned to London. My client mentioned he had never met Michael Broadbent. Would I ask him to lunch? Michael was happy to be invited to Scott's. We sat down, and I promptly handed him the wine list. 'Oh, no, dear boy. Why don't you pick the wine?' he asked. I instantly felt put on the spot – Michael was my idol.

I looked at the list as the three of us discussed what to eat. Oysters, lobster and Dover sole were the order of the day. I had a sudden inspiration: 'Michael, what do you think of Champagne for lunch?' 'Don't be silly!' he shot back, 'I had that for breakfast.' Of all the skills I learned from my mentor, the most useful was without doubt the art of advising wisely. We settled on a Chablis Grand Cru Les Clos from François Raveneau, to the general satisfaction of everyone. **D**

The perfect MARTINI

Vodka or gin? Lemon or olive? Shaken or stirred? There's no right answer – or is there? Here's what the world's best Martini-makers have to say on the matter

STORY ALICIA MILLER

The most enduring of classic cocktails, the Martini is simple to make and infinitely customisable. But how do you create the very best one possible? We asked the top mixologists in London's Martini business – Agostino Perrone and Giorgio Bargiani of The Connaught Bar, Alessandro Palazzi of Dukes Bar and Brian Silva of Rules. Here are their thoughts...

THE SPIRIT: VODKA VS GIN

None of our bartenders would badmouth the Vodka Martini. And yet, all name gin as their go-to spirit base, because it has so much more flavour. It seems their customers agree: both Palazzi and the Connaught duo say 70% of the Martinis they sell are made with gin. Silva's numbers are similar, though the Boston native notes an exception: 'American customers seem to prefer vodka.'

As for the perfect gin? Choose something classic and juniper-forward. The Connaught Bar, known for both precision and world-leading innovation, uses its own gin, infused with hand-crushed juniper, coriander seeds, liquorice, angelica root, orris root, mace, Amalfi lemon and red wine – but also uses Tanqueray No10.

Silva's preference is a gin that's 'as ginny as possible', and he cites the likes of

Tanqueray, No3 (from Berry Bros & Rudd), Plymouth and Sipsmith. Palazzi, meanwhile, prides himself on experimenting with a number of smaller gin brands, but he considers Beefeater, No3, Plymouth and Tanqueray to be reliable, easy-to-find picks.

When vodka is involved, full-flavoured spirits get the nod. Palazzi and the Connaught team often use Konik's Tail, a blend of spelt, rye and wheat. Though for his popular Vesper Martini – a James Bond-inspired blend of gin and vodka – Palazzi uses one-part rye Potocki vodka to three-parts No3 gin, with amber vermouth.

THE VERMOUTH: WET VS DRY

'It's very wrong not to have vermouth – otherwise it's not a cocktail,' Palazzi points out. In every bartender's eye, even the driest Martini must contain some vermouth, giving the drink balance and flavour. In fact, now that there are so many quality vermouths on the market, it's sometimes a case of the more, the better. Palazzi can tell a customer is in the drinks business if they order their Martini 'wet': '99% of the time industry people ask for more vermouth; they appreciate the aroma and balance it brings.'

The preferred ratios vary. Palazzi, when he wheels his Martini trolley out to customers, famously doesn't measure; he coats the inside of a freezer-chilled

Martini glass in vermouth then, in his signature move, shakes out the excess on the bar carpet. 'People think it's all going on the floor, but actually there's still plenty of vermouth in the glass,' he explains.

Meanwhile, Perrone and Bargiani use a five-to-one ratio in their signature Connaught Martini – 75ml spirit to 15ml vermouth – and Silva prefers a classic 60ml to 10ml.

Palazzi often uses Sacred's vermouth, a product he helped to develop. But both the Connaught team and Silva use a house blend of commercial vermouths – the former employing a mix of extra-dry, dry and sweet to create a rounded pour that can work with many serves. But our bartenders recommend that home mixologists just plump for something good quality; Noilly Prat and Cocchi (which has just released a new extra-dry with Martinis in mind) were both named as favourites.

THE CHILL: SHAKEN VS STIRRED

Sorry, 007: all our bartenders say they would never shake a Martini, unless explicitly asked to do so by a customer. It comes down to control. Stir a cocktail in a mixing glass, and you can keep a close eye on how fast the ice is melting. Shaking is less precise; it can result in a lighter cocktail, but also ice shards – ultimately causing over-dilution.

And yet, some dilution is essential. 'Ice is the third ingredient,' says Silva, who mixes room-temperature gin and vermouth with large chunks of ice in a mixing glass to achieve his perfect serve. 'As you stir, the spirit and vermouth will melt the ice, adding around 10ml water to your final cocktail – the perfect balance.' For home bartenders who might not know how long it takes to achieve that 10ml of melt, he suggests using a straw to sample the drink every 5-10 seconds while stirring. 'If it's still tasting rough, then you know you're not quite there.' With practice, you should get a sense of how long to mix for – though you'll have to adjust timings to fit different spirits. Higher-abv ones, for example, might need longer.

The quality of your ice is crucial. In fact, Perrone and Bargiani say this is the number one thing people get wrong when making Martinis. 'The rest is personal taste,' says Perrone, 'but use bad ice or a bad garnish, and it won't be right.'

At The Connaught they use only crystal-clear commercial ice, because frosty chunks from a normal freezer are full of impurities. It's hard for home bartenders to get hold of, but you can make your own cheat's version. Perrone and Bargiani suggest filling an insulated picnic cooler with water and placing it uncovered in the freezer.

'It's very wrong not to have Vermouth, otherwise it's not a cocktail'

—— Alessandro Palazzi, Dukes Bar

The ice will freeze very slowly, giving impurities time to settle to the bottom, and when you remove the ice block you can simply chip these away. 'I did it all the time at home during lockdown,' says Bargiani.

Meanwhile, Palazzi takes a different approach to chilling. He neither shakes nor stirs his Martinis in the conventional sense, preferring to pour icy spirit direct from freezer-chilled bottles into the vermouth-coated glass and allowing them to mingle naturally. This lack of water dilution makes his smooth-tasting Martinis notoriously strong – especially as the cold temperature delays the alcoholic punch. If you

Agostino Perrone & Giorgio Bargiani, The Connaught Bar

How to make the perfect Martini at home

Play around with the quantities, timings and spirits of choice to get a Martini that suits your taste.

60ml London dry gin
10ml dry or extra-dry vermouth, plus another 10ml to flavour the ice (optional)
1 fresh unwaxed lemon
Large-chunk quality ice

1 Twenty minutes before making your Martini, chill a small (125ml) drinking glass in the freezer. Five minutes before making it, fill a cocktail mixing glass to the brim with large-chunk quality ice and (optional) 10ml vermouth.

2 When ready, remove your glass from the freezer and pour any melted liquid away from your ice-filled cocktail mixing glass. Add your gin and 10ml vermouth to your mixing glass, then stir continuously for 10-15 seconds.

3 Strain the Martini into your drinking glass. Cut a length of lemon peel using a vegetable peeler, and twist over your Martini to release the oils. Garnish with the peel and enjoy immediately.

use his method at home, just remember that there's a reason why Palazzi limits customers to a maximum of two Martinis each per seating.

THE GARNISH: LEMON VS OLIVE

There's no right or wrong answer here – if you're drinking a vodka Martini, at least. When it comes to gin, our bartenders all prefer a lemon peel garnish because it enhances, rather than clashes with, the spirit's botanicals. (For the same reason, gin Dirty Martinis, using olive brine, are considered a no-no.)

For Palazzi, lemon enhances the overall drinking experience too. 'You drink the cocktail first with your nose – the lemon is fragrant. Olives don't smell of anything.' Not just any lemon will do. Both Palazzi and the Connaught team exclusively use organic Amalfi lemons for their thick skin and aromatic, slightly sweeter profile. But the most important thing is that the lemon is unwaxed, so all those citrus oils can escape from the peel into your Martini.

There's no need for fancy knife skills. All our bartenders simply cut long, chunky lengths using a vegetable peeler, then pinch or twist it over the Martini. You've done it right if you can see tiny drops of lemon oil floating on top of your drink. Most bartenders finish by resting the peel inside the Martini glass, though Silva is an exception: 'there's no need as you've already extracted the flavour'. He prefers to serve his Martini naked.

As for any other serving tips? The Connaught team break from tradition and add bitters to their drinks to make them customisable. Before pouring the prepared Martini, **Perrone and Bargiani** personalise each glass with a drizzle of the customer's choice of housemade bitters: lavender, coriander, tonka, cardamom or 'Dr Ago' blend. Palazzi, meanwhile, uses a dash of Angostura bitters in his Vesper Martini. ◨

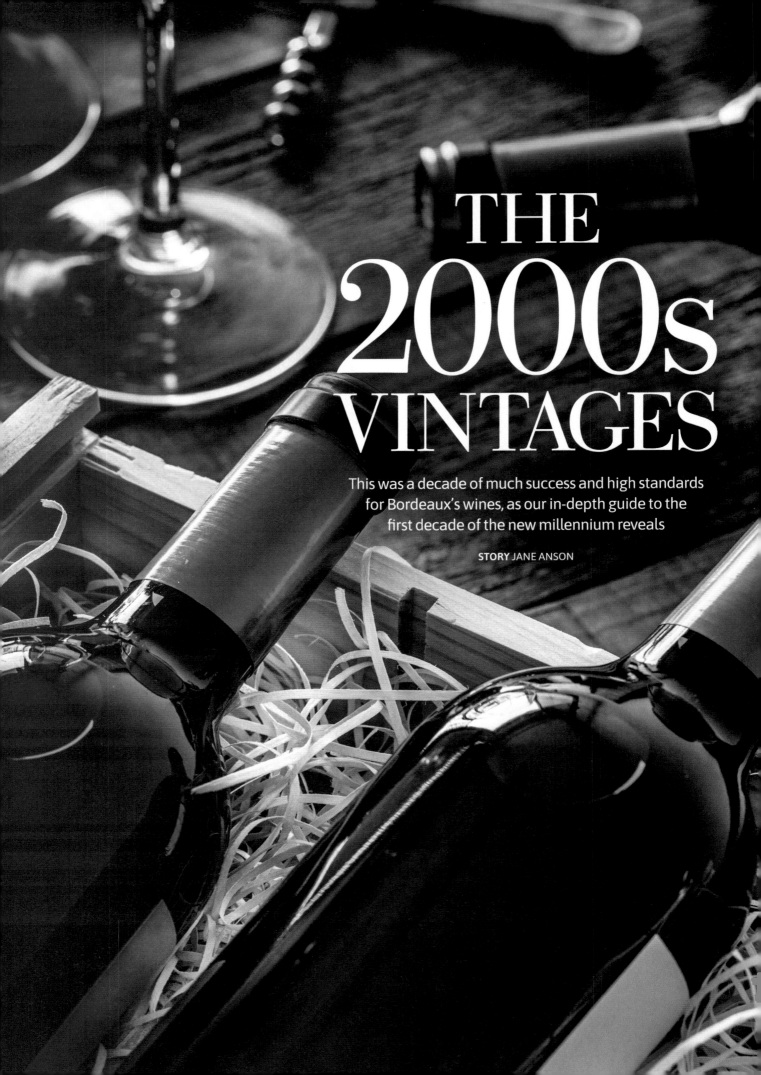

THE 2000s VINTAGES

This was a decade of much success and high standards for Bordeaux's wines, as our in-depth guide to the first decade of the new millennium reveals

STORY JANE ANSON

Where the 1990s gave Bordeaux winemakers a number of difficult challenges, the first 10 years of the new millennium were far kinder. Looking back at the decade today, not a single vintage was a complete disaster. There were challenges, unquestionably – 2002, 2004 and 2007 all had tough moments, and 2003 was in a league of its own for sustained drought that lasted through the entire season (although it was greeted with great acclaim at the time by many). But there were also a number of standout vintages, notably 2000, 2005 and 2009, with 2001 becoming a cult classic, and 2008 an underrated star that delivered some of the best prices of the decade. Not a bad 10 years in all.

These were also years of significant change in Bordeaux. New wineries sprang up, notably at Château Pichon Baron in 2007 with its vast underground cellar. Cranes were a regular sight, although it was the revenue from the successful 2009 vintage that would cause building fever to pick up pace from 2010 onwards.

Technology was moving fast, and both new and existing cellars were invariably moving towards smaller vats that allowed plots in the vineyard to be isolated and followed more carefully from beginning to end, even if the green revolution in classified properties of the following decade had not yet fully blossomed, with just Châteaux Pontet Canet in Pauillac and Guiraud in Sauternes flying the flag for organics, and most estates still following traditional practices in the vineyards.

Many of the current generation of Bordeaux owners arrived during this decade. Ronan Laborde arrived at Château Clinet, Pomerol, in 2003; Jean-Charles Cazes took over from his father Jean-Michel at Château Lynch Bages, Pauillac, in 2006; and Prince Robert of Luxembourg became president of Domaines Clarence Dillon (Châteaux Haut-Brion and La Mission Haut-Brion, Pessac-Léognan) in 2008. Today's leading directors were also getting settled; Thomas Duroux arrived at Château Palmer, Margaux, in 2004 and Olivier Berrouet took over from his father Jean-Claude Berrouet at Petrus, Pomerol, in 2008. Other high-profile arrivals were Silvio Denz at Château Faugères, St-Emilion, in 2005, and the first Chinese owner in 2008, with trading company Longhai International buying Château Latour Laguens in Entre-deux-Mers. Within a few years

there would be hundreds of articles written about the arrival of dozens more investors from China.

Michel Rolland still reigned as consultant on the Right Bank, with Nicolas Thienpont arriving at Château Larcis Ducasse, St-Emilion, in 2002 – a key moment in the widening of his influence. On the Left Bank, Jacques Boissenot was still the leading name, consulting to four out of five first growths along with almost the entire range of 1855 estates, although he was already working alongside son Eric who took over entirely on Jacques' death in 2014.

PRICES & INVESTMENT

This was also a decade when interest in fine wine trading was growing. Burgundy was becoming a serious investment vehicle, threatening to eclipse Bordeaux at times, and new investors were on the scene, most notably – buying châteaux as well as wines – from Hong Kong and mainland China.

The impact that this had on wine prices became more apparent after the economic crisis hit in 2008. This led to a collapse in demand from traditional markets, with power shifting towards a number of Asian buyers who were happy to pick up the slack – and pay for it. The fallout was only seen in the following decade.

It's also notable that, following the dot.com boom and bust of the late 1990s, fine wine began more seriously turning towards online sales. Wine-searcher.com was founded in 1999 and had an increasing impact on transparency around Bordeaux pricing. Liv-ex, the fine wine trading platform, was launched in 2000, and similarly grew to have a significant impact on opening up transparency in the fine wine market.

Its figures for the decade under consideration here show that, for the Bordeaux Left Bank first growths during the 2000-2009 vintages, 2009 is the most traded Bordeaux vintage (by both value and volume). Between September 2017 and September 2021 it accounted for 11.5% of trade by value, followed by the 2005 (9.7%), then the 2008 (7.7%).

BROAD PRICING TRENDS

That doesn't mean that 2009 has performed the best for investors. Based on the wines included in Liv-ex's Bordeaux 500 index, looking at the average increases of all wines from release to now, those from the 2000 vintage have seen the biggest price rises on average, up 653%, followed by 2001 (393%), 2002 (366%) and 2004 (310%).

The success of the 2000 vintage is led by one particular wine, Château Mouton Rothschild 2000, which has risen 1,142% since its release (ex-London) at £1,580 per 12x75cl, and it currently commands a market price of £19,634 on the Liv-ex exchange – not least because of its striking black and gold ram label design.

'There were a number of standout vintages, with 2001 becoming a cult classic, and 2008 an underrated star'

▶

Bordeaux 2000s – every vintage rated

2000 ★★★★

The pressure was on for this to be a stellar vintage, and for the most part it delivered, although not without a few stress points along the way. Harvest began on 18 September, lasting right through until mid-October, and you can find wines from both Right and Left Bank that are still delivering.

The sweet wines were affected by rain on 10-15 October. But for the most part 2000 performed the much sought-after trick of delivering quality and quantity, with yields high in most places, and wines that were rich, tannic and deeply coloured.

This was certainly the most consistent vintage since 1990, but it needed patience. Only in the last few years have I really started to find large numbers of 2000s that have opened up. Today they are starting to come into their own, and if you pick a big name from a good appellation, it's hard to go wrong.

Château Canon, St-Emilion 1GCC 2000 95
£123.34-£146.67 (ib) **Berry Bros & Rudd, Farr Vintners, Montrachet**
A beautiful moment to be drinking this wine as it edges towards tertiary flavours. Beginning to soften around the edges now, with waves of brushed leather, walnut, dried roses and earth, together with the fresh acidities of its limestone soils. Supple tannins, finessed and fine, with juicy raspberry puree and blackberry fruits. 75% Merlot, 25% Cabernet Sauvignon; 55% new oak. **Drink** 2022-2032 **Alcohol** 13%

① **Château Montrose, St-Estèphe 2CC 2000** 95
£141.67 (ib)-£260 **Berry Bros & Rudd, Bibo, Cru, Farr Vintners, Goedhuis & Co, Jeroboams, Millésima, Montrachet, Salusbury Winestore, Tanners, The Good Wine Shop, Wineye**
Just beginning to open after a stubborn few decades. Tobacco and crushed mint leaf sit against blackberry and bilberry fruits held by a firm frame of tannins. A stately Montrose with a long future ahead, packed with the power and finesse that is a signature of this estate. First year in the new stainless steel vat room. 63% Cabernet Sauvignon, 31% Merlot, 4% Cabernet Franc and 2% Petit Verdot. **Drink** 2022-2035 **Alc** 13%

2001 ★★★★

A vintage that was undervalued for a long time and has now become something of a cult year, offering elegant, classically styled wines with great aromatics. Particularly impressive for Sauternes

Château Canon, St-Emilion

and Barsac, with Château d'Yquem legendary. The best reds also offer an unusual combination of elegance, freshness and delicate fruits, and the majority are in a sweet spot right now.

It's less consistent overall than 2000, although the gap between the two is only just starting to become apparent as they click into their third decade. Most will not be as long-lasting as the 2000s, but offer tons of pleasure and there are real spots of brilliance. Château Figeac, St-Emilion, has long been one of my favourite wines of this vintage, as has Château Haut-Bailly, Pessac-Léognan. In terms of price rises over the 20 years since launch, Carruades de Lafite, Pauillac 2001 is in the top spot, up 1,733% according to Liv-ex data.

② **Château La Conseillante, Pomerol 2001** 94
la-conseillante.com
A finessed and balanced vintage, this is full of soft bramble fruits, tobacco and campfire notes, with sculpted fine tannins at 20 years old. Bernard Nicolas was the owner and winemaker at the time, with no outside consultant, so a very different set-up at the château from the one you'll find today. 80% Merlot, 20% Cabernet Franc; old-school and utterly charming. **Drink** 2022-2034 **Alc** 13%

Château Léoville Poyferré, St-Julien 2CC 2001 94
£85 (ib)-£147 **Amathus Drinks, Crump Richmond Shaw, Montrachet, Richard Kihl, Wilkinson Vintners**
The finesse of St-Julien comes through clearly in the glass, heightened by both bottle age and the character of the 2001 vintage itself. Expect cured leather, baked earth and cigar-box spice, with softened blackberry and bilberry fruits. Totally moreish. 75% Cabernet Sauvignon, 20% Merlot, 5% Petit Verdot; 80% new oak. **Drink** 2022-2036 **Alc** 13.5%

Château Beauregard, Pomerol

Château Mouton
Rothschild 2002

2002 ★★

Mixed quality overall, with a difficult spring and a summer that refused to get going. A beautiful September proved to be the saviour of wines that were able to take advantage of the late harvest that lasted through to mid-October, and today you can find plenty of classically balanced bottles, particularly on the Left Bank.

Overall, Cabernet Sauvignon did better than Merlot, and you'll find lots of classically styled wines that are ready to begin drinking. On recent tastings, look out for St-Julien and Pauillac wines, with Mouton Rothschild a particular success.

③

③ Château Lafleur, Pomerol 2002 95

£376.68 Justerini & Brooks

Always one of the most aromatic of Bordeaux wines, the 2002 effortlessly overperforms and is on its way to becoming a classic Lafleur. It's seen as a Cabernet vintage, and certainly even at 17 years old the Cabernet Franc (40%, with 60% Merlot) is taking the lead in this wine. The austerity of the young wine has now softened but it's still showing plenty of structure, tannic hold and fresh acidity, with tons of bracken, grilled rosemary and violet-edged florality. You can drink now but it will very happily – and beneficially – wait another few years. This was the first year in which Jacques and Sylvie Guinaudeau were sole owners, making things official after renting from Jacques' aunt for 15 years. **Drink** 2022-2040 **Alc** 13.5%

2003 ★★★

Undoubtedly the 2000s vintage with the most column inches written about it, for both good and bad reasons, 2003 saw a heatwave across Europe that lasted throughout the growing season, with temperatures regularly climbing up to 40°C. Bordeaux joined many other regions by recording some of the earliest picking dates on record for both white and red grapes – the veraison colour-change was 20 days in advance of average over the previous 50 years and many estates recalled their staff from their August holidays to begin bringing in the scorched grapes.

The result was high alcohols and low yields, and a year when terroir counted if estates were to avoid cooked or dried fruit flavours. Overall, Cabernet Sauvignon withstood the extreme summer heat better than Merlot, but rather than grape variety, I would suggest looking instead for fresh terroirs, such as limestone on the Right Bank and the clays of St-Estèphe, or those along the Gironde in the Médoc – I have recently tasted a good number of Pauillacs that are still delivering, from Lynch Bages to Latour. Excessively dry or hot soils had more issues with water stress and blockages, and sugar concentration was exacerbated by evaporation due to high temperatures.

Overall I would say 2003 has survived better than I expected, but start drinking up now.

Château Beauregard, Pomerol 2003 91

chateau-beauregard.com

A hot vintage that is showing well now, with a highly attractive spice character and still plenty of tannins, giving the fruit something to lean on. Easy to approach, this wine has traces of black chocolate and the lovely tobacco character that is so Pomerol. The fresh edge of Cabernet Franc (25%, with 75% Merlot) helps add a little lift and structure. Not as much persistency as some vintages, but full of pleasure and one that's good for drinking today. **Drink** 2022-2038 **Alc** 13.5%

▶

2004 ★★★

A vintage that you often hear described as 'classic', and it's a favourite with a number of old-school Bordeaux lovers for its understated charm, and generally for its good-value wines.

Yields were high as the vines made up for their low yields the year before. Good weather at flowering, and at harvest, but more challenging in between – meaning once again that it's the top estates of Bordeaux, who could afford the time and effort in the vineyard, that really shone. Among the star risers of the vintage, up 640% from release between 2004 and 2022, is Château Beychevelle, St-Julien, according to Liv-ex figures.

Château Pichon Baron, Pauillac 2CC 2004 94

£102.50 (ib)-£180 **Bordeaux Index, Bowes Wine, Lay & Wheeler, Montrachet, Shrine to the Vine**
Tasting great right now. Still muscular and a little bit foursquare, but with concentrated cassis and blackberry, waves of fresh mint leaf and eucalyptus on the finish. This is juicy and enjoyable. Jean-René Matignon was technical director and Eric Boissenot consultant. 65% Cabernet Sauvignon, 30% Merlot, 5% Cabernet Franc; 80% new oak. **Drink** 2022-2045 **Alc** 13%

2005 ★★★★★

One of the greatest vintages of the past 50 years, with near-perfect weather conditions across the region and Bordeaux University's Faculty of Oenology remarking how it would 'remain long in the memory for its quality'. The wines have proved more stubborn to get going than many initially thought, because although they were not exuberant when young, they had a high tannin count and needed time to soften. Many are starting to really blossom: balanced and nuanced, yet full of fruit. Easily my favourite vintage of the past few decades, and although it was hot and dry, it was less intense than 2003, as cumulative temperatures over July and August show – a total of 760°C in 2003, with six days hitting 40°C, compared with 632°C in 2005, and only two days over 35°C.

④ Château Trotanoy, Pomerol 2005 98

£175 (ib) **Corney & Barrow**
From the first great vintage of the new era: by this point there were smaller tanks, allowing more precision between harvesting and the winery, and fine-tuning of sorting (separating out parts of plots they weren't happy with). The 2005 is on the cusp between tight young fruit and a more complex array of ageing characteristics – and it's gorgeous. It has rich, sweet fruit, wonderful balance and liquorice alongside olive paste, chocolate and cassis puree, embraced by firm but flexible tannins. If you're a fan of classic Pomerol seduction, you'll want to get hold of this wine. Merlot with 3% Cabernet Franc. **Drink** 2022-2040 **Alc** 14%

⑤ Château Grand-Puy-Lacoste, Pauillac 5CC 2005 97

£93.75 (ib)-£165 **Christopher Keiller, Cru, Frazier's, Hedonism, Montrachet, Richard Kihl, The Oxford Wine Co**
The 2005 is taking its time to fully come around and this will still improve over the next five to 10 years, but it is starting to live up to expectations. Packed with truffles and tar, together with cigar box, soy, black tea, campfire smoke and smoked earth. A classic Grand-Puy-Lacoste from an effortlessly balanced vintage. 78% Cabernet Sauvignon, 22% Merlot; 70% new oak. **Drink** 2022-2040 **Alc** 13.5%

④ ⑤

Château Cantenac Brown owner Tristan Le Lous (left) with winemaker José Sanfins

2006 ★★★

Another classic vintage, plenty of good-quality wines starting to come into their sweet spot at just over 15 years old. The weather was variable, with hot spells in July and September, a cool August and storms in mid-September that threatened rot. The weather was fine through the last two weeks of September, although rain in October put pressure on many Médoc estates that did not have early-ripening terroirs. The Faculty of Oenology commented that 'Merlot planted on clay and Cabernet on the finest gravel soils withstood the weather conditions of this vintage better than those planted on sandy or silty soils' – this means you should look at both Pomerol and Pauillac for wines that are tasting good today.

Château Cantenac Brown, Margaux 3CC 2006 93

£46.25 (ib)-£89.99 **Crump Richmond Shaw, Frazier's, Majestic, Montrachet**
Subdued on opening, but after 30 minutes in a carafe it spills out rich pencil lead and liquorice notes, with blackberry fruits and smoky vanilla spice. A classic Margaux 2006, with fairly high acidity that emphasises a floral character, alongside refined tannins. Just beginning to evolve towards an older wine. An unusual vintage at Cantenac Brown, where only 30% of the harvest was used for the first wine, reflecting a new regime of greater precision in harvesting and sorting. 75% Cabernet Sauvignon, 25% Merlot; 60% new oak. **Drink** 2022-2040 **Alc** 13.5%

⑥ Château Nénin, Pomerol 2006 92

£42 (ib) **Crump Richmond Shaw, Montrachet**
The 2006 vintage is not always generous, but it is now beginning to be fully open with Merlot-dominated wines such as Nénin – and this is at a sweet spot for drinking. With expansive blackcurrant and bilberry fruits, held firmly in place by still well-structured tannins, this is enjoyable and well balanced, if less sleek than you find in more recent vintages from this estate. 76% Merlot, 24% Cabernet Franc; 20% new oak. **Drink** 2022-2035 **Alc** 14%

2007 ★★

A classic example of why you shouldn't dismiss the less-media-friendly vintages in Bordeaux. It was a difficult vintage weather-wise, with a damp summer that meant lighter-styled wines in the main, and an early-drinking year. But the best spots delivered delicious, sculpted wines. Some of my favourite bottles in recent years, perfect for unfussy sharing with friends, have been from this vintage – I can particularly point to a brilliant Château d'Armailhac, Pauillac 2007. Some excellent white wines also, still going strong in most cases, particularly from Pessac-Léognan, and one of the best years for Sauternes and Barsac in the new millennium, comparable to 2001.

Château d'Yquem, Sauternes 1CC 2007 97

£223 (ib)-£380 **Berry Bros & Rudd, Bordeaux Index, Cru, Crump Richmond Shaw, DBM Wines, Hennings, Honest Grapes, Millésima, Montrachet, VinQuinn, Vinum, Wineye**

▶

Soft gold in colour, packed full of generous stone fruit, nectarine and white peach, with honeysuckle, white truffle, saffron-laced lemon curd and bitter orange peel, all wrapped up in the satiny texture that makes drinking Yquem feel like the most indulgent of moments. The 2007 vintage was a fairly generous 18hl/ha yield, with 130g/L residual sugar; 80% Semillon, 20% Sauvignon Blanc. The winemaker was Sandrine Garbay. **Drink** 2022-2050 **Alc** 13.5%

2008 ★★★

Plenty of classic wines, particularly those from estates that waited to take full benefit of the Indian summer which allowed for long, slow ripening after a more difficult early season. Even the white wines did not really get under way until 15 September. This was also one of the rare years when en primeur prices came out at extremely reasonable levels due to the financial crisis that had erupted during the second half of 2008. Châteaux Lafite, Latour and Margaux released an opening tranche at €110 per bottle, with Mouton at €100, and Haut-Brion at €130, which still gave early movers a huge opportunity. Not everyone displayed the same restraint, but on the whole this was the last of the really affordable en primeurs.

⑦ Château Malartic-Lagravière, Blanc, Pessac-Léognan CCG 2008 94

£45.83 Millésima

A delicious 2008, singing with the salinity that takes pole position in older whites without sacrificing minerality or juiciness. It has flavours of white pear and finely drawn citrus, with the saffron-edged sweetness of age. 85% Sauvignon Blanc, 15% Semillon. Perfect for drinking now. **Drink** 2022-2030 **Alc** 13%

2009 ★★★★★

The decade signed off with an excellent year, rivalling both the 2000 and the 2005, but altogether different in style: more exuberant and easy to love from its first moments. Much of the growing season was hot and dry combined with fresh nights that encouraged good aromatics, and the wines themselves were richly structured. It has also proven to age well, and is now beginning to show the terroir characteristics that were sometimes missing in the early years. The more I taste it as it hits its second decade, the more I think 2009 just might be the modern-day 1982. Sauternes and Barsac also saw some excellent successes in this vintage. The biggest drawback? The prices, which saw huge rises on 2008 as the Chinese buyers came in strongly. This set up all

kinds of problems for the following decade, but for now, back in 2009, it was smiles all round.

Château Latour's landmark tower surrounded by its Pauillac vineyards

⑧ Château La Serre, St-Emilion GCC 2009 93

moueix.com

Soft ruby red in colour, this delivers plenty of signature limestone character. The fruit majors on blackberry, wild strawberry and softened raspberry puree, with clear salinity, giving a mouthwatering finish that gently holds on. A softer expression of this brilliant vintage, this is almost at the perfect moment for opening. The consultant was Stéphane Toutoundji. 80% Merlot, 20% Cabernet Franc; 50% new oak. **Drink** 2022-2035 **Alc** 14.5%

Château Poujeaux, Moulis-en-Médoc 2009 93

£36.67 (ib)-£71.26 Berry Bros & Rudd, Bordeaux Index, Christopher Keiller, Cru, Crump Richmond Shaw, Four Walls, Hedonism, Honest Grapes, Ideal Wine Co, Montrachet, The Sampler, VinQuinn, Wineye

One of the best-value 2009s you can find in terms of its ability to deliver signature Moulis-Médoc character without having to wait too long or think too hard. Dark bramble fruits, tannins that are now soft and melted, with layers of cigar box, mint leaf, crushed stones and saffron. No need to wait to drink but plenty to enjoy – and even better out of magnum if you can find it. 51% Merlot, 41% Cabernet Sauvignon, 4% Petit Verdot, 4% Cabernet Franc; 40% new oak. **Drink** 2022-2032 **Alc** 14% **D**

Red Graves 2016

It's a good time to stock up – our judges enjoyed plenty of high-scoring wines showing fleshy fruit and depth yet structure and freshness, too

REPORT ANDY HOWARD MW

Over in Bordeaux, the 2016 vintage is acknowledged as one of the finest of the century – so far! This added extra interest to an exciting tasting of red wines from Graves and Pessac-Léognan, already notable for being the last ever *Decanter* panel tasting to be held in its former Canary Wharf office, before the company's move to offices in Paddington, west London.

The judges were highly impressed with 2016's winning combination of succulent, ripe fruit interwoven with fine tannins and an enduring freshness on the finish. Out of 65 wines tasted, six were awarded scores of 95 points (and above), with almost one third of the wines tasted scoring 93pts or more.

Graves and Pessac-Léognan are located southwest of Bordeaux on the Left Bank of the river Garonne. 'Graves' refers to the gravel deposits which characterise much of the region's soils. Although larger in area than the Médoc, Graves produces about 50% of the volume of wine and is, with the exception of a couple of top estates, less revered.

The wines of the Graves can be beautifully perfumed and often have an earthy, mineral character which distinguishes them from the more blackcurrant and lead-pencil style of many Haut-Médoc wines.

Graves was first granted appellation status in 1953, with Pessac-Léognan separated out from it as an appellation and confirmed in 1987. This tasting did not feature Châteaux Haut-Brion, La Mission Haut-Brion, Les Carmes Haut-Brion or Smith Haut Lafitte, but included several of the Pessac-Léognan cru classé estates. These did live up to their higher AP status, with six out of the seven wines present scoring 93pts and above, and three rated Outstanding – Pape Clément, Carbonnieux and Latour-Martillac.

Tim Triptree MW was impressed, stating that 'overall quality was high and confirmed the outstanding quality of the 2016 vintage'.

Triptree found 'the best examples were harmonious and powerful, rich – wines with depth of black fruit flavours, yet balanced with freshness and elegance, and silky ripe tannin'. Robert Mathias, Bordeaux buyer for Bibendum Wine, agreed, commenting: 'Almost all wines had a freshness and acidity which can often be lacking with wines that are fleshy on the palate.'

The panel noted the range of grape varieties used within the blends. Although Merlot or Cabernet Sauvignon dominate, judicious use of Cabernet Franc, Malbec and Petit Verdot was appreciated. Triptree observed: 'Blending grape varieties is important, with many of the top-scoring wines having a decent amount of Cabernet Sauvignon which added freshness, as well as well-judged additions of Cabernet Franc and Petit Verdot.'

Mathias also felt 'the wines had good concentration of fruit, the best being very detailed on the palate with a lot of power and energy behind them'. He was intrigued by the number of wines incorporating a higher proportion of one grape in particular: 'What was interesting was the growing use, and successful integration, of Petit Verdot'. And although a couple of wines were a little tannic as a result, this 'added an extra dimension'.

The quality of 2016 Graves and Pessac-Léognan wines is undoubtedly high, while the relative value they present is likely to be more attractive than for many leading Haut-Médoc or St-Emilion wines.

Combined with the distinctive Graves character, and excellent ageing potential, these 2016s are classic Bordeaux wines, and well worth stocking up on.

THE SCORES 65 wines tasted

Exceptional 0 **Outstanding** 6 **Highly recommended** 42 **Recommended** 17
Commended 0 **Fair** 0 **Poor** 0 **Faulty** 0

Entry criteria: producers and UK agents were invited to submit their Pessac-Léognan and Graves AP red wines, from the 2016 vintage only

THE JUDGES

Andy Howard MW
is a *Decanter* contributing editor and DWWA Regional Chair. A former retail wine buyer for more than 30 years, he now runs his own consultancy Vinetrades, focusing on wine education, judging, investment and sourcing, and has a house in southwest France

Robert Mathias
is a wine buyer for London-based Bibendum Group, responsible for sourcing wines from France as well as fine wine purchasing. He has been a DWWA judge since 2019, tasting across a range of regional categories

Tim Triptree MW
is the international director of wine and spirits at Christie's, responsible for the planning and execution of Christie's wine and spirits auctions internationally. A Master of Wine since 2018, at DWWA 2021 he was a judge on the Rhône and Bordeaux panels

Outstanding 95-97pts

Château Pape Clément, Pessac-Léognan GCC

Andy Howard MW 96
Robert Mathias 95
Tim Triptree MW 96
£62.50 (ib)-£97.50 **Widely available via independent merchants**
The 60ha of vineyards are situated on an ancient alluvial terrace topped by a thin layer of more recent Garonne gravel. The winery's 28 wooden fermentation vats correspond to individual parcels, and the grand vin red (in 2016, equal parts Cabernet Sauvignon and Merlot) is aged for 18 months in 70% new oak barrels.
Andy Howard MW Intriguing wine with an extra layer of aromatics. Floral, leafy, a touch herbal. Great purity allied with fresh acidity and integrated oak. A very fine Pessac.
Robert Mathias A brooding nose, coffee, cedar and dried tobacco. Broad structure with black cherry fruit. Tannins very fine, some warmth on the finish.
Tim Triptree MW Hedonistic aromatics of ripe black cherry, plum and blackberry, complex notes of smoke and cedar, leather, dried meats, tobacco and cinnamon spice. Opulent, ripe, great balance and length. Harmonious, ageworthy Pessac.
Drink 2022-2040 **Alcohol** 14%

Château Brown, Pessac-Léognan

AH 95 **RM** 95 **TT** 95
£18.25 (ib) **Crump Richmond Shaw**
After falling into decline in the 1950s, Château Brown was revived after it was bought by businessman Bernard Barthe in 1994, to be taken over again 20 years later by the Mau family. Now led by fifth-generation Jean-Christophe Mau, its 26ha of red vines consist of 53% Cabernet Sauvignon, 45% Merlot and 2% Petit Verdot. The 2016 (5% Petit Verdot) was aged in French oak barrels, 40% new, for 12-15 months.
AH Appealing, ripe, dark fruit on the palate. Bright acidity and firm tannins, a little angular at the moment. Bitter cherry flavour, should drink even better in 18-24 months.
RM Dark chocolate and cocoa with robust black fruits. Very fine on the palate. Excellent concentration of black fruits with complexity and clove spice. Tannins are very fine, with a youthful finish.
TT Bright and intense plum aromas, black cherry and cassis notes to the fore, intermingled with pencil lead, tobacco and cedar and cigar box. Full-flavoured with firm structure and a good balance of vibrant acidity and fruit ripeness.
Drink 2022-2040 **Alc** 14.5%

Château Cantelys, Pessac-Léognan

AH 95 **RM** 96 **TT** 95
smith-haut-lafitte.com
This 20ha estate has been owned since 1994 by Florence and Daniel Cathiard, who also own Château Smith Haut Lafitte. Today, its 15ha for reds are planted to 70% Cabernet Sauvignon and 30% Merlot, on mostly gravel soils with some clay. Grapes are handpicked and sorted twice, whole-berry fermented in large oak vats before ageing 14 months in 25% new French oak barrels.
AH Damson and cherry dominate the nose. Fleshy palate, bright acidity and some firm but ripe tannins. Hint of bitterness on the finish, but this adds to the feeling of freshness. Long, lingering, a classy Pessac.
RM Nose is closed but has lots of detail: clove, anise, cedar and coffee. Great concentration, firm and fine-grained tannin. Energy with a spicy liquorice and black pepper finish.
TT Rich and complex aromatics, great fruit intensity with well-integrated oak. Generous ripe plum, red and black cherry, with fine tannins and persistence.
Drink 2022-2035 **Alc** 13.5%

Château Carbonnieux, Pessac-Léognan GCC

AH 95 **RM** 94 **TT** 95
£21.84 (ib)-£46.70 **Berry Bros & Rudd, Crump Richmond Shaw, Haynes Hanson & Clark, Millésima**
Château Carbonnieux has returned to traditional working of the soils and is trialling organic farming methods. The property consists of 119 plots with a range of clay, gravels, sand and limestone soils. The 2016 blends 50% Cabernet Sauvignon, 40% Merlot, 5% Cabernet Franc and 5% Petit Verdot, aged 16-18 months in 35% new oak barrels.
AH Toasty oak on the nose, but there's plenty of concentration to allow this to integrate over time. Dark fruit, berry and cherry. Crisp acidity with a bitter cherry edge to the finish.
RM Nose is quite closed, but quite classical with savoury spice and good concentration of black fruits. Refreshing acidity and firm, sinewy tannin.
TT Intense aromatics, earthy and savoury, cedar, leather with ripe black berries and plum. Opulent, great Pessac typicity.
Drink 2022-2040 **Alc** 13.5% ►

Château Latour-Martillac, Pessac-Léognan GCC

AH 95 **RM** 94 **TT** 96
£24.67 (ib)-£41.67 **Crump Richmond Shaw, Millésima**
The estate takes its name from the remnant of a 12th-century fort in the main courtyard. Grapes for the red wines are rigorously sorted before fermentation in stainless steel. The 2016 blends 60% Cabernet Sauvignon, 32% Merlot and 8% Petit Verdot, aged for 16 months in French oak barrels, 40% new, produced under the direction of Loïc Kressmann and winemaker Valérie Vialard.
AH Wonderful nose: intense, dark fruit, vibrant yet has a balance of cool menthol. Plush palate, soft, generous ripeness and perfectly integrated oak.
RM Smoked wood and clove with richness and generosity of fruit, more open on the palate with a fine texture and very good intensity and freshness.
TT Ripe black cherry, plum and blackberry fruits leap from the glass, revealing complex cedar, leather and cinnamon spice nuances. Full and opulent fruit palate, fine-grained tannins and vibrant acidity. **Drink** 2022-2040 **Alc** 13.5%

Château Léognan, Pessac-Léognan

AH 95 **RM** 95 **TT** 96
chateauleognan.fr
Château Léognan's 6ha of vines were first planted on a vein of gravel and sand in the early 20th century and, prior to its purchase by Philippe and Chantal Miécaze in 2006, the property had supplied fruit for neighbouring Domaine de Chevalier. Now comprising 70% Cabernet Sauvignon and 30% Merlot, grapes are hand-havested and manually sorted twice before traditional vinification by parcel.
AH Intriguing floral nose and smooth, dark fruit on the palate. Elegance and persistence, a classy Pessac with lovely structure and finesse.
RM Dark chocolate and rich black fruits lead to ripe and well-rounded texture on the palate with fleshy black fruits. Well-managed tannin with full body and a long finish.
TT Hedonistic and complex nose, spice and cedar, notes of mint and graphite minerality. Mouthfilling flavours of cassis, plum and black cherry, firm structure and mouthwatering acidity. Starting to drink well now but has potential to age. **Drink** 2022-2035 **Alc** 13%

Highly recommended 90-94pts

Château La Louvière, Pessac-Léognan
AH 94 **RM** 94 **TT** 93
£21.09 (ib) **Crump Richmond Shaw**
Complex nose of cigar box, crushed stones, cedary wood and fleshy dark fruits. Very smooth palate, rich and fleshy with a lovely tannic structure. Intriguing, with a long and harmonious finish. **Drink** 2022-2035 **Alc** 13%

Clos Marsalette, Pessac-Léognan
AH 94 **RM** 92 **TT** 96
£16.67 (ib)-£34.35 **Crump Richmond Shaw, Haynes Hanson & Clark, Nickolls & Perks**
Layered aromas of roses, violets, plums, toasty notes, cedar and savoury hints. Fruit expands on the palate, lingering mineral aftertaste. **Drink** 2022-2035 **Alc** 13%

Château Bouscaut, Pessac-Léognan GCC AH 94 **RM** 93 **TT** 92
£20.50 (ib)-£30 **Crump Richmond Shaw, The Wine Society**
Toasty nose showing cigar box, Asian spices and plush dark berries, nuances of leather and mocha. Opulent with a velvety texture, long silky finish. **Drink** 2022-2040 **Alc** 14.5%

Château de Beau-Site, Graves
AH 94 **RM** 94 **TT** 91
chateaudebeausite@wanadoo.fr
Attractive scents of sweet oak spice, ripe red bramble fruit, vanilla and fragrant violet nuances. Mouthfilling, with freshness and a nice concentration. Rounded, with purity of fruit. **Drink** 2022-2038 **Alc** 13.5%

Château de France, Pessac-Léognan
AH 93 **RM** 94 **TT** 93
POA **Via UK importer New Generation Wines**
Restrained aromatics, subtle black cherry and cassis notes mingled with pencil lead, tobacco and cedar and cigar box. Powerful palate with silky texture. Serious, with a lot of finesse. **Drink** 2022-2035 **Alc** 13.5%

Château de Rouillac, Pessac-Léognan
AH 95 **RM** 92 **TT** 92
chateauderouillac.com
Fresh aromas of peppery black fruits, pure cassis and spicy notes with roasted coffee undertones. Earthy palate with a mineral edge. Complex and concentrated, firmly structured. **Drink** 2022-2035 **Alc** 13.5%

Château Haut-Bailly, Pessac-Léognan GCC
AH 93 **RM** 93 **TT** 94
£84.17 (ib)-£146.67 Berry Bros & Rudd, Cru, Cult Wines, Goedhuis & Co, Ideal Wine Co, Grand Vin, Millésima, Mumbles Fine Wines, Richard Kihl
Brooding nose, liquorice, black pepper and charcoal. Powerful, with broad-shouldered tannins and intensity of black fruit. Long and dense. **Drink** 2022-2040 **Alc** 13.5%

Château Lamothe-Bouscaut, Pessac-Léognan
AH 93 **RM** 93 **TT** 93
£26.99-£32.99 Corks, Exel, Liberty Wines, KWM, NY Wines, Salusbury Winestore, Shelved Wine
Fresh dark fruits, cherry and blackcurrant with herbs on the nose. Very precise, delineated and fine in texture. Lovely tannins, finely layered, and well-judged oak use. **Drink** 2022-2035 **Alc** 14%

Château Le Thil, Pessac-Léognan
AH 93 **RM** 94 **TT** 92
£15.84-£23.17 (ib) Cru, Starling Wines, Wineye
A rather opulent nose, showing fresh and dried black cherry and raspberry, dark chocolate, liquorice and cigar box notes. Very fine in the mouth with silky tannins and an excellent concentration of fruit. **Drink** 2022-2035 **Alc** 14%

Château Luchey-Halde, Pessac-Léognan
AH 94 **RM** 93 **TT** 93
luchey-halde.com
Leafy notes on the nose beneath notes of tobacco, dried meat, ripe plums and black cherry aromas. Has fresh, red fruit on the palate with good concentration and purity. Quite a lot of structure here. **Drink** 2022-2035 **Alc** 13%

Château Olivier, Pessac-Léognan GCC
£20.92 (ib)-£45 Adnams, Crump Richmond Shaw, Millésima, The Bordeaux Cellar, The Suffolk Cellar, Vintage Cellars
AH 92 **RM** 94 **TT** 92
Warm nose showing fine details of olive tapenade, smoked wood, roasted coffee and blackberries. Fleshy and weighty on the palate, opulent yet balanced by a vibrant refreshing acidity. **Drink** 2022-2040 **Alc** 14%

Château Picque Caillou, Pessac-Léognan
AH 92 **RM** 96 **TT** 90
£15 (ib)-£31.99 Blanco & Gomez, Christopher Keiller, Corney & Barrow, Cuchet & Co, Haynes Hanson & Clark, Huntsworth Wine Co, Millésima, Private Cellar
Vibrant aromas of cassis, kirsch, wood shaving and savoury spices. Elegant, with acidity supporting its luscious fruit character. Long. **Drink** 2022-2040 **Alc** 13.5%

Château Roche-Lalande, Pessac-Léognan
AH 93 **RM** 93 **TT** 94
domaines-rodrigues-lalande.fr
Serious nose of wet stones, cocoa, red brick, ripe black cherry and plum. Firm structure of fine-grained tannins, crunchy acidity and earthy length. **Drink** 2022-2035 **Alc** 13.5%

Clémentin de Pape Clément, Pessac-Léognan
AH 94 **RM** 91 **TT** 93
£22.92-£30.34 (ib) Christopher Keiller, Cru, Crump Richmond Shaw, Wineye
Intriguing nose: earth, iron, violets, leather, nuances of cinnamon and tobacco leaves. Soft, plush texture with lovely black cherry character. Fresh. **Drink** 2022-2035 **Alc** 13.5%

Domaine de Grandmaison, Pessac-Léognan
AH 93 **RM** 93 **TT** 93
domaine-de-grandmaison.fr
Black and red cherry, plum and cassis notes, hints of spice and cedar from the integrated oak. Full-bodied with generous ripe fruit flavours. **Drink** 2022-2035 **Alc** 13.5%

Château Brondelle, Graves
AH 91 **RM** 93 **TT** 93
chateaubrondelle.com
Smoky nose with some warm gravel and sweet spice under toasty notes of oak and cassis overtones. Lovely purity with a classical texture on the palate. Fresh, with an earthy finish. **Drink** 2022-2035 **Alc** 13.5%

Château Couhins, Pessac-Léognan
AH 92 **RM** 93 **TT** 90
£28.33 Millésima
Black chocolate on the nose with mocha, showing some opulence. Intense black fruit with a touch of cocoa nib. Fine-grained texture on the palate, with ripe tannins and a long finish. **Drink** 2022-2035 **Alc** 14.5%

Château Couhins-Lurton, Pessac-Léognan
AH 90 **RM** 94 **TT** 92
POA Theatre of Wine
Evolved aromatics, from tobacco and cedar to nuances of leather and spice with hints of ripe black cherry and blackberry notes. Harmonious, with refreshing acidity and concentration. **Drink** 2022-2032 **Alc** 13.5% ▶

Château Ferran, Pessac-Léognan
AH 91 **RM** 93 **TT** 91

£17.25 Goedhuis & Co

Tobacco and coffee on the nose with ripe bramble fruit. Elegant on the palate with good freshness and energy. Quite a long finish. **Drink** 2022-2035 **Alc** 14%

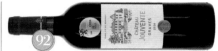

Château Jouvente, Graves
AH 93 **RM** 92 **TT** 92

chateau-jouvente.fr

Dried mushroom and dried meat with light balsamic character and oriental spice nuances. Firm tannins on the palate with a nice balance. **Drink** 2022-2035 **Alc** 14%

Château Malartic-Lagravière, Pessac-Léognan GCC
AH 93 **RM** 91 **TT** 93

£35.42 (ib)-£63.95 Crump Richmond Shaw, Davy's, Farr Vintners, Ideal Wine Co, Millésima, The Vinorium, Uncorked

Violet, vanilla and blue fruit aromatics, coffee notes. Finely textured with pure fruit, vibrant acidity. **Drink** 2022-2035 **Alc** 13.5%

Château Seguin, Pessac-Léognan
AH 92 **RM** 93 **TT** 92

chateauseguin.com

Cigar box and cedar with light notes of leather and game. Elegant black fruits with freshness and some dried meat on the palate. Ripe, fleshy tannins on the finish. **Drink** 2022-2032 **Alc** 14%

Château Villa Bel-Air, Graves
AH 93 **RM** 92 **TT** 92

£13.89-£20 (ib) Berry Bros & Rudd, Christopher Keiller

Ambitious nose with forward aromas of chocolate and vanilla and leafy nuances. Ripe and fleshy black fruits, with opulence on the palate and a spicy finish. **Drink** 2022-2040 **Alc** 13%

Grand Enclos du Château de Cérons, Graves
AH 92 **RM** 93 **TT** 90

US$34.99 DB Fine Wines, The Wine Source, Vigneron Imports

Savoury nose showing cassis, plum and black cherry with mineral earthy notes. Generous black fruit flavours on the palate with firm, structured tannins, good balance of acidity. **Drink** 2022-2035 **Alc** 14%

Le Petit Haut Lafitte, Pessac-Léognan
AH 92 **RM** 93 **TT** 91

£20 (ib)-£34.58 Christopher Keiller, Cru, Crump Richmond Shaw, Farr Vintners, Jeroboams, Starling Wines, Vinum, Wineye

Restrained scents of subtle black cherry, pencil lead, violets and toasted wood. Very attractive: concentrated yet elegant despite the weight. **Drink** 2022-2035 **Alc** 13.5%

Les Demoiselles de Larrivet Haut-Brion, Pessac-Léognan
AH 92 **RM** 92 **TT** 92

larrivethautbrion.fr

Charcoal and cigar box nose with polished red cherry fruit and nuances of mocha and floral notes. An elegant wine with fine-grained tannins and refreshing acidity. **Drink** 2022-2032 **Alc** 13%

Château de Cérons, Graves
AH 90 **RM** 90 **TT** 92

£19.50-£21 Highbury Vintners, JN Wine

Fleshy black fruits on the nose with some coffee aromas. Medium body with pleasant plum and black fruits on the palate. Harmonious. **Drink** 2022-2030 **Alc** 12.5%

Château des Fougères, Clos Montesquieu, Graves
AH 93 **RM** 89 **TT** 92

chateaudesfougeres.fr

Appealing nose, showing plenty of pure, dark berry fruit. Soft and generous on the palate with fresh acidity and long finish. **Drink** 2022-2032 **Alc** 13.5%

Château Haut-Bergey, Pessac-Léognan
AH 93 **RM** 91 **TT** 88

US$31-$44.99 Bedford Wine Merchants, The Wine Cellarage, Total Wine, Watergate Vintners

Toasted wood, black pepper, coffee aromas and ripe black fruits. The palate is generous, with fleshy black fruits and some weight. **Drink** 2022-2035 **Alc** 13%

Château La Garde, Pessac-Léognan
AH 92 **RM** 91 **TT** 91

£15.60 (ib)-£32 Berry Bros & Rudd, Crump Richmond Shaw, Farr Vintners, Millésima

Liquorice, toasted wood and black pepper aromas around a core of ripe black fruit on the nose. Ripe tannins with vibrant acidity. **Drink** 2022-2035 **Alc** 14%

Château Lafargue, Pessac-Léognan
AH 90 **RM** 91 **TT** 92

chateaulafargue-france.com

Warm stones, dried tobacco and aromas of clove spice. An elegant example that shows dark berry and cherry fruit character, and smooth tannins along with lively acidity. **Drink** 2022-2030 **Alc** 13.5%

Château Lafont Menaut, Pessac-Léognan
AH 91 **RM** 92 **TT** 90

vignobleperrin.com

Dark fruits, brooding character but there is plenty of freshness here. Some liquorice and anise notes, with ripe, firm tannins. **Drink** 2022-2035 **Alc** 13.7%

Château Le Bruilleau, Pessac-Léognan
AH 90 **RM** 94 **TT** 90

chateau-le-bruilleau.monsite-orange.fr

Rich and generous nose with cocoa nibs, mocha and ripe black fruits. Well-defined palate, clean and focused, with poise. **Drink** 2022-2040 **Alc** 14%

Château Magneau, Graves
AH 92 **RM** 91 **TT** 89

US$23-$25.99 Charlestown Wine & Spirits, Daily Wine Co, Liner & Elsen, Park Avenue Fine Wines

Pronounced aromatics with black cherry and cassis notes mingling with mocha, toast and cedar from the new oak. Full-bodied and mouthfilling. **Drink** 2022-2035 **Alc** 13%

Château Pont Saint-Martin, Pessac-Léognan
AH 90 **RM** 92 **TT** 91

domaines-rodrigues-lalande.fr

Notes of leather and dried meat with some woodsmoke. Ripe bramble fruits with fine texture and quite a classical feel in the mouth. **Drink** 2022-2030 **Alc** 13.5%

Château Caillivet, Graves
AH 92 **RM** 90 **TT** 89

caillivet.fr

Blue fruits and stewed plums on the nose with some notes of sweet spices, then ripe and fleshy fruit character on the palate. **Drink** 2022-2030 **Alc** 14%

Château de Chantegrive, Graves
AH 89 **RM** 92 **TT** 90

£9.17 (ib)-£19 Cru, Millésima, Nickolls & Perks, Starling Wines, Waitrose

Rich and complex nose of ripe black fruits and hints of savoury spice and cedar. Grainy tannins, rich and fleshy. **Drink** 2022-2038 **Alc** 13.5%

Château Haut Nouchet, Pessac-Léognan
AH 89 **RM** 91 **TT** 91

hautnouchet.com

Youthful nose with sweet oak spice, savoury wet stones and fleshy black fruits. Rich on the palate with mouthwatering acidity. **Drink** 2022-2035 **Alc** 13.5%

Château Mancèdre, Pessac-Léognan
AH 90 **RM** 90 **TT** 91

US$42 Saratoga Wine Exchange, Underground Bottle Shop

Nice purity of red fruit with liquorice and hints of mint and leather. Bright acidity on the palate with firm tannins. **Drink** 2022-2030 **Alc** 13.5%

Château Roche-Lalande La Croix, Pessac-Léognan
AH 91 **RM** 91 **TT** 88

domaines-rodrigues-lalande.fr

Restrained aromatics with subtle black cherry and cassis notes and hints of game and cedar. Fresh with plenty of length. **Drink** 2022-2035 **Alc** 13.5%

Château Simon, L'Empreinte, Graves
AH 91 **RM** 90 **TT** 88

chateausimon.fr

Attractive red fruit aromas with leafy notes and hints of sweet oak. Crisp acidity on the palate, and a spicy feel on the finish. **Drink** 2022-2030 **Alc** 14%

Château Tourteau Chollet, 1760, Graves
AH 90 **RM** 90 **TT** 90

lesvignoblesdemaxime.com

Dried meats and bramble fruits with a lick of cedar. Sweet-fruited on the front of the palate supported by firm, chewy tannins. **Drink** 2022-2035 **Alc** 14.5%

▶

Recommended 86-89pts

Wine	Score	AH	RM	TT	Tasting note	Alc	Drink	Price	Stockists
Château Crabitey, Graves	89	88	92	88	Restrained nose with earthy and cedar notes over black and red cherry fruit. Finely textured ripe tannins.	13%	2022-2035	£20.99 -£22	Amathus Drinks, Borders Wines, Harrods
Château Rahoul, Graves	89	87	92	88	Elegant aromas of pencil shavings, cocoa and black fruits. Lovely intensity, sinewy tannins. Savoury finish.	13.5%	2022-2032	£23-£27	C&C Wines, Christopher Keiller, The Good Wine Shop
Château Roquetaillade La Grange, Graves	89	90	89	89	Profound nose of dark plummy fruit, chocolate and liquorice hints. Fresh palate with firm structured tannins.	13.5%	2022-2032	N/A UK	vignobles-guignard.com
Château Tour Bicheau, Graves	89	89	90	88	Attractive, red berry aromas. Plump and juicy, with crisp acidity and fleshy red and black fruits on the finish.	14%	2022-2032	N/A UK	chateau-tour-bicheau.fr
Château Tour de Castres, Graves	89	90	86	90	Coffee and smoke on the nose with some black tea. Energetic acidity with quite a light structure.	13.5%	2022-2030	N/A UK	domaines-rodrigues-lalande.fr
Château de Castres, Graves	88	90	87	88	Balsamic edge on the nose, with sweet spice, coffee and vanilla. Mouthfilling, with a lingering mineral finish.	13.5%	2022-2030	N/A UK	domaines-rodrigues-lalande.fr
Château de Respide, L'Inattendu, Graves	88	88	87	88	Earthy and leafy notes under attractive brambly aromas. Ripe, broad-grained tannins with a persistent finish.	13.5%	2022-2030	N/A UK	respide.fr
Château Fernon, Graves	88	88	92	84	Perfumed nose, some violets and hints of beeswax. Fleshy, soft palate with dark fruit and gentle tannins.	13.5%	2022-2035	N/A UK	vignobles-boudat-cigana.com
Château Haut-Gramons, Graves	88	89	90	86	Dark berry and damson fruit aromas. Smooth tannins on the palate, dense, with purity of fruit.	13.5%	2022-2035	N/A UK	vignobles-boudat-cigana.com
Château Larrivet Haut-Brion, Pessac-Léognan	88	90	85	90	Lovely plump red fruit character with nice oak integration. Brambly palate with fine-grained tannins.	13%	2022-2030	£24 (ib) -£49.50	Bakers & Larners of Holt, Crump Richmond Shaw, Millésima, The Vinorium
Agora du Château des Places, Graves	87	88	85	89	Dried mushrooms, dark chocolate and black fruit aromas. Refreshing on the palate with grainy tannins.	13.5%	2022-2030	N/A UK	vignobles-reynaud.fr
Château d'Arricaud, Graves	87	88	86	87	Wild nose with hints of game and notes of cassis. Appealing ripeness with a warm finish.	14%	2022-3035	N/A UK	chateau-darricaud.fr
Château Haut Selve, Reserve, Graves	87	88	87	87	Savoury nose with graphite minerality and strawberry notes. Full-bodied and oaky. Impressive on the palate.	14%	2022-2028	£25	Castelnau Wine Agencies
Château Le Bourdillot, Graves	87	86	88	88	Cedary wood and a hint of leather and liquorice under plummy and cherry aromas. Fleshy and juicy.	13%	2022-2030	N/A UK	chateau-le-bourdillot.com
Château Saint-Jean des Graves, Graves	87	86	84	91	Easy-drinking, red fruit style with some meat juice notes. Light body with firm structured tannins.	13%	2022-2030	N/A UK	chateauliot.com
Château Tourteau Chollet, Graves	87	85	87	89	Ripe cassis and plum, cocoa and leafy notes. Chewy and a bit grainy on the palate.	14.5%	2022-2038	N/A UK	lesvignoblesdemaxime.com
Château Haut Selve, Graves	86	85	89	84	Restrained crunchy red berry and cherry fruit nose. Vibrant acidity, easy drinking.	12%	2022-2035	US $34.99	L&P Wines & Liquors

The Decanter guarantee

Our buying guide provides you with trusted, independent, expert recommendations on what to buy, drink and cellar.

Each panel tasting is judged by three experienced tasters chosen for their authority in the category of wine being rated. All wines are tasted blind and are pre-poured for judges in flights of 8-10 wines. Our experts taste and score wines individually but then discuss their scores together at the end of each flight. Any wines on which scores are markedly different are retasted; however, judges are under no obligation to amend their scores.

Judges are encouraged to look for typicity in wines, rewarding those that are true to their region. When judging, experts are aware of wine price bands – under £15, £15-£30 and over £30 – with the aim of recognising and rewarding quality and value.

The tastings are held in the controlled environment of *Decanter*'s tasting suite: a quiet, purposely designed room, with natural light. We limit the number of wines tasted to a manageable level – a maximum of 85 per day – allowing judges to taste more thoroughly and avoid palate fatigue.

Drink-by dates indicated are based on how long it is prudent to keep the wine in question. However, some wines will have a longer ageing capacity if stored in pristine conditions throughout their lifespan.

SCORING SYSTEM

Tasters rate the wines using the 100-point scoring system. The overall *Decanter* rating is the average of all three judges' scores. The ratings are as follows:

98-100 Exceptional A great, exceptional and profound wine

95-97 Outstanding An excellent wine of great complexity and character

90-94 Highly Recommended
A very accomplished wine, with impressive complexity

86-89 Recommended A well-made, straightforward and enjoyable wine

83-85 Commended An acceptable, simple wine with limited personality

76-82 Fair Correctly made, if unexciting

70-75 Poor Unbalanced and/or bland with no character

50-69 Faulty Displays faults due to winemaking, transit, storage or cork taint

For the Exceptional and Outstanding *Decanter* ratings, judges' individual scores and tasting notes are listed in addition to the average score.

For the Highly Recommended and Recommended wines, individual and average scores are also listed but tasting notes are a combination of the three judges' notes.

Southwest France
a buyer's guide

The wide range of obscure grapes and unusual styles from France's rural southwest makes it fascinating yet mysterious – and there are great wines to be found at bargain prices too. Here are the key appellations and producers, plus 10 top bottles to try

STORY ANDY HOWARD MW

It may lack the glitz and glamour of areas in the south of France, but the country's southwest is a beautiful region, much loved by visitors from around the world. Yet, despite the region's popularity as a tourist destination, the wines of the southwest have had a low profile abroad – a great pity given the region's cornucopia of terroirs, its huge and diverse range of unusual grape varieties and wine styles, and its inspirational winemakers.

In a recent article, *Decanter* contributing editor, DWWA Co-Chair and leading wine writer Andrew Jefford posed some questions: 'What is France's greatest undiscovered wine region? Where do you find the greatest value for money in French wine? Where would you look around France to find potential fine-wine quality at affordable prices? Three questions from me, and the same answer to each: southwest France.'

INTRIGUING COMPLEXITIES

So, what is it that makes the southwest such a rich source of alternative, great-value and high-quality wines? It is a region shaped by both similarity and diversity. The similarities include the influence of the maritime climate driven from the Atlantic ocean; the unremittingly beautiful countryside ranging from the foothills of the Pyrenees to the limestone causses (limestone plateaux and gorges) of the Tarn, Dordogne and Lot; the influence of major, westward-flowing rivers; and historical factors – most importantly the legacy of the Romans, the influence of the church, the changes in the wine trade and the effects of phylloxera.

Cahors vineyards overlooking the village of Albas and the meandering Lot river

▶

Another unifying factor is the presence of rare, often unique, grape varieties. Only found in the southwest are whites Camaralet, Lauzet, Len de l'El, Raffiat de Moncade and Verdanel, and reds Duras and Prunelard; with white Arrufiac, Ondenc and Petit Manseng, and reds Abouriou and Négrette on the 'almost' exclusive list. The Agence de Développement Economique Région Occitanie (AD'OCC) describes the southwest as 'a reservoir of diversity with more than 300 varieties of grape, 120 of which are indigenous'.

Diversity is also seen in the varying size of the region's appellations. Bergerac, Cahors, Gaillac and Madiran are the largest, while Irouléguy and Marcillac are a tenth of the size. Even smaller (and hardly ever seen in France, let alone the UK) – are the tiny appellations of St-Sardos, Côtes de Millau, Entraygues-Le Fel and Estaing – the last two covering just 18ha and 14ha.

Underlying rock structure and soils also contribute to the variety of styles found in the southwest, with iron oxide-rich soils in Marcillac (Aveyron), limestone influences in the Dordogne, Lot and Tarn, and red sandstone in the Pyrenees.

The southwest can be roughly divided into seven parts, running from the east towards the Atlantic: the hilly areas of the Aveyron (Marcillac); the Tarn (Gaillac); Toulousain (Fronton); the Lot (Cahors); Dordogne (Bergerac); Gascony, or Gascogne (St-Mont/Madiran/Pacherenc du Vic-Bilh); and the Pyrenees (Irouléguy/Jurançon).

AROUND THE REGIONS

Marcillac is a small (about 200ha) AP and produces distinctive, individual wines. Located in the Aveyron, close to the small city of Rodez, almost 90% of production is red wine from the Braucol grape (also known as Pinenc in Gascony and Fer Servadou in other areas). Although found through much of the southwest, here it is known as Mansois, where it thrives on iron oxide-rich soils (rougiers) to give spicy, liquorice and blackcurrant notes, allied with firm tannins and a slightly wild edge.

Gaillac, a significant appellation in terms of area – about 3,150ha for AP wines and some 3,650ha more for IGP and others, with annual production close to 40 million bottles in total – is one of France's most ancient vineyards, with evidence of a thriving wine trade dating back to the second century BC. Red wine accounts for about 60% of production, with white and rosé 25% and 15%. Gaillac has an impressive range of appellations covering red, rosé and dry whites (the latter with the additional, higher designation of Gaillac Premières Côtes); the slightly spritzy perlé; excellent sweet wines ranging from doux (minimum 45g/L residual sugar) to vendanges

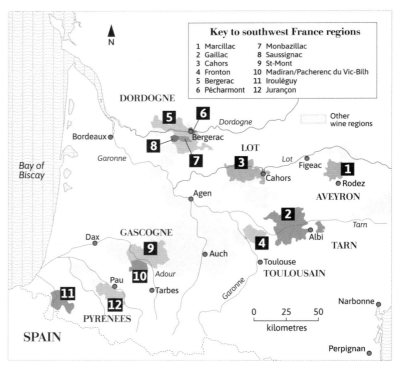

Key to southwest France regions

1	Marcillac	7	Monbazillac
2	Gaillac	8	Saussignac
3	Cahors	9	St-Mont
4	Fronton	10	Madiran/Pacherenc du Vic-Bilh
5	Bergerac	11	Irouléguy
6	Pécharmont	12	Jurançon

tardives (100g/L or above), which you may find described as moelleux or liquoreux; a carbonic maceration AP Gamay Primeur sold in November; and two sparkling wines – méthode

Big names in Cahors, clockwise from top left: Château de Chambert; Jean-Luc and Sabine Baldès from Clos Triguedina; Jean-Marc (left) and Pascal Verhaeghe at Château du Cèdre

traditionelle and what used to be known as méthode Gaillacoise (now ancestrale). The latter, like Clairette de Die in Limoux, is produced by a single fermentation in bottle, giving less pressure, lower alcohol and more sweetness than found in twice-fermented sparkling.

The Gaillac vineyard area is divided into three main zones, with the Premières Côtes on steep slopes to the north of the Tarn, above which lies the limestone-dominated plateau leading towards the famous hilltop town of Cordes. The other significant area is the left bank (south),

where alluvial deposits dominate with *graves*, a pebbly soil mixed with clay on a chalky subsoil. The finest producer here is Domaine Rotier, with Alain Rotier being one of the key winemakers driving the rise in quality of one of Gaillac's exclusive white grape varieties – Len de l'El (also known as Loin de l'Oeil). Gaillac is a hunting ground for many of the southwest's unique varieties. Like Len de l'El, Verdanel is an exclusive white grape with tiny production, while Ondenc (with small plantings in Australia) produces very fine sweet wines such as Domaine Plageoles' Vin d'Autan. Reds Duras and Prunelard (or Prunelart) are only found in Gaillac, with the latter of interest being one of the parents of Malbec.

An hour northwest of Gaillac lies **Cahors**. This is an important appellation which has only started to fully recover in the past few decades from the ravages of phylloxera. Only red wines are permitted within the AP, and Malbec (known locally as Auxerrois or Côt/Cot) is the main variety, supported by Merlot and Tannat. Cahors once had a name for its 'black wine', but this was not fully representative of the appellation, as that wine was actually a heated, concentrated, distilled wine of dubious quality. Today there are an increasing number of high-quality domaines ranging from older, established producers ▶

Above from left: Château d'Aydie vineyards; Château Montus and its vines – both properties are in Madiran

(Château du Cèdre, Clos Triguedina) to relative newcomers to the area (Château de Chambert, Château Lagrézette).

Cahors wines are deep in colour with intriguing violet and herbal aromas and spicy, meaty notes on the palate. Malbec here has traditionally been very different to that found in Mendoza, with many producers now adapting their style to benefit from the Malbec 'brand' – as established by Argentina's varietally labelled bottlings – through better management of tannins and emphasising fruit ripeness, while still retaining the wilder, individual side of Malbec from the causses.

An hour south of Cahors, heading towards Toulouse, one enters the territory of another intriguing grape – Négrette. This area is the Toulousain and its primary appellation **Fronton**. Like Gaillac, winemaking in Fronton dates back to Roman times. Négrette is reputed to have been brought to the area from Cyprus by the Knights of St John, although more recent studies suggest it is related to Auxerrois. The grape is proving highly successful as a dark-coloured, fruit-driven, early-drinking red which retains plenty of floral notes and supple juiciness. Négrette is also leading a rapidly developing rosé sector, very popular in the bars of Toulouse.

Covering some 13,000ha in all, and incorporating 13 appellations, the extended **Bergerac** vineyard is by some way the largest wine region in the southwest. Perhaps due to its proximity and historical trading links, Bergerac seems more oriented to Bordeaux, often being viewed (incorrectly) as a satellite appellation. While it is true that grape varieties are more closely aligned with Bordeaux, with Cabernet Sauvignon, Merlot, Sauvignon Blanc and Semillon much more common than in other southwest vineyards, there is plenty to interest the wine enthusiast here.

Bergerac is a source of great-value, good-quality dry wines, with **Pécharmant** a specific, high-quality red wine AP to the east of the region, benefiting from a mineral-rich subsoil. Bergerac is perhaps best known for its wonderful sweet

SOUTHWEST FRANCE: PRODUCERS TO KNOW

MARCILLAC
Domaine du Cros
Domaine Matha

GAILLAC
Château L'Enclos des
Rozes
Domaine d'Escausses
Domaine de Brin
Domaine Rotier
Robert Plageoles

CAHORS
Château du Cèdre
Château Lagrézette
Clos de Gamot
Clos Triguedina

FRONTON
Vinovalie

**BERGERAC,
PECHARMANT**
Château de Tiregand
Château Tour des Gendres
Domaine de l'Ancienne
Cure

**MONBAZILLAC,
SAUSSIGNAC**
Château Tirecul
La Gravière

ST-MONT
Producteurs Plaimont

**MADIRAN, PACHERENC
DU VIC-BILH**
Château Bouscassé/
Montus
Château Laffitte-Teston
Domaine Capmartin
Château d'Aydie
Domaine du Crampilh

JURANÇON
Clos Lapèyre
Domaine Cauhapé

IROULEGUY
Domaine Arretxea
Domaine Ilarria

wines, from **Haut-Montravel**, **Rosette**, **Saussignac** and **Monbazillac**. Unlike many other southwest vineyards, botrytis thrives here, often yielding stunning results and some amazing value for sweet wine.

VOYAGE OF DISCOVERY

Gascony is the large region situated south of Bordeaux, west of Toulouse and stretching as far south as the Pyrenees. It is the source for the single biggest IGP in the southwest – **Côtes de Gascogne** – which covers more than 12,000ha, according to the regional syndicat. Here, 85% of production is dry white wines based around Ugni Blanc (Trebbiano Toscano in Italy, key also in the production of Armagnac in the same region here), Colombard and Gros Manseng. Gascony is also home to some important appellations – Madiran, Pacherenc du Vic-Bilh and St-Mont.

St-Mont is an AP producing very distinctive wines, with many UK supermarkets stocking a blend made by Producteurs Plaimont. This significant, quality-focused cooperative has been responsible for putting many of the wines of

'Individuality is the key in the southwest: it's best to explore as many different areas as possible'

southwest France on the map, with much of this down to the vision and leadership of André Dubosc. St-Mont only came about through the drive of Dubosc, achieving AP status in 2011 for red, white and rosé wines, mostly using blends of unusual varieties, and all offering great value. Arrufiac is a key component of many of the best whites, adding delicate aromas and finesse to Gros Manseng and Petit Courbu, with reds dominated by Pinenc (Fer Servadou) along with Tannat, both Cabernets and Merlot.

André Dubosc (who retired in 2006) may have put Gascony and St-Mont on the viticultural map, but another individual – Alain Brumont (Châteaux Bouscassé and Montus) – did the same for **Madiran**. This is one of the southwest's most intriguing wines – dominated by the Tannat grape, with a reputation for full-bodied wines

▶

capable of (and sometimes needing) long ageing. Cabernets Sauvignon and Franc are used in most of the blends, with the latter's fruitiness perhaps a better foil for Tannat than the more austere Cabernet Sauvignon. Despite their vin de garde reputation (wines intended for keeping), modern Madirans are often quite approachable in their youth, displaying intriguing floral notes and rounded tannins. As well as the Brumont wines, excellent Madiran is produced by Château d'Aydie, Domaine Capmartin and Domaine Labranche Laffont.

Pacherenc du Vic-Bilh is a white-only wine appellation covering the same area as Madiran. Traditionally the wines were sweet (and of high quality), but today there is also a dry white AP labelled as Pacherenc Sec. Much of the character and quality of both sweet and dry whites is down to the grape varieties – Arrufiac, Gros Manseng and Petit Manseng. The latter has thick skins and can remain on the vine until late in the autumn, encouraging the production of fine sweet wines.

Jurançon is located south of Pau and produces sweet and dry whites based around Gros Manseng, Petit Manseng, Petit Courbu and two rare varieties – Lauzet and Camaralet. Jurançon produces high-quality wines – in the 13th century, according to Paul Strang's book *South-West France* (UC Press, 2009), the rulers of Béarn were the first in France to introduce the concept of 'cru' to designate quality. The climate here is unusual – wet spring seasons enable water reserves to replenish, while long, dry summers and autumns allow for the development of fine late-harvest sweet wines. As with Pacherenc, dry wines must be labelled Jurançon Sec. Clos Lapèyre and Domaine Cauhapé are two of the leading producers.

'The southwest is such a rich source of alternative, great-value and high-quality wines'

Further south again, one approaches the wines of the Basque Country and the Pyrenees mountain region. **Irouléguy** is primarily a red wine produced from Tannat, Cabernet Sauvignon and Cabernet Franc, and today covers more than 230ha (source: *Aquitaine Online*). Soils here are reddish sandstone, mixed with alluvial deposits washed down from the mountains. Low yields and manual labour in the vineyard add to the price of the wines, but they are worth seeking out for their individuality. Top producers include Domaines Arretxea and Ilarria.

STRENGTH OF CHARACTER

It's impossible to characterise and describe the wines of the southwest as one, given the variety of grapes, diverse terroirs and dynamic producers all adding to a potpourri of wines which really emphasise a 'sense of place'. Individuality is the key, with consumers' best option being to explore as many different areas as possible. In addition to those described here, it's well worth looking out for some of the other APs and IGPs which I've been unable to cover in this short piece – such as Buzet, Côtes de Duras and Coteaux du Quercy.

Unfortunately, with the exception of Bergerac, Côtes de Gascogne and St-Mont, relatively few southwestern wines are available outside their local area. But if you get the opportunity to search them out, you won't be disappointed.

Above: Iban and Teo Riouspeyrous, at Domaine Arretxea

Howard's 10: pick of southwest France

① Domaine Rotier, Renaissance, Gaillac 2019 93

£13.50 The Wine Society

On the domaine's gravel soils, Alain Rotier focuses on organic methods and champions the Len de l'El grape, which in Renaissance is blended with 20% Sauvignon Blanc, co-fermented in barrel prior to 10 months' maturation in wood, with 20% in acacia. Concentrated, fresh and precise on the palate, showing crisp acidity and nutty characters combined with fresh citrus. A standard-bearer for Gaillac. **Drink** 2022-2025 **Alcohol** 13%

② Domaine l'Ancienne Cure, Jour de Fruit, Bergerac Sec 2019 91

£10.06/35cl Les Caves de Pyrene

Christian Roche is the fifth-generation winemaker at this family-owned 50ha estate. A fine dry white blend of 70% Sauvignon Blanc and 30% Semillon. Very fragrant nose of boxwood and lime leaf, with bright, zesty citrus character on the palate. Plenty of concentration and lots of complexity at this price level. Organic. **Drink** 2022-2022 **Alc** 13.5%

③ Château du Cèdre, Cahors 2018 94

£18.95-£25.99 Connaught Cellars, Eton Vintners, Exel, Lea & Sandeman, Les Caves de Pyrene, The Dorset Wine Co, The Good Wine Shop, The Wine Reserve, Waud Wines

Pascal and Jean-Marc Verhaeghe have driven this family estate to new levels of quality. From three distinct terroirs, this is a complex, incisive and very fine example of Cahors Malbec. Deep in hue, with a haunting, fragrant, floral nose and vibrant dark fruit on the palate with a spicy edge and slightly wild character. 90% Malbec, 5% Merlot, 5% Tannat, aged in foudre/barrel for 20 months. Capable of long ageing. Organic. **Drink** 2022-2028 **Alc** 13.5%

④ Domaine Ilarria, Irouléguy 2018 93

£21 Yapp Bros

This Tannat-Cabernet Sauvignon blend has soaring floral notes combined with spicy red berries and a touch of menthol. Although concentrated on the palate this is not a clumsy, tannic beast; instead there is plenty to enjoy with blackcurrant and damson fruit, and beautifully integrated wood. An intriguing, elegant and classy wine with a refined finish. Organic and biodynamic. **Drink** 2022-2026 **Alc** 13%

⑤ Producteurs Plaimont, Le Faîte Rouge, St-Mont 2016 93

£20.95 Corney & Barrow, House of Townend

Le Faîte is a top-of-the-range St-Mont with an intriguing nose of wild flowers and leafy raspberry. Oak needs a little longer to fully integrate. Weighty palate with concentration, dark berry fruit, ripe tannins and fresh acidity keeping everything in balance. A fine example of how good St-Mont can be. **Drink** 2022-2026 **Alc** 14.5%

Château d'Aydie, Odé d'Aydie, Madiran 2016 92

£11.95 The Wine Society

Chateau d'Aydie's 49ha are predominantly planted on clay-limestone soils. A fine Madiran with smoky, scented notes on the nose of violet and rose petal. 100% Tannat, deep and dark, with masses of dark berry and damson fruit on the palate. Aged in barrel for a little more than a year with firm, supple tannins for long ageing, though drinking well now. **Drink** 2022-2027 **Alc** 14%

Château de Tiregand, Pécharmant 2018 92

£14.95-£17.40 PDN Wines, Tanners

The soils in the east of Bergerac are sand and gravel mixed with clay and iron deposits, giving Pécharmant wines a distinctive flavour. This Merlot and Cabernet Sauvignon-dominated blend is matured partly in used barrels from Château Mouton Rothschild. With notes of cassis and dark cherry, supple tannins and well-integrated oak, this is a classy Bergerac red which will age very well. **Drink** 2022-2026 **Alc** 14.5%

Domaine Jean-Luc Matha, Cuvée Laïris, Marcillac 2016 92

£16.49 Les Caves de Pyrene

A real 'wine of the land', Cuvée Laïris is 100% Mansois (Fer Servadou). Hand-harvested, this is a distinctive, deep, dark wine which needs aerating to open up. Very elegant, with pure red berry and currant fruit, crisp red-apple acidity and plenty of drive and lifted floral notes. Impressive concentration for a wine with 11.5% alcohol. Spicy finish and firm tannins. Biodynamic. **Drink** 2022-2025 **Alc** 11.5%

⑥ Château Tirecul La Gravière, Les Pins, Monbazillac 2020 92

£14.50/50cl Lea & Sandeman

Muscadelle is Tirecul's speciality, accounting for 40% of its plantings. Les Pins is the entry-level sweet wine from younger vines with less botrytis than the Cuvée Madame, but it still shows classic botrytis notes of orange peel and mushroom on nose and palate, with purity of tropical/citrus fruit and cleansing acidity to finish. Deftly treads the fine line between sweetness and freshness. Excellent value. Organic. **Drink** 2022-2025 **Alc** 12.5%

Domaine Cauhapé, Ballet d'Octobre, Jurançon 2019 91

N/A UK jurancon-cauhape.com

The 40ha estate's entry-level sweet wine is produced from 100% Petit Manseng. Harvested at the end of October, this has remarkable clarity and finesse. Not overly sweet, with cleansing acidity on the palate, it is a delicious doux that's great as an aperitif, or to accompany cheese and desserts. **Drink** 2022-2024 **Alc** 13% **D**

The new Super-Italians

This is the very best in modern Italian winemaking. New ideas, new enthusiasm and new styles. Our experts pick 12 excellent wines to showcase the renaissance

INTRODUCTION JAMES BUTTON; **CONTRIBUTORS** MICHAELA MORRIS, RICHARD BAUDAINS, ALDO FIORDELLI, SUSAN HULME MW

Today, the wine landscape of Italy is reaping the benefits of change. A new generation of winemakers are bringing energy and innovation to complement the knowledge and experience of their forebears.

So we thought it was time to highlight this reinvigorated Italy. Loosely inspired by the SuperTuscans – those wines that side-stepped Tuscan traditions and regulations five decades ago to forge a new path for quality-minded producers – our concept of the 'new Super-Italian' is to group together wines from across Italy that merit attention for their forward-looking, even groundbreaking philosophies.

These new Super-Italians are not only excellent wines in their own right, they represent the best that the future of Italian winemaking has to offer.

We asked four of our Italy experts to nominate three wines each from their respective regions of speciality. And the wines they chose certainly reflect the new, progressive Italy.

High-altitude and morning sun-facing vineyards are becoming increasingly important as a way to combat the ever-warming climate – indeed, the Brunello di Montalcino authorities have removed the region's upper altitude limit of 600m, effective from the 2016 vintage.

Fungus-resistant 'PIWI' hybrid varieties are gaining traction too, especially in the cool northeast, to reduce pesticide usage and provide a gateway to organic farming (*piwi-international.de*).

Indigenous varieties are championing terroir and sympathetic winemaking on a scale not seen before. Meet the new Super-Italians.

▶

'The new Super-Italians represent the best the future of Italian winemaking has to offer'

In Campania, the barrel cellar
at Mastroberardino features
handpainted frescoes

Northwest

Escalating land costs in Barolo and Barbaresco combined with the changing climate have drawn attention to Nebbiolo's lesser-known, cool alpine zones. These stretch from Valtellina in Lombardy all the way to the border with France and Switzerland, where the Valle d'Aosta is located, abutting Piedmont's minuscule appellation of Carema. After years of abandonment due to the gruelling mountainous terrain, a dynamic new generation is slowly reversing this.

The same can be said of Alto Piemonte's multiple denominations. Among these, Gattinara was thriving as long ago as the 1500s but fell into decline after its 19th-century apogee. It is now on the path to its former glory – helped by one of Italy's most revered names, Roberto Conterno.

Beyond Nebbiolo, rare native grapes are enjoying a booming revival in the northwest. Simmering with potential, the once almost-extinct Timorasso stands out for its complex, ageworthy whites as exemplified by one young gun who has returned to his roots.

Northwest Italy's new Super-Italian trio represents a safeguarding of native grapes and precious terrain. They ally respect for tradition with modern expertise. What is new is old; what is old is new. *Michaela Morris*

① Vigne Marina Coppi, Fausto Timorasso, Colli Tortonesi, Piedmont 2018 93

£40.99 Carruthers & Kent, Liberty Wines

After completing winemaking studies, Francesco Bellocchio established vineyards on land in the tiny village of Castellania that had belonged to his cyclist grandfather Fausto Coppi. Joining Colli Tortonesi's Timorasso revival, he has drawn on the diversity of vine material that had been recovered locally. Mineral-driven and savoury with a steely backbone, his Fausto is emblematic of the Timorasso grape. Still youthfully restrained, it is flinty with subtle hints of blanched nuts, grapefruit and white peach. A tactile mouthfeel and underlying concentration suggest this will flesh out with time. This demonstrates that Italy's native whites can offer complexity and character without relying on international varieties or ageing in oak – and that Timorasso deserves a place in the cellar. **Drink** 2023-2029 **Alcohol** 14%

② Nervi Conterno, Gattinara, Piedmont 2017 94

£25-£36.50 (ib) Appellations, Asset Wines, Atlas Fine Wines, Cru, Seckford Wines

Roberto Conterno's purchase of the historic Cantina Nervi in 2018 signals a new Super-Italian reality, casting a spotlight on this underrated denomination. Conterno saw the 2017 vintage through élevage and decided not to bottle the estate's famous Molsino and Valferana crus separately. With some coaxing, alpine flowers, red cherry and juniper emerge from a dark, earthy backdrop. The palate is further nuanced by bitter roots, chinotto citrus, liquorice bark and a crushed granite mouthfeel. Refined tannins build up, with textural grip closing in on the finish. Tanginess and energy are evident throughout, underscoring the promise of cooler regions as global temperatures rise. **Drink** 2025-2042 **Alc** 14.5%

③ SorPasso, Carema, Piedmont 2018 93

£32.50 (ib) Cru, Ultravino

While Carema has long been dominated by a very good cooperative, a handful of intrepid 30ish-year-olds are piecing together small parcels to make their own wines. Local oenologist Vittorio Garda and his wife Martina launched SorPasso in 2012. Four plots total a mere 1ha and span a steep 350m-700m, and with each successive vintage Garda continues to fine-tune his craft. This co-fermentation of Nebbiolo with hyper-local varieties Neretto and Ner d'Ala gives scents of roasted chestnut, dried leaves and brushwood, raspberry and rose. The palate is stony in minerality, bracing in acidity and gracefully composed in tannins. It captures the crispness and clarity of the area, as well as the resolute persistence of the winemaker. **Drink** 2022-2028 **Alc** 14%

With the Alps in the distance, Roberto Conterno stands in a Nervi-Conterno Nebbiolo vineyard, Gattinara DOCG. Below: Thomas Niedermayr (see p56)

'A renewed mindfulness has washed over several Italian regions, stimulated by the threat of global warming'

Veneto & northeast

'Super-wines' have that wow factor that makes you sit up and take notice; that special character that makes them memorable. But more than that, they each have a story that makes them stand out. It might be to do with a terroir, a grape or an inspirational winemaker, or often a combination of all three. Here are three such stories.

Col del Vent is a unique plot of ancient vines in Valdobbiadene that Nino Franco has rescued in order to affirm the individuality of terroir in the context of a wine – in this case, Prosecco, which is often perceived as a standardised, commercial product.

Kristian Keber from Collio, meanwhile, is one of the rising stars of natural wine – a horrendously inadequate term, but one with undeniable currency. He has given an already highly respected family winery a new dimension.

►

> 'Such wines are grounded in a rich Italian viticultural tradition but deliver something that lifts them above their peers'

—— Susan Hulme MW

Finally, Thomas Niedermayr from Alto Adige is a pioneer of PIWI varieties, which represent the new frontier in organic viticulture. He has won over sceptics of the genre with wines of class and character. *Richard Baudains*

④ Nino Franco, Nodi Brut, Prosecco Conegliano-Valdobbiadene Superiore, Veneto 2019 96

£24.30-£25 **Lay & Wheeler, Sommelier's Choice**

When Nino Franco discovered the Col del Vent vineyard in 2014, he said it was like taking a step back in time. He found the tiny plot above Valdobbiadene hosted, in excellent health, 100-year-old vines of biotypes of Glera that have long since been replaced in the region by modern clonal selections. The following year, with the help of master pruner Marco Simonit (consultant among others to Yquem, Latour and Roederer), he produced the first wine from the vineyard. He named it Nodi, or 'knots', referring to the gnarled trunks of the ancient vines. The 2019 has aromas of herbs, spring flowers and white fruit, a distinct mineral nuance and a crisply incisive palate of extraordinary length and crystalline purity. A wine of great finesse. **Drink** 2022-2028 **Alc** 11.5%

⑤ Edi Keber, Collio, Friuli Venezia Giulia 2019 95

£23.99 **All About Wine**

A typical Collio estate may produce up to a dozen monovarietal wines from local and international grapes. Edi Keber was the first in the region to eliminate international varieties and produce a single-estate wine with the traditional blend of Friulano, Ribolla Gialla and Malvasia. His son Kristian (*pictured right*) has taken the concept of terroir a stage further, converting to organic and more recently biodynamic farming, and adopting a holistic approach in the cellar. The varieties for this wine (70% Friulano with equal parts Ribolla and Malvasia) ferment together at natural temperatures with their own yeasts, before ageing on the lees for 18 months. The nose unfolds gradually with the classic lime blossom and sweet white fruit of the Collio, while the palate bursts with energy. Long, tangy and irresistibly moreish. **Drink** 2022-2026 **Alc** 13%

⑥ Thomas Niedermayr, Hof Gandberg Souvignier Gris, Mitterberg, Alto Adige 2018 95

thomas-niedermayr.com

Hof Gandberg is on the high slopes of Appiano on the right bank of the Adige. The Niedermayrs began the conversion to PIWI in the 1990s; with the exception of a small plot of Pinot Bianco, today they exclusively cultivate these fungus-resistant hybrids. Numerically, the most important is Souvignier Gris, which includes Gewürztraminer and Riesling in its parentage. Thomas Niedermayr vinifies the grape in two styles: a macerated 'orange', and this splendidly rich, white organic version, fermented with indigenous yeasts and aged on the fine lees for eight months. Enticing, complex nose, sweet florals with lime, mango and autumn leaf hints. Great volume on the palate, with an undertow of succulent acidity and an intriguingly long, aromatic finish. **Drink** 2022-2028 **Alc** 14%

Tenuta di Biserno winery and vineyards. Below: Kristian Keber and his sister Veronika

Tuscany & central Italy

A renewed mindfulness has washed over several Italian regions stimulated by the threat of global warming and a market that is relentless in its quest for biodiversity. In this context, one can interpret the role of Pievalta – which lays claim to being, since 2008, the first certified biodynamic estate in Marche on the Adriatic coast – as 'Super-Italian'. Its San Paolo Riserva Verdicchio dei Castelli di Jesi Classico Superiore has already demonstrated its elegance and ability to age, and the latest vintage is the first to be partially fermented in oak.

If Super-Italian to you means 'super-premium', then the wise collector should add Tenuta di Biserno's Lodovico to their cellar. This Cabernet Franc-based blend from Bibbona, just above Bolgheri, is made by Lodovico Antinori, founder of Ornellaia and Masseto.

In Montalcino, the warming climate is redrawing some of the best plots. San Filippo's Le Lucére is an elegant, fresh Brunello made with flair by Roberto Giannelli. It has consistently been one of the best wines within the appellation for the past four or five vintages. *Aldo Fiordelli*

⑦ **Pievalta, San Paolo Riserva, Verdicchio dei Castelli di Jesi Classico Superiore, Marche 2019** 95

£18.50 (2017) **Vintage Roots**
The San Paolo vineyard lies on the right bank of the Esino river, on Monte Follonica. A steep hill with a 20% gradient and northeastern exposure, the biodynamic vineyard sits on clay and marl, with an

▶

important outcrop of sandstone from the Pliocene era. In the 2019 vintage, a cool July preserved an ideal canopy. Gently pressed and fermented with an indigenous yeast starter for 18 days, this vintage is the first time the wine has been partially fermented and aged in oak. A restrained, clean and mineral-driven nose is enhanced by Canary melon and scents of Eau d'Orange Verte. White lemon peel perfectly weaves into an elegant, chalky yet not phenolic palate with refreshing acidity. A detailed wine with huge ageing potential. **Drink** 2022-2032 **Alc** 13.5%

⑧ Tenuta di Biserno, Lodovico, Tuscany 2018 98

£300 (ib) **Atlas Fine Wines**

Produced since 2007 in Bibbona, bordering Bolgheri, Lodovico is a relatively young label managed by Lodovico Antinori. Annual production is below 10,000 bottles, and the exact blend is not revealed. Cabernet Franc-based, blended with tiny amounts of Merlot and Petit Verdot, the wine is fermented in stainless steel and aged 16 months in barrique, with notably less racking compared to an equivalent Bordeaux. The 2018 is not completely representative (try the outstanding and more concentrated 2016), but it describes fairly well the graceful, Margaux-like elegance of this SuperTuscan. Parma Violets, cedar, eucalyptus, wild raspberry and coffee grounds outline its complexity. Silky tannins are integrated with refreshing acidity. **Drink** 2022-2038 **Alc** 14.5%

⑨ San Filippo, Le Lucére, Brunello di Montalcino, Tuscany 2017 96

£49.60 (ib) **Farr Vintners**

Le Lucére is a single vineyard of 3.5ha planted in 1996 below Salvioni and La Cerbaiona in Montalcino and producing about 13,000 bottles annually. Gentle fruit handling and a short maceration contribute to

Alessandro Fenino and Silvia Loschi, Pievalta

'One can interpret the role of Pievalta — which lays claim to being, since 2008, the first certified biodynamic estate in Marche on the Adriatic coast – as "Super-Italian"'

—————— Aldo Fiordelli

the graceful style of this Brunello. It ages in a combination of big oak casks and small barrels for a total of two years. What, in my opinion, could explain the exceptional freshness and the unwavering elegance of this Brunello is the eastern exposure of the vineyard on the northern side of the village. The dried cherry fruit is lifted with thyme and blood orange, a touch of wax and deep hints of smoky woodland. The palate is dense and velvety, with greatly refined tannins and predominantly floral flavours. Organic. **Drink** 2022 2037 **Alc** 14.5%

South & islands

The term 'Super-Italian' conjures up a wine that has an extra magical factor — an excitement that stops you in your tracks. Such wines are grounded in a rich Italian viticultural tradition but deliver something that lifts them above their peers. Southern Italy and its islands have a great potential to develop wines in this vein, due to their incredible wealth of indigenous grape varieties and their many old-vine heritage vineyards.

My three nominations from southern Italy are all exciting not just because they taste great and are supremely well made, but also because each

Massimo Ruggero, Siddùra

represents a new, surprising twist on a strong local tradition: Mastroberardino's Stilèma is an innovative new wine in a range of three from Campania's most historical producer; Sardinia's Siddùra puts an intriguing spin on Vermentino di Gallura; and Idda is a new Sicilian collaboration between two wine-producing giants, Gaja from Piedmont and Graci on Etna. *Susan Hulme MW*

⑩ Mastroberardino, Stilèma, Greco di Tufo, Campania 2017 95

£31.67 **Millésima**

When tasted blind during judging week at the DWWA last year, this was immediately awarded a Gold medal. It was a thrill to discover later that it was by Mastroberardino – still innovating and experimenting in Campania after all these years. Stilèma is the result of a two-decade, heritage-based project to stylistically reference the region's finest wines of the 1970s and 1980s. It is bright, zesty and modern, yet reflects a return to the best practices of the past. A blend from three different vineyards, it's fermented and kept on the lees for 30 months. Ripe yellow fruits, orchard fruits and honeysuckle aromas turn into a distinctive waxy, Riesling-like note, typical of mature Greco di Tufo. The palate has a laser-like focus, very pure and linear with a long, savoury, salty, lime-peel finish. Set to become a modern classic. **Drink** 2022-2026 **Alc** 13%

⑪ Siddùra, Bèru, Vermentino di Gallura Superiore, Sardinia 2016 94

£35.95 **Independent Wine**

Siddùra impressed me so much when I first came across the estate in 2016. The wines are lively, fresh and – just like the winery itself – super-stylish. Newly built in 2008, it sits right in the heart of Siddùra's vineyards in Gallura, Sardinia's only DOCG, where Vermentino grows on the area's famous granite and clay soil. Bèru is an interesting variation on the estate's classic Vermentino di Gallura; the team has

given the wine some gentle oak treatment, which produces a fuller, rounder, creamier texture with some potential to age – all of this without losing its crunchy, green, vivid Vermentino identity. Handpicked and gently pressed, it ferments in small French oak barriques. **Drink** 2022-2026 **Alc** 14%

⑫ Idda, Blanco, Sicily 2020 93

£33-£41.10 **Harvey Nichols, Hedonism, Museum Wines, Petersham Cellar, Vin Cognito**

This wine represents a collaboration between two leading producers, Gaja from Piedmont and Graci from Etna. They bring all their skill and knowhow to this venture, focusing on the largely unexplored, warmer southern slopes of Mount Etna and on local white variety Carricante – one of Italy's most exciting, characterful white grapes. Fruit from five hectares of newly planted Carricante vines was included in the 2020 vintage and it really makes a difference, bringing a brightness and intensity to the wine. Aromas of cream, waxy lemon rind and smoke are followed by lively, zesty Sicilian lemon and white flowers enveloped in a creamy texture. It's a vibrant and energetic wine that manages to be gentle at the same time. **Drink** 2022-2029 **Alc** 12.5% **Ð**

SICILY
Sun & sustainability

A push towards sustainability is driving change on the fabled wine-growing island of Sicily. Indigenous grape varieties are being rediscovered, and its diverse climate and geology are adding even more excitement to the wines being made today

STORY FILIPPO BARTOLOTTA

For years, Sicily was known for its production of sun-driven, jammy reds and creamy, round, robust whites. On my most recent trip to Sicily in October last year, however, I was blown away by the quality of the wines I encountered. The sheer complexity of the island's terroir *(see p62)* means that an article about Sicily should really begin by focusing on the wines from the 'different Sicilies'. There's a dizzying array of climatic, geological and cultural features that translates into the kaleidoscope of colours, scents and flavours we can enjoy in our glass.

REVIVING A HERITAGE

You'll encounter the same diversity in the palette of grape varieties that winemakers draw from. In the past, old varieties were abandoned to give space to more productive clones vinified to get more extractive and alcoholic wines suitable for blending. But today, thanks to the research and protection work put in place by the Consorzio di Tutela Vini DOC Sicilia body, Sicily has rediscovered more than 70 indigenous varieties.

The vine germplasm study, in collaboration with the Sicily ministry of agriculture, University of Palermo and F Paulsen centre, is showing how the key varieties of Lucido (Catarratto), Grillo and Nero d'Avola can be used as a litmus test, clearly expressing the different terroirs of the island. The study has also discovered these indigenous varieties to be much more resistant to climate change than more recent additions.

During my visit to Riofavara winery *(riofavara. it)* at Ispica in the southeast, owner Massimo Padova could not contain his joy at seeing butterflies and an abundance of different flowers. 'See, on this hill we planted Recunu, and Cutrera and Rucignola further below.' Padova stopped

and turned to me, smiling. 'They are relic varieties. Those which had disappeared because they did not produce enough in the 1980s. We planted a few vines, taking the grafting propagated at the Palermo Botanical Garden, thanks to the consorzio.'

I tasted some of his wines while he watched me, waiting for a nod of approval. There was no need to tell him anything: my reactions were enough. I was pleasantly surprised by the fragrance and the almost mountainous character of his wines, with their balsamic traits and exciting freshness.

SUSTAINABILITY PUSH

In addition to having the largest area under vine in all of Italy, Sicily also lays claim to the largest organic vineyard area, with a little more than 30,000ha of its approximately 98,000ha total *(data source: Mipaaf, 31 July 2020)* cultivated according to methods of environmental, social

'Sicily manages to transmit its richness and biodiversity through the kitchen as much as through the glass'

and economic sustainability, thanks to Fondazione SOStain Sicilia (*fondazionesostainsicilia.it*). This foundation, a joint project by the consorzio and the Assovini Sicilia winemakers' association, aims to promote the sharing of best practices, and stimulate research and higher education to develop a culture of eco and ethical sustainability.

Sicily is already in itself a garden of organic viticulture. 'The sustainable vocation of Sicily,' explains Antonio Rallo, CEO of the historic Donnafugata company and president of the Consorzio Sicilia, 'is a natural factor thanks to its favourable climatic conditions and soil variety and biodiversity.' The dry, continental yet ventilated climate favours crops and protects them from disease – three treatments based on

sulphur and copper have always been enough to combat powdery and downy mildew. To this natural advantage has been added, in the past 20 years, an institutional policy aimed at the transition to organic viticulture.

SOStain Sicilia is the sustainability programme for Sicilian viticulture promoted by the foundation, with the purpose of certifying the sustainability of the island's wine industry. The SOStain specifications are based on 10 requirements that member companies must comply with to obtain the certification. These 'integrated farming methods' cover not only cultivation but the entire production cycle, including the prohibition of chemical weeding, the protection of biodiversity, use of eco-friendly and local raw materials, the use of energy-efficient technologies, and the reduction of bottle weight. Members are also required to issue an annual 'sustainability report'.

Scattered throughout the region, 26 Sicilian wineries have already joined the foundation, representing 4,617ha of certified vineyard area, equivalent to 19 million bottles. 'It is a project that is gaining great support because it allows companies, from small properties of only 1ha to the largest wineries, to create a system, share and spread good practices to respect the ecosystem,' says Alberto Tasca, CEO of Tasca d'Almerita and president of the SOStain foundation.

Antonio Rallo

SICILY: A TOUR OF ITS TERROIR

Sicily's **southeast** is the furthest extent of the African tectonic plate that pushes on the Eurasian plate and emerges from under the sea. Vines here have their roots in the robust, sandy, loamy carbonate base, giving whites based on Inzolia (Ansonica) or Moscato a mineral character, and reds that are very light, salty and reactive with strong floral notes. Frappato, airy and floral, is often mixed with Nero d'Avola in a classic blend of the only Sicilian DOCG, Cerasuolo di Vittoria.

In the **northeast**, altitudes exceed 1,000 metres with the wines of Etna, the largest active volcano in Europe. To its north lie the metamorphic rocks on whose soils Nerello Mascalese, Nero d'Avola and Nocera grow to give transparent and energetic ruby-red wines.

It's the **western** part of the island, however, where 85% of Sicily's wine is produced and where there are myriad terroirs: the clay hills of the northwest with important chalky and calcareous veins that give structure and generous flavour; the stretches of looser sandy soils of the extreme western tip where once Carricante and Grillo (the backbone of Marsala) were harvested overripe and vinified in an oxidative style, but

today appear as whites vinified in a reduced style with strongly mineral and crunchy traits. Down in the **southwest**, the micro-terroirs of the Menfi area deserve an article all to themselves. On the coast, the scenic Scala dei Turchi ('Turkish steps'), a bright white, limestone-marl stepped cliff, rises up out of the sea.

The **central-western** area is characterised by a coastal area with sandy limestone terraces that give more saline and savoury wines, and inland areas of more impervious hills where soils with a more significant presence of clay emerge. Here, Nero d'Avola is typically more structured and powerful than in the southeast, although in recent years the wines have developed a juicier and more contrasted side. Grillo from vineyards of altitude shows a richer profile with almost Sauvignon Blanc-like pyrazine aromas. These are vertical whites, tense, with a strong acid component; but as you near the coastal sands they turn more savoury and almost saline.

The small **islands** off the coast of Sicily, volcanic in nature, are known for aromatic white wines that in the past were almost all vinified sweet, but now also as dry wines – and deliver strong gastronomic traits.

BRIGHT FUTURE

The sustainability programme can be an important driver of competitiveness, giving visibility to the Sicilian territory and to its wine companies, and representing an effective tool for local development – as I witnessed at Giasira winery *(lagiasira.it)*, north of Rosolini. Owners Isabella and Giovanni Boroli, who decided to move here from the north of Italy, offered a Sicilian welcome: a buffet full of cheeses of all kinds, prickly pears, rustic focaccia and pasta 'alla Norma'. Sicily manages to transmit its richness and biodiversity through the kitchen as much as through the glass. Afterwards, I tasted samples of Nero d'Avola that were extremely vibrant.

The foundation's project, plus research carried out by the consorzio, is changing the oenological face of the island, from a marginal region to a protagonist of quality wines. It's a wine region in collaborative and strategic ferment, guided by the strength of the Grillo, Lucido and Nero d'Avola varieties as ambassadors of its different terroirs.

Although the journey down this path began more than a decade ago, the results are already quite tangible. Among the approximately 250 wines I tasted during my visit, a good percentage displayed precise fruit and good expressiveness. If we take into account that most of the wines are not 'high-end' (more than 90% cost between £7 and £15), the results are even more encouraging. Organic and sustainable wines generally cost 10%-20% more than their non-sustainable counterparts, but this should be considered a positive because it allows winemakers to reinvest in further sustainability projects, thus activating a virtuous circle for the benefit of all.

As Tasca says: 'Sharing means owning together, which I interpret as safeguarding together.'

Bartolotta's pick: 10 top sustainable Sicilians to try

① Tasca d'Almerita, Fondazione Whitaker Mozia Grillo 2020 94

£23.33 **Millésima**

A saline, juicy and vibrant style of Grillo from the tiny Phoenician island of Mozia, off the western tip of Sicily. The nose shows some very delicate notes of aromatic herbs and lime with an orange blossom touch. On the palate there's a pleasant dialogue between sweet tropical fruit and a generous, zesty citrus juiciness with a mineral finish. **Drink** 2022-2027 **Alcohol** 14%

② Alessandro di Camporeale, Vigna di Mandranova Grillo 2020 92

£18.30 (2021) **Tannico[†]**

From the high hills of the Belice valley, not too far from Palermo, this organic Grillo is a great example of how the variety can bring Sicily to a totally different game when it comes to zesty, mineral and salt-driven whites. I love the super-fragrant citrus aromas combined with an almond and anise edge and a delicious, sweet prickly pear complexity. **Drink** 2022-2027 **Alc** 12.5%

③ Cusumano, Lucido 2020 90

£13.80 **Tannico[†]**

A very floral Lucido – a biotype of the most-cultivated variety in Sicily, Catarratto. The nose is a wonderful combination of gentle honeysuckle, lemon and tangerine citrus with a remarkable complexity of Mediterranean herbs. A pretty, full-bodied white with plenty of alcoholic power offering a very round texture that's balanced by grapefruity acidity and a nice mineral finish. **Drink** 2022-2027 **Alc** 12.5%

Donnafugata, SurSur Grillo 2020 90

£15.10-£17.49 **Carruthers & Kent, Valvona & Crolla, Vinvm, Wine Direct**

Produced in the southwest, this pale white has a lychee and melon nose opening up to reveal some very pleasant scents of white peach, lemon and basil. The palate seems to show the character of the two varieties from which Grillo was born in the 19th century: the creaminess and viscosity of Catarratto and the floral aromatics of Zibibbo. **Drink** 2022-2027 **Alc** 14%

Principi di Butera, Carizza Insolia 2020 90

£17 **Zonin UK**

A really generous white from the ancient variety Inzolia (Ansonica) cultivated on the chalky, limestone terroir of the southern-central part of Sicily near Licata. Wildflowers, almonds and honeydew melon aromas lead to a very fruit-driven palate with a smooth touch and a very generous pear, tropical fruit and vanilla finish. **Drink** 2022-2027 **Alc** 12.5%

④ Casa Grazia, Laetitya Frappato 2020 95

casagrazia.com

This demonstrates just how Frappato from the southeast (near Gela) can show the elegant and light side of Sicilian reds. It's a very aromatic, light-bodied organic red that has a seductive nose of rose petals, hibiscus, mountain strawberries and black pepper. On the palate it shows a really inviting crunchy, juicy character with so much drinkability and energy. **Drink** 2022-2032 **Alc** 13.5%

⑤ Salvatore Tamburello, 306 Nero d'Avola 2020 94

£19.45 (2017) **Independent Wine**

Try this organic Nero d'Avola grown in the eastern part of the island for an intriguingly light and crunchy version of Sicily's most famous red variety. There's no oak involved here, but so much red berry crush that it jumps right out of the glass. It's all about the redcurrants with orange peel and a gunflint complexity. Agile, savoury and really refreshing. **Drink** 2022-2028 **Alc** 14%

⑥ Planeta, Nocera 2018 93

£20.40-£23.50 **Carruthers & Kent, Great Wines Direct, The Great Wine Co, Vinvm**

Up at the northeast tip of the island, there's a little-known variety called Nocera. This has so much complexity – a Mediterranean herb and pomegranate-driven red – yet it is so easy to drink. A lovely sapidity develops on the palate, which almost becomes salty and reflects its seaside character, along with plenty of wild fennel and liquorice. **Drink** 2022-2030 **Alc** 12.5%

Duca di Salaparuta, Passo delle Mule Nero d'Avola 2020 92

£20.95-£22.49 **Club Vini, Moreno, North & South**

A really approachable Nero d'Avola, contrasting the maturity resulting from very hot days and windy nights with the reactive savouriness possibly provided by the limestone and silex soils. Sour cherries, redcurrants and a touch of vanilla, mild oak spice adding some depth to this well-designed red. **Drink** 2022-2030 **Alc** 13.5%

Terre di Gratia, 170 Perricone 2020 91

terredigratia.com

It's pretty rare to come across Perricone *in purezza* – it's an austere, tannic, tough-to-produce variety often blended with Nero d'Avola. This wine, from western Sicily, is all about its blue flowers and blue berries, with intense tobacco and balsamic notes then a mocha-like finish. A lot of structure, but smoother and rounder than expected. Organic. **Drink** 2022-2032 **Alc** 13% **D**

The Algarve

Its year-round sun and dramatic coastline mean it's already a much-loved beach holiday destination. But this southern Portuguese hotspot is upping its game, providing plenty to tempt wine lovers inland for a taste of something different

STORY BRIDGET MCGROUTHER

When the Romans reached the southwestern point of the Algarve, they thought it was the end of the world, where the waters of the ocean boiled at sunset. Yet despite the impending sense of doom (or perhaps because of it), they planted vines in the region, finding the temperate climate and fertile terroir a nirvana for wine-growing.

Fast forward to present times and it isn't just the grapes that relish soaking up the rays, as beach lovers, walkers, cyclists, golfers and water sports enthusiasts all bask in their share of a reputed annual 300 days of sunshine. At first, the coastal vineyards lost out to the consequent package holiday boom of lucrative hotels and seaside resorts developed from the 1960s onwards. But in a land deeply rooted in wine-growing traditions, artisanal viticulture is re-emerging in a flourishing revival of indigenous red and white grape varieties, especially the revered Negra Mole (meaning 'black soft').

As enterprising estate owners become increasingly recognised for award-winning results, a new set of adventurous wine tourism thrill-seekers is fast being drawn to Portugal's south. This final frontier of western Europe still has so many grapes yet to be tasted and explored, along with the region's rich gastronomy, culture and dramatic landscapes.

Spectacular limestone cliffs and Arcos Naturais double sea arch, as seen from the popular Praia da Marinha beach

▶

'This final frontier of western Europe still has so many grapes yet to be tasted and explored'

Many vineyards are concentrated inland in what is known as the barrocal, bookended between the Atlantic and the rugged uplands with soils of sand, limestone, clay, shale and alluvium. Producers are working hard to safeguard the distinctive properties of the Algarve's wines, particularly in the region's four DOCs (or DOPs, west to east): Lagos, Portimão, Lagoa and Tavira.

MAKING MEMORIES

Warm, velvety reds include Negra Mole, Castelão and Trincadeira, while top DO white wines such as Arinto, Malvasia Fina and Crato Branco (Síria) taste delicate and smooth. A significant number of Algarve Vinho Regional wines also allow producers even more versatility, with sparkling and late-harvest wines recently released.

Although harvest can start as soon as late July, early September is a good time to catch it. At family-run **Quinta dos Vales** (*quintadosvales.eu*) in Lagoa, the enterprising Winemaker Experience package includes the opportunity to rent or even own a vineyard along with the facilities to make your own wine at this colourful, art-loving estate (*pictured right*) decorated with voluptuous sculptures amid rolling vines, stylish villas, tennis courts and pools (private and shared).

For a slightly less ambitious start to a career in winemaking, the three-hour bottle blending workshop allows you to handpick grapes before

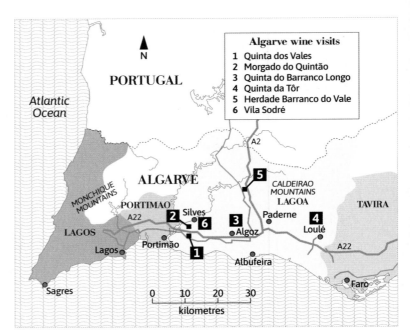

Algarve wine visits
1 Quinta dos Vales
2 Morgado do Quintão
3 Quinta do Barranco Longo
4 Quinta da Tôr
5 Herdade Barranco do Vale
6 Vila Sodré

How to get there

Low-cost airlines from regional UK airports fly to Faro's international airport. Rent a car on arrival for the approximate hour-long drive to the heart of the Algarve wine region. For more information go to *visitalgarve.pt*

sitting down with experts to glean tips on tasting and combine different proportions of native and international varieties. You can create your own blend (I chose 40% Touriga Nacional, 40% Cabernet Sauvignon and 20% Aragonês), before hand-corking and labelling bottles, mine since set aside for an impending special birthday...

A private bash at **Morgado do Quintão** (*morgadodoquintao.pt*) would be idyllic, and tours, tastings, lunches, weddings and authentic farm stays in vineyard cottages are popular here. To spend time sitting in the shade of a 2,000-year-old olive tree overlooking Negra Mole, Crato Branco and Castelão vines at a farmer's table of Algarvian delicacies paired with excellent estate wines is truly memorable.

First founded in 1810 by the Count of Silves and located in a wine-rich region sandwiched between the Monchique mountains and Lagoa, this historic winery is still owned by the fourth generation of the original family. Their passion for preserving the inherited indigenous grapes is undiminished, championing centuries-old styles such as palhete and clarete – both light, pale-hued reds, the former made by mixing with up to 15% white grapes. Yet a modern vision to return to organic production has resulted in prize-winning wines which, since first being produced in 2016, have

Vila Vita Parc, Porches (see p68)

Quinta dos Vales

MY PERFECT DAY IN THE ALGARVE

MORNING

An al fresco breakfast of a still-warm pastel de nata with a freshly squeezed orange juice and hot, strong coffee is, in my books, obligatory in the Algarve. The spectacular, golden cliff coastline is best appreciated from the sea, so set sail from Albufeira marina with **AlgarExperience** (*algarexperience.com*) on a thrilling two-hour speedboat tour, with fun commentary on the bays, caves, dolphins, lighthouses and celebrity homes.

AlgarExperience

LUNCH & AFTERNOON

Keep the adrenalin going with an **Extremo Ambiente** (*extremoambiente.pt*) Jeep Safari to the breathtaking Monchique mountains – you can be picked up from Albufeira, and opt to stop off for an atmospheric lunch and wine tasting near historic Silves, at fascinating family cellar **Vila Sodré** (*residencialvilasodre.pt*). It's a treasure trove of fortified and still wines dating back as early as 1890. Knowledgeable and enthusiastic sommelier Andre will pour glass after glass of Portuguese wines, from a local Al-Mudd Negra Mole rosé 2020 to a Messias 1966 vintage Port from the Douro, at tables laden with Algarvian cheeses, homemade bread, sausages, olives, sardine pâté, carob cake and almond tart. On the steep, winding uphill climb, fortify yourself with the local brandy Medronho and Melosa liqueur, made from honey and wine, at a mountain village cave before enjoying one of the most stunning panoramic views at sunset.

Restaurante Veneza

EVENING

For a memorable menu paired with the best vintages, **Restaurante Veneza** (*restauranteveneza.com*) is in Paderne, an 11km drive inland from Albufeira. You'll be surrounded by 2,000 different fine wines, on sale by the glass or to take away by the bottle. Each delicious wine and dish is described and served by knowledgeable staff in this friendly, family-run establishment which started out as grandfather Manel's grocery store. If you don't want to drive, dinner here can also be added to the action and wine-packed Extremo Ambiente Jeep Safari.

►

already won annual awards from *Revista de Vinhos* magazine for 'Best Wine in Portugal: Algarve' in 2019 and 2020.

Perhaps it's no surprise that the wines at **Quinta do Barranco Longo** (*quintadobarrancolongo.com*) have reached the top division, as owner Rui Virgínia's two footballing sons have both had stints in the English Premier League! Located in rural Algoz, the winery's use of modern technologies combined with innovative winemaking methods have resulted in fine wines from blends of native and international grape varieties, such as the vibrant Grande Escolha (Arinto, Chardonnay, Encruzado) or refreshing Aragonês-Touriga Nacional rosé. This year, a new tasting room will open with a rooftop restaurant, which promises to be an incredible place to drink in both spectacular wines and scenery.

ANCIENT & MODERN

You can lap up grape views while taking a dip in the infinity pool during a tasting tour at **Quinta da Tôr** (*quintadator.com*), now owned by Mário Santos, local-lad-made-winemaker, who as a boy used to go swimming in the nearby river. The historic Roman bridge that leads to Tôr village, just north of Loulé, adorns the labels of the estate wines, which are known for their unusually high alcohol content, such as the robust 17% Syrah.

Surrounded by cork, carob, olive and pine trees, **Herdade Barranco do Vale** (*hbv.pt*) offers stunning panoramas of the Caldeirão mountains when you take a tour of the estate on foot or by tractor.

Owner Ana Chaves still tends the Negra Mole vines that were first planted here by her grandfather in the 1960s, as well as 20-year-old Aragonês and Castelão vines, but the latest family generation has now also introduced first-class white grape varieties such as Antão Vaz, Arinto and Alvarinho.

While the fine wines in northern Portugal have long been internationally revered, the Algarve wine-producing region is only now coming of age. It's an exciting time for discerning wine lovers who will undoubtedly relish heading to the 'ends of the earth' for the dawning of a new wine era – and perhaps stock up on some bargain bottles in the process.

> 'In a land deeply rooted in wine-growing traditions, artisanal viticulture is re-emerging'

YOUR ALGARVE ADDRESS BOOK

ACCOMMODATION

3HB Faro
The first five-star boutique property in the Algarve capital with a rooftop infinity pool, cocktail bar and gourmet restaurant with panoramic views. Only 15 minutes by taxi from Faro airport, there are stylish rooms and a modern spa. *3hb.com/home/3hb-faro*

São Rafael Atlântico
A contemporary five-star hotel in Albufeira with spacious rooms and a spa as well as direct beach access and three outdoor pools in its tropical gardens. Breakfast can be enjoyed on the terrace, with pancakes and other treats made freshly for you. *saorafaelatlantico.com*

Vila Vita Parc
This five-star resort on the coast in Porches offers private tastings in the exclusive wine cellar or dinner in 10 different restaurants, including Michelin two-star Ocean. Many of the rooms, apartments and villas have sea views; others look out over the lush gardens with fountains, pools and resident swans. *vilavitaparc.com*

RESTAURANTS

O Pátio
Head to coastal Carvoeiro for delicious

O Pátio

seafood. This is one of the oldest and best restaurants in the area. The original water well has been converted into a wine cellar. *opatiocarvoeiro.com*

Restaurante Ramires
Don't miss another signature Algarve dish, piri-piri chicken. This friendly, family-owned restaurant in Guia, Albufeira, has been serving it since 1964. *restauranteramires.com*

Tertúlia Algarvia
Doubles as a restaurant and cooking school in Faro. Learn to cook a traditional seafood

stew in the iconic, clam-shaped cataplana, enjoying the fruits of your labour afterwards on the sunny terrace. *tertulia-algarvia.pt*

SHOPPING & LEISURE

Adega-Museu de Odeceixe
The winery museum near Aljezur is housed in an early 20th-century winery. Visitors can discover the history of wine production through antique tools of the trade. *visitalgarve.pt/pt/438/adega---museu-de-odeceixe.aspx*

Mercados de Olhão
Head to this vibrant market in Olhão with your friendly **Portugal4U** guide before catching a water taxi to Culatra island in the Ria Formosa lagoon, where you learn about oyster harvesting. Wine tours are also available. *pt4u.pt/tours*

Seven Hanging Valleys Trail
Hike the seven-mile track from Praia da Marinha to Praia do Vale de Centeanes in Carvoeiro above some of the world's best beaches with cliff-edge viewpoints. For longer routes, walkers and cyclists should follow the Coastal Ecovia (along the whole southern Algarve coast) or the inland Via Algarviana, as many lead to wineries. *walkalgarve.com* ▣

The stunning sea
cave at Benagil

THE JUNIPER HUNTERS

A small number of British distillers are choosing native juniper rather than popular imported European options to make their gins

STORY PETER RANSCOMBE

Above: the berry-like seed cones of juniper, the key ingredient in flavouring gin

While it may trace its roots back to Belgium and the Netherlands' genever, gin has become the most quintessential of British drinks, whether it's being served in London's taverns or on colonial verandas. Yet the key ingredient in 'British' gin now seldom comes from Britain.

Juniper's seed cones give gin its distinctive pine aroma and resinous flavour. This pioneering shrub was one of the first species to recolonise the British Isles following the last ice age, with its habitat stretching from pine woods and moors to cliff tops and heath.

Overgrazing in some areas and a lack of grazing in others reduced its range, and its ability to burn with a near-smokeless flame made it the ideal fuel to chop down for illegal whisky stills. More recently, *Phytophthora austrocedrae* – a fungus-like pathogen, similar to the species that caused Ireland's 19th-century potato famine – has decimated the UK's remaining stocks.

Gin makers have turned to European sources, importing dried juniper cones from Italy and the Balkans. Yet a handful of British distillers continue to use local juniper – both wild and home-grown – as part of their recipes.

ECOLOGY FIRST

Rather than simply harvesting wild juniper from his estate in Northumberland, Hepple Spirits founder Walter Riddell has taken two steps to help the bushes. The first involves picking ripe cones that Lucy, his wife and a trained gardener, propagates into seedlings, which they plant on their moor; the second uses cows and horses to break up the soil to promote natural regeneration.

'We've put ecology at the heart of our management decisions, even ahead of economics, because we believe that if we get the ecology right then it will make the economics right,' Riddell explains. The estate's rewilding work is supervised by ecologist Mary Gough in partnership with the Northumberland National Park and government conservation agency Natural England.

Hepple's gins use juniper in three ways. While most distillers select the ripe, dark blue-black juniper cones to make gin, distiller Chris Garden instead harvests the green cones from Hepple and distils them in a vacuum to give his gins freshness.

Meanwhile, he uses traditional ripe Italian juniper in a pot still to give smoothness, and organic Serbian juniper for 'supercritical extraction' – a technique borrowed from the perfume industry – to give depth of flavour.

'We source juniper from beyond Hepple because I don't want to put too much pressure on things here,' Riddell says. 'The Italian juniper is different to what we have – it's almost chocolatey.

'We're not absolutely fanatical about only going local because we've been trying to make the very best gin we can, using whatever means to make it. Both from an ecological point of view and for

'Juniper is part of our national DNA'

—————— Hamish Martin, The Secret Garden *(above)*

saplings with bottles sold through supermarket chain Waitrose, while wine merchant Berry Bros & Rudd's No3 London Dry Gin, which distils Italian juniper, supported conservation charity Plantlife's efforts to map wild British juniper and provided grants to landowners to promote natural regeneration.

Plantlife, which works nationally and internationally to save threatened wild plants, also works with The Maidstone Distillery in Kent and Rémy Cointreau's Botanist brand from Islay.

Several Scottish micro-distilleries also harvest juniper from local estates for their gins, including Badvo in Perthshire, Inshriach in Strathspey, and Loch Ness Spirits. Each of the distilleries makes its gins in small batches, allowing for their juniper to be gathered sustainably.

Crossbill, which launched in Aviemore in 2012, moved production to Glasgow's legendary Barras market in 2017, but it continues to forage for botanicals in the Highlands. In recent years, the distillery has produced a special-edition gin made from juniper harvested from a 200-year-old plant.

Other Scottish distilleries are rearing their own shrubs, with Arbikie near Montrose planting about 600 juniper bushes each year since 2015. The distillery – which already makes its own base spirit from crops grown on its farm – aims initially to produce a small batch gin using its own juniper, with the potential to eventually supply all its needs.

flavour, we'd like to raise the Hepple component, but that's a super-long-term project.'

Hepple accounts for about a fifth of the juniper Riddell uses overall but, with about 200 seedlings being planted each year, he hopes to become self-sufficient eventually. 'The changes we want to see on the land need a 50-year perspective or more – the natural world moves slowly up here,' he adds.

THE JUNIPER REGENERATION

Other gin brands have also played a role in growing Britain's juniper stocks over the years. In London, Portobello Road Gin – which uses Tuscan juniper in its recipe – gave away juniper

▶

Helen Stewart, Badvo

At the foot of the Pentland Hills on the edge of Edinburgh, Hamish Martin and his family are celebrating a decade at the Secret Herb Garden, where they grow more than 600 plant varieties, and run the Secret Garden Distillery.

After a career importing wine, Martin retrained as a herbologist, and grows his plants without synthetic chemicals. All 12 botanicals in his Secret Garden Wild Gin *(see notes, right)* grow on site and are harvested by hand, with the recipe even including some of his own juniper.

Martin planted some 1,500 juniper bushes in the garden. 'Just as you can't harvest grapes from vines to make wine for four or five years, you have to wait until juniper is about four years old before it starts to fruit,' he explains. 'Juniper is part of our national DNA. We only have two wild spices in the UK – juniper and wood avens root, which tastes like cloves.'

Having planted the first batch of juniper in dense, wide rows, the next 2,000 bushes are being positioned in narrower rows and staggered diagonally, making them easier to harvest. While only a small proportion of the juniper he uses is grown on site at present, Martin hopes to cultivate all the juniper he needs for his wild gin within the next four years.

While other distillers have said juniper is notoriously difficult to grow, Martin gives a modest shrug of his shoulders when asked about his success with the plant. 'For us, it's been a journey of experimentation, and the juniper has flourished,' he replies.

'It's not rocket science. I don't have the arrogance to say I know what I'm doing or pretend to be a professional. For me, it's about a relationship between us and the plants.

'So much of modern farming is about take, take, take, but I believe we need to give something back. We don't use chemicals, and we always leave parts of our lavender, roses and other plants for wildlife.'

Five to try: gins with British juniper

SELECTED BY PETER RANSCOMBE

① Badvo Gin

£39.95/70cl **Badvo, Craft Bottle Shop, Craft56, Master of Malt**

Helen Stewart opened Badvo distillery on her family's farm at Pitlochry in Perthshire in 2018 when she was just 22. Her Scottish juniper delivers damp pine, blaeberry, and a savoury tang on the nose, developing into delicious orange zest and runny honey on the palate. **Alcohol** 45%

② Becketts Type 1097 London Dry Gin

£32-£39.99/70cl **Beckett's, D&R Group, Master of Malt, Noble Green**

Made in London using juniper from Box Hill in Surrey and mint from Kingston-upon-Thames, Beckett's offers gentle mint and lemon aromas, with spearmint and lime flavours balanced by a rounded texture and spicy black pepper notes on the finish. **Alc** 40%

③ Crossbill Small Batch Scottish Dry Gin

£36-£45.99/70cl **Craft56, Crossbill, Czerwik Fine Wines, Drinkmonger, Inverurie Whisky Shop, Lockett Bros, Master of Malt, The Good Spirits Co, Valvona & Crolla**

Just two botanicals – juniper and rosehip from the Highlands – are used to make Crossbill. The juniper is joined by spicy notes on the nose before leading into a warm and textured palate, with sweeter blackcurrant and mint notes. **Alc** 43.8%

④ Hepple Gin

£32.49-£45.99/70cl **Czerwik Fine Wines, Master of Malt, Spirits Kiosk, The Bottle Club, The Drink Shop, The Good Spirits Co, The Whisky Exchange, Virgin Wines**

Bright pine and marmalade aromas give way to richer dark chocolate, peppermint, and lemon zest flavours. Hepple harvests juniper from its moorland estate in Northumberland to be used in one of the components in its three complex distillation processes. **Alc** 45%

⑤ The Secret Garden Wild Gin

£35-£36/50cl **After Noah, Harvey Nichols, Kew.org, Royal Mile Whiskies, The Secret Garden, Yumbles**

Some of the juniper used to make Wild Gin is grown within the Secret Herb Garden on the outskirts of Edinburgh. Floral and citrus notes on the nose lead into a complex mix of black pepper, lemon curd and rose Turkish delight on the palate. **Alc** 39% **D**

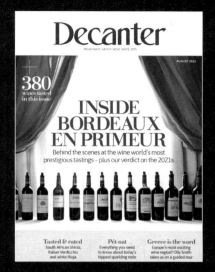
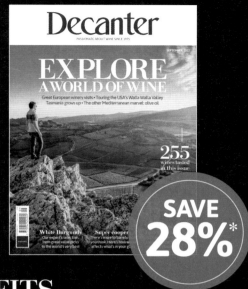

EUROPE
in 12 top winery visits

If you're clever about it, you can have some amazing holiday winery experiences, and keep your non-wine-loving partner happy too. These estates really do offer something for everyone

STORY CHRIS LOSH

UFO sculpture *Chitonia* (2008) by Sylvie Fleury, part of a previous art exhibition at Champagne Pommery

After two years of sofa tourism, European travel is finally back on the agenda this summer. This, clearly, is great news. And even allowing for some of the winery-related activities that didn't make it through the pandemic, wine lovers are still spoiled for choice; all but the most introverted wineries offer tastings – and often tours too.

In fact, the problem is not what's on offer – it's what (and how much) you can convince your travelling companion(s) to take part in. After all, strange as it may seem, not everyone likes to spend sunny afternoons standing around in a barrel cellar.

This article picks out a dozen of the best visits that offer so much more than just wine, ensuring everyone goes home happy. Booking in advance is essential in most cases.

FRANCE

Champagne Pommery, Champagne

GET YOUR ART ON

Domaine Pommery's huge estate is close to the centre of the cathedral city of Reims. At 30 minutes' walk from the train station, this is a visit you could do on a day-trip from Paris (45 minutes by train).

Lots of the grandes marques in Champagne have impressive visitor experiences (Taittinger just down the road is very good, for instance: *taittinger.com*). But it's the non-wine elements that make this one stand out – particularly for those visitors who are less into wine. As well as

the art nouveau/art deco Villa Demoiselle building, there are curated exhibitions of artworks from local and international artists. These are on display all year round (apart from changeover times), mostly 30m below ground, where Pommery's famous 'crayères' (old chalk pits) form excellent galleries for contemplation. They can add a uniquely thought-provoking, amusing, poignant, and occasionally baffling element to your visit. Open every day, 10am-5pm, tickets from €24. *vrankenpommery.com* ▶

Patrice Legrand in the Cave aux Coquillages he has created at Champagne Legrand-Latour

Champagne Legrand-Latour, Champagne

MEET A FOSSIL

Every wine lover knows that Champagne's terroir is all about limestone. And at Champagne Legrand-Latour in Fleury-la-Rivière, just northwest of Epernay, the team are keen to show you what it's all about. In their Cave aux Coquillages ('cellar of seashells'), they have put together a globally respected collection of more than 300 prehistoric shells – some of them unnervingly large – encased and preserved in limestone from 45 million years ago, when France's coolest wine region was a tropical beach.

For those keen to know more or to get more involved, there's everything from a half-hour introductory explanation of fossil-hunting to half-day and full-day workshops where you get to excavate your own molluscs from the rock. Obviously, it'll be fun to see if you can taste the limestone terroir in the wines afterwards. Open every day, with visits from €13; workshops from €50, available Monday to Friday, minimum number of students required. *geologie-oenologie.fr*

Pathways to explore at Domaine Laroche

Above: the vineyard trail at Domaine du Lycée Viticole de Beaune in Burgundy. Above right: students visit the Hameau Duboeuf 'wine theme park' in Beaujolais

Domaine du Lycée Viticole de Beaune, Burgundy

HIKE THE COTES

The wine school in Beaune is a kind of 'learn on the job' winery, where students go to learn how to be the next star grower or winemaker. 'La Viti', as it's known locally, is about half a kilometre from the centre of the town at the foot of Beaune's premier cru vineyards. And the joy of this visit is that you can get out among the vines, following a 10km way-marked trail designed to help you discover six of the 'climats' belonging to the estate. Taking you up and down the slopes of the Côte de Beaune, the student-designed tour is not a gentle stroll, but it's a good way to work up an appetite while engaging with the subtleties of the region's terroir. It's dog-friendly too. Download the free map online. *lavitibeaune.com/vins*

Domaine Laroche, Chablis

PICNIC IN THE VINES

If hiking the vineyards is a bit strenuous, then Domaine Laroche could be more your thing. It's something of a one-stop shop in Chablis, with a good restaurant, accommodation and numerous tasting options, all located in and around the medieval 'Obédiencerie' monastery – part of a

ninth-century abbey – in the centre of the town. There are plenty of leisurely food and accommodation packages available, plus the more entertaining option of heading out into the vineyards on an e-bike. You'll be provided with a picnic and a map, which should allow you to explore the chalky pathways of the Chablis crus without working up too much of a sweat, and also give you a bit of downtime on the south-facing slopes. Most visits available year round; cycling tours (including wine tasting and Obédiencerie visit) from April to October, Monday to Saturday, 10.30am, €69. *larochewines.com*

Hameau Duboeuf, Beaujolais

BRING THE KIDS

Children, it's safe to say, aren't likely to be interested in most wine-themed visits, so options for wine-loving parents with little 'uns in tow are pretty limited. But if you're in (or passing through) Beaujolais, Hameau Duboeuf should keep both parties happy.

Billing itself as 'Europe's first wine theme park', Hameau Duboeuf tries hard to make wine – and wine culture – digestible, not least in a 4D cinema where you can 'fly' over the crus of Beaujolais.

The gardens, open from April to September, are a good place for a stroll or picnic (or aimless juvenile charging about), and kids who aren't interested in the winemaking centre can ride pedal bikes or play crazy golf instead. The 100 vintage drinks advert posters from 1890 to 1950 are practically worth the admission fee alone.

It's just off the main A6 between Lyon and Mâcon, or a local train to Romanèche-Thorins will drop you straight in the park. Park open most of the year, Wednesday to Sunday, 10am-6pm; tickets from €10 (children €6). *hameauduvin.com* ▶

Château Smith Haut Lafitte, Bordeaux

FOOD AND SPA LUXURY

This Pessac-Léognan estate has won a lot of tourism awards down the years, so no surprise to see it included here. The chance to be a winemaker for a couple of hours and fiddle around (supervised, of course) in the winery and cellar might be aimed more at wine geeks than those with a passing interest. But a tour focusing on the estate's biodynamic ethos could have wider appeal. You might even see a horse ploughing in-between the vines.

The five-star Les Sources de Caudalie hotel has a two-star Michelin restaurant and a spa offering a variety of treatments, often involving grape produce. Try the crushed Cabernet scrub, for example, and you can sample the terroir inside and out. Château tours from €22; hotel from €335 per night for a double room; tasting menu from €165; half-day spa rituals from €302; workshops POA. *smith-haut-lafitte.com*

FRANCE

Château L'Hospitalet, Narbonne

JAZZ UNDER THE STARS

The south of France doesn't, on the whole, feature the glitzy tourist attractions of the wealthier wine regions. However, former rugby player Gérard Bertrand's 1,000ha Languedoc estate in La Clape is a magnificent exception. There are plenty of interesting tour options, of which the one-hour electric scooter tour of the vineyards plus winery tour and tasting is the most eye-catching. But if you decide to stay in the château then the less wine-engaged can happily amuse themselves in the spa or the winery's beachfront restaurant while you feed your inner geek.

That said, the big attraction here, without doubt, is the annual jazz festival. It's six nights of outdoor eating and drinking in the gentle warmth of a Mediterranean July evening, followed by a concert. There's a different artist each night, and over the past 20 years it's attracted some really big names. Open year round, with tours from €19; electric scooter tour, Saturdays only, €40. *chateau-hospitalet.com; jazzhospitalet.com*

ITALY

Castello di Volpaia, Chianti Classico

VISIT A MEDIEVAL 'BORGO'

Just to the north of the walled town of Radda in Chianti – well worth a visit in itself – is the ancient borgo (hamlet) of Volpaia. Once abandoned, it is being painstakingly turned into a quirkily beautiful food and wine destination. There's a restaurant, a bakery, olive oil and of course (this being Italy) artisanal ice cream. There's also a winery, with its various production and ageing facilities scattered among the old basements, manor houses and former churches of the 12th-century village. So a tour here is as much a wander through the past as a viewing of vats and barrels – something that will appeal to foodies and historians alike. The estate has also teamed up with cycling company Ciclismoplus to offer personalised one-day bike tours of the area. Open year round, with group tours and tastings from €21; bike hire and bike tours, POA. *volpaia.com; ciclismoplus.com*

Above: the restored medieval hamlet of Volpaia in Chianti. Below: the spa at Les Sources de Caudalie in Bordaux has a natural hot spring water bath

Jazz at Château L'Hospitalet

PICTURE: FEDERICA MASCHERONI FEDERICA@VOLPAIA.COM

Bodegas Muga, Rioja

UP, UP AND AWAY!

In Spain's north, Bodegas Muga is one of Rioja's five-star producers, handily located in Haro's famous Barrio de la Estación. With the likes of La Rioja Alta, López de Heredia and Roda all clustered around the station, this is a great place for wine lovers to spend the day. But Muga has been one of the more creative in its offerings, with the standout attraction being an evening hot-air balloon ride over the vineyards.

Where the balloon goes obviously depends on the wind, but it's a magnificent way to take in the topography, landmarks and wine villages of the region. Vineyard tours on a Segway could be an alternative for anyone suffering from vertigo. Guided tours and tastings available Monday to Saturday, from €25; Segway tours (including picnic and winery visit), €100; balloon flights available at weekends and during holidays (weather dependent), €180pp (€900 for a private flight). *bodegasmuga.com* ▶

Hot-air ballooning at
Bodegas Muga, Rioja

SPAIN

Bodegas Monje, Tenerife

UNDERWATER TASTING... REALLY

In the Canary Islands, Bodegas Monje does everything it possibly can to make wine and food interesting – and if you're ever on this volcanic island it should be a must-visit.

Food-wise, as well as great brunches and lunches, there are wine and tapas matching sessions, while aspiring chefs (including children) can learn how to make the famous local 'mojo' sauces. Creatives can learn to dye fabrics with natural materials such as flowers and grapes. Also on offer are helicopter tours round the island, a night-time picnic and tasting, and (most bizarrely of all) an underwater wine tasting. You'll need to be able to dive (obviously), but heading down into an underwater tasting room in the Atlantic to try the 'sea-aged wines' in situ is weirdly wonderful. Open year round, with tours and tastings from €12; wine and tapas pairing sessions from €19; underwater wine-tasting experience, from €675; helicopter tours from €945. *bodegasmonje.com*

'The chance to stroll the cloisters with a glass of wine accompanied by live Gregorian chants makes for a uniquely atmospheric experience'

Clockwise from top left: an underwater tasting experience at Bodegas Monje; the hotel at Quinta do Vallado in the Douro; Kloster Eberbach by candlelight

PORTUGAL

Quinta do Vallado, Douro

SAIL/CANOE PORT COUNTRY

The Douro is one of the most beautiful parts of the wine world, so even non-wine enthusiasts should be happy to spend some time here. Quinta do Vallado's bijou hotel, just outside Regua, has a good restaurant, a pool and lots of activities that make the most of the region's natural beauty. There are walking trails, picnics and Jeep tours in the vineyards. For this writer, however, the best way to capture the Douro is from the river, with the famous whitewashed terraces stretching up the steep arid slopes on either side of you. A Vallado-organised boat tour on the river looks fun; the chance to self-navigate on a canoe down the smaller Corgo river, even better. Contact via the website for more details. *quintadovallado.com*

GERMANY

Kloster Eberbach, Rheingau

MONKS, RIESLING AND BIG SEAN

This is a visit that will interest fans of German Riesling (ie, 99% of *Decanter* readers) and fans of Sean Connery (ie, 99% of people ever). Why? Because as well as hosting various wine-related visits and activities (plus shop), the 900-year-old abbey was also the setting for the film of Umberto Eco's book *The Name of the Rose*. The abbey offers these various elements separately, but it's more fun when it combines them. The chance to stroll the cloisters with a glass of wine accompanied by live Gregorian chants or taste and tour by candlelight make for a uniquely atmospheric experience. Open year round, with monastery tours from €17.50; wine tastings and tours from €34.50. *kloster-eberbach.de* Ⓓ

Willamette Valley
PINOT GRIS

Pinot Gris has found the perfect home in Oregon's well-known Willamette Valley region, but it's only now starting to reach its full potential – in affordable, easy-drinking styles as well as more serious, ageworthy bottlings

MAIN STORY CLIVE PURSEHOUSE **WINES** MICHAEL ALBERTY

While it doesn't enjoy the profile of Willamette Valley's renowned Pinot Noir or rising star Chardonnay, Pinot Gris remains an important wine for the region's growers and producers. The acknowledged founding father of Willamette Valley, the late David Lett of The Eyrie Vineyards, planted

varieties based not on a Burgundian model but rather on what made climatic sense. Pinot Gris was a big part of those early calculations. In his 1992 speech entitled 'The Emergence of Pinot Gris', Lett joked that the variety was still emerging at the time, recalling the slow sales that Pinot Gris found in the early days at Eyrie.

He claimed to have bartered much of his annual 25-case production from 1971 to 1981 with regional salmon fishermen, given the tough time he had selling it.

Lett was responsible for America's first commercial Pinot Gris. Bringing 'about 160' cuttings north from the University of California, Davis variety collection, these were among Eyrie's original vineyard rows. There are now a few Pinot Gris wines coming from Oregon's more southern wine-growing regions, primarily the Umpqua and Rogue Valleys, but only a handful. It is the Willamette Valley leading the charge.

KEY STYLES

While it is a broadly cool growing region, the Willamette Valley AVA contains plenty of climatic variety – there are 11 sub-appellations as of 2022. Three styles have consequently emerged. First are the nearly ubiquitous bright, fresh wines made in stainless steel that highlight their crisp, fruity character and zippy acidity. Secondly, there has also been a surge in skin-contact Pinot Gris, most (correctly) referred to as ramato. These wines follow the winemaking tradition of Italy's Friuli region, specific to the Pinot Grigio grown there.

Finally, a few producers are making a style of Pinot Gris that's more associated with the traditional wines of The Eyrie Vineyards. These are complex, ageworthy, premium-priced white wines, often from old vines or well-sited vineyards, using neutral oak or concrete.

Today, Pinot Gris is the second most widely planted variety in the state of Oregon (though it only represents about a quarter of the total of the state's Pinot Noir). But, despite the volume, Pinot Gris seems to lag behind Pinot Noir, Chardonnay and arguably even Riesling when it comes to local cachet and buzz.

However, the global popularity of easy-drinking, wallet-friendly Italian Pinot Grigio has been an unexpected benefit: by comparison, Willamette Valley Pinot Gris has developed a national reputation thanks to its superior quality.

King Estate has almost single-handedly buoyed the variety's market share, committing to the grape and producing more than 1.2 million bottles a year. The self-proclaimed 'King of Pinot' makes about 10 variations of Pinot Gris (all biodynamic), including single-vineyard and limited-availability cuvées. The grape's popularity has helped fashion a broader Willamette style – approachable

King Estate buildings and vineyards, to the southwest of Eugene city, Oregon

Jason Lett, The Eyrie Vineyards

aromatically fruit-forward, light-bodied, fresh, crisp and easy-drinking.

Perhaps equally importantly, these wines are affordable – often below $20 in the US market. Though also, perhaps, in the establishment of that signature style, Willamette Pinot Gris has hemmed itself in. Is this approachable, easy-drinking style the full realisation of the variety's potential here? Does this ubiquity limit producers' and consumers' aspirations?

A FRESH APPROACH

Should there be any doubt about the potential of Willamette Pinot Gris to produce a more contemplative wine, look no further than The Eyrie Vineyards' Original Vines Pinot Gris. Made with grapes from vines of more than 50 years old – the valley's first – it has depth, seriousness and noteworthy ageability. It's far more grand cru in its stature than easy-drinking.

For Eyrie's second-generation winemaker and David's son Jason Lett (*pictured above*), however, there is a sense of frustration. 'There was a time when Pinot Gris was being explored seriously for things like site specificity. Between what my father was doing and other pioneers such as Don Lange, there was a real commitment to making Pinot Gris with a sense of place.

'That is not how the wine is being approached today. I believe the Willamette Valley is quite possibly *the* place where a kind of grand cru Pinot Gris can be made. It's really about climate: Pinot Gris ripens best in cool conditions, and that's what we have here. This is really where it belongs.' Lett is excited about burgeoning producers who

FIVE WILLAMETTE VALLEY PRODUCERS TO KNOW

SELECTED BY MICHAEL ALBERTY

These talented young Pinot Gris producers have a lot in common. They largely avoid the Pinot Noir arena, are self-taught and their winemaking practices embrace skin contact, minimal intervention and modest alcohol.

CHAMPIONSHIP BOTTLE
Based in Amity, winemaker Saul Mutchnick makes a variety of minimal-intervention whites for his Championship label, including an exceptional Pinot Gris. In 2020, Mutchnick abandoned skin contact to make his Out on Love Pinot Gris as a white wine. Its clean, acid-driven beauty has Mutchnick thinking he might just keep his Pinot Gris white in future vintages. *championshipbottle.com*

Cyler and Taralyn Varnum

FAIR MOON WINE
Fair Moon is a one-woman natural winemaking operation out of Amity, where Jessica Wilmes believes Pinot Gris' purpose in life is to be orange. Her debut skin-contact Pinot Gris, the Sunshine Effect 2020, is a worthy homage to two producers who inspire her: Gravner and Radikon. Wilmes added Auxerrois and Tinto Cão to her line-up in 2022, so keep an eye out. *fairmoonwine.com*

MALOOF WINES
Bee and Ross Maloof stay out of nature's way as much as possible while making some of the Willamette Valley's best Pinot Gris

Bee and Ross Maloof

in Forest Grove. Before winemaking, Bee was a materials engineer in the aerospace industry, while Ross was a sommelier for a vegan restaurant in Philadelphia. They both love pizza, as their 'eat pizza, suck glass' winery motto makes clear. *maloofwines.com*

MIJITA WINE CO
Lizzy Esqueda's first wine for her Mijita label is a skin-contact Pinot Gris aged in neutral oak and old acacia barrels. It is absolutely brilliant juice: I wish Pinot Gris lovers everywhere could taste it. Esqueda makes her wines at PDX Revolution in downtown Portland, one of the world's few all-female winery incubator/cooperatives. Wherever Mijita moves next, I'm following. 2025 SE 7th Ave, Portland, OR 97214

VARNUM VINTNERS
Based in Amity, Cyler and Taralyn Varnum (*above*) lighten their carbon footprint by using lighter 37.5cl glass beer bottles to house some of their red, white, pink and sparkling wines. My current favourite wine to serve from a beer bottle is a Pinot Gris rosé that was aged on its skins for two weeks. Innovation plus good wine is a winning equation. *varnumvintners.com*

are raising the profile of Pinot Gris among new wine drinkers, sommeliers and chefs. Wineries such as Maloof and Fossil & Fawn are breathing new life into the variety. The focus on Pinot Gris at Fossil & Fawn is a nod back to David Lett's 1992 speech in which he said: 'It is high time viticulture and grape variety adaptation become the focus of premium winemaking on the West Coast.'

That spirit drives Fossil & Fawn's Jim Fischer and Jenny Mosbacher *(pictured, right)*. 'We did not endeavour to revolutionise Pinot Gris in Oregon,' Mosbacher says. 'I wish I could say we did. Our mission from the beginning was to do our best to represent the care that went into tending the grapes by making the best wines we could.'

GREATER UNDERSTANDING

Skin-contact, ramato or vin gris wines are leading the next wave of Pinot Gris from the Willamette Valley. Electric-hued wines with mouthfeel and texture are a great fit for the new demographic of wine drinkers and the always-edgy Portland restaurant scene clamouring for orange wines.

For Fossil & Fawn, it's not about being on trend, but treating the wine in a way that makes the most sense. 'It's wild to think that Santa Margherita [in Italy's Alto Adige] is credited with making the first white Pinot Grigio in 1961,' Mosbacher says. 'Since 2014, we've been making

Jenny Mosbacher and Jim Fischer, Fossil & Fawn

Pinot Gris exactly as we do our Pinot Noir. For us, it makes sense to vinify these two varieties in the same way: to treat Pinot Gris with the same sort of reverence in the cellar as we do Pinot Noir.

'As a wine community, now more than ever we have a greater understanding of the genetics of Pinot Noir and Pinot Gris – the only difference being a few select pigment markers in the DNA.'

Thanks to its myriad sub-AVAs, styles and price points, Willamette Valley Pinot Gris offers a style for all – from the popular, affordable fresh and crisp Pinot Gris (in cans as well as bottles) to more earnest, ageworthy wines that reflect their terroir, as well as ramato-style wines for hipster wine bars. It's time to find the one for you.

Willamette Valley: 12 top Pinot Gris wines to enjoy

SELECTED BY MICHAEL ALBERTY

Ponzi Vineyards, Old Vine, Chehalem Mountains 2018 96
A dazzling wine made with fruit from a section of the original Ponzi estate vineyard planted in 1970. After fermentation with native yeasts and six months of lees stirring, the wine stays in neutral Pinot Noir barrels for almost two years. The wine possesses an otherworldly texture, accompanied by aromas and flavours of butterscotch, papaya, orange blossoms and cardamom spice. Wow! **Drink** 2022-2032 **Alcohol** 13.6%

① The Eyrie Vineyards, Estate, Dundee Hills 2020 95
£28.43 (2017) Christopher Keiller
This is the bar by which many Willamette Valley producers measure their own Pinot Gris. Made with certified organic grapes, the wine's pale moonbeam colour casts its glow on aromas of orange blossom honey, lemon verbena and a trace of vanilla.

Flavours of honeycomb, lemon sorbet and white grapefruit complement a lithe texture backed by acidity that packs a pop. **Drink** 2022-2034 **Alc** 12.8%

② Alexana, Terroir Series 2018 94
£24.99-£25.95 Eton Vintners, The Wine Twit, Vineyard Cellars
While Alexana is well known for its Pinot Noirs, this producer is equally adept when it comes to Pinot Gris. The Terroir Series has fresh, floral aromatics including gardenias, wild roses, lemon tea and a few drops of rainwater. The palate is creamy and rich, with modest acidity and flavours such as lemon chiffon cake, cantaloupe and thyme. **Drink** 2022-2028 **Alc** 13.5%

Evesham Wood, Blanc du Puits Sec, Eola-Amity Hills 2021 94
This Pinot Gris blend includes a portion of Gewürztraminer and homeopathic

amounts of Pinot Blanc, Traminer, Rieslaner and Kerner. The wines are co-fermented in barrel, followed by six months in neutral French oak. It is spicy, lithe and elegant, with aromas and flavours of lemon, lychee, ginger, orange blossom and wet concrete drying in the sun. Its acidity will spark the imagination. Organic. **Drink** 2022-2030 **Alc** 12.5%

Brooks, Estate, Eola-Amity Hills 2021 93
POA Ester Wines
Brooks may be known for its Riesling and Pinot Noir, but this biodynamic producer also makes a fine Pinot Gris with fruit from 43-year-old estate vines. The aromas and flavours of this wine produced in stainless steel are dominated by peaches, Granny Smith apples, lemon zest, pears and a saline note that will have you pining for the sea shore. **Drink** 2022-2030 **Alc** 13%

▶

Elk Cove Vineyards, Estate 2021 93

£23.50 **Amathus Drinks**

This is an excellent Pinot Gris from one of the region's standard-bearers. Made with 100% estate fruit that was whole-cluster-pressed into stainless steel tanks, the straw-coloured wine smells like white peaches and toasted coconut. Pear and peach flavours are joined by hazelnuts on the rich, full palate. The wine's zippy acidity is like a surprise ending to a movie. **Drink** 2022-2030 **Alc** 13%

③ Lange Estate, Reserve, Dundee Hills 2021 93

£41 (2017) **Humble Grape**

The Lange family uses neutral French oak and concrete tanks for fermentation and ageing, claiming the oak lends silkiness while the concrete adds weight. The wine's lemon colour is the perfect segue to scents of lemon sorbet, peach and honeysuckle, then a velvety mouthfeel accompanies flavours of ripe orchard fruit and lemon hard candies. The acidity comes across as just right. **Drink** 2022-2030 **Alc** 13.3%

④ Maloof, Temperance Hill, Eola-Amity Hills 2020 93

Direct-pressed then fermented and aged on the lees without stirring for 10 months in Burgundy oak barrels, this wine is the colour of a faded sunflower, and has aromas of fresh-cut grass, earth, orange peel, beeswax, saline and sweet baked carrots. Flavours like pear, lemon verbena and fresh-baked bread glide on a rich

palate, with enough acidity to trigger a tingle. Organic. **Drink** 2022-2030 **Alc** 12%

⑤ AD Beckham, Amphora, Chehalem Mountains 2019 95

£31.67 **Iconic Wines**

This magenta-coloured wine was fermented and aged on skins for up to 10 months in amphorae made by winemaker Andrew Beckham. The aromas of grilled peaches and crispy salmon skins made my mouth water. The flavour combination of quince, rhubarb and hazelnuts is equally compelling. Toss in a one-two punch of bold tannins and elevated acidity for good measure. **Drink** 2023-2033 **Alc** 12.3%

Fossil & Fawn 2020 94

Jim Fischer and Jenny Mosbacher think Pinot Gris reaches its full potential with extended maceration. Their oak-aged Pinot Gris made as a red wine has been

successfully making the point since 2014. This year's model is the colour of blood orange juice, with aromas and flavours of nectarines, strawberries, saline and white pepper. The tannins clearly announce their presence. **Drink** 2022-2030 **Alc** 12.2%

Vincent Wine Co 2019 92

Vincent Fritzsche treats his Pinot Gris fruit to three weeks on the skins to extract colour and tannin structure. It is darker than most rosés yet lighter than most Pinot Noirs. With fine-grained tannins and flavours like blackcap raspberries, orange zest, hibiscus and black pepper, if you close your eyes you might think you are drinking a red wine. **Drink** 2023-2030 **Alc** 12.5%

⑥ The Marigny, Carbonic Maceration 2021 91

Andy Young throws one impressive whole-cluster carbonic maceration party. The big-time rock drummer-turned-winemaker transforms his Pinot Gris fruit into a tangerine-coloured brew that smells like a warm croissant smeared with apricot jam. The wine's dominant flavours of orange and hibiscus are joined by traces of white tea and tonic water. It has modest tannins and an acid beat you can dance to. **Drink** 2022-2027 **Alc** 12.1% **D**

Michael Alberty writes about wine for *The Oregonian*, a daily newspaper based in Portland. His column on Oregon's more unusual wines appears monthly in *Oregon Wine Press*

PHOTOGRAPH JIM FISCHER

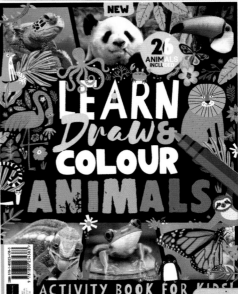

Mendocino
wine country

In the centre of Mendocino County is the bucolic Anderson Valley, home to a string of renowned
wineries, superb restaurants and effortlessly excellent places to stay, all within a short drive

STORY BROOKE HERRON

Now a destination in its own right, the Anderson Valley has developed into more than just a stopover for visitors on their way to the Pacific coast. And a good place to base yourself when exploring this northerly cool-climate wine region is the idyllic coastal town of Mendocino.

It was founded in 1851 but fell into economic decline with the dissipation of the logging industry, and didn't really bounce back until the late 1950s, when it became a haven for artists.

Since then, Mendocino's quaint charm has made it beloved by visitors near and far – a town frozen in time, thanks to much of it being on the National Register of Historic Places and many of its original buildings qualifying as California Historical Landmarks.

About 50km inland, in the Anderson Valley, development was slower. It wasn't until the

The Sea Rock Inn looks out over one of the cliffs that surround the picturesque town of Mendocino, on a remote stretch of coastline in northern California

The tasting patio at Pennyroyal Farm Left: Navarro Vineyards (p80) offers free tastings

1970s, more than a century after early settlers arrived here, that the first commercial wineries planted vineyards. Due to the cool weather, making it harder for thicker-skinned red wine grapes to fully ripen, the initial focus was on white varieties such as Riesling, Chardonnay and Gewürztraminer. This was still the case when Anderson Valley was officially designated an American Viticultural Area (AVA) in 1983.

While small amounts of Pinot Noir were planted in the 1970s, its popularity increased in the 1990s, and the potential for the grape in Anderson Valley was more widely recognised. Today, Mendocino County produces considerably more Pinot Noir than it did in the 1980s – some 1,200 tonnes were crushed in 1980 compared to more than 6,700 tonnes in 2021 (source: California Wine Institute) – with much of that grown and made in the Anderson Valley.

ALONG THE WINE TRAIL

In the centre of the valley, about 60km southeast of Mendocino along Highway 128, is **Pennyroyal Farm** (pennyroyalfarm.com) one of the region's newest estates. Proprietor and head winemaker Sarah Cahn Bennett – daughter of the founders of **Navarro Vineyards** (see p92) – practises regenerative and sustainable farming on her 40ha property, growing vegetables, herbs and fruit, including 10.5ha of Pinot Noir and Sauvignon Blanc. The Pennyroyal team hosts tastings by

'A favourite with visitors for almost five decades, Navarro is also one of the few wineries in the valley where tastings are still free'

reservation on the outdoor patio from Thursday to Monday, and picnic tables are available to those wanting to stop for a glass of wine and something from the 'Farm Fare' menu.

Driving back up the highway toward Philo you'll arrive at the **Drew Family Wines** (drewwines. com) tasting room at The Madrones complex, where visitors can enjoy award-winning Pinot Noir and Chardonnay made from fruit grown primarily in the winery's cool, fog-shrouded, high-elevation Mendocino Ridge vineyards. The tasting room (where you're likely to find owners Molly or Jason Drew serving) is open by appointment on weekends but walk-ins are accommodated if space permits.

Toulouse Vineyards (toulousevineyards.com) is just a two-minute drive back up the highway. Offering one of the nicest views in the valley from the rear deck, overlooking the Navarro river and Hendy Woods state park, it is the perfect place to stop on a sunny day for an afternoon tasting of

Mendocino County: the facts

Planted area (2020)
7,070ha

Main grapes (by area)
Red Pinot Noir, Cabernet Sauvignon, Zinfandel, Merlot, Syrah, Petite Sirah, Carignan, Grenache, Sangiovese, Barbera
White Chardonnay, Sauvignon Blanc, Gewürztraminer
AVAs Anderson Valley, Cole Ranch, Covelo, Dos Rios, Eagle Peak, McDowell Valley, Mendocino, Mendocino County, Mendocino Ridge, North Coast, Potter Valley, Redwood Valley, Talmage Region, Ukiah Valley, Yorkville Highlands

SOURCE: MENDOCINO WINEGROWERS

MY PERFECT DAY IN MENDOCINO WINE COUNTRY

LUNCH AND AFTERNOON

Arrive in Boonville, in the centre of the Anderson Valley, and enjoy a farmstead cheese and charcuterie board with a wine tasting flight at **Pennyroyal Farm** *(see p90)*. After lunch, head back up Highway 128 to **Navarro Vineyards** *(p92)* for a wine tasting on the patio. From there, take a 40-minute drive towards the coast to check into your room at **The Harbor House Inn** *(p92)* in Elk, south of Mendocino, before enjoying a walk down to the inn's private cove and beach to search for abalone shells or watch for dolphins, sea lions and birds at play.

EVENING

Take your seat at The Harbor House restaurant, which offers views of the chef's gardens and the coastline. This isn't just a meal, though – it's an interactive experience, as your server and sommelier describe each dish and wine and the origin of the ingredients. End the day with a book by the fire in your room, or bundled up on your deck, stargazing and listening to the ocean.

The Harbor House Inn

NEXT MORNING

After breakfast, visit the charming town of Mendocino for a scenic walk along the remote, rugged headlands, beginning at the visitor centre. Breathe in the crisp air mixed with the fresh scent of saltwater, bay and redwoods and let the hypnotic sounds of crashing waves lull you into a zen-like state. After your walk, stop at the **Goodlife Cafe & Bakery** *(goodlifecafemendo.com)* in the centre of town for a freshly made sandwich, a hearty salad or a bowl of soup.

▶

aromatic whites and Pinots. The ambience here is relaxed and fun, just the way that owners Vern and Maxine Boltz like it. You'll find one of the winery's slogans proudly displayed on a sign outside: 'Too tense? Toulouse'.

A further three-minute drive along Highway 128 brings you to **Navarro Vineyards & Winery** (*navarrowine.com*), set against a gorgeous backdrop of rolling hills and vineyards. Founded in the 1970s by Ted Bennett and Deborah Cahn, Navarro was one of the first commercial wineries in the Anderson Valley, and is best known for its aromatic, Alsace-style white wines and friendly, casual atmosphere. A favourite with visitors for almost five decades, Navarro is also one of the few wineries in the valley where tastings are still free.

Roederer Estate (*roedererestate.com*) is just up the road, about 45km from Mendocino. While the roots of this property are tied to the venerable Champagne house that created Cristal, the estate itself is humble, choosing to highlight the natural beauty and relaxed style of the Anderson Valley. Seated tastings are offered indoors or outdoors and feature flights of the winery's estate-bottled traditional-method sparkling wines, with or without food prepared by the winery's chef. At weekends, visitors can also enjoy a picnic with bottle service.

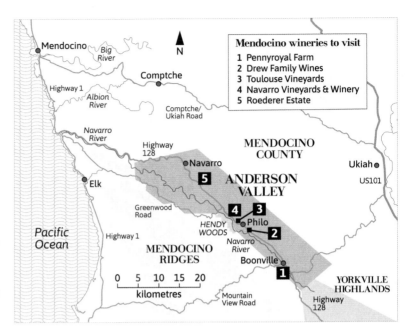

How to get there

It's a 2.5- to 3-hour drive from San Francisco International Airport to the Anderson Valley. Or it's just over an hour's drive from the smaller Sonoma County Airport, which offers flights to/from US destinations including Los Angeles, San Diego, Portland, Seattle, Las Vegas and Phoenix.

YOUR MENDOCINO WINE COUNTRY ADDRESS BOOK

ACCOMMODATION

Little River Inn
On Highway 1, just 5km south of the town of Mendocino, this fifth-generation, family-run oceanfront hotel and resort gives guests an expansive view of the Pacific, comfortable rooms equipped with jacuzzi tubs and fireplaces, and an on-site restaurant and golf course. There are also pet-friendly rooms. *littleriverinn.com*

The Boonville Hotel
A cosy, understated but upscale rural roadhouse, this is an institution in the Anderson Valley. Originally built in the late 1800s, it has 17 accommodation options, including a few 'casitas' or cabins, offering additional privacy and space. The concept throughout is 'simplicity by design', rejecting clutter for quality. *boonvillehotel.com*

The Harbor House Inn
Perched on a cliff overlooking the Pacific, The Harbor House Inn features six luxurious rooms and five private cottages, a two-star Michelin restaurant (*see right*), expansive gardens and access to a private cove and beach. Built in the early 1900s and renovated in 2018, the property exudes effortless and comfortable elegance. *theharborhouseinn.com*

RESTAURANTS

The Harbor House Inn Restaurant
Run by chef Matt Kammerer (among the first to earn a Michelin Green Star), this offers an immersive dining experience. Ingredients are sourced from within a small area, focusing on regenerative farming methods. For dinner, the Full Experience tasting menu is paired with mainly local and often rare wines. *theharborhouseinn.com*

Wickson
Opened in late 2020, this is a partnership between chefs Alexa Newman and Rodney Workman and the owners of The Madrones complex where it is located. Wickson is an homage to the Wickson apple variety, historically grown in the Anderson Valley before grapes became the main crop. The focus is on wood-fired dishes and pizzas, and on working with the farmers, foragers, fishermen, brewers and vintners of Mendocino and Sonoma counties. *wicksonrestaurant.com*

SHOPS

Farmhouse Mercantile, Boonville
Featuring items made or designed by local artists, this has the look of a country store and the feel of a workshop. It features simple but expertly crafted items such as handmade plates and bowls, leather bags, kitchen linens and carved utensils made (as far as possible) using natural resources and repurposed materials. *farmhouse128.com*

Mendocino Art Center
Founded in 1959 by artists who spurred the cultural revival of the town, this is a gallery showcase of paintings, photography, sculptures, ceramics and other mixed media creations by local talent. The centre runs regular exhibitions, classes and workshops, and sponsors several artists in residence throughout the year. *mendocinoartcenter.org* D

PHOTOGRAPHS GEORGE ROSE/GETTY IMAGES, ALL CANADA PHOTOS/ALAMY STOCK PHOTO, BRENDAN MCGUIGAN, WILL PATTERSON PHOTOGRAPHY. **MAPS** MAGGIE NELSON

Little River Inn hotel
and resort, ocean
views at sunset

NEW WAVE
American whiskey

US distillers are pushing the boundaries of whiskey production,
experimenting with different raw materials and processes to create
new flavours – which is great news for the adventurous spirits lover

STORY RICHARD WOODARD

For a country not known for being short on confidence and self-belief, the US has spent much of the past century on the back foot when it comes to its whiskey. Blame Prohibition, which lasted from 1920 until 1933, decimated domestic whiskey production, and turned the drinking population on to the joys of illicit Scotch and Canadian hooch instead.

Blame vodka too. Smirnoff famously rose to prominence on the back of advertising that proclaimed: 'Smirnoff White Whiskey – No Smell, No Taste'. In a new world in love with the light and the neutral, the ripe, rich joys of a well-aged bourbon or rye were yesterday's story.

By the 1980s, American whiskey resembled a wasteland, devoid of creativity and, beyond the remnants of its ageing fanbase, all but forgotten by the country that created it. Then attitudes began, slowly, to shift. Partly this was driven by a natural consumer cycle – just as one generation rejects the things their parents love, so the one after tends to discover them all over again – and partly by a fresh sense of determination on the part of distillers. If the Scots can sell their whisky for big bucks, they said, why the hell can't we?

The explosion of craft brewing spawned, in its wake, an army of small distillers who had no interest in aping the mainstream. Their only rule was to have no rules, beyond an imperative to create new flavours that people loved and kept coming back for.

THE RISE OF RYE

Some of those 'new' flavours, however, were anything but. America's first whiskey was rye, not bourbon, made by the European immigrants who planted it in Maryland, Pennsylvania and West Virginia in the mid-18th century.

'Rye was frequently consumed for close to 200 years, and then had a precipitous fall,' explains Joe Magliocco, president of Michter's Distillery. 'When we began our work in the 1990s to resurrect the Michter's brand in Kentucky, the market for American rye was close to non-existent. It was the bartenders and some whiskey aficionados in retail stores who championed quality American rye and reintroduced it to the public, both in the US and abroad.'

Now, rye's distinctively spicy, peppery punch has found an eager new audience, and Michter's has started distilling with estate-grown rye from its own farm in Springfield, Kentucky. This practice is in keeping with another hallmark of today's whiskey distillers – a concern with the quality of raw materials.

When Waco-based Balcones Distilling released the first whiskey in Texas since Prohibition, it was Balcones Baby Blue – a corn whisky (they spell it without the 'e') made by distilling roasted Hopi blue corn and ageing it for a short time in tiny five-gallon (22.7-litre) casks. With its combination of sweet chilli heat, buttery corn and spiced tropical fruit, it became an instant classic.

SINGULAR STYLE

Balcones also makes bourbon and rye, but most of its production is devoted to single malt – a rising star of American whiskey that provides the template for some of the finest liquid around today.

Matt Hofmann, co-founder and managing director of Westland Distillery in Washington State, reckons there are more than 170 producers making American single malt today, and a legal definition underpinning its identity is imminent. The Westland approach, with its laser focus on the flavour-giving properties of whiskey's base ingredient, the cereal grain, is uncompromising.

'There's a certain type of whiskey consumer that's been drinking the same product for a long time and has no desire to try something new,' Hofmann explains. 'They usually aren't for us. But there's a huge segment of younger, more diverse whiskey drinkers who are really attracted to our unique philosophy of whiskey-making, one that is truly connected to provenance and agriculture.'

The latest manifestation of this ethos is Colere, an annual-release whiskey that takes its name from the Latin verb meaning to cultivate, and that moves the Westland philosophy beyond the mere pursuit of flavour, and into issues of ethics and the environment.

The aim is to use barley varieties that are new to whiskey, sourced from more sustainable and regenerative agricultural systems, explains Hofmann. 'While we've always looked at malted barley as being a critical source of flavour in whiskey (in contrast to most of the industry today), what we've been able to do with Colere is to push innovation with barley in a way that has never been done in this sector, by getting outside of the commodity grain system and developing a somewhat new relationship to agriculture. The whiskey's been well received, but so too has the intent that went into it.'

WORLD CLASS

All of this invention and innovation is, in turn, having a positive knock-on effect on the quality of mainstream styles such as bourbon, as Magliocco explains. 'Our goal is to make the greatest American whiskey, and we pay tremendous attention to details such as having barrels made from wood cured for 18 months or more outdoors, toasting our barrels in addition to charring them, and heat-cycling our rickhouses,' he says, referring to a complex process whereby ▶

barrels are subjected to additional temperature variations during the colder winter months to increase complexity.

The results are there for all to see, and to taste; and distillers are no longer shy about trumpeting their credentials to the watching world. Westland recently concluded The Judgement of Westland, a four-month-long series of independently run blind tasting events featuring four unnamed single malts from the US, Australia, India and Scotland.

The results placed the US and Australia marginally ahead of Scotland, followed by India – but that's not really the point. As the contest shows, the real winners are the consumers, because never before, in its long and chequered history, has American whiskey been as diverse, innovative and damned enjoyable as it is today.

Matt Hofmann of Westland Distillery in Washington State

WHISKEY AMERICA
six innovative spirits to try

SELECTED BY RICHARD WOODARD

① Balcones Baby Blue Corn Whisky, Texas

£40-£49.95/70cl **Widely available**
Corn gives whisky sweetness and an oily, mouthcoating texture; here, it's also youthful, only adding to the punch of toffee, vanilla and popcorn, plus a little lemon verbena. Hugely flavoursome, with tropical notes and a sweet chilli heat. **Alcohol** 46%

② Horse With No Name Spirit Drink, US/Germany

£43.85-£45.45/50cl **Drink Supermarket, Gerry's, House of Malt, Master of Malt, The Whisky Exchange**
The concept of combining bourbon with a habanero chilli distillate made in the Black Forest in Germany is bizarre, but it works: oaky, sweet, ultra-fruity, but with none of the hot chilli kick you might expect. **Alc** 45%

③ Michter's US *1 Small Batch Bourbon, Kentucky

£46.95-£55/70cl **Widely available**
Its ryes are excellent, but don't overlook this class act from Michter's. It elevates the typically rich sweetness found in bourbon with complex notes of dried fruit, white pepper and freshly baked bread. **Alc** 45.7%

④ Westland Colere 1st Edition, Washington

£170-£174.95/70cl **Berry Bros & Rudd, Whisky Kingdom**
Made from Skagit Valley-grown Alba, a six-row winter barley given full expression by four years in used casks. Aromatic pineapple and a persistent cereal thread, alongside a punchy, peppery spice character. **Alc** 50%

⑤ Westward American Single Malt, Oregon

£58.75-£69.95/70cl **Distillers Direct, Hard to Find Whisky, House of Malt, Milroy's, Restless Spirits, The Bottle Club, The Drink Shop**
A very American single malt, using local barley, ale yeast and lightly charred barrels to create a richly sweet mix of baked plum, cinnamon, coffee bean and cigar smoke. Opulent and highly enjoyable. **Alc** 45%

⑥ WhistlePig Small Batch Rye Aged 10 Years, Canada/Vermont

£69.80-£83/70cl **Widely available**
Now here's a curiosity: a Canadian rye whiskey, but aged 'over the border' in Vermont, USA, at the WhistlePig Farm. It's rye personified, with bags of peppy spice and oak char, underscored by orange, red cherry and butterscotch. **Alc** 50% Ⓓ

Premium South American whites

Putting wines at £20 and above through their paces, our judges delighted in a 'thrilling' array of styles from the varied terroirs of the South America

REPORT AMANDA BARNES

I'm giving scores of above 90 like I've never given before!' exclaimed fellow panel taster Dirceu Vianna Junior MW, as we were getting to the end of a long, but delicious day of tasting. 'I have been involved with *Decanter* for more than 10 years and I cannot remember such a success rate.'

Vianna was not alone in his enthusiasm. Together we tasted 75 wines, and 72% of those wines scored 90 points or above. At *Decanter*, that means it is a wine that has complexity and precision – a benchmark wine. Anything that touches, or even nearly touches, Gold at 95pts is not only exemplary but thrilling. And we tasted some thrilling wines.

Chardonnay, the great terroir interpreter, is certainly serving as testimony to the increasing mastery of South America's winemakers. 'Clearly Chardonnay is finding its feet in terms of terroir, viticulture and winemaking in South America to produce wines that can now proudly sit among the world's most delectable,' commented Ben Gubbins. 'Limarí, Aconcagua Costa and Gualtallary are producing Chardonnays of real elegance and personality, and while stylistically nodding towards Burgundy, each distinctly reflects its unique terroir.'

While we had a diverse spread of wine regions from across Argentina, Chile and Uruguay (sadly nothing from Brazil), there was one that stood out for top quality across the board. 'There were some delicious wines from Argentina and Uruguay, but overall Chile was clearly the country that seems to be showing more ambition,' summarised Vianna.

'Within Chile, the area that impressed me the most was Limarí for its sheer quality and class. The wines were characterful, displayed great concentration and wonderful freshness.'

That being said, our top Chardonnay was from Aconcagua Costa *(see right)*. So there are always exceptions to the rule. And while we also had some excellent Sauvignon Blanc wines in the tasting, it was some of the less common varieties that stood out for their fantastic potential and distinction.

One of my favourite wines in the tasting was a gloriously textured, spicy and complex Chenin Blanc from Maule. And there were some stellar Semillons that really showed purity and focus. We also had some really enjoyable wines from Riesling, Pedro Ximinez, Albariño, Torrontés and Petit Manseng.

Winemaking techniques were delightfully diverse – some with a bit of skin contact, others with richness from lees work, and oak clearly taking a back seat in most of the top wines. It was this diversity of styles, varieties and regions that made the tasting so thrilling. 'South America's blessing of diversity of terroir is only just at the beginning of what promises to be a very interesting, exciting trip ahead,' concluded Gubbins.

South America may well be dominated by its red wines in volume, but, as this tasting showed, make way for South America's premium whites. They may have been a long time coming, but South America's premium white wines are here to stay. And there are more than a few that deserve a space at the high table.

THE SCORES 75 wines tasted

Exceptional 0 **Outstanding** 6 **Highly recommended** 48 **Recommended** 21
Commended 0 **Fair** 0 **Poor** 0

Entry criteria: producers and UK agents were invited to submit white wines with availability in the UK or US priced at £20/$20 or above, single varietal or blends, from any grape and any vintage

THE JUDGES

Amanda Barnes
is a writer and presenter specialising in South American travel and wine. A DWWA judge, she is author of the award-winning *South America Wine Guide* (£35 south americawineguide.com)

Ben Gubbins
is general manager and WSET wine educator at Vagabond Wines in London. A native of Chile, he was previously with UK wine merchant Oddbins, moving into the buying department in 2010, then working as UK & Europe sales director for Dos Andes Wines before joining Vagabond in 2013

Dirceu Vianna Junior MW
is a wine writer, consultant, educator and broadcaster. Moving to the UK in 1989, he spent much of his career as wine director for some of the UK's most prominent wine distributors, and in 2008 he became the first South American male to obtain the Master of Wine title

Outstanding 95-97pts

96

Errazuriz, Las Pizarras Chardonnay, Aconcagua Costa, Chile 2019

Amanda Barnes 97
Ben Gubbins MW 95
Dirceu Vianna Junior MW 96
£49.99-£64.15 Berry Bros & Rudd, Bon Coeur, Burnett & Herbert, Farr Vintners, The Surrey Wine Cellar
Viña Errazuriz was founded in 1870 by Don Maximiano Errázuriz. The estate majored on European varieties from the early days – an influence still seen today with the focus on international varieties. The grapes for Las Pizarras come from three small plots located on the mid-slopes of the Aconcagua Costa estate, which has significant deposits of slate, basalt and andesite in the soils and enjoys substantial cooling influences from the nearby Pacific ocean. Fermentation is with indigenous yeasts in

French oak barrels with 25% of the wine completing malolactic fermentation. The wine is then aged in 400-litre French oak barrels, of which 19% are new.
Amanda Barnes Notes of lavender and lemon balm ring through the glass; great texture, balance and extraordinary length. Pure class.
Ben Gubbins MW Very elegant wine, green and citrus fruit, pith, oak barely discernible but adding texture. Beautiful note of lemon on a long finish.
Dirceu Vianna Junior MW Sophisticated, restrained style, elegant aromas of ripe yellow fruits, citrus, sweet spices and beautifully judged oak. Excellent concentration of fruit, freshness and balance. **Drink** 2022-2035 **Alcohol** 13%

96

Longaví, Cementerio, Huerta de Maule, Maule Valley, Chile 2020

AB 97 **BG** 96 **DV** 94
£35 Bibendum Wine
Longaví originated as a joint venture between Julio Bouchon and David Nieuwoudt a decade ago. They settled right away in the Maule Valley, producing a variety of wines from both local and international grape varieties. Cementerio is 100% Chenin Blanc from Maule, the grapes coming from the Cementerio estate which is dry-farmed and sits on granite-based soils. The grapes are whole-bunch pressed and fermented in barrels using indigenous yeast. Sulphur is not used and the wines are aged for 12 months on fine lees in old 400L French oak barrels.
AB Shows a flinty, struck-match character on the nose but also

honeysuckle, camomile and talcum powder notes, with racy acidity on the palate yet a mouthfilling finish. Ticks so many boxes, and just delicious.
BG Flint, nutmeg, asparagus, dairy, quince and apple on the nose, with a rich ripe palate balanced with singing acidity. Ceamy texture, good balance, a delectable wine.
DV Intriguing, complex style with lots of personality. Flinty, floral notes, apples, citrus and attactive spiciness. Vibrant, refreshing and persistent.
Drink 2022-2035 **Alc** 13.5%

Errazuriz, Las Pizarras vineyards

Catena Zapata, Adrianna Vineyard White Stones Chardonnay, Gualtallary, Mendoza, Argentina 2020

AB 95 **BG** 95 **DV** 95
£78-£88.40 Hedonism,
Lay & Wheeler, NY Wines

Catena Zapata was founded in 1902, with a focus on high-altitude plantings in Mendoza. Its famed Adrianna vineyard sits above 1,450m, ensuring a quality crop with good acid retention as a result of the cool night-time temperatures. The wine is 100% Chardonnay from a small selection of vines on stony, free-draining soils with a topsoil of oval-shaped white stones. Fermented in French oak, the wine also goes through partial malolactic fermentation before ageing 12-16 months in seasoned French oak barrels with batonnage throughout.

AB Great purity and wet stone character. Vibrant acidity and great tension on the finish.
BG Fresh, light and vibrant with red apple skin, lemon, good intensity and tension.
DV Graceful and attactive with lovely aromas of citrus fruits, yellow plum, star fruit, fresh dough and hints of sweet spices. Refined, silky texture and beautiful underlining freshness.
Drink 2022-2032 **Alc** 12.5%

Undurraga, TH Chardonnay, Quebrada Seca, Limarí Valley, Chile 2021

AB 95 **BG** 95 **DV** 95
£20 (2020) Hallgarten Wines,
Strictly Wine

At the western end of the Limarí Valley, the plots of Chardonnay clone 548 used for this wine are grown on gravel- calcareous soils and are significantly influenced by the Pacific ocean, getting a mixture of misty mornings, windy afternoons and cool nights. The grapes are hand-harvested and pressed before the must undergoes a short and controlled pre-fermentation oxidation. Native yeasts are used during the fermentation, 70% in concrete eggs and the remaining in 500L Burgundian barrels, after which the wine is aged for 10 months on its fine lees.

AB A classy expression of Limarí, mouthwatering acidity with a rounded finish. Elegance with texture and tang: stylish.
BG Very well balanced and appealing, riper fruit, some stone fruit and melon along with grapefruit. Rounded, fresh.
DV Flinty and restrained, shows notes of citrus fruits, star fruit and fresh dough. Lovely concentration, well-judged oak, excellent texture, persistent.
Drink 2022-2032 **Alc** 12.5%

Undurraga, TH Sauvignon Blanc, Quebrada Seca, Limarí Valley, Chile 2021

AB 95 **BG** 95 **DV** 95
POA Hallgarten Wines

A 100% Sauvignon Blanc grown in vineyards on the northern end of the Limarí river, adjacent to the Fray Jorge national park. The vines here are planted on limestone soils with constant cooling influences coming from Pacific breezes that sweep through the valley all day. The grapes are harvested by hand and pressed gently into stainless steel for fermentation at cool temperatures, before the completed wine is aged for five months on fine lees.

AB An inviting nose of lemon zest and fine herbs, great intensity on the nose and palate. Racy! Ideal for oysters.
BG Asparagus, green bell pepper, citrus zest, passion fruit and a savoury note. Crisp, light, elegant and refreshing with a long citrus finish. Complex yet very enjoyable.
DV Remarkable aromas of tropical fruits, asparagus and citrus jump out of the glass. Shows great concentration of fruit, lovely texture and a persistent, refreshing finish.
Drink 2022-2028 **Alc** 13.3%

Undurraga, TH Sauvignon Blanc, Leyda Valley, San Antonio, Chile 2021

AB 94 **BG** 95 **DV** 95
£20 Hallgarten Wines, Strictly Wine

The Leyda vines for this TH bottling are 14km inland, so are cooled by ocean breezes, and benefit from a high diurnal temperature range. The Sauvignon Blanc vines used are 95% Davis I clone with the remaining 5% being French 107. After a pre-fermentation cold soak, 95% of the must was fermented in stainless steel and the remaining 5% in used French oak barrels. The wine was then aged on its fine lees for five months before bottling.

AB Textural, mineral and subtle in style, this is a sophisticated Sauvignon Blanc with drive. Mouthwatering and slightly chalky on the finish.
BG Asparagus and stone fruit, capsicum, touch of sour cream. Full-bodied, textured but vibrant at the same time, lively zesty fruit and a long finish with notes of grass and green apple.
DV Delicious, vibrant, exotic with intense notes of passion fruit, guava and citrus. Great concentration with creamy texture and racy freshness.
Drink 2022-2028 **Alc** 13.2%

Highly recommended 90-94pts

Casa Marin, Miramar Vineyard Riesling, Lo Abarca, San Antonio, Chile 2021
AB 94 **BG** 94 **DV** 94
£25 Alliance Wine
Defined and focused, lime, lemon peel, and a hint of white flowers. So much energy and an almost sizzling acidity. Youthful but should open up and grow in complexity with time. **Drink** 2022-2035 **Alc** 12.5%

Matias Riccitelli, Old Vines from Patagonia Semillon, Río Negro, Patagonia, Argentina 2021
AB 95 **BG** 94 **DV** 92
£41 Hallgarten Wines, Selfridges, Shelved Wine
Flinty, butternut, citrus fruit and fresh dough. Pure with razor sharp acidity, great concentration and definition. Wait a couple of years if you can. **Drink** 2022-2035 **Alc** 12%

Matias Riccitelli, Old Vines from Patagonia Torrontés, Río Negro, Patagonia, Argentina 2019
AB 94 **BG** 93 **DV** 94
£41 Hallgarten Wines, Taurus Wines
Mint and lime leaf jump from this aromatic amphora-aged Torrontés. The palate shows more lemon zest and zingy acidity, leading to a citrussy finish. **Drink** 2022-2026 **Alc** 12%

Carmen, Quijada Semillon, Apalta, Chile 2020
AB 94 **BG** 94 **DV** 91
£31.20 (2019) Hedonism
Lime, wet stones, green apple and fresh dough. Lively Semillon with good purity, direction and a faint hint of smoke. Classy. **Drink** 2022-2030 **Alc** 12.5%

Rutini, Apartado Gran Chardonnay, Gualtallary, Mendoza, Argentina 2019
AB 94 **BG** 93 **DV** 93
£44 Viñals Wine & Food
Ethereal and inviting, with complex aromas of yellow fruits, hazelnuts, bruised apples and sweet spices. A sophisticated wine that will age well. **Drink** 2022-2035 **Alc** 13.6%

Cerro Chapeu, 1752 Gran Tradición Petit Manseng-Viognier, Montevideo, Uruguay 2019
AB 90 **BG** 94 **DV** 91
cerrochapeu.com
Aromatic nose with white peach, green melon, apple and blossom. Full-bodied and round, backed up by lively acidity with a silky finish. **Drink** 2022-2029 **Alc** 13.5%

Concha y Toro, Terrunyo Sauvignon Blanc, Casablanca Valley, Chile 2021
AB 91 **BG** 94 **DV** 92
POA Concha y Toro UK
A lean and mouthwatering Sauvignon Blanc with attractive gooseberry and thyme notes. On the palate it is refined, refreshing and persistent. **Drink** 2022-2027 **Alc** 12%

Falasco, Hermandad Chardonnay, Uco Valley, Mendoza, Argentina 2019
AB 91 **BG** 91 **DV** 94
£21.99 Widely available at independent merchants via UK agent Condor Wines
Restrained, elegant aromas, notes of citrus, fresh apples and a hint of sweet spices. The palate is lively, with lingering notes of citrus. **Drink** 2022-2028 **Alc** 13.5%

Finca Suarez, Semillon, Paraje Altamira, Mendoza, Argentina 2021
AB 90 **BG** 94 **DV** 93
£24.50 Carruthers & Kent, Tiny's Tipple
Fresh, slightly creamy, displaying notes of whites peach, citrus and fresh dough. On the palate it is delicate, refined and delicious with a beautiful, refreshing finish. **Drink** 2022-2028 **Alc** 12%

Garces Silva, Amayna Chardonnay, Leyda Valley, San Antonio, Chile 2019
AB 91 **BG** 93 **DV** 93
£21.80 Buckingham Schenk
Elegant and sophisticated aromas include notes of peach, citrus and hazelnut. This wine has a nice balance and brings plenty of joy. **Drink** 2022-2029 **Alc** 14%

Garzón, Petit Clos Block #27 Albariño, Maldonado, Uruguay 2020
AB 93 **BG** 92 **DV** 90
bodegagarzon.com
Youthful with delicate aromas of citrus fruits, fresh apple and fresh dough. The palate has good weight and concentration. A full-bodied Albariño with great drive and length. **Drink** 2022-2027 **Alc** 14%

La Cayetana, Criolla Blanca, Lavalle, Mendoza, Argentina 2019
AB 92 **BG** 91 **DV** 94
£19.99-£23 Roberts & Speight, Terroir Wines, Tiny's Tipple
Orange zest, ripe apricot, jasmine and white orchard fruit. On the palate a wonderful creamy texture, good concentration with a delicate finish. **Drink** 2022-2027 **Alc** 13.5% ▶

101

Norton, Altura White Blend, Uco Valley, Mendoza, Argentina 2021
AB 91 **BG** 93 **DV** 92
£21 Last Drop Wines
A blend of Sauvignon Blanc, Semillon and Gruner Veltliner. Smoky mineral, layered aromas of fine herbs and citrus fruit. Beautifully structured on the palate, with vibrant freshness. **Drink** 2022-2029 **Alc** 13%

Santa Rita, Floresta Field Blend Blanco, Apalta, Chile 2020
AB 91 **BG** 96 **DV** 90
£25 Santa Rita Estates Europe
Complex wine with layers of savoury and sweet aromas between spices, tea leaves, bergamot, cardamom, blossom and dried fruit. A slight salinity on the finish and great freshness. **Drink** 2022-2028 **Alc** 13.3%

Viña Cobos, Bramare Los Arbolitos Chardonnay, Mendoza, Argentina 2019
AB 92 **BG** 93 **DV** 90
£42.99 Alliance Wine, House of Wine Leeds, The Beckford Bottle Shop
Tangy acidity and attractive notes of Meyer lemon, blossom, honey and nuts. Round and full but vibrant acidity keeps it fresh. Full of character. **Drink** 2022-2030 **Alc** 14.5%

Zuccardi, Polígonos Chardonnay, San Pablo, Uco Valley, Mendoza, Argentina 2021
AB 90 **BG** 92 **DV** 93
£25.25 Hatch Mansfield, Mr Wheeler, The Oxford Wine Co
Notes of yellow fruits, florals and brioche. Displays beautiful texture, harmony and exudes finesse. **Drink** 2022-2028 **Alc** 13%

Zuccardi, Polígonos Semillon, Tupungato, Mendoza, Argentina 2021
AB 93 **BG** 92 **DV** 92
£25.25 Hatch Mansfield
Butter, toast, green apple and lime. On the palate it is rich, concentrated and beautifully balanced by attractive freshness. **Drink** 2022-2028 **Alc** 13%

Bouza, Albariño, Montevideo, Uruguay 2021
AB 90 **BG** 92 **DV** 92
£24.95 Jeroboams
Youthful and vibrant with notes of pear, red apple, lemon and jasmine. Lots of energy and crunchy fruit combined with a persistent and refreshing finish. **Drink** 2022-2028 **Alc** 13%

Bouza, Riesling, Pan de Azucar, Maldonado, Uruguay 2020
AB 93 **BG** 91 **DV** 89
£24.95 Jeroboams
Inviting notes of rubber boots and petrol will drive Riesling fiends wild. The palate has good concentration, ripe lemon and white peach, leading to a gradual and long finish. **Drink** 2022-2032 **Alc** 13.5%

Bouchon, Granito Semillon, Maule Valley, Chile 2020
AB 93 **BG** 90 **DV** 90
£35 Condor Wines
Honey and hay notes with hints of quince. Racy, crisp, lean and attractive Semillon that promises a long future. **Drink** 2022-2030 **Alc** 13%

Casa Marin, Cipreses Vineyard Sauvignon Blanc, Aconcagua Valley, Chile 2021
AB 92 **BG** 87 **DV** 93
£22.99 Alliance Wine, Sandhams
Bright, clean and seductive on the nose displaying notes of passion fruit, fresh cut grass and elderflower. Bright and extremely enjoyable. **Drink** 2022-2027 **Alc** 13.5%

Casa Silva, Lago Ranco Riesling, Región Austral, Patagonia, Chile 2021
AB 93 **BG** 90 **DV** 89
£21.95 De Burgh Wine Merchants
Graceful and attractive with citrus fruit, fresh dough and bruised apples with a racy acidity that is tamed by off-dry sweetness. Chile's equivalent of a Mosel-style Riesling. **Drink** 2022-2032 **Alc** 11.5%

Concha y Toro, Marques de Casa Concha Chardonnay, Quebrada Seca, Limarí Valley, Chile 2020
AB 92 **BG** 90 **DV** 92
£14.11 Nethergate Wines
Fresh dough, citrus peel, green apple and vanilla. Full-bodied with breadth from oak ageing, but still with a lively acidity and Limarí typicity. **Drink** 2022-2029 **Alc** 13.9%

De Martino, Tres Volcanes Chardonnay, Malleco Valley, Chile, 2017
AB 93 **BG** 90 **DV** 89
£23.67-£29.50 Great Wines Direct, Hic, KWM, The Fine Wine Co, The Great Wine Co
Honey and custard tart characters envelop this full-bodied Chardonnay, which has a solid structure, but retaining freshness and lively fruit. **Drink** 2022-2028 **Alc** 13.5%

Familia Deicas, Preludio Barrel Select White, Juanico, Canelones, Uruguay 2021
AB 91 **BG** 93 **DV** 90
£25.50 (2020) Christopher Keiller
Lively, youthful and full of attractive fruit including apple, melon and citrus fruits. Lovely precision and focus with good ageability. **Drink** 2022-2030 **Alc** 13%

Garces Silva, Amayna Sauvignon Blanc, Leyda Valley, San Antonio, Chile 2021
AB 89 **BG** 93 **DV** 92
£20 Buckingham Schenk
Lime leaf, capsicum and grass, with notes of mango, passion fruit and white flowers. On the palate it is ripe, rich, forward and carries good acidity. **Drink** 2022-2026 **Alc** 14%

Garces Silva, Amayna Cordón Huinca Sauvignon Blanc, Leyda Valley, San Antonio, Chile 2021
AB 90 **BG** 91 **DV** 93
£26.50 Buckingham Schenk
Gunflint and oyster shell notes. On the palate it is full of energy, vibrancy of fruit and carries on with a persistent and refreshing finish. **Drink** 2022-2028 **Alc** 13.9%

Matías Riccitelli, Blanco de la Casa, Mendoza, Argentina 2021
AB 91 **BG** 91 **DV** 90
£23.75-£26.95 Fintry Wines, Hallgarten Wines, Hic, Shelved Wines, Strictly Wine
Youthful, attractive and vibrant, showing plenty of orchard fruits and a hint of fresh dough and spice. Nice freshness and texture. **Drink** 2022-2030 **Alc** 12.5%

Rutini, Colección Sauvignon Blanc, Gualtallary, Mendoza, Argentina 2022
AB 93 **BG** 90 **DV** 90
£20 Viñals Wine & Food
Racy acidity and a cool-fruit profile with crunchy green apple, mountain herb and citrus zest. Delicate, young and promising. **Drink** 2022-2028 **Alc** 13.2%

Santa Rita, Floresta Chardonnay, Limarí Valley, Chile 2020
AB 92 **BG** 90 **DV** 91
£25 Santa Rita Estates Europe
Bright notes of apple and camomile are emphasised by coastal freshness. On the palate it is rich and creamy with fresh, vibrant acidity. **Drink** 2022-2028 **Alc** 13%

Tabalí, Talinay Sauvignon Blanc, Limarí Valley, Chile 2021
AB 91 **BG** 93 **DV** 90
£20 D Byrne & Co, Highbury Vintners, John Hattersley
Delicate notes of dill, green bell pepper, grass and elderflower embrace the cool climate of Limarí. Well made, balanced and very enjoyable. **Drink** 2022-2028 **Alc** 14%

Viña Cobos, Vinculum Chardonnay, Mendoza, Argentina 2019
AB 90 **BG** 94 **DV** 89
£44.99 Alliance Wine, KWM, Reserve Wines, The Vinorium
Nutty complexity with notes of hazelnut and butterscotch with voluptuous Chardonnay underneath. Full-bodied, persistent and still has a while to go. **Drink** 2022-2028 **Alc** 14.5%

Viña Edén, Chardonnay, Pueblo Edén, Maldonado, Uruguay 2019
AB 91 **BG** 90 **DV** 92
vinaeden.com
Lemon peel, tropical fruits, bright and refreshing with a delicious coastal character of tangy sea salt. Precise, pure and showing excellent varietal typicity and overall balance. **Drink** 2022-2029 **Alc** 12.3%

Zuccardi, Polígonos Verdejo, San Pablo, Uco Valley, Mendoza, Argentina 2021
AB 92 **BG** 92 **DV** 90
£25.25 Hennings, The Halifax Wine Co
Delicately perfumed including aromas of passion fruit and floral notes. The palate has texture, with fresh and vibrant green fruit. Bright and enjoyable with nice purity. **Drink** 2022-2028 **Alc** 13%

Bouchon, Granito Semillon, Maule Valley, Chile 2019
AB 92 **BG** 85 **DV** 92
£31.95-£35 GrapeSmith, Kernowine, Theatre of Wine, The Dorset Wine Co, The Secret Bottle Shop, Vineyards of Sherborne, Wadebridge Wines
Flinty, smoky green fruit. Texture and just a touch of petrol from bottle age. Rich and voluptuous, underpinned by a beautiful refreshing finish. **Drink** 2022-2032 **Alc** 13.5%

Bouza, Chardonnay, Montevideo, Uruguay 2020
AB 90 **BG** 88 **DV** 92
£24.95 Jeroboams
Refined, inviting, attractive aromas of citrus, apple, pear and a hint of sweet spice. There's a pleasing balance of fruit and freshness with a silky finish and touch of creamy complexity. **Drink** 2022-2030 **Alc** 14%

►

BraccoBosca, Memoriter, Atlántida, Uruguay 2021

AB 91 **BG** 90 **DV** 90

£30 Hispamerchants

Attractive dried fruits, grilled nuts and sweet spice aromas lead into a mouthfilling and broad, spicy oaked wine that shows a note of citrus peel on a persistent finish. **Drink** 2022-2027 **Alc** 12%

Casa Silva, Lago Ranco Sauvignon Blanc, Región Austral, Patagonia, Chile 2021

AB 92 **BG** 88 **DV** 90

£21.95 Frank Stainton

Snow peas and custard apple on the nose. On the palate it has great concentration, silky texture and good balancing acidity. **Drink** 2022-2027 **Alc** 12.5%

Casas del Bosque, Pequeñas Sauvignon Blanc, Casablanca Valley, Chile 2021

AB 89 **BG** 91 **DV** 89

£24.99 ABS Wine Agencies

Juicy Sauvignon Blanc, with notes of capsicum, green apple, green melon. Some richness on the palate, yet it remains fresh and lively. **Drink** 2022-2027 **Alc** 13.5%

Concha y Toro, Amelia Chardonnay, Quebrada Seca, Limarí Valley, Chile 2020

AB 90 **BG** 88 **DV** 92

POA Concha y Toro UK

A complex, barrel-aged Chardonnay with lashings of toasty notes. A rich ripe style, showing good concentration and length. **Drink** 2022-2032 **Alc** 13.9%

Finca Suarez, Chardonnay, Paraje Altamira, Mendoza, Argentina 2019

AB 91 **BG** 88 **DV** 92

£21-£24 Carruthers & Kent, Dunell's, Highbury Vintners, House of Townend, Quercus Wines, The Horsham Cellar, The Secret Cellar

Gently fragrant and complex, yellow and citrus fruits, fresh and delicate with a filigree structure. **Drink** 2022-2028 **Alc** 13%

Garzón, Single Vineyard Albariño, Maldonado, Uruguay 2020

AB 90 **BG** 88 **DV** 91

£31.99 Liberty Wines, The Fine Wine Co, Tim Syrad

Pretty nose of blossom and orchard fruits, while on the palate it has a medium body and attractive fruit, underpinned by fresh acidity with a lasting note of lemon leaf. **Drink** 2022-2027 **Alc** 14%

Garzón, Single Vineyard Sauvignon Blanc, Garzón, Maldonado, Uruguay 2021

AB 91 **BG** 90 **DV** 90

bodegagarzon.com

White peach, lemon and a touch of grass and wet stones. Youthful, sophisticated. Good length shows a more serious side, will develop well. **Drink** 2022-2028 **Alc** 12.5%

Hacienda Araucano, Clos de Lolol, Lolol Valley, Colchagua Valley, Chile 2017

AB 90 **BG** 89 **DV** 90

£20.99 Bonafide Wines, Good Pair Days, House of Townend, South Downs Cellars

A mature and toasty oaked Sauvignon Blanc, notes of roasted nut pastry, toffee, mango and quince. Ageing gracefully, still with vibrancy. **Drink** 2022-2026 **Alc** 13.5%

Piedra Negra, Jackot Organic, Uco Valley, Mendoza, Argentina 2022

AB 92 **BG** 90 **DV** 89

£20.99 Condor Wines

Bright, zesty but with intriguing mountain herbs and yellow fruit. On the palate it has good concentration of fruit and good freshness. Approachable aromatic white, easy to enjoy. **Drink** 2022-2030 **Alc** 13%

Rocamadre, Blanco, Paraje Altamira, Mendoza, Argentina 2021

AB 90 **BG** 91 **DV** 90

£29 Pip of Manor Farm, Quaffology, Valhalla's Goat

Cider apple notes keep this cloudy Chardonnay lively. Citrus-pith tannins, good acidity, tense, light yet expressive and long. A good example for those getting into skin contact whites. **Drink** 2022-2027 **Alc** 12%

Ver Sacrum, Geisha Dragon del Desierto, Uco Valley, Mendoza, Argentina 2021

AB 90 **BG** 88 **DV** 91

£22.99 House of Townend, Speciality Drinks, The Horsham Cellar

Toasty aroma followed by white peach and some floral notes. On the palate it is dry, well balanced and smooth on the finish. **Drink** 2022-2027 **Alc** 12.5%

Viña Progreso, Overground Viognier, Progreso, Canelones, Uruguay 2022

AB 89 **BG** 90 **DV** 90

£25.50 Dunell's, Ucopia Wines

Ripe peach and honeyed apricot with a note of almond. A fragrant and bright Viognier that has a slight oiliness on the finish. **Drink** 2022-2027 **Alc** 13%

Recommended 86-89pts

Wine	Score	AB	BG	DV	Tasting note	Alc	Drink	Price	Stockists
Bodega Sottano, Maria Magdalena Chardonnay, Mendoza, Argentina 2021	89	90	89	89	Ripe, toasty nose with citrus and tropical fruit notes. Creamy texture and balancing freshness.	14.2%	2022-2029	£39	Vindependents
Bodega y Viñedos Catena, Catena Alta Chardonnay, Mendoza, Argentina 2020	89	90	87	89	Aromas of ripe tropical fruits, ripe apples, brioche and hints of spice. An enjoyable style of oaked Chardonnay with complexity and plenty of brightness.	13.6%	2022-2027	£26.99	Majestic
Bouchon, Skin, Maule Valley, Chile 2020	89	89	92	86	Bergamot, orange blossom and smoky spice. The palate is quite rich and the tannins are very gentle.	13.5%	2022-2028	£23.96	Condor Wines
Dom Bousquet, Gaia Organic White Blend, Gualtallary, Mendoza, Argentina 2021	89	87	92	89	Vibrant palate with citrus and some tropical notes. Good tension, refreshing and appetising.	13%	2022-2027	£20	Vintage Roots
Finca Ferrer, Block C2 Chardonnay, Uco Valley, Mendoza, Argentina 2019	89	89	87	90	Buttery with some herbal aromas, hints of honey and tropical fruit with a silky mouthfeel.	13.8%	2022-2030	£29	Slurp, Waitrose
Hacienda Araucano, CLO de Lolol Organic, Lolol Valley, Colchagua Valley, Chile 2021	89	92	87	89	Marzipan, melon, passion fruit and elderflower aromas. On the palate it is light, elegant and refreshing.	13.5%	2022-2026	£25	Condor Wines
Los Cerros de San Juan, Lahusen Gewürztraminer, Colonia, Uruguay 2020	89	88	88	91	Warm floral notes of orange blossom combine with peach melba. Elegant, subtle and sophisticated.	12.3%	2022-2026	N/A UK	bodegaloscerrosdesanjuan.com
Los Cerros de San Juan, Lahusen Riesling, Colonia, Uruguay 2020	89	90	88	90	A hint of kerosene graces this lively Riesling, easy to enjoy with pleasant citrus fruits underpinned by a racy freshness of acidity.	12.3%	2022-2032	N/A UK	bodegaloscerrosdesanjuan.com
Luis Felipe Edwards, Marea Sauvignon Blanc, Leyda Valley, San Antonio, Chile 2021	89	88	87	92	Exuberant tropical fruit characters with refined herbal notes. Rich attack on the palate with a herbaceous finish.	13%	2022-2027	N/A UK	lfewines.com
Marichal, Reserve Collection Albariño, Etchevarría, Canelones, Uruguay 2022	89	88	89	91	Good intensity of lemon peel, pineapple, and a touch floral. Harmonious with great texture and a pleasant, refreshing finish.	12.7%	2022-2029	N/A UK	marichalwines.com
Rutini, Colección Chardonnay, Gualtallary, Mendoza, Argentina 2021	89	91	87	89	Bony minerality on the palate with a hint of blossom and white pear. Vibrant and youthful.	13.9%	2022-2029	£20	Viñals Wine & Food
Viña von Siebenthal, Riomistico Viognier, Panquehue, Aconcagua Valley, Chile 2018	89	90	89	87	Luscious, full-bodied style of Viognier. Peach, vanilla and butterscotch. Rich, powerful with a creamy texture.	15.6%	2022-2028	£31.50	Terroir Wines Lauder, The Cellar Lymington
Bodega Rolland, Mariflor Sauvignon Blanc, Mendoza, Argentina 2019	88	89	87	89	Asparagus and lemon verbena on the nose. Well balanced with a pleasant texture and refreshing finish.	14%	2022-2027	£21.99	Wine Embargo
Casa Marin, Casona Gewürztraminer, Lo Abarca, San Antonio, Chile 2021	88	87	89	89	Floral with hints of rose and Turkish delight. Lovely freshness on the palate and a spicy note to the finish.	13.5%	2022-2026	£25	Alliance Wine
Familia Deicas, Extreme Sub Suelo Chardonnay, Garzón, Maldonado, Uruguay 2020	88	89	87	89	Rich, creamy, nutty character on the nose. Palate has tension and freshness with a round texture.	13%	2022-2027	N/A UK	familiadeicas.com
Garzón, Single Vineyard Albariño, Maldonado, Uruguay 2021	88	91	85	88	Subtle nose with floral and stone fruit notes. On the palate it is light and refreshing.	12.5%	2022-2028	N/A UK	bodegagarzon.com
Cerro del Toro, Singular Fósiles de Mar Chardonnay, Piriápolis, Maldonado, Uruguay 2020	87	85	87	89	On the nose it shows caramelised fruits, nutty notes and hints of spices. Oily texture, with a sweet spicy finish.	12.5%	2022-2026	£49.99	Vinos Latinos
Dom Bousquet, Gran Organic Chardonnay, Gualtallary, Mendoza, Argentina 2021	87	87	86	87	Ripe apple and biscuit aromas and flavours, with a broad texture. A full-bodied Chardonnay style.	14.2%	2022-2027	£20	Vintage Roots
Luis Felipe Edwards, Marea Chardonnay, Leyda Valley, San Antonio, Chile 2021	87	85	88	89	Woody asparagus on the nose. Riper style, yet it retains freshness and vibrancy.	13%	2022-2026	N/A UK	lfewines.com
Pisano, RPF Chardonnay, Progreso, Canelones, Uruguay 2020	87	86	89	86	Acacia and exotic spice come through on this: a very accomplished example of Chardonnay from Uruguay.	13%	2022-2027	N/A UK	pisanowines.com
Zorzal, Eggo Blanc de Cal, Tupungato, Mendoza, Argentina 2019	86	85	88	86	Baked butter biscuits, a herbaceous note and white pepper. Rich, creamy and has a nice grip.	11.5%	2022-2024	£20.49	Hallgarten Wines, Strictly Wine

Mexico's *other* agave spirits

There's more to Mexican spirits than tequila, so start exploring the territory of mezcal, raicilla and bacanora and discover a whole new dimension to the agave plant

STORY LAURA FOSTER

While tequila is Mexico's most famous spirit by far, it's not the only one produced in the central American country. A clutch of others also exist, with the majority also made from agave, just as tequila is. As consumer awareness and appreciation of tequila grows, a ripple effect is occurring across these other spirits categories, as new products make their way beyond Mexico's borders.

So what are these spirits, and what sets them apart? Let's explore their similarities first, starting with the agave.

Agave is a genus of plants that boasts about 270 different species, and while their characteristics vary widely, it can be said that they all take a number of years to mature, and they all have a piña, or heart of the plant, which is used to ferment and make distilled spirits. While tequila can only be made from one variety – Agave Tequilana Weber Azul, often known as 'Blue Agave' or 'Blue Weber', most other agave spirits may use any number of different varieties.

When it comes to production there is a process that's more or less the same for all agave spirits: the agave is harvested and its leaves removed, the heart of the piña is cooked, and then milled or shredded. The resulting juice (and sometimes the crushed fibres, too) is fermented and then distilled. Variations in cooking, pressing and distillation methods will be found everywhere,

A worker walks through an agave field in Santa Catarina Minas, Oaxaca, the heartland of mezcal production

but there is no real uniformity of approach within the categories themselves – stills might be made from stainless steel, copper, or even have chambers made out of tree trunks. The cooking process can be huge and industrial, or involve brick ovens, or even pits in the ground.

Each producer has hit upon their own personal production approach after many years of experimentation – often, methods have been developed, passed down and tweaked from generation to generation in one family. It is this slightly freewheeling, sometimes madcap approach that makes Mexico's spirits some of the most exciting for consumers to explore.

MEZCAL
The smoky one

Mezcal's star has slowly been rising in the UK and US for more than a decade now. While tequila is produced in the northern state of Jalisco, and is made only from Blue Weber agave, mezcal is allowed to be produced in nine different states, from a much wider selection of agave varieties. The most commonly used varietal in mezcal production is Espadin, which has sword-like leaves, and produces a clean, pure taste.

While there are some larger, more industrial mezcal brands, the majority of mezcals are made in a more traditional, artisanal way than most tequilas. One of the main differences is the way the agave is cooked in order to prepare it for crushing to extract the sugars. Most mezcal producers use a brick-lined pit in the ground that is pre-heated with a wood fire. The pit is filled with the agave, and then covered with agave fibres and earth, which allows the agaves to slowly roast over three days, with the wood fire embers imparting a distinctive smoky flavour.

'If you're a whisky drinker you will appreciate the mezcals from different regions, because you are used to peated single malts,' says Eduardo Gomez, founder of London festival Tequila & Mezcal Fest (now in its fifth year: *tequilafest.co.uk*) and sales director of specialist food and drink importer Mexgrocer.

The most prolific state in terms of production is Oaxaca in the south of Mexico, with various sources putting the proportion of overall mezcal production anywhere between 70% and 90%. The states of Durango, Guanajuato, Guerrero, Michoacán, Puebla, San Luis Potosi, Tamaulipas and Zacatecas share the rest.

'Mezcal is the biggest in territory in terms of having a DO, and the most diverse,' says Gaby Moncada, agave ambassador at drinks agency Speciality Brands. 'In Oaxaca, spirits are much more punchy, and they take pride in high abvs and lots of flavours of smoke.

'In Michoacán the altitude is totally different; there are forests and mountains, it's very green, [and the resulting spirit has] flavours of eucalyptus, rosemary and earth. In Zacatecas, which is close to Jalisco, the climate is very similar and they use Blue Weber agave, but the smoke flavours get so absorbed that you get barbecue and dried chilli flavours in it.'

Laura Foster is an awarded and widely published freelance journalist and writer with a particular focus on spirits and cocktails

Tasting mezcal can be a wild, exhilarating ride – most people coming to it don't forget their first experience of this category.

One to try ① **Del Maguey Vida**

£40.80-£47.50/70cl **Amathus Drinks, Drinks & Treats, Hedonism, House of Malt, Master of Malt, Spirits Kiosk, The Drink Shop, The Whisky Exchange, The Whisky Shop**

An entry-level mezcal made from Espadin agave in the village of San Luis del Río, Vida is an all-rounder that's perfect for sipping or mixing (see also **QuiQuiRiQui Matatlan** for an alternative: £39.95 **The Whisky Exchange**). Barbecue smoke mingles with sweet spice, lime, stone fruits and banana. **Alcohol** 42%

RAICILLA
The one that was left behind

Raicilla became a spirits category in its own right due to circumstance. The spirit, which has been made in the state of Jalisco for more than 500 years, was originally classified as mezcal.

The name 'raicilla' means 'little root', inspired by the baby plants that grow at the bottom of the agave when it reproduces. 'The historic name for raicilla was actually *vino del mezcal raicillero*,' explains Esteban Morales, the founder of La Venenosa, a label that sells various raicilla made by different producers. 'Mezcal was always the name of what we were drinking, raicilla was the nickname.'

However, when mezcal's denominación de origen was created and the states in which it could be produced were defined, Jalisco was left off the list. This meant that producers of what was technically mezcal in the state were left high and dry.

'[Jalisco was excluded] because Jalisco has tequila,' says Morales. 'So that pushed some people to ask for a new recognition with the name raicilla.'

A DO was created for raicilla in 2019, which ironically has excluded some producers who were previously labelling their spirit as raicilla. 'Now it's even worse because the denomination makes things more complicated,' declares Morales.

One to try ② **La Venenosa Puntas**

£120-£122.50/70cl **Casa Agave, Cool Chile, Master of Malt, The Whisky Exchange**

Made by Don Gerardo Peña for the La Venenosa brand, Puntas is made with 100% Maximiliana agave. A fresh, zesty nose leads onto an initially sweet palate that gives way to intense chilli spice, green agave and then a floral hit of violets and quinine. **Alc** 64%

BACANORA
The spirit of Sonora

Made in the state of Sonora, which sits on the western side of the US border, bacanora production has clung on despite a 77-year-long prohibition in the area. Named after a town in

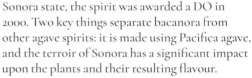

Most mezcal producers cook the agave in brick-lined pits that are pre-heated by a wood fire

'Tasting mezcal can be a wild, exhilarating ride'

Sonora state, the spirit was awarded a DO in 2000. Two key things separate bacanora from other agave spirits: it is made using Pacifica agave, and the terroir of Sonora has a significant impact upon the plants and their resulting flavour.

'Sonora is in the middle of the country; it's hot and arid, not much grows there,' says Mexgrocer's Eduardo Gomez. 'It's so hot during the day – a summer day in Sonora can reach 47°C, and in the night it can get to -5°C. So there are dramatic changes in temperature, and the soil is really rich. Seven years of the plant living in those conditions causes it to be very stressed and strong, so you get complex earthy, spicy flavours of the agave.'

There are only a handful of producers left thanks to the long-running prohibition in the area, but the spirits that they make have been hitting the right notes with consumers. 'Guests really like it,' says Deano Moncrieffe, owner of the Hacha agave spirits bars in London. 'It's almost a bridge between mezcal and tequila. I think it's a bit of a gateway spirit. From a flavour point of view there are greener notes and more pepperminty flavours. It's less smoky than mezcal, and it has an earthier note to it. I paired one with Polo mints.'

One to try ③ **Santo Pecado Bacanora Artesanal**

£57.60/70cl **Mexgrocer**

Made by master bacanorero Rumaldo Flores Amarillas, the agave are roasted in underground pits fired with mesquite wood. The result is a dry, distinct spirit with aromas of rubber, gherkins, cracked black pepper and lime, and flavours of leather, earth and charcoal smoke, with a peppermint note in the background. **Alc** 45% **D**

DISCOVER THE GREATEST WINES FROM ACROSS THE GLOBE

From the sunny vineyards of McLaren Vale to the looming chateaux of Bordeaux, take a tour of the world's most famous wine regions and find out how the industry is evolving in all four corners of the world

SOUTH AFRICA FOCUS:
Bordeaux blends

In some ways old, in other ways new, South Africa occupies a unique place in the wine world. The country has some of the oldest soils on the planet and a history of wine production extending back more than 360 years, yet it's only in the last 30 or so that the wine-producing nation has experienced a rebirth.

South Africa's wine industry has seen an explosion of well-qualified winemakers exploit the country's vast diversity of terroirs, and quality-driven red Bordeaux blends have proven to be among the nation's best, with characteristic New World fruit and concentration balanced by Old World complexity.

Setting an international benchmark for quality, results from the Decanter World Wine Awards offer annual insights into the calibre of wine regions and nations, and in 2021 South Africa saw standout results, including a record-breaking

number of Gold medals awarded. In 2022, the nation managed to equal its top Gold medal count, with almost 50% awarded to red wines, and a wide diversity of grape varieties and styles on show. From top-quality Pinotage to Cinsault and Pinot Noir to Shiraz, there's not one clear identifier of what South Africa does best – but Bordeaux blends did gain a foothold in 2022.

On the judging, DWWA Regional Chair for South Africa Fiona McDonald commented: 'What makes a wine a Gold is it's got to be true to its varietal character. It's got to have balance, to be elegant, to be harmonious – but it also has to have an X-factor. That X-factor is that indefinable pixie dust.'

Below, discover 15 Bordeaux blends that stand out amid 2022 results, with many more award-winning South African wines to discover at *awards.decanter.com*.

Cape Town

Groot Constantia, Gouverneurs Reserve, Constantia 2018
95 **Gold**
£32-£36 **Widely available via independent merchants**
48% Cabernet Sauvignon, 24% Merlot, 21% Cabernet Franc, 7% Malbec. A classical Cape Bordeaux blend with attractive hints of cherry cola, blackcurrant and grilled herbs. Creamy and plush, deliciously vibrant fleshy fruit and an elegant finish. **Alcohol** 14.2%

Durbanville Hills, The Tangram, Durbanville 2018
93 **Silver**
POA **Cape Wine**
60% Cabernet Sauvignon, 15% Cabernet Franc, 15% Merlot, 7% Malbec, 3% Petit Verdot. Black plum, blackcurrant, cherry and chai tea nose. The texture is sleek and polished, very elegant and cool with a lovely fresh blueberry-fruited finish. **Alc** 14.6%

Constantia Glen, Five, Constantia 2019
92 **Silver**
£35.25 **NY Wines**
31% Cabernet Sauvignon, 27% Merlot, 17% Petit Verdot, 15% Cabernet Franc, 10% Malbec. Aromas of cedar spice, grilled herbs and black plums. Elegant and finely poised with silky tannins, sweet tobacco, blackcurrant and a long, finessed finish. **Alc** 14.5%

Paarl

Babylonstoren, Nebukadnesar, Simonsberg-Paarl 2019
95 **Gold**
£28.75-£32.99 **Banstead Vintners, Glug, Novel Wines, Vinotopia, Wanderlust**
46% Cabernet Sauvignon, 25% Merlot, 14% Cabernet Franc, 10% Petit Verdot, 5% Malbec. Brooding, ripe dark fruit, cedarwood and mint. Opulent and extracted, yet balanced. Polished tannins and savoury. **Alc** 14.5%

Glen Carlou, The Collection Red Blend, Simonsberg-Paarl 2019
95 **Gold**
£26.90 **K&LWines, Port2Port**
86% Cabernet Sauvignon, 7% Cabernet Franc, 7% Merlot. Cacao nib, smoke, baked cherry pie and coffee mingle on a youthful, structured palate. Christmas pudding richness, cranberry acidity and savoury, spicy highlights. A smart, softly textured wine. **Alc** 14.5%

Stellenbosch

Ridgeback, Signature C 2018
95 **Gold**
£66.25 (2017) **Charles Mitchell**
58% Cabernet Franc, 17% Merlot, 17% Cabernet Sauvignon, 8% Petit Verdot. Rich, complex ripe black fruit, Christmas cake, old leather books, juniper and liquorice. The creamy palate is fresh and complex. Spicy vibrancy and touches of herb add complexity to a cohesive, layered palate. **Alc** 14.5%

Stellenbosch 1679, The Legacy 2018
97 Platinum

koelenhof.co.za

50% Cabernet Sauvignon, 12.5% each of Cabernet Franc, Malbec, Merlot and Petit Verdot. Gentle plum pudding and spice on the nose open into a deeper palate of blackcurrant, cherry, clove and cigar smoke. Tannin is balanced by fruit concentration and freshness. **Alc** 14%

Franschhoek Cellar, The Last Elephant 2019
96 Gold

£34-£38 **Widely available via independent merchants**

48% Merlot, 28% Cabernet Sauvignon, 12% Cabernet Franc, 12% Malbec. Alluring perfumes of fruitcake, black cherry coulis, tobacco, clove, bay leaf and cocoa, echoed on the palate. Succulent, with ripe, pure fruit, layered and nuanced, with inky depth and a long tail. **Alc** 14%

Jordan, Cobblers Hill 2018
95 Gold

£35.55 **ABS Wine Agencies**

73% Cabernet Sauvignon, 17% Merlot, 5% Cabernet Franc, 5% Petit Verdot. Gamey characters accompany leafy blackcurrant notes, cassis, damson, leather and tobacco. The palate shows a complex granite earthiness with accents of potpourri, pencil shaving, cedarwood and deep black fruits. Great potential. **Alc** 14%

Uva Mira Mountain Vineyards, OTV 2018
95 Gold

£125 **Museum Wines**

59% Cabernet Franc, 41% Cabernet Sauvignon. Brambles, damson, black cherry, and prunes in brandy, some curry leaf spice. A succulent palate has a silky texture with a whip of gravelly acidity. Long and refined with an attractive cherry-pip finish. **Alc** 14.5%

Spier, Creative Block 5 2019
93 Silver

POA **Freixenet Copestick**

42% Cabernet Sauvignon, 32% Merlot, 11% Petit Verdot, 11% Cabernet Franc, 4% Malbec. Chocolatey oak with bramble and toffee notes join cherry tobacco and a hint of forest floor. Finishes with a firm grip. **Alc** 14.4%

Aslina, Umsasane 2020
92 Silver

£19 **The Wine Society**

70% Cabernet Sauvignon, 18% Cabernet Franc, 12% Petit Verdot. Black fruit flows from the glass offset by capsicum, rosemary, bay leaf and hedgerow. Well-integrated warm oak spice and tannin. **Alc** 14.5%

Delheim, Grand Reserve 2018
92 Silver

£26 **The Wine Society**

63% Cabernet Sauvignon, 19% Petit Verdot, 12% Cabernet Franc, 6% Merlot. Fruitcake richness with notes of juniper, boozy red cherries, blackcurrant pastilles and a lovely mint lift. A promising future. **Alc** 14.5%

Oldenburg Vineyards, Rhodium 2020
92 Silver

£35 (2018) **Wine & Something**

60% Cabernet Franc, 30% Merlot, 10% Cabernet Sauvignon. Rose, musk, sweet baking spice, violet, talcum powder and black fruit with a brush of dried herbs. An elegant and nuanced wine. **Alc** 14%

Western Cape

Vilafonté, Seriously Old Dirt 2020
92 Silver

£27-£29.99 **Handford, Hard to Find Wines, Port2Port, Roberson, Wine Direct**

86% Cabernet Sauvignon, 8% Merlot, 4% Malbec and 2% Cabernet Franc. Bramble and hedgerow fruit, a brush of herbs, incense and sandalwood, a touch of milk chocolate. Savoury elegance, with firm tannins. **Alc** 13.5%

Tasmania

The wines coming out of this unique island state today are fresh, complex and lively.
Their quality is testament to the winemakers who spotted its potential in the 1980s,
overcoming serious climatic challenges to produce some exemplary wines

STORY DAVID SLY

Australia's island state of Tasmania has long been earmarked as a wine region of great potential, largely for the distinctive quality of its pristine cool-climate fruit. Now there is proof on the table of potential realised. Popping open the House of Arras' 2001 Blanc de Blancs, you can only marvel at the freshness and vitality of a 20-year-old wine just entering maturity. Extraordinary grapes have been caressed and framed masterfully in the winery in a way not seen on the Australian mainland, nor rarely elsewhere in the world.

LEARNING PROCESS

It has been a slow journey to reach this point. From the 1980s, boutique growers began planting the right grape varieties in the right sites, with a particular focus on Chardonnay and Pinot Noir. But early efforts were often clumsy, as winemakers struggled to properly harness the intensity of unusually persistent acidity in the grapes and the island's maddeningly fluctuating vintage conditions.

It's a tricky landscape for growers to read. The temperature is seriously cold here – a daily average of 9°C in some parts – and the next landfall beyond Australia's southernmost point is Antarctica.

But Tasmania is also dry, with the eastern span of vineyards lying in the rain shadow of a range of mountains that splits the isle. All this promotes slow flavour development in the fruit and an extraordinary acid line that ensures complexity while retaining freshness.

House of Arras *(houseofarras.com.au)* winemaker Ed Carr was among the early true believers to stake his winemaking reputation on the potential of Tasmanian fruit. When his bosses at Hardys Wines (now part of Accolade Wines) gave Carr free rein in the late 1980s to source whatever fruit would bring wine show trophies and prestige to the company, he chose only Tasmanian Pinot Noir and Chardonnay grapes.

Since its launch in 1995, the success of Arras as a sparkling wine brand of global significance has

'It's the complexity of the components from different areas that I'm most excited about – that brings the elegance and nuance to the wines'

—— **Ed Carr, House of Arras** ▶

inspired confidence to accelerate growth and double its 240,000-bottle annual production. This will lead to a significant expansion of Tasmanian vineyards, a prospect that delights Carr.

'We don't see Tasmania as a single vineyard,' says Carr. 'It's the complexity of the components from different areas that I'm most excited about, because that brings the elegance and nuance to the wines. It's a unique resource.'

THE VERY BEST

Carr's colleagues at Hardys took notice – most notably senior winemakers Peter Dawson and Tim James, who have both now retired from positions in large wine corporations to create their own boutique label. While they live in McLaren Vale in South Australia, the duo source only Tasmanian fruit for their Dawson James wine brand.

'We wholeheartedly believe Tasmania can produce the very best Chardonnay and Pinot Noir in Australia,' enthuses Dawson, 'and that's why it's the only place we source fruit from.'

Dawson and James are primarily excited by the personality of a specific site: a portion of the Meadowbank vineyard in Coal River Valley, which they lease from growers Gerald and Sue Ellis. The duo demand particular management of their leased vines and, as a result, their wines are significantly different to the Meadowbank wines made by Peter Dredge (another former Hardys/ Accolade winemaker who has now settled in Tasmania), along with his own Dr Edge wines (dr-edge.com). 'The very varied wine personalities that can come off this one site means this can be like Burgundy,' says Dawson.

Tolpuddle Vineyard (see right), also in Coal River Valley, is arguably Tasmania's most valued and important site. Established in 1988, it was purchased by cousins Michael Hill Smith MW (one of Decanter's four DWWA Co-Chairs) and Martin Shaw in 2011. The pair transfer the grapes by refrigerated transport to their Shaw & Smith winery in South Australia's Adelaide Hills.

It's a big investment that Hill Smith says is entirely justified. 'The vineyard has focus. It shows place,' he says. 'It's uplifting to be making wines from such a recognisable site.'

When the first vintage of Tolpuddle Vineyard was issued in 2012, Shaw and Hill Smith chose a Tasmanian identity for the label rather than brand it as part of their existing Shaw & Smith portfolio. Hill Smith says that this was vital to respect the integrity of the site, and to elevate an elite Tasmanian entity.

'People around the world are so curious about this frontier island, and they find the notion of Tasmania's remoteness hugely interesting,' Hill

Smith says. 'The story ties in with the fruit quality to drive respect for a distinctive Tasmanian identity – and there's great value attached to that.'

The big challenge now facing Tasmania is consistent and reliable output. Wild vintage variations due to harsh weather patterns result in variable annual yields, along with unpredictable flavours from fruit of younger vines. Despite such obstacles, many winemakers from Australia's mainland have embraced the challenges and now live in Tasmania.

REALISING POTENTIAL

New Zealand-born Sam Connew (pictured right) came to Tasmania in 2016 following stints in Oregon, a decade at Wirra Wirra Vineyards in McLaren Vale and two years at Tower Estate in the Hunter Valley. She chose island life because she wanted to make the best possible Riesling, Chardonnay and Pinot Noir – today the focus of her Stargazer label (stargazerwine.com.au), which she established in 2012. 'Tasmania is the only place I know that excels in all three varieties,' Connew says, 'and I understand instinctively just how great this region can be. To me it instantly felt like home – like a perfect combination of Australia and New Zealand.'

Having taken the plunge to buy a vineyard in Coal River Valley in 2016 and plant more vines, Connew has now built a winery in partnership with Greg Melick of Pressing Matters (pressingmatters. com.au), for whom she also makes wines. 'We believe in the potential of this place,' she

Tasmania at a glance

Producers 184
Area planted 2,000ha
Proportion Represents 1% of Australia's total harvest volume but 4.2% of national sales by value
Wine regions Seven in total: North West (near Davenport), Tamar Valley and Pipers River hugging the north coast; East Coast (from St Helens to Freycinet); in the south, Coal River Valley, Derwent Valley and Huon/ d'Entrecasteaux Channel
Climate Temperate maritime, cooled by westerly winds off the Southern Ocean; daily mean average is 9°C-12°C
Key varieties Pinot Noir (48%), Chardonnay (25%), Pinot Gris (9%), Riesling (6%). Note that 76% of Chardonnay and 45% of Pinot Noir is allocated to sparkling wine production

SOURCE: WINE TASMANIA

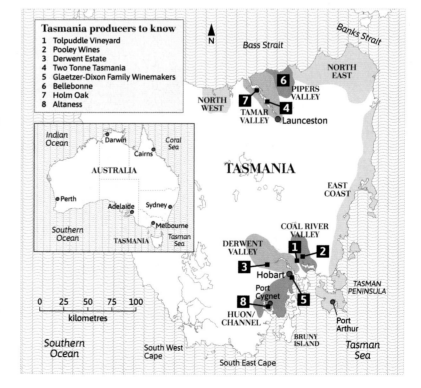

Tasmania producers to know
1 Tolpuddle Vineyard
2 Pooley Wines
3 Derwent Estate
4 Two Tonne Tasmania
5 Glaetzer-Dixon Family Winemakers
6 Bellebonne
7 Holm Oak
8 Altaness

Tasmania: eight producers to know

Altaness

Having sold their Cascabel Winery in South Australia's McLaren Vale to pursue cool-climate winemaking, Susana Fernandez and Duncan Ferguson are now making notable Chardonnay, Pinot Noir and pétillant naturel wines from deep in the Huon Valley. *altaness.com*

Bellebonne

Former Jansz winemaker Natalie Fryar has launched her own boutique sparkling wine venture, with the first vintages of her Bellebonne Blanc de Blancs and Rosé cuvées showing great finesse and structure. This small, dedicated sparkling wine brand is destined to build a big reputation. *bellebonne.wine*

Derwent Estate

A long-time provider of elite grapes to Penfolds, Derwent Estate now retains most of its fruit for estate wines. A lithe, textural Riesling stands out as an exemplar of the style in Tasmania, but winemaker John Schuts is equally fixated on the top-quality Chardonnay and Pinot Noir. *derwentestate.com.au*

Glaetzer-Dixon Family Winemakers

Barossa-born winemaker Nick Glaetzer

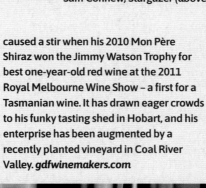

'We believe in the potential of this place. The story of excellent-quality Tasmanian wines is just beginning'

———— Sam Connew, Stargazer (*above*)

caused a stir when his 2010 Mon Père Shiraz won the Jimmy Watson Trophy for best one-year-old red wine at the 2011 Royal Melbourne Wine Show – a first for a Tasmanian wine. It has drawn eager crowds to his funky tasting shed in Hobart, and his enterprise has been augmented by a recently planted vineyard in Coal River Valley. *gdfwinemakers.com*

Holm Oak

Best known as a white wine specialist, winemaker Bec Duffy is reading her Tamar Valley vineyard cleverly to produce serious barrel-fermented Chardonnay. The brand also has notable Riesling, Pinot Gris and Sauvignon Blanc, along with the best example of Arneis grown on the island. There's also a smart range of Pinot Noir expressions. *holmoakvineyards.com.au*

Pooley Wines

Significant among Tasmania's pioneer grape-growers, the Pooley family's shift from primarily farming to a serious wine business has propelled them on a quest for the highest quality. Winemaker Anna Pooley is now focused on specialising in single vineyards within the large Pooley range. *pooleywines.com.au*

Tolpuddle Vineyard

This estate sets a lofty new benchmark for vineyard management and winemaking finesse in Tasmania, with exceptional Pinot Noir and Chardonnay coming from an elite single site in Coal River Valley. It has benefited greatly from a decade of investment and vineyard improvement undertaken by its owners, cousins Michael Hill Smith MW and Martin Shaw (*pictured, p47*). *tolpuddlevineyard.com*

Two Tonne Tasmania

The attention to detail of winemaker Ricky Evans, with his small parcels of Tamar Valley fruit, has resulted in a small portfolio of very interesting, particular wines. He explores a raft of different ideas, from use of whole bunches in his Dog & Wolf Pinot Noir to the Ziggurat range, which is his playground for experimentation. *tttwine.com.au* ▶

Bec Duffy of Holm Oak, near Launceston

emphasises. 'The story of excellent-quality Tasmanian wines is just beginning.'

Another with long-term belief in Tasmanian wine is Robert Hill-Smith, former CEO and now chairman of historic Barossa Valley estate Yalumba. His curiosity in the island's potential was piqued in the mid-1980s, when Tony Jordan of Domaine Chandon Australia planted grapes for sparkling wine production there, and then Champagne Louis Roederer followed, partnering with Heemskerk Wines to create the Jansz (jansz. com.au) sparkling wine label. 'That European insight into the possibility of Tasmania signalled something of importance to me,' says Hill-Smith.

When the opportunity emerged to buy Jansz in 1998, he pounced. 'I felt a sense of adventure by being among the first to recognise the potential of Tasmania and embarking on improvement and specialisation,' he explains, having just opened a new winery at the Pontos Hills Vineyard estate in Coal River Valley for the Jansz sparklings. 'Now, we can see that our belief in consistently making wines of great quality has been entirely justified.'

Key Tasmanian vintages to seek out

2021 Signs are good for wines across the most recent vintage release, with pristine Chardonnay, bright and lively Pinot Noir and a diverse array of Riesling styles showing great texture and balance between ripe fruit and persistent acidity. Broach from 2022, drink to 2033.

2020 The best examples of Pinot Noir yet seen from Tasmania. The benefits of a long, even growing season have been coupled with more finesse and an assured touch by winemakers to produce Pinots of heightened delicacy and complex structure. Broach from 2023, drink to 2033.

2018 A superior Chardonnay vintage, showing luscious fruit character and sharp minerality, built around a firm spine of acidity that will ensure long-lasting freshness and vitality. Drink 2022-2035.

2011 Unfairly tarnished with criticism due to a prolonged wet ripening season across mainland Australia, the 2011 vintage in Tasmania offers many exceptional wines showing the true benefits of the island's renowned acidity. Key examples are Dawson James' Chardonnay, showing remarkable freshness a decade on, and Glaetzer-Dixon's Mon Père Shiraz. Drink 2022-2030.

Sly's taste of Tasmania: a selection of 14 of the island's best

① House of Arras, Arras Grand Vintage Extra Brut 2013 98
houseofarras.com.au
Opulence on a grand scale, from its rich, persistent mousse, through the surging complex flavours that wash luxuriously across the palate. With 62% Chardonnay showing radiant personality and assured citrus flavours, everything in this blend is perfectly balanced: bright fruit, mineral drive, depth of flavour, refreshing acidity, extraordinary palate length and firm persistence. **Drink** 2022-2040 **Alcohol** 12.5%

House of Arras, Arras Blanc de Blancs Brut 2006 96
£24.59 (2004) Christopher Keiller
Made by winemaker Ed Carr since 1995, this is an assured sparkling wine, driven by bright, intense citrus flavours cased in savoury secondary notes thanks to seven years on its lees. The rounded palate is marvellously complete, from the lick of oyster shell and sea spray to brioche and baking spices. A rich, persistent mousse draws everything together through a luxurious finish. **Drink** 2022-2035 **Alc** 12.5%

Pirie, Vintage, Tamar Valley 2017 91
tamarridge.com.au
Three years on its lees has added a

distinguished tone to this blend, led by 52% Pinot Noir, with roasted nut and savoury notes gripping the palate. Driven by a clean acid line, it has bright flavours of lemon curd and green apple with a yeasty complexity, giving a serious nod to French tradition. **Drink** 2022-2030 **Alc** 12%

② Jansz, Vintage Rosé 2018 94
£17.50 (ib)-£33 (2017) Harvey Nichols, Lay & Wheeler, VinQuinn, Wine Direct
Rose petal perfume leads to a sharp crunch of raspberry that defines the front palate, but it's the soft, creamy texture that proves most seductive. This generous vintage amplifies strawberry plushness from the 100% Pinot Noir, with two-and-a-half years on lees adding brioche and nougat. A firm acid spine gives this lean, understated rosé length and focus. **Drink** 2022-2030 **Alc** 12%

③ Dawson James, Chardonnay, Derwent Valley 2018 97
£54.99 Liberty Wines, The Fine Wine Co, VinQuinn
Fascinating to see the different treatment afforded to this fruit, sourced from part of the Meadowbank vineyard, and how beautifully it responds to a powerful Burgundian-style approach. Flavours are concentrated yet focused, the strong acid line amplifying freshness but also tempered by smart oak

usage to frame the wine's magnificent architecture. **Drink** 2022-2035 **Alc** 12.7%

Tolpuddle, Chardonnay, Coal River Valley 2019 97
£35 (ib)-£69.88 Cru, Cuchet & Co, Hedonism, Mummy Wine Club, Oz Wines, Vin Cognito, Wineye
Understated purity defines filigree flavours. Pretty white flowers of a citrus orchard in bloom, notes of struck flint: a delicate balance between fruit and minerality. The creamy texture is sublime, underpinning rolling flavours of lemon pith, grapefruit and a lick of slate. Each nuance completes a superb portrait. **Drink** 2022-2035 **Alc** 13%

④ Stargazer, Chardonnay, Coal River Valley 2021 95
£55 Blas ar Fwyd, Great Wines Direct, The Great Wine Co
There is great strength here but also judicious balance between the gentle oak, long acid line, an arresting silky texture and robust flavours. Bright preserved lemon leads out fleshy nectarine, grapefruit and a hint of roasted nuts through to a lingering savoury finish. **Drink** 2022-2032 **Alc** 13.4%

Holm Oak, Chardonnay, Tamar Valley 2021 91
£20 (2019) Villeneuve Wines

Martin Shaw (left) and
Michael Hill Smith
MW, Tolpuddle

Fleshy flavours of apricot and lemon pith, with spiced oak providing good framework and savoury tones. For this vintage, 60% malolactic fermentation has helped balance the high minerally acidity, and extended time on lees provides a lovely rich texture. **Drink** 2022-2027 **Alc** 12.5%

Stargazer, Riesling, Coal River Valley 2021 95

£37.50 **The Fine Wine Co, The Great Wine Co**
A firm embrace of pretty citrus blossom aromas alongside the crunch of green apple freshness. The 5% of fruit fermented on skins provides textural muscle that adds strength to the lemon pith and brûlée flavours that roll through the mid-palate. The texture is soft and playful, the finish long and satisfying. **Drink** 2022-2035 **Alc** 12%

Stargazer, Palisander Riesling, Coal River Valley 2021 94

£44 **The Great Wine Co**
Ten months on lees in a ceramic egg has given great chalky texture as well as heightening the subtlety of lemon curd, dried flowers and briny, oyster-shell tones. A taut acid line contributes tension and nervy energy to the sinewy palate and the bone-dry finish emphasises its slatey minerality. **Drink** 2022-2032 **Alc** 12.7%

⑤ Tolpuddle, Pinot Noir, Coal River Valley 2020 98

£59.95-£69.50 **Alexander Hadleigh, Cru, Hedonism, KWM, Lockett Bros, Natty Boy Wines, Oz Wines, Philglas & Swiggot, The Secret Bottle Shop, Vin Cognito**
The best Pinot Noir offering yet from this

esteemed estate. Seductive aromas of bright red cherry and raspberry then a vibrant array of black fruits on the palate with lively spice and a velvety texture of real power and purpose. The seamless structure is sustained by an unwavering acid line that carries each element with grace and poise. A complete package. **Drink** 2022-2035 **Alc** 13%

Dawson James, Pinot Noir, Derwent Valley 2020 96

£74.99 (2018) **John Hattersley, The Drink Shop, The Fine Wine Co, VinQuinn**
Sourced from a portion of the Meadowbank vineyard curated to the particular specifications of winemakers Peter Dawson and Tim James, whose unobtrusive winemaking ensures real purity of fruit. Rose petal, dusty red earth and red fruit aromas leap from the glass. The silky,

seductive palate is all strawberries and cream, framed by gently gripping tannins. **Drink** 2022-2035 **Alc** 12.6%

Stargazer, Pinot Noir, Coal River Valley 2021 94

£55 **The Great Wine Co**
A seductive nose makes an immediate impression: fresh berries, sooty stalks and stone. There is rich intensity to the full-bodied, creamy palate of dark plum, rhubarb and blackcurrant, allowing gentle sweetness to ride over a sour lick. The flavours resonate long, riding on unobtrusive tannins. **Drink** 2022-2032 **Alc** 13.5%

⑥ Holm Oak, The Wizard Pinot Noir, Tamar Valley 2019 89

£30 **Villeneuve Wines**
A fuller, funkier style, boasting ripe dark cherry and spicy plum. Prominent French oak makes this seem rather chubby, but the palate firms up on the finish with savoury tannins, suggesting it will bloom with a few more years. **Drink** 2022-2032 **Alc** 13.5% **D**

① ② ③ ④ ⑤ ⑥

PHOTOGRAPHS ROBERT HARDING/ALAMY STOCK PHOTO; JESSICA CLARK PHOTOGRAPHY. MAP MAGGIE NELSON

New Zealand Sauvignon Blanc

If you love the fruity-zingy style of Sauvignon Blanc there are still many great, wallet-friendly buys to be found, from Marlborough and beyond

REPORT ROGER JONES

New Zealand wines – particularly Sauvignon Blanc – suffered severe shortages in the 2021 vintage, so it was gratifying to see such a large number entered for this two-day tasting. In our discussions during and following it, we three judges considered regional and vintage differences as well as the range of Sauvignon Blanc styles, notably considering whether there is a lighter, more focused style emerging.

Highlights came from Wairarapa on North Island, which showed real quality and refinement, thanks in part to the free-draining alluvial gravels and clay silts of the terraces which produce small, concentrated berries. On South Island, wines from Waipara showcased a fresh, clean style that impressed. Likewise, it was pleasing to see what Central Otago (especially the Bannockburn sub-region) can produce – it is certainly a region to watch.

Marlborough dominated, with the Wairau sub-region a positive. Notably, we questioned whether Marlborough producers were moving away from punchy, fruity styles (that made the region's name and which many consumers still love) to a more elegant 'European' style. Melanie Brown wondered if Marlborough winemakers were 'scared to own their classic style', or whether Mother Nature and financial circumstances had forced them into higher yields, thereby producing lighter-styled wines.

Roger Jones considered whether producers were just responding to consumers' changing palates. 'Maybe Marlborough Sauvignon Blanc drinkers are moving away from old favourites that had oak and big bold flavours? Obviously plenty still enjoy these flavour-packed styles, however as a global Sauvignon Blanc standard, not just within Marlborough, it is pleasing when refinement, quality and depth combine to give a perfect wine.'

'There's been lots of hype about the 2021 vintage,' said Rebecca Palmer. 'The gross generalisation is that because yields were down then quality was up, almost as if that's a given. But the relationship between yield and quality isn't linear. The growing season was stop-start, affected by frost then cool weather at flowering. And hang-time is crucial to the development of aroma and flavour.'

Brown agreed: 'I do wonder whether this was a factor in the wines submitted here: far too many I'd describe as "decent enough" but lacking the personality and balance we might have hoped for in order to give more Highly recommendeds and Outstandings.'

Due to Covid restrictions, New Zealand only fully opened its borders on 31 July 2022, and has been partially or totally locked down since March 2020. This resulted in few container ships docking, meaning delays of more than three months to take stock out of the country, not to mention the cost hike.

But it is not all doom and gloom. The 2022 vintage is looking promising, shipping should become easier and NZ Sauvignon Blanc will remain a favourite, despite this temporary mid-life crisis. Until the 2022 vintage makes it on to retailer shelves and wine lists, *Decanter* readers have some excellent wines to try from this panel tasting, showcasing New Zealand Sauvignon Blanc at its very best.

THE SCORES 116 wines tasted
Exceptional 1 **Outstanding** 5 **Highly recommended** 40 **Recommended** 45
Commended 21 **Fair** 4 **Poor** 0

Entry criteria: producers and UK agents were invited to submit their latest releases of still white wines made with 100% Sauvignon Blanc from any region in New Zealand

THE JUDGES

Roger Jones
is the retired former owner of The Harrow at Little Bedwyn restaurant in Wiltshire. He is now a wine writer, judge and consultant with a particular interest in the hospitality trade, as well as helping charities. He is a DWWA judge, with a focus on New World regions

Melanie Brown
is founder and CEO of Heist Group, which includes New World-focused online wine merchant Specialist Cellars and The Laundry restaurant, Brixton. From New Zealand, she arrived in the UK in 2015 to work as a chef for the likes of Raymond Blanc, Peter Gordon and more

Rebecca Palmer
is associate director of Corney & Barrow, based in the UK, Shanghai, Hong Kong and Singapore. She heads up the commercial buying team, covering most world regions. At DWWA 2022 she judged in the New Zealand and USA & Central America categories

Exceptional 98-100pts

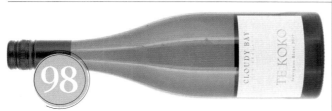

98

Cloudy Bay, Te Koko, Wairau Valley, Marlborough 2019

Roger Jones 98
Melanie Brown 98
Rebecca Palmer 98
£42.99-£56 **Amazon UK, Clos19, Laithwaites, Majestic, Sainsbury's, Selfridges, Specialist Cellars, Tesco**
Established in 1985, Cloudy Bay has become one of the world's most recognised New Zealand wine brands. Te Koko is made from fruit from four prime vineyard parcels. It's barrel-fermented with 'wild' indigenous yeasts for four to five months before spending 15 months on fine lees.

Roger Jones Thai rice pudding with kaffir lime. Clean, focused and lingers for an age. The luxurious feeling at the end is immense; this is a stunning wine.
Melanie Brown Opulent and alluring. Shows how oak can heighten flavours and texture. Soft white peach and florals on a citrus base. Creamy centre with caramel popcorn and a pristine acid line. Beautiful.
Rebecca Palmer Attractive key lime characters, oak melding to create the silky, sleek palate.
Drink 2022-2025 **Alcohol** 13%

The Cloudy Bay Shed tasting room close to lake Dunstan at Cromwell, Central Otago

Outstanding 95-97pts

96

Craggy Range, Te Muna Vineyard, Martinborough, Wairarapa 2021

RJ 97 **MB** 95 **RP** 96
£13.50-£18 **Cadman, Harvey Nichols, ND John, NZ House of Wine, Specialist Cellars, The Wine Society**
Family-owned winery Craggy Range was founded in 1998 in Hawke's Bay, and the family has pursued a single-vineyard approach to winemaking. For this wine, grapes are grown on limestone-speckled stony soils in Martinborough. It is fermented in a mixture of oak and stainless steel followed by four months ageing in barrique.

RJ A mellow, yellow wine with buttercups, green herbs and rosemary flowers, a silky purity and freshness. Stunning.
MB The perfect collaboration of sweet fruit and vegetal aromas. Grapefruit, elderflower and sweet pea shoots, plus lively acid and purity galore. This is next-level elegant.
RP Tart lemon-lime and whitecurrant notes with hint of spice. Silky texture, lifted by oak. Spice notes on the finish.
Drink 2022-2024 **Alc** 12.8%

95

Palliser Estate, Pencarrow, Martinborough, Wairarapa 2021

RJ 95 **MB** 95 **RP** 95
£9.40-£10.85 **Field & Fawcett, Justerini & Brooks**
In recent years the team at Pallister Estate have been working hard to convert to organic farming practices across their seven vineyards. For this wine, 70% of the fruit was taken from older vines from the estate's Clouston Vineyard. The wine goes through a cool fermentation and has some post-fermentation less stirring.

RJ Delicate, floral and refined, with acaia honey and buttercups. Racy acidity and layers of complexity; a fresh and buoyant wine.
MB Concentrated and pure. Lemon sherbet nose leads to a tasteful and pristine palate. Acid is lively and enticing.
RP Clean, fresh and light, with lemon-lime aromas. It has a subtle, silky mouthfeel with some rose petal aromatics coming through. Medium length. **Drink** 2022-2023 **Alc** 13% ▶

Seifried Estate, Aotea, Nelson 2020

RJ 96 **MB** 95 **RP** 95
£17-£20.77 Banstead Vintners,
New Zealand House of Wine,
Specialist Cellars, T Wright Wine
Seifried was established in
Nelson in 1973 by Austrian-born
Hermann Seifried *(right)* and his
New Zealand wife Agnes, and
their Aotea series represents
specially selected, single-
vineyard wines. The fruit for the
2020 Sauvignon Blanc comes
from the stony, free-draining
soils of the Brightwater
Vineyard, just 15km from the
coast. It was de-stemmed and
pressed immediately after
harvest, before undergoing cool
fermentation in stainless steel.
RJ Savoury, with herbaceous
notes and textured spice. Some
age coming through to give it
legs. Clean and focused, this
will impress people, especially
when served with food.
MB Tropical hints on the nose,
with subtle floral nuances
flowing across the palate.
Poised and elegant, with fresh
and lively acidity that feels
balanced.
RP This has a light, delicate
aromatic profile with some
lime/lime leaf characters.
Drink 2022-2025 **Alc** 13%

Hermann Seifried,
Seifried Estate

Spring Creek, Wairau Valley, Marlborough 2021

RJ 95 **MB** 95 **RP** 95
£12 Castang, MWH Wine Merchants,
Underwood
Founded in Marlborough in
1995, Spring Creek Estate
originally championed a blend
of Chardonnay and Sauvignon
Blanc, but as consumer
preferences changed, so did the
wines, and its focus is now on
single-varietal wines. The
grapes for this wine come from
the stony riverbed soils of the
renowned Rapaura district in
the Wairau Valley, and their
freshness is maintained by
ageing in stainless steel.
RJ Bright and fresh, with
passion-fruit ice cream, tropical
spices and guava, and a spiced
herbaceous feel. A refreshing,
creamy palate; the finish has
some spice and citrus acidity.
MB Impressively ripe (but not
overripe) tropical fruit salad.
Playful and rich characters
entwine with lively flint. A fuller
style with heaps of character.
RP Bright and clean, with citrus,
pear and rose petal. Has
something of an Alsatian
accent. Down-the-line steeliness;
light and precise. A cleansing
finish. **Drink** 2022-2024 **Alc** 12%

Vineyard Productions, Fincher & Co, Awatere, Marlborough 2021

RJ 95 **MB** 95 **RP** 95
£13.95 Widely available via UK
agent Global Wine Solutions
A collaboration between British
Master of Wine Liam
Steevenson and celebrated
Marlborough winemaker Ben
Glover, Fincher & Co highlights
the diversity of single-vineyard
sites. Fruit for this wine comes
from the Dashwood region on
the northern bank of the
Awatere river, where it's cooler
and drier than the rest of
Marlborough. Grapes are
machine harvested, followed by
cool tank fermentation.
RJ A zippy wine, with tangerine,
Williams pear and gentle
spices, delicate tropical fruit
and hidden hints of passion fruit
and fresh green herbs.
MB Beautifully pure example of
Sauvignon Blanc. Fresh, lively
and green, with hints of tropical
fruits and a playful acidity. An
elegant style that speaks of the
Awatere. A ripper wine for
under £15.
RP This has bright, expressive
New Zealand Sauvignon Blanc
aromatics. It's a punchy and
zesty wine, with tropical green
fruit. **Drink** 2022-2024 **Alc** 13%

Highly recommended 90-94pts

Hunter's, Wairau Valley, Marlborough 2021
RJ 94 **MB** 95 **RP** 92

£14.95-£16.99 Castang, Experience Wine, Field & Fawcett, Gorey Wine Cellar, Guest Wines, Jeroboams, Laithwaites

Pristine fruit characters. Citrus-green, rose petal aromas. A poise that champions Sauvignon. **Drink** 2022-2023 **Alc** 13.5%

Johner Estate, Gladstone, Wairarapa 2020
RJ 95 **MB** 93 **RP** 93

£16.99 Virgin Wines

Plentiful lemon balm, zest, bright juicy pineapple, cape gooseberries and kaffir nuances. The mid-palate is so clean and focused; has a delicate acid line and long, enticing finish. **Drink** 2022-2024 **Alc** 13.5%

Delta Estate, Lower Wairau Valley, Marlborough 2021
RJ 94 **MB** 94 **RP** 92

£14.99 Hennings

Refined excellence. Textured and layered, and the depth of flavour is immense. The balance between citrus freshness and cool restrained tropical fruit is perfect. Layers of complexity. **Drink** 2022-2024 **Alc** 13%

Glover Family Vineyards, Tanners, Wairau Valley, Marlborough 2021
RJ 94 **MB** 94 **RP** 90

£13.95 Tanners

Beautiful fruit purity running seamlessly from nose right through to abundantly long length. Pink grapefruit and gentle layers of restrained mango; creamy and focused on the finish. **Drink** 2022-2023 **Alc** 13%

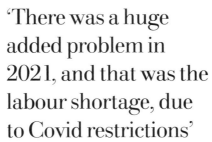

> 'There was a huge added problem in 2021, and that was the labour shortage, due to Covid restrictions'
>
> —— Rebecca Palmer

Main Divide, Waipara Valley, North Canterbury 2021
RJ 93 **MB** 94 **RP** 92

£16.75-£17.75 Grape to Glass, NZ House of Wine, Oak N4, The Grocery, Vinvm

Freshly cut grass dances between ripe lemons, limes and passion fruit. Racy on the mid-palate. Zippy and sassy with oodles of complexity. **Drink** 2022-2023 **Alc** 13.5%

Astrolabe, Taihoa Vineyard, Kēkerengū Coast, Marlborough 2020
RJ 92 **MB** 92 **RP** 91

£30 Armit

Restrained elegance that gently simmers to the top. The integration of oak is harmonious. Has an aytpical, cinnamon-cardamom-spiced profile. Length is clean and full. **Drink** 2022-2023 **Alc** 13.5%

Forrest Wines, The Doctors', Wairau Valley, Marlborough 2021
RJ 95 **MB** 86 **RP** 95

£9.75-£11.99 Cadman, Frontier Fine Wines, Gerrard Seel, JN Wines, Luvians, Majestic, T Wright, Tesco, Waitrose, Wine Down

Expressive citrus and fruit salad. Very clean, pure and refined. Impressive example of a lighter ABV wine. **Drink** 2022-2024 **Alc** 9.5%

Gladstone Vineyard, Estate, Gladstone, Wairarapa 2020
RJ 92 **MB** 92 **RP** 92

£13.99-£17 Bottles Worcester, The Vineking, Vindependents, WoodWinters

Limey, fresh aromatics – bright, upbeat and tingly. There's a sense of refinement here, almost Sancerre in style, with a saline edge. **Drink** 2022-2023 **Alc** 14%

Isabel Estate, Marlborough 2021
RJ 93 **MB** 91 **RP** 92

£19.99 Widely available via UK agent Bancroft Wines

Crushed fresh peas sit playfully with citrus, hints of nettles and a gunpowder matchstick uplift. A well-balanced wine. **Drink** 2022-2026 **Alc** 13%

Mount Brown Estates, Waipara Valley, North Canterbury 2021
RJ 92 **MB** 94 **RP** 90

£13.95 Davy's, Hennings

Freshness! Passion fruit, kaffir and custard apple. Linear and crisp acidity lines, full of promise and delivers across the palate with integrity. **Drink** 2022-2023 **Alc** 12%

Mount Fishtail Wines, Mount Fishtail Sur Lie, Wairau Valley, Marlborough 2021
RJ 92 **MB** 92 **RP** 91

POA Barton Brownsdon & Sadler

Kaffir lime, guava and elderflower on the palate. Juicy, aromatic and restrained passion fruit. **Drink** 2022-2023 **Alc** 13%

►

Mt Difficulty, Bannockburn, Central Otago 2021
RJ 93 MB 93 RP 90

£18.50-£19.50 Cadman, Ellis Wines, NZ House of Wine, Specialist Cellars

Abundantly green and vivacious. Green apples, taut acid and fine delicate vegetals. Layered rather well. A lean but perfect example. **Drink** 2022-2023 **Alc** 14%

Rimapere Vineyards, Plot 101, Rapaura Road, Marlborough 2021
RJ 94 MB 90 RP 92

£24.99 DBM Wines, Majestic, Ocado, Waddesdon Wines

Salted lemons and briny character; spicy, silky, uplifting. Bright acidity, with hints of passion fruit and wet grass. A real crowd-pleaser. **Drink** 2022-2024 **Alc** 14%

Steve Bird, Wairau Valley, Marlborough 2021
RJ 93 MB 90 RP 93

£19 The Wine Arcade

Sweet perfume dominates the nose. Ripe and fresh stone fruits bring this wine alive. Concentrated and fresh, with a mouth-cleansing texture. Steely, impressive length. **Drink** 2022-2023 **Alc** 13%

Borthwick Vineyards, Paper Road, Gladstone, Wairarapa 2021
RJ 92 MB 89 RP 91

£17 Armit

Crisp, clean, enticing nose and palate. Alphonso mango with sweet grilled pineapple. Wonderful depth and complexity of fruits supported by lively acid and a spiced finish. **Drink** 2022-2023 **Alc** 13.6%

'We three judges considered whether there is a lighter, more focused Sauvignon Blanc style emerging'

— Roger Jones

Catalina Sounds, Sound of White, Waihopai Valley, Marlborough 2019
RJ 90 MB 92 RP 90

£20 Amps, D Byrne & Co, Hoults, NY Wines, WoodWinters

Expressive and zesty with umami characters. A lovely persistence, with oak integration providing an incredible backdrop for delicate tropical notes and sweet spice. **Drink** 2022-2023 **Alc** 12.5%

Church Road, Grand Reserve, Hawke's Bay 2019
RJ 91 MB 90 RP 91

church-road.com

Expressive nuances of ripe mango and pineapple. An intuitive use of oak complements the ripeness of the fruit. This has complexity and depth, and is crying out for fish and chips. **Drink** 2022-2023 **Alc** 13%

Foley Wines, Grove Mill, Wairau Valley, Marlborough 2021
RJ 90 MB 94 RP 89

£9.50-£10 Co-op, The Wine Society

Aromatic with bursts of lime, florals and crushed fresh peas. Passion fruit, guava and elderflower notes. Has a minerality that creates structure and poise, letting the fruit shine. **Drink** 2022-2023 **Alc** 13%

Kim Crawford, Spitfire Small Parcels, Wairau Valley, Marlborough 2021
RJ 92 MB 88 RP 92

£21.99 Liberty Wines, Martinez Wines, WoodWinters

Clean and fresh, with lychee, passion fruit, guava, thai lime and kaffir. Flinty nuances provide further complexity. Quite long on the finish. **Drink** 2022-2023 **Alc** 13%

Palliser Estate, Martinborough, Wairarapa 2021
RJ 94 MB 90 RP 90

£11.40 Justerini & Brooks

Lovely vegetal aromas including sweet peas, asparagus and peppers. Buttercups, floral notes and a stunning perfume on the front palate. Textured and spiced, with apricots and nectarines, plus a gooseberry and elderflower hit. **Drink** 2022-2023 **Alc** 13%

Saint Clair, Barrique, Marlborough 2020
RJ 92 MB 89 RP 91

£20.25 Hallgarten Wines, NZ House of Wine, Strictly Wine

Citrus, pear, vanilla and cardamom oak. This has a purity of fruit that excels alongside alluring texture, which is silky, helping to give the impression of body. Well managed. **Drink** 2022-2024 **Alc** 12.5%

Settlement, Heritage, Wairau Valley, Marlborough 2021
RJ 90 MB 94 RP 90

£14.50 The Wine Society

Bright lemon pith, with fresh lime and fine herbs. Delicate vegetal undertones creep across the palate, along with opulent fruits. This is light on its feet, and well balanced. **Drink** 2022-2023 **Alc** 13%

Te Mata Estate, Hawke's Bay 2021
RJ 90 MB 92 RP 90
£20.99 Vinvm, Wine Direct
This wine is definitely an extrovert! A wonderfully pungent nose of green bell peppers, tomato leaf and saline. Spices and tiny clusters of dancing fruit on the palate, with citrus hints, lemon and lime. Focused. **Drink** 2022-2023 **Alc** 13%

Te Pā, Reserve Collection Seaside, Lower Wairau Valley, Marlborough 2021
RJ 91 MB 92 RP 90
£15 Buckingham Schenk
Ripe fruit profile with passion fruit and crème anglaise; bright and focused. Struck match is prevalent from nose to palate. Sense of harmony and fullness, and yet light. **Drink** 2022-2023 **Alc** 13.5%

Ant Moore, Central Wairau, Marlborough 2021
RJ 90 MB 92 RP 89
£13.99 Cellar Twelve, The Sipster, Vinotopia, Walkers Wines
Pure and damn fine! Lime leaf, citrus, guava, tropical fruit. So crisp and clean it's pristine. Spiced acidity, fresh on second taste. Evolves more volcanic and pure, with a focus. **Drink** 2022-2023 **Alc** 13%

Brancott Estate, Classic, Marlborough 2021
RJ 90 MB 92 RP 88
£9.50-£10 Asda, Cellier, Co-op, Morrisons, Sainsbury's, Tesco, Waitrose
Classic crowd pleaser, tropical with clean focused fruit, paw paw, guava and alphonso mango. The zippy refreshing acid directs the flavours to a pure and long, lively finish. **Drink** 2022-2023 **Alc** 13.5%

Clouston & Co, Wairau Valley, Marlborough 2021
RJ 90 MB 90 RP 91
£16.95 Slurp
Restrained but bursting with passion fruit from start to finish. Lemon-lime marmalade with gentle spices, some baked apples, cordial and lime curd. Finishes with poise and attitude. **Drink** 2022-2023 **Alc** 12.5%

Craggy Range, Marlborough 2021
RJ 91 MB 90 RP 89
£15.99-£18.50 Harvey Nichols, Waitrose Cellar
Light, appealing lemon-lime and pear cordial characters, like cut grass on a summer day. The synergy of savoury and sweet makes this an exemplary bottling. **Drink** 2022-2026 **Alc** 13%

E&J Gallo Winery, Whitehaven, Marlborough 2021
RJ 91 MB 92 RP 88
£13.99-£16 Cadman, Vivino
Welcome aromas of honeyed bananas and soft citrus fruits. Complexity enhanced by silky texture and weight. Well balanced, with a decent finish. **Drink** 2022-2025 **Alc** 13%

Elephant Hill, Hawke's Bay 2018
RJ 92 MB 86 RP 92
£15.95 Corney & Barrow
Fruits are slowly turning tertiary. Full of flavour, from buttercups to stone fruit to racy fruit. This has character, depth and freshness. **Drink** 2022-2023 **Alc** 12.5%

Framingham, Marlborough 2021
RJ 91 MB 90 RP 90
£16.99-£17.50 Liberty Wines, NZ House of Wine, Nickolls & Perks, NY Wines, Specialist Cellars
Kaffir lime-focused, with stony, flinty nuances across the mid-palate. Concentrated but bright, fresh and limey, with delicate quince and crab apple at the end. **Drink** 2022-2026 **Alc** 13.5%

Greystone, Organic, Waipara Valley, North Canterbury 2020
RJ 90 MB 88 RP 92
£15.99-£18.99 Cadman, Frontier Fine Wine, The Wine Centre Great Horkesley, Waitrose
Restrained, elegant and refined, with layers of ripe banana peel and pineapple leaves underpinned by elderflower and nettles. **Drink** 2022-2023 **Alc** 13.5%

Invivo X, SJP, Marlborough 2021
RJ 90 MB 90 RP 90
£15-£18 Harvey Nichols, Ocado, Tesco, Wine Delivered
Clean and fresh aromatics here; tropical and citrus fruits with some herbs. The frisky line of acidity provides attitude and fun. **Drink** 2022-2025 **Alc** 13%

Marisco Vineyards, Emma Marris, Waihopai Valley, Marlborough 2021
RJ 90 MB 92 RP 88
£11.99 Majestic
Fresh-forward and approachable, this wine has hints of red apples and passion fruit as well as a touch of herbaceous coriander. Ripe-fruited and expressive, with zingy acids. **Drink** 2022-2023 **Alc** 13%

►

Nautilus, Marlborough 2021
RJ 91 **MB** 90 **RP** 88
£13-£18 Cadman, Co-op, Specialist Cellars
Perfectly ripe stone fruit unveiled across the mid- and back-palate. Richly textured and full flavoured, this is evolving. Abundant patches and complexity of fruit unfold and the length is full of flavours and personality. **Drink** 2022-2026 **Alc** 13.5%

Peregrine, Mohua, Wairau Valley, Marlborough 2021
RJ 90 **MB** 90 **RP** 91
£15.95 The Great Wine Co
An archetypal Sauvignon wine, with an abundance of tropical notes interlaced with a herbaceous thread. Rich in flavour and texture. A well-balanced wine with some silky length. **Drink** 2022-2023 **Alc** 12.5%

Saint Clair, Reserve, Wairau Valley, Marlborough 2021
RJ 90 **MB** 90 **RP** 90
£22.85-£25.99 Cadman, Fintry Wines, Hay Wines, Hallgarten Wines, Majestic, Wine Republic
Savoury in style, with abundant vegetal aromas of asparagus and bell peppers on the nose. Has a crisp, focused and rippling finish. **Drink** 2022-2023 **Alc** 13%

Seifried Estate, Nelson 2021
RJ 92 **MB** 90 **RP** 88
£14.99-£15.99 Liquorice, NZ House of Wine, Waitrose
Bright, focused and polished, with Williams pear and orchard fruit. Structurally balanced between acidity and fruit concentration. Notes of flint on the finish. **Drink** 2022-2023 **Alc** 12.5%

Steve Bird, Manu, Wairau Valley, Marlborough 2021
RJ 90 **MB** 92 **RP** 89
£17.50 The Wine Arcade
Concentrated lime, citrus and *fines herbes*. Focused precision, restrained fruit, layered and textured. Fresh, clean acidity leaving a tingling palate. **Drink** 2022-2023 **Alc** 13%

Yealands Estate, Single Vineyard, Awatere, Marlborough 2021
RJ 90 **MB** 92 **RP** 87
£13.95-£14.99 Booths, Chiltern Wines, Majestic, ND John, NY Wines, The Great Wine Co
Struck match and flint dominate the nose. Classic asparagus meets citrus and rose. Concentrated fruit aromas and saline, synchronised by a pulsing acidic backbone. **Drink** 2022-2023 **Alc** 13%

Recommended 86-89pts

Wine	Score	RJ	MB	RP	Tasting note	Alc	Drink	Price	Stockists
Astrolabe, Marlborough 2021	89	89	90	89	Refined, savoury and herbaceous, with lime curd. The palate is pure-fruited with some texture and length.	13.5%	2022-2023	£19.70	Armit
Bladen, Little Angel, Renwick, Marlborough 2020	89	89	89	88	Expressive, bright and uplifting lemon-lime and herbs. It's full of fun grapefruit vibes, with a refined elegance.	13%	2022-2023	£12.99	Hard to Find Wines
Greywacke, Wild Sauvignon, Marlborough 2020	89	90	90	88	Baked apple style, rather atypical with tart rhubarb acids. Concentrated and rich, finishing poised.	13.5%	2022-2026	£29.99 -£31.99	Liberty Wines, Majestic, North & South, Philglas & Swiggot, Specialist Cellars
Mike Paterson, Lay of the Land Destination, Marlborough 2021	89	90	89	88	Apples and pears with a lovely citrus feel; touches of sherbet lift the texture.	12.5%	2022-2023	£17.99	Naked Wines
Rod Easthope, Reserve, Hawke's Bay 2021	89	89	90	89	Delicate notes of peach, pineapple and fruit salad. Lots of fruity layers with a creamy complexion.	13%	2022-2023	£15.99	Naked Wines
Seresin Estate, Organic, Southern Valleys, Marlborough 2020	89	90	90	87	A textural style still exemplifying Sauvignon charisma. Smooth crème anglaise with passion fruit curd.	13%	2022-2023	£21.50 -£22	Specialist Cellars, The Great Wine Co
Smith & Sheth, Cru, Wairau Valley, Marlborough 2021	89	89	85	92	Herbs, citrus and rosewater, and a richness to the palate. It's racy but has a refined feel.	13.7%	2022-2024	£17-£22.50	Selfridges, Specialist Cellars, Tesco, The Drink Shop, Wine Direct, WoodWinters
Bladen, Renwick, Marlborough 2020	88	90	84	91	There's some green apple here, with subtle florals and lychee aromatics. Long finish with a lovely purity.	13%	2022-2024	£13.99	Hard to Find Wines
Boutinot, Passing Giants, Marlborough 2021	88	89	89	86	Bold and bright with a poised backbone, racy on the mid-palate with spices, fresh kiwi, sweet gooseberries.	13.5%	2022-2025	£17-£18	NY Wines, Wild Wines
Esk Valley, Hawke's Bay 2021	88	87	86	92	Steely profile, pithy, lime. Powerful and well balanced with a crisp mid-palate and a clean fresh finish.	13.5%	2022-2024	£14.50	NZ House of Wine, WoodWinters
Foley Wines, Vavasour, Awatere, Marlborough 2021	88	88	89	88	Bright aromatics, a mix of tropical, citrus and green fruits. Exceptional fruit purity and resistance.	13.5%	2022-2023	£10-£12.99	Co-op, Majestic, Matthew Clark-Bibendum

Wine	Score	RJ	MB	RP	Tasting note	Alc	Drink	Price	Stockists
Jackson Estate, Stich, Waihopai Valley, Marlborough 2021	88	89	89	87	Pristinely pure, with clean fruits smothered by the crisp and lively acidity. Refreshing and focused.	13.4%	2022-2023	£12.99 -£14.99	Christopher Piper, Majestic, Ocado, The Secret Bottle Shop, Waitrose
Kelly Washington, Southern Valleys, Marlborough 2018	88	88	88	89	Hints of pineapple and mango. Acidity is quite lean. Harmonious finish.	12.5%	2022-2023	£20-£24.95	Jeroboams, The Wine Society
Lake Chalice, The Falcon, Marlborough 2020	88	87	89	87	Delicate aromas of elderflower and gooseberry. Citrus acidity uplifting the grassy notes and refined fruit.	12.5%	2022-2026	£15.99	Hallgarten Wines
Lobster Reef, Marlborough 2021	88	89	89	86	Abundantly savoury with fresh asparagus present on the nose. Sharp and focused on the palate.	13%	2022-2026	£14.49	Widely available via UK agent Bancroft Wines
Mount Brown, Catherine's Block, Waipara Valley 2017	88	88	86	89	Fresh lime, cooked pineapple and butterscotch, with floral and spicy hints. Silky mouthfeel.	13%	2022-2023	£16.95	Davy's
Nika Tiki, Marlborough 2021	88	88	92	85	Savoury talc, spices and juicy ripe fruit. Textured with fresh passion fruit cream. Rich, vibrant finish.	13.5%	2022-2025	£12.50 -£13.95	Lanchester Wines, Mr Wheeler, Tanners, The Secret Bottle Shop
Rapaura Springs, Rohe, Blind River, Marlborough 2021	88	88	89	87	Voluptuous, ripe and brooding, a good food-matching wine. Sherbety finish and abundant tropical nuances.	13.5%	2022-2023	£16.95 -£19.50	Harvey Nichols, Laithwaites, ND John, Oddbins
Schubert, Martinborough, Wairarapa 2020	88	89	88	88	Baked and waxy fruits on the nose, pure and refined. Decant and let it open up.	12.5%	2022-2024	£24.75	Ellis Wines
Spy Valley, Waihopai Valley, Marlborough 2021	88	89	90	85	Layers of citrus, gooseberry and elderflower, supported by a refined acidity with just the right amount of restraint.	13%	2022-2023	£12.95 -£14.49	Constantine Stores, Must Wine, ND John, North & South, The Drink Shop
Squealing Pig, Marlborough 2021	88	89	88	88	Mango-papaya profile, tropical brightness. Flavours are concentrated and long, and fill the palate with ease.	13%	2022-2024	£10	Asda, Morrisons
Tiki, Maui, Waipara Valley, North Canterbury 2021	88	88	89	86	Underpinned with a delicate fruit structure of guava, passion fruit and a hint of flint. Straightforward profile.	13%	2022	£15.99	Castelnau Wine Agencies
Tiki, Single Vineyard, Waipara Valley, North Canterbury 2021	88	87	89	88	Ripe, forward fruit, with whitecurrant, lime and creamy passion fruit; some savoury nuances.	13.5%	2022-2023	£18.99	Castelnau Wine Agencies
Tohu, Awatere, Marlborough 2021	88	90	89	84	An undercurrent of salinity sits across the palate with lime marmalade and mellow, restrained stone fruit.	13.5%	2022	£15.99 -£17	Adnams, CE Fine Wines, Ocado
Auntsfield, Single Vineyard, Marlborough 2021	87	87	88	87	Green apples, gooseberries and ample citrus fruits. Some pleasant spices on the back-palate.	13%	2022-2023	£15-£17.75	Caviste, Harrods, Hic, North & South, Vinvm, Wines with Attitude
Babich, Select Blocks, Organic, Wairau Valley 2021	87	88	88	86	Tart rhubarb and apple with biscuity aromas that fall through to the palate.	13%	2022-2023	£12	Berkmann
Baron Edmond de Rothschild, Rimapere, Marlborough 2021	87	89	85	87	Lime, mango and dried pineapple with vanilla spice. Fresh acidity with a clean finish.	13%	2022-2023	£17.95 -£19.99	Cheers, Hic, Majestic, Waddesdon Wines
Deep Down, Blenheim, Marlborough 2021	87	88	86	88	Nettle, citrus and rose petal. The palate is full of ripe nectarines and autumnal fruits.	12%	2022-2023	£19.95 -£20.99	Ellis Wines, Mumbles Fine Wines, The Wine Reserve, Wadebridge Wines
Dog Point Vineyard, Marlborough 2020	87	88	85	88	Granny Smith and custard apples. With bright acids, this is upbeat and has some weight.	13.5%	2022-2024	£17.99-£18.49	Widely available via UK agent Bancroft Wines
Greenhough, River Garden, Nelson 2020	87	88	90	84	Pithy lime aromatics. Ripe mango, banana and hints of toasted brioche instantly envelop the palate.	13%	2022-2027	£14.50	Tanners
Hāhā, Marlborough 2021	87	87	89	86	Peach and passion fruit galore. Light, but there's a sense of balance with everything in the right proportion.	12.5%	2022-2023	£13.90	The Northern Wine & Beer Co
LeftField, New Zealand 2021	87	88	85	87	Guava, passion fruit and mango with a herbal edge. Full-flavoured with soft acidity.	12.5%	2022-2023	£15.30	NZ House of Wine
Oyster Bay, Marlborough 2021	87	88	86	86	Lime and lemon. Bright and focused, with sharp acidity and lots of fresh, bright flavours.	13%	2022-2024	£10-£11.49	Asda, Cellier, Co-op, Majestic, Morrisons, Ocado, Sainsbury's, Tesco
Stanley Estates, Awatere, Marlborough 2021	87	88	86	86	Tropical fruit, *fines herbes* and lime leaf with wonderfully crisp acidity and a lovely long finish.	13.3%	2022-2023	£13-£16.95	Booths, Derventio Wines, Frontier Fine Wines, Promotion Wine, Vino Direct, Wine Boutique
Stoneleigh, Wairau Valley, Marlborough 2021	87	88	86	88	Clean and refreshing, with lemon-lime aromatics. There's a real softness to the fruit here.	13.5%	2022-2023	£10-£10.95	Asda, Cheers, Morrisons, Ocado, Sainsbury's, Waitrose
Waipara West, Waipara Valley, North Canterbury 2020	87	88	88	86	Ginger spice, creamy and textured. Fresh and pouncy acid structure brings an excitable nature to the wine.	13.5%	2022-2023	£15.50	Lant Street Wine, Private Cellars
Blank Canvas, Abstract, Dillon's Point, Marlborough 2018	86	84	86	89	Ripe and savoury fruit with a matchstick note. Opulent use of oak here.	13.5%	2022-2023	£26.99	Liberty Wines, NY Wines
Dog Point Vineyard, Section 94, Marlborough 2019	86	89	85	83	Ginger spice from oak on the nose; white peaches, grassy notes and some raw asparagus.	14.5%	2022-2026	£26-£27.99	Bancroft, Sandys Fishmongers, Specialist Cellars, Sterling Fine Wines, Wine Yard
Forrest Wines, Forrest, Marlborough 2020	86	86	85	88	Slightly flinty, mineral profile with pear notes. Restrained fruits and high acid give this real attitude.	13.5%	2022-2024	£14.99	Adnams

Wine	Score	RJ	MB	RP	Tasting note	Alc	Drink	Price	Stockists
Loveblock, Awatere, Marlborough 2021	86	87	84	86	Rhubarb and dried tangerine, with flinty nuances. Textured and has some length.	13%	2022	£17.95 -£20	Aitken, Curious Liquids, Luvians, Old Garage, Palate Bottle Shop, Pop Wines, Vinarius, Vin Santo
Misty Cove Wines, Kēkerengū Coast, Marlborough 2021	86	85	84	88	Delicate white floral notes on the nose. A nicely textured wine with lovely balance.	13%	2022-2023	POA	Anthony Byrne
Mt Beautiful, North Canterbury 2020	86	89	82	87	Spiced and full of herbaceous goodness. Texture amplified by oak and well managed.	14.5%	2022-2023	£14	Nectar Wines
Saint Clair, Sea Change, Marlborough 2021	86	87	84	87	Guava, passion fruit and sweet pea nuances. Tart gooseberry skin concentration – one for acid-lovers.	13%	2022-2023	£16.99	Sea Change Wine
Te Pā, Signature Series, Marlborough 2021	86	87	85	85	Floral notes with fresh savoury herbs. A restrained and refreshing wine.	13.5%	2022-2024	£10	Asda, Morrisons, Tesco
Te Whare Ra, Awatere, Marlborough 2021	86	87	85	86	Tingling freshness with clementine, quince, nettles and whitecurrant.	13.3%	2022-2023	£17-£17.50	Widely available via UK agent Les Caves de Pyrene

Commended 83-85pts ■ **Caythorpe, Marlborough 2021** 85, 13%, 2022-2023, £14 Wanderlust Wine ■ **Churton, Marlborough 2021** 85, 14%, 2022-2023, £16.95 Tanners ■ **Lake Chalice, The Raptor, Marlborough 2021** 85, 13%, 2022-2025, £19.50 Hallgarten Wines, Strictly Wine, Wine Republic ■ **Spoke, Resolute, Dillon's Point, Marlborough 2021** 85, 13%, 2022, £21.95 Via UK agent Global Wine Solutions ■ **Spy Valley, E Block, Waihopai Valley, Marlborough 2021** 85, 13.5%, 2022-2023, £12 All About Wine, M&S ■ **Te Awanga, Wildsong, Hawke's Bay 2021** 85, 13%, 2022-2023, £14.99 Adnams, Kwoff, Love Wine, South Downs Cellars, Vino Fandango ■ **The Marlborist, Alpine Rift, Marlborough 2021** 85, 13%, 2022-2024, £21.99 9 Elms Wines ■ **Villa Maria, Reserve, Clifford Bay, Marlborough 2021** 85, 14%, 2022-2023, £15 NZ House of Wine, Waitrose Cellar ■ **Yealands Estate, Single Block L5, Awatere, Marlborough 2021** 85, 13%, 2022-2023, £17-£19 ND John, NY Wines, NZ House of Wine, The Great Wine Co, Wines Direct ■ **Zephyr, Dillon's Point, Marlborough 2021** 85, 13%, 2022, £15.99-£16.95 Banstead Vintners, Borders Wines, Kwoff, Regency Wines, Talking Wines, The Fine Wine Co ■ **Allan Scott, Marlborough 2021** 84, 12.5%, 2022-2024, £13.65-£16.99 Ellis Wines, Fine Wines Direct UK, Great Grog, The Wine Centre ■ **Black Cottage, Marlborough 2021** 84, 12.5%, 2022-2025, £13-£13.95 Chapel St Wines, Field & Fawcett, Glug, Shelved Wine, Slurp, Sociovino, Streatham Wine House ■ **Churton, Best End, Marlborough 2019** 84, 13%, 2022-2023, £26 Tanners ■ **Invivo, GN, New Zealand 2021** 84, 12.4%, 2022-2023, £9 Asda, Morrisons, Wine Delivered ■ **Marisco Vineyards, The King's Favour, Waihopai Valley, Marlborough 2020** 84, 13%, 2022-2023, £15.99 Majestic ■ **Rose Family Wines, Reserve, Blenheim, Marlborough 2021** 84, 12.5%, 2022-2023, £16.75 Ellis Wines, Wolseley Wine Loft ■ **Sileni, Straits Grand Reserve, Marlborough 2021** 84, 13%, 2022-2023, £13-£15 Kwoff, Premier Cru Fine Wine, Thind Wine Merchants ■ **Bill & Claudia Small, Small & Small, Marlborough 2021** 83, 13%, 2022-2023, £15.99 Naked Wines ■ **Catalina Sounds, Waihopai Valley, Marlborough 2021** 83, 13%, 2022, £12.67-£14.25 D Byrne & Co, Kwoff, NY Wines ■ **Giesen Estate, Marlborough 2020** 83, 12%, 2022-2023, £10 Bibendum Wine, Morrisons ■ **Marisco, Leefield Station, Waihopai Valley, Marlborough 2020** 83, 13.5%, 2022, £12-£13.99 Hillside Brewery, The Crafty Vintner, The Sipster, The Vineyard Belfast, The Vintage Wine Merchants

Fair 76-82pts ■ **Brancott Estate, Letter Series B, Marlborough 2021** 82 ■ **Little Beauty, Pounamu, Marlborough 2020** 82 ■ **Seresin Estate, Mārama, Marlborough 2018** 82 ■ **Walnut Block, Nutcracker, Marlborough 2021** 82

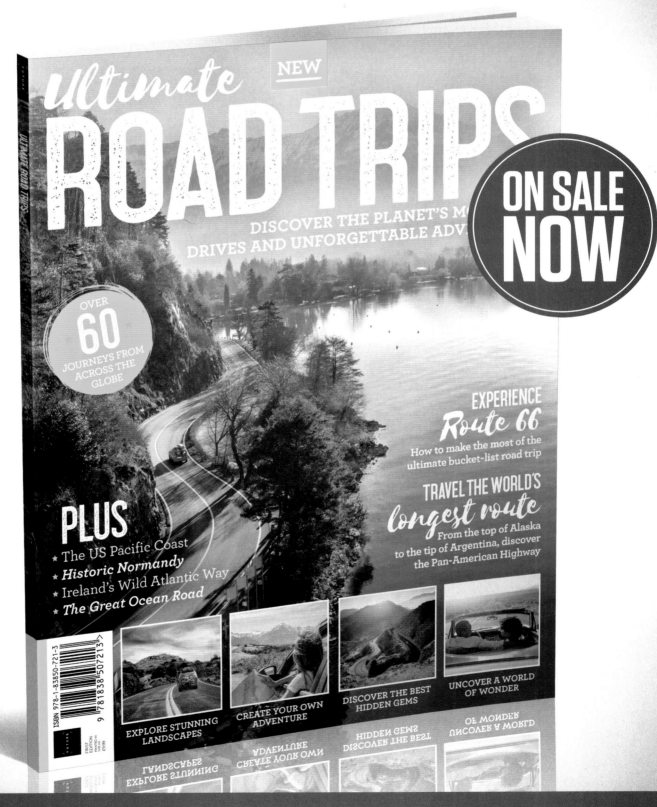

Decanter®
FINE WINE ENCOUNTER
LONDON
25TH ANNIVERSARY

The world-famous Decanter Fine Wine Encounter London returns

We are thrilled to announce the highly anticipated return of Decanter Fine Wine Encounter London 2022, which will be held on Saturday 5 November at The Landmark London.

Following huge success in NYC, join us this Autumn for Decanter's flagship Encounter for an iconic wine tasting experience in the heart of the capital. Taste over six hundred fine wines and meet the world's best wine producers all under one roof.

This year's festivities also marks the 25th anniversary of our Fine Wine Encounters, celebrating with an extraordinary programme you won't want to miss. You will have the opportunity to experience an atmospheric walk-around **Grand Tasting**, access the *new* **Cellar Collection Room**, attend sensational **Masterclasses** with highly regarded producers and learn from the experts in the **Discovery Theatres**.

Bringing prestigious producers, sommeliers and wine enthusiasts together, don't miss out on what will be an unforgettable day in the world of fine wine.

Decanter Premium and magazine subscribers can enjoy priority booking from Friday 29 July. Tickets go on general sale from Friday 5 August.

■ Grand Tasting

£95

11am-5.30pm

This is a walk-around tasting offering guests the opportunity to taste sensational fine wines and meet prestigious producers.

■ *New* Cellar Collection

10.30am-5.30pm

A new addition to the Grand Tasting, this VIP room will feature 20 producers, each showcasing a mini-vertical of one top wine. Access with a Grand Tasting ticket.

SCAN OR VIST WWW.DECANTER.COM